Loving The Reaper

Fire & Death

Silver Falls University
Book 2

Lola King

Cover art by Wild Love Designs
Editing by Mackenzie at Nice Girl Naughty Edits
Alpha reading by Lauren Pixley

the alphabet's letters are my tribe
and I mean to live quietly among them
bending my body into meaningful shapes
perhaps entangled with yours
using our whole persons to confess
what can't be, by any other means,
comprehended or expressed

— Amy Gerstler

To all the women who smile when they want to scream.
I got you, darling.
Sit back
And watch it all burn.

CONTENT WARNING

Hello, and thank you for picking up this book.
Before going in, please note this book is a dark romance for
readers aged 18+ only.

If you've read my books before - please note that while this
book doesn't have a 'shopping list' of TW, it is still dark
romance.
Wren Hunter might not be as dark as my other MMCs but
he must be in control, and that comes with darkness.

It's important for you to know your limits, and that what
matters the most is your mental health and your wellbeing.
Reading is fun, fiction is great, but you matter the most.
Please note the following possible triggers in no specific
order:
Blackmail
Dubcon
Manipulation
Toxic relationship
Murder

Playlist

You and Me - David Kushner
Hell of a good time - Haiden Henderson
Kids Say - Henry Morris
Afraid - The Neighbourhood
Family Line - Conan Gray
OXOX - Dutch Melrose, Lost Boy
God Needs The Devil - Jonah Karen
Precious - Omido, Nic Dean
Teeth 5 Seconds of Summer
Nightmare - Halsey
Demons - MISSIO
Scream My Name - Thomas LaRosa
Can you love me? - Croixx
In The Woods Somewhere - Hozier
Poison - David Kushner
.Goëtia. - Peter Guidry
Hayloft - Mother Mother
Burn - David Kushner
Angel - Camylio
Bottom Of The Deep Blue Sea - MISSIO

Playlist

Make Me Wanna Die - The Pretty Reckless
SEX LOVE DRUGS - Dutch Melrose, Lost Boy
THE RIDE - Omido, Kai
EXTRA EXTRA, Chandler Leighton
The Darker The Weather // The Better The Man -
MISSIO
I love it - Croixx
Paradise - Henry Morris
Yours - Conan Gray
Trouble - Camylio
No Angels - Stellar
Craving' - Stiletto, Kendyle Paige
Used to This - Camila Cabello
Sinner - Shaya Zamora
Reflections - The Neighbourhood
Carry You Home - Alex Warren
Hayloft II - Mother Mother
Pretty Boy - Cavale
Bonnie and Clyde - Dutch Melrose, HARRY WAS HERE
Burning Down - Alex Warren
Breathe In, Breathe Out - David Kushner
LABOUR - the cacophony - Paris Paloma
Littlest things - Camylio
My Home - Myles Smith
Ordinary - Alex Warren

Wisdom & Power

Welcome back to
Silver Falls University

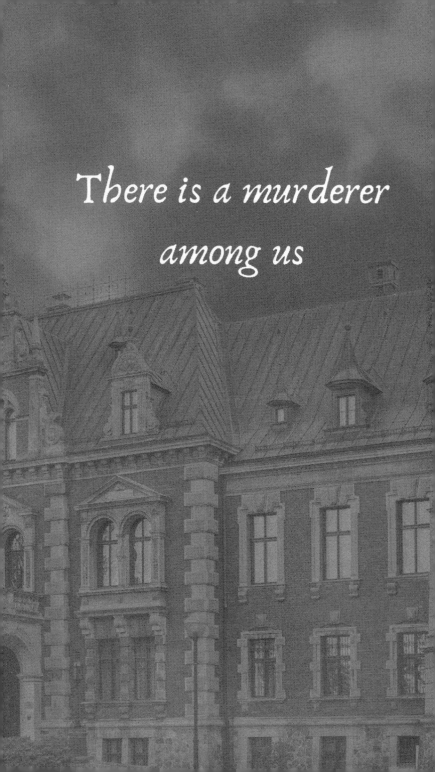

There is a murderer among us

-metal IS NOT the same as punk.
-She's still allergic to shellfish and cat hair
-Always leave the green olives to her
-We don't like metal anymore.
-Tea tree and peppermint shampoo
-Don't forget the peri-peri powder on her fries
-Bake and shake every first Tuesday of the month.
-No more sugar in her coffee. It makes her feel sick
-DO NOT bother me during girls' night Wren
-Spiced honey on pepperoni pizza
-Check the triangle freckles on her right shoulder
frequently. Dermatologist said to keep an eye.

Prologue

Wren

You and Me – David Kushner

Her palm cups my cheek ever-so-softly.

Soft isn't a word I'd ever use for her, but God, this feels like everything I've ever needed.

"We're drunk," she rasps.

"Not drunk enough for it to be an excuse." Our voices are so quiet we can barely hear each other.

This is a secret. This is something we'll never tell anyone. Her standing in front of me, green eyes shining with need. Me with my head lowered so I can take in every inch of her face. So I can observe every precise shift of her features. We're close enough to feel each other's breaths on our skin. She smells sweet, of the spiked punch she's been drinking all night, a hint of weed mixing with it.

Above her face, my forehead practically touches hers, her lips skimming mine.

"You're seeing someone."

I shake my head subtly to make sure my gaze doesn't leave her eyes. They look so innocent that way, looking up into mine. Mine feel hooded from the pleasure of *barely* touching her. From the drunkenness of her palm keeping me prisoner with the slightest pressure.

"I saw her a few times. She means nothing."

Her quick thinking catches up right away, the only conscious thing leaving her as her subconscious needs take over. "Tell me why you're seeing her."

The corner of my mouth tips. She wants to hear it, doesn't she? That vixen.

"Because your jealousy is the only way to get your attention, Peach. I did what I had to."

She bites her lower lip, and I bring my thumb to it, pulling the plush flesh from between her teeth, then lower, until it bounces back into place. I press my finger to her mouth, and her reflex is to bite on it.

That's what Peach does. She bites, and she fights. She will drag your sanity out of you before she ends you.

"Gentle," I murmur. "Let's not do this. No push and pull. Please, just tonight. Be sweet to me, and I'll leave the side of me you hate behind."

Sensing my need for a truce, she follows me down that path. I know what got her. Me saying *please.* Her bite turns into nibbling my thumb, and when her tongue rolls around it, my eyes flutter shut.

"Fuck, Peach..."

As she sucks on my finger, I bring my other hand to her narrow waist, grabbing her tightly. So tightly, I feel every quick breath she takes. Her ribs push against my grip.

"We said *gentle,*" she snarls around my thumb.

I relax my fingers around her waist, caressing her skin instead. She's only wearing a bikini top with a flowing, see-through beach skirt. The two sparkly black triangles stay in place through the sheer force of the flimsy strings and the holy spirit holding the whole thing together. One pull at the back and I would have access to her breasts that are now pressed against my chest. The thought has my dick pushing so eagerly against my jeans, I think the zipper might burst.

I wonder if she's as wet as I am hard. I wonder if she can take what she needs out of us playing nice.

I pull my thumb out of her mouth, slide the wet finger down her throat, then her collarbone, and until I've reached her left nipple.

Shit. It's already poking through the elastic material of her bikini.

When all I do is circle it over and over again, she sucks in a sharp inhale. Her hand on my cheek goes to the back of my neck. It isn't so soft anymore, her true self showing.

She pulls, and our foreheads press firmly against each other. I slip the triangle to the side to get better access to her beautiful breast. As I flick her nipple, her eyes flutter shut, and the tiniest moan escapes her.

"We could do it," I say against her lips. "You and me. We both want to."

For the first time since we're grown-up enough to understand our feelings toward each other, Peach doesn't deny our attraction. She nods, licking her lips as she blinks her eyes open.

"We could." The green in her gaze deepens, saturated with emotions. "I could fall for you, Wren Hunter. If only you weren't such a dominating fuck."

"I don't want us to fight this anymore. I don't want to have to show you that you like me through jealousy. You're worth so much more to me."

She nods again, her breathing accelerating as my hand lowers, skimming her stomach before I push past the elastic band of her skirt, and under her bikini.

I groan when I feel the wetness at her seam, and my middle finger breaches between her lower lips, pressing against her entrance.

Shifting her hips forward, she moves against my hand.

"Kiss me," she whispers.

I can already taste the sweetness of her lips, even though they're barely touching mine. I'm *dying* to kiss her. That's all I've ever wanted. She's the only woman I'd move heaven and earth for a chance to kiss.

But I slow us down, moving my mouth to her cheek and smiling against her skin.

"Say please."

She startles, attempting to push away, but my hand at her waist tightens.

"Don't. You're getting wetter."

Her breathing becomes erratic, her hips thrusting in the slightest, silently pleading with me to go further. I've never exerted so much self-control in my entire fucking life.

"Give in," I beg her. "You can do it for me. I won't tell anyone. I promise you, this stays between us."

I nibble her earlobe, and she tilts her head to the side to give me better access as she sighs. She's getting there. It's *finally* happening.

"Ask for a kiss," I say in her ear. I want her to know this is our secret. "The first step is the hardest. But then you'll beg me to push my fingers inside you."

She freezes completely.

"Wait—"

"I *knew* you wouldn't play nice," she hisses as she pushes me away. I stumble back and she steps to the side.

"Wait, Peach. I take it back."

She rearranges her bikini top, pointing an accusing

finger at me. "You can't fucking do it. You *have* to take control."

"You liked it," I say calmly. "I could feel it."

"You asked me to be gentle, and I was. You said you'd leave your shitty dominant side behind if I played nice. I did. You couldn't do it. Fuck you."

Running a hand over my face, I step in front of the door as she tries to grab the handle. I can suddenly hear the party behind it. Everything had disappeared while we were close, but the real world is right out there. Her badass reputation she holds so dearly. Our friends teasing us about being into each other. The whole college knowing I want no one but her. Our friendship she desperately wants to preserve. It's all so real now.

"I'm sorry." I put a hand in front of me, but she takes a step back, staying out of reach.

Suddenly, this bedroom feels so huge. It was narrow a minute ago, like we'd have to push the walls if we wanted to separate. Now I can see she has places to be, away from me. That she was touching me because she *wanted to*.

This was the closest we ever got to kissing. To having sex. To being together, and I fucking blew it because I couldn't control myself.

"Get out of the way."

"I can't," I admit immediately. "We were so close. Peach, I already wanted you, but now I can't give up."

Her face hardens, her eyebrows pulling together in anger. "Your infatuation isn't my fucking problem. Get. Out. Of. The. Way."

My heart pulses in my ears, panic throbbing through my skull.

"We almost kissed and you're going to go back to pretending you don't want me?"

She snorts. "It's not that hard, Wren. Believe me. I can just have someone keep my mind off—"

"I wouldn't finish that sentence if you want to get out of this room."

A sarcastic laugh explodes from her mouth as she throws her head back.

"Here it is." She can be so condescending. It's a super-power she has. "Wren, *the asshole*, Hunter. Ooh, so dominant." She pretends to shake. "Move. Go back to Ania. I bet she gets on her knees every time you snap your fingers. I bet she *begs* you to kiss her."

I run my tongue against my teeth. She wants the asshole? Fine, we'll get back to the usual.

"She'd bark if I asked her," I say, voice low. "She'd do anything for me to choose her instead of you. You want me to go back to her? I will. I'll kiss her, don't you worry. I'll make her come because she begs so well, how could I not?"

She squares her jaw, but the best sight is her fists tightening at her sides. Frustrated little thing she is.

"If that's what you need to feel in control, don't let me get in the way."

"I will do it, Peach," I say in all seriousness. "And when your jealousy gets the best of you, because we both know it will, I'll bring her to all our gatherings with the rest of the group. I'll parade her in front of you, and I'll watch that cute vein pop on your forehead every time she holds my hand." I point at it, smiling smugly. The way she hates.

She breathes in through her nose, nostrils flaring.

"Have a blast."

"I will."

"Good," she snarls through gritted teeth.

Fucking. Brat.

"Great."

6

I don't know what I expected. You don't make Peach fold by challenging her stubbornness.

We stand in silence for God knows how long until a sigh leaves me.

"Have a good night," I huff.

I turn around, open the door, and go back to the party, leaving behind what might have been my only chance to get the woman I wanted.

My only *legal* chance.

Ania

My erratic breaths break the silence of the dark forest. It's proof of the pain puncturing the side of my stomach and the burning in my lungs.

This is what running for your life feels like. Tight muscles, urine trailing down your legs, everything blurring apart from what's right in front of you.

I stop on the bank of the Silver Snake River, the open night sky finally allowing me to breathe.

The party I was attending at my sorority house is too far away for me to even hear the bass of the music anymore. I ran through the entire back of campus, through the thick woods, the painful branches.

It's silent out here, apart from the sound of the wild current of the river. I can't even hear the person who was chasing me. I think I might have lost them. Whoever they were.

A sob bursts past my lips. I can feel everything so vividly now. Leaning over the barrier, I vomit all the alcohol I ingested earlier tonight.

Did I survive an attempted murder?

Why?

What did I do? Who did I piss off?

My thoughts swirl, bumping against my skull as a headache comes over me. I vomit some more, disgustingly wiping my mouth with my forearm.

A beautiful, free laugh resonates behind me, and someone stumbles my way, leaning next to me.

I shake my head, trying to process that this is reality as I turn to the stranger.

"I need help," I rasp. "I-I was attacked."

I get no verbal answer, only two hands violently wrapping around my throat. A cough cuts my shriek short. My already tight lungs instantly feel the lack of oxygen.

All I see is a flash of fiery red hair. It can't be missed even in the dark night.

As I lose consciousness and am pushed into the wild waters below, my last hope is for one thing only.

That the world one day learns my murderer was Penelope Sanderson-Menacci.

-metal IS NOT the same as punk.
-She's still allergic to shellfish and cat hair
-Always leave the green olives to her
-We don't like metal anymore.
-Tea tree and peppermint shampoo
-Don't forget the peri-peri powder on her fries
-Bake and shake every first Tuesday of the month.
-No more sugar in her coffee. It makes her feel sick
-DO NOT bother me during girls' night Wren
-Spiced honey on pepperoni pizza
-Check the triangle freckles on her right shoulder
frequently. Dermatologist said to keep an eye.

Chapter One

Wren

Hell of a good time - Haiden Henderson

T*hree months later...*

Penelope Sanderson-Menacci.

How did I fall so deeply in love with her?

How was it so easy to know that our friendship would never feel like *friendship* to me. That in a room full of people, she would always be the one my eyes would search for. That when I hug my friends, she would be the one I kept close a little longer.

Men *want her*. And why wouldn't they?

I watch her pour tequila in a shaker she pulled out of the fridge, throwing her long, thick red hair over her shoulder and smiling at the guy flirting with her, impressed when he says how quickly she can prepare a margarita.

It's her favorite, I think to myself. Her go-to on any night out, friends' night in, *bake and shake* afternoon with her girls.

I lick the salt off my lips. She made me one earlier—before everyone arrived at the house my best friend Achilles and I share on campus. September first also means the first party of the year at SFU, and since we're in our last year, we decided to host.

That guy was staring at her ass for twenty minutes before he gathered the courage to come and talk to her. The same ass that earned her the nickname *Peach*.

Penelope *Peach* Sanderson-Menacci. One of my best friends with a stupid nickname that reduces her to a part of her body. A name that caught on since high school and that I, of course, use without shame. Because calling her *my love, baby, queen of my life*, doesn't exactly scream *friends since elementary school,* does it?

She still hasn't said anything to Fuckboy Number One of the night. She's letting him enjoy everything there is to enjoy about her. A gorgeous body sculpted by years of cheerleading. Beautiful, vibrant hair. A mix of brown, auburn, and red no dye could compete with. Bright green eyes that sparkle the second she finds something amusing. This week, she's also sporting a small bruise on her cheek from a violent protest. She got in a fight with a protester who was trying to block the entrance to the women's shelter she volunteers at. It's not taking anything away from her beauty. If anything, imperfections on Peach somehow make her look more perfect.

Enjoy while you can, buddy.

Because while Peach is someone you can appreciate from afar, you can only fall for the idea of her. A pretty princess that could come straight out of a Disney film—

"What the fuck are you looking at, Hunter?"

Until she opens her mouth.

She cocks an eyebrow at me, the fact that she called me by my last name making my stomach do somersaults. I hate that last name. So, why does it sound so hot coming from her? She silently dares me to say something about the guy who's still hovering around her, even though she hasn't answered any of his advances.

My chest tingles. The sensation travels up my throat and forces the corner of my mouth to tilt up. She doesn't expect any answer from me, turning to Fuckboy Number One.

"Go bother someone else. Can't you see you're punching above your weight here?" Her voice is as warm as a winter night.

Yeah, he didn't expect those words to leave such pretty lips. His jaw drops open, his expression hardening as he tries to save face.

"You're not all that."

"I am, in fact, all that. Now shoo."

She shakes her head, walking to our group of friends, and this time, I don't stop my smile.

Men don't like Peach. They like how beautiful she is, and they all want to fuck her despite themselves. Peach? She eats them alive. Which makes her even more attractive, because everyone likes a good challenge. She was late to the sex party. Lost her virginity freshman year of college and suddenly decided she gets a kick out of putting men on their knees, pushing them to desperation.

It only lasted our first year, though. I quickly grew tired of it and put a stop to that behavior.

"He's new," Achilles says to me as Peach starts talking to our friends, Alex and Ella. "He must be if he didn't get the memo about hitting on Peach."

"He can always try." I shrug, taking a sip of my drink. "That's the quickest way to learn to stay away from her."

"It's also the quickest way to get your legs broken around here," my friend adds. He sounds excited about it, like the psycho he is.

I stare at her as she complains to her friends that, even if she had found Fuckboy Number One hot, she knows he would have given up before having sex with her.

"Or was he cute? Because my vision has lowered. My left eye is minus 3.25 now, and I haven't received my new contacts." She huffs. "Never mind. It doesn't matter, anyway. I swear they're scared of me." She laughs. "I'm doomed to stay celibate at this point."

Truth is, the men on campus aren't scared of her. They're scared of me. But she doesn't need to know that, right? She's not wrong, though. Men with big egos and small dicks are scared of strong women.

I don't fear Peach. As a friend, I ground her when she's about to explode. I defuse the ticking time bomb that she is. I know her by heart, and I'm the only one capable of cooling her down when she's burning hot. Our friends know I'm the one to call when she's about to get herself in trouble. And that works well for us...as *fucking. Friends.*

But here's the issue; Peach dominates as a hobby, and I dominate to keep myself alive. It's more than something I enjoy. It's how I live, survive, *thrive.*

I am not a mean man. I don't do it to hurt people. But the world is my playground, and I must not only succeed in everything, but be the best. I breathe success. Dominant is a weak word for who I am. It's in my *soul.*

And that's where Peach and I clash. She can't take that. Her pride gets in the way of everything and all the ways I could make her happy.

"Seriously, your weirdness is showing, Wren. Why are you staring at me so hard tonight?"

Our friends Ella and Alexandra burst out laughing. Chris, Ella's boyfriend, shakes his head, smiling knowingly.

"The way you guys flirt is so weird." Alex giggles. "But we love it."

It's not a secret to anyone that I've had the biggest crush on Peach since forever. She likes to insist nothing happened or will ever happen. I like to lean into it and make her mad. Our best friends enjoy pointing out that I've never dated. That she's never had a serious boyfriend. Some say I have her on a leash, and others say that she'll put me on my knees one day.

The game is fun, but the truth is so *real*.

I'm in love with Peach.

Because her beautiful, soft, feminine traits often harden with the power that hides within her. Because she looks like a little kitten but carries the intensity of a lioness. There's fire in her soul, in her entire being.

Peach has always been my biggest challenge. But God, I will put her back in her place one day. She won't see it coming.

She would look so gorgeous on her knees for me, her beautiful eyes looking up into mine, narrowing from the anger of submitting and yet not able to help it.

"We don't flirt," Peach snaps. "That's weird to say. Everyone, stop being weird." She takes a gulp of her margarita. "Bet ya I can down it quicker than you?" she taunts as she looks at my glass.

I hold back a smile to not show my excitement. This girl loves to show how she's faster, tougher, smarter. She has a constant need to prove herself, and I'm always the one she chooses because I take her up on it every time. If it means I have her attention, I'll probably do it.

I place the rim of the glass to my lips and cock an eyebrow at her as she does the same. I finish before her... obviously. That cute little mouth of hers can't compete with me gulping down a glass.

"Ugh. That wasn't fun," she huffs.

"That's because you lost." I chuckle. "What do I get for winning? A date?"

"No."

I tilt my head, eyebrow quirked. "We can skip straight to the wedding."

"You're really not hot enough to be making suggestions like that."

I put a hand on my chest, pretending to be hurt. Fuck, I love teasing her. "The rest of the SFU population disagrees with you, Peach darling. Even you can't deny I'm hot."

She looks me up and down, pretending to be analyzing me even though we grew up together and have seen every phase a human can go through.

"You're lukewarm at best, Wren *darling*." Turning to her girls, she says, "Is it me or is this party boring?"

"I think it's the curse of being a senior," Ella says with a sigh. "Nothing is that exciting anymore."

I stare down at her as her eyes travel around the room.

"Don't," I say, voice low. "You'll make your night worse."

Every time Peach states something is *boring* or *dead*, the part that comes after isn't fun. Too much drinking, drugs, trouble. She becomes a hurricane ready to destroy everyone and everything in her wake. She blacks out and doesn't remember anything the next day, especially not me cleaning up after her mess.

Smiling brightly at me, her eyes flicker. She starts walking backward and into the crowd of people drinking and dancing together.

"Don't tell me what to do."

Two middle fingers aimed at me, and she's gone.

Penelope Sanderson-Menacci. You'll be the end of me one day, and I can't wait.

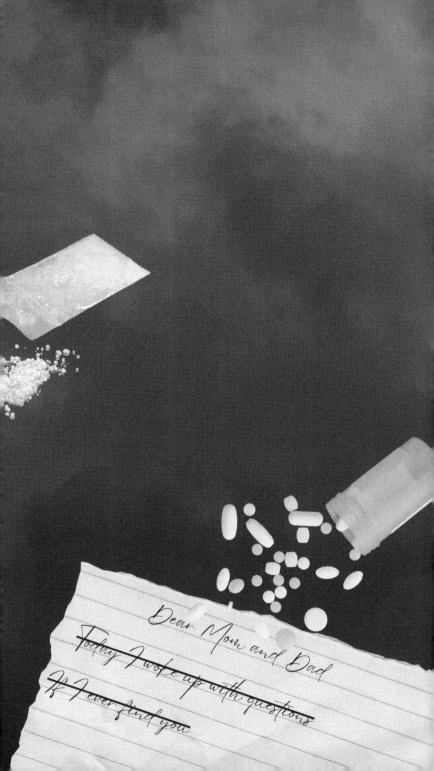

Chapter Two

Peach

Kids Say – Henry Morris

"Holy shit," I gasp as my phone rings loudly, jolting me out of a deep sleep.

Wait. Not a deep sleep. A fucking blackout.

I tap around me in the bed, feeling it vibrate against the mattress but incapable of getting my hands on it. I can't see shit, only able to squint one eye open to stop the headache on the side of my head from spreading to the rest of my skull.

Finally wrapping my fingers around my phone, I answer my dad, putting it on speaker right away so I don't have to press it to my aching head.

"H—" I cough, scratching my throat when I realize how dry it is. Too much alcohol.

And I can feel that disgusting taste at the back of my throat. Too much coke.

"Hey," I try again. "How are y—"

"*I'm leaving*," he cuts me off. It's Dad Menacci, as opposed to Dad Sanderson.

I like to call them by their last names. They tried to introduce one and two when I was little. Dad and Daddy. Dad and Papa. Daddy George and Daddy Georgio. But seriously, who dates someone who has the same name as them in a different language? That shit is confusing for a kid.

No, I make my own rules, and I quickly decided it would be Dad Menacci and Dad Sanderson. I tried *the old one* and *the young one* when I was a teen, but Dad Sanderson really didn't like me pointing out the twenty-year difference. What really happens is, I call them both Dad. And if they're in the same room, I add their last name when they both go *Yes, Principessa?* Or *Yes, Penny Pickle?*

"Dad," I huff. "You know you're not leaving." Every Saturday morning is the same.

"*He did it again. Who in their right mind cheats on me? I'm younger than him. I'm hot. I was a movie star, for fuck's sake.*"

In Italy. He was a movie star in Italy for a few years when he was young. Then he met my dad and moved to Stoneview, Maryland, to live the life of the *truly* rich and famous.

I unlock my phone, checking for messages from my friends as he keeps talking.

"*I should have left the first time it happened. I should have taken you back to Italy with me. You were just a kid, you know? It was barely a year after we got you.*"

Something stirs in my stomach, making me feel sick. I don't like when he mentions *getting me*. There are too many questions they've always refused to answer, and that I gave up on asking. But the worst is the reminder that there was a time I thought no one would love me enough to bring me home with them. I'm one of *those* kids…the ones old enough to realize they're not wanted. Who watched the newborns get snatched up like everyone's favorite candies. The kind of kid who was told she was *lucky* to be adopted just before six years old, because more often than not, we just end up in the system. Couples want babies to start their families, not strays.

"Did you hear me?" he insists on the other end of the line.

"Dad, if you really want to leave him, leave. Don't just say you'll leave." We have this conversation two to three times a month. Every time my dad cheats on him, really.

I scroll through messages from Ella and Alex in the group. Ella sent all the selfies we took at the party, and I can see the way I gradually worsened during the night. Alex liked all of them with a pink heart. She disappears from the pictures at some point, then there's a message that her boyfriend Xi picked her up and she's going to the home they share off campus. Now that we're in senior year, she spends less and less time in the campus house Ella, her, and I share.

According to the texts I sent around two a.m., I ended up kissing that guy who was hitting on me at the beginning of the night. He really wasn't my type, way too clingy. But my choice of men has been limited. I'm hit on a lot, but every time I try to take it further, they ghost me like I threatened their grandma. I've been ghosted so many times, I'm a haunted house at this point. A horny haunted house.

"It's more complicated than that, Penelope." He sighs, like nobody gets him.

But I get him. He wants to leave the man who doesn't give him attention anymore, just doesn't want to leave his money. And Dad Sanderson has always been a rich man. That prenup was watertight.

"I'm not sure what you want me to say," I mumble.

I catch a picture of me and my friend Elijah that Ella sent. I'm clearly drunk off my face. Elijah is kneeling next to me, and my belt is wrapped around his neck while I stand next to him, holding it like a leash.

I barely stop myself from laughing. My dad is still going on about Dad Sanderson cheating.

Clicking forward, I look for Elijah's number. We're always chatting, so our conversation is right below the girls'.

I add a message to the picture.

> Peach: I'm glad you finally learned your place...

"...and you need to tell him that he's destroying this family with his actions. He's irresponsible. Selfish. He's hurting both you and me."

I roll my eyes. Do you know what's exhausting? Parenting your parents. And my dads are so bad at communicating that they will forever be unhappy. No matter what I do.

"Why don't you tell him yourself? I'm not your couple's therapist."

"About that. Did you know he hasn't shown up to the last two sessions?"

I smile to myself when I get a text back from Elijah.

> Elijah: Any guy who gets to be on his knees beside you is a lucky dude. ;)

Excitement buzzes through me as I bite my lip. I like Elijah. He's not scared of admitting things other men would be embarrassed about. Not scared of accepting parts of him that fit with mine. We've always been friends, but he had left to study in Europe for college, so I hadn't seen him in ages, and I thought I wouldn't see him again until graduation. A lot of kids from our town go away for a year. Money can buy us anything, and when you're from Stoneview, you can easily afford to study anywhere you want. But Elijah said he was leaving for good.

I was surprised when he came back unannounced during the summer, but we quickly became inseparable again. He's a year younger, now a junior at Silver Falls University. Sometimes, it feels like he and I were made for each other. He can take my craziness and doesn't try to tame me, and I make him a little less boring every time we hang out. Taking that man out of his shell is a full-time job. He's not like the other guys at SFU. He's as rich as any of us, has the world in the palm of his hand, and the kind of privilege only the richest people in the world do. And yet... he's a good person. A *real* good guy. I take pleasure in making him blush. Or getting him drunk and ending up in compromising positions. With my belt around his neck, for example.

Nothing's ever happened between us, though. And there's a reason for that.

Elijah Hunter is Wren's younger brother. And Wren and I are a whole different topic. A whole different problem. If Elijah and I feel like meant to be, Wren and I feel like forbidden lovers who could never work yet can't help desiring the danger of it. It's as electrifying as it is impossible. Both men would be a terrible idea, and I don't often make good decisions, but staying purely friends with both of them is the best one I ever made.

"...*Penelope, are you even listening?*"

I jolt out of my daydreaming, looking down at my phone.

"Yes, Dad. But I'm not going to get involved in this. We have the same conversation every time."

"Please, come home for the weekend. I'll send a driver now. Your dad is so much more loving when you're around."

"He's also so much more loving when he's at a public event for work. I'm sure you two have one of those soon."

"Principessa, per favore," he begs in Italian.

Shaking my head, I huff. The emotional blackmail is real. "Dad, I left two days ago. It's the first weekend back at college. Be a big boy and go talk to your husband."

I don't listen as he lists all the reasons he'll feel so much better if I go home today. Instead, I open the SFU app. This is pretty much the only social app we use because only people from our college have access to it.

As I scroll down, I barely register all the similar pictures everyone is posting of our gorgeous campus. The signature red brick castle is all over my feed. Some people are inside the castle quad, posting selfies with their summer St Barts tans by the Athena statue in the west quad, saying how excited they are for their whatever year, and some by the Poseidon statue in the east quad... They're ready to "work hard and party." Most people in this college could party their way through the four years and still have Mommy and Daddy get them a very nice job somewhere.

I check my DMs, making sure I haven't sent anything stupid while I was partying a little too hard yesterday. I'm about to leave the app, when the noise of something moving through the air rings out from my phone.

Hermes posted.

That fucker, whoever they are, has a kink for me and my friends. Whenever they post, we can all fear to be the target. Because Hermes loves the popular students. It wouldn't be such a big problem if they just posted stupid shit. But they don't. They tend to post secrets we truly don't want revealed. And their motto is my worst nightmare.

Your secrets are safe with me. Until they aren't.

I tap on their post and my mouth twists. It's not about me. But it's bad.

Welcome back to campus, everyone. Did you miss me over the summer? I'm starting the year nice and easy...just a quick update that the ugly Hunter brother is back at SFU.
Some say Elijah spent a couple years studying in France. I say, he was trying to hide while he was glowing up, and um... he's done hiding, but where's the glow up?
I'm still a Wren fan, if you ask me. But I'll let you vote in the comments.
Welcome back, Elijah. We didn't miss you, because we were too busy drooling over Wren.
I'll find out why you came back, ugly duckling.
Remember, your secrets are safe with me...
Until they aren't.
#uglyduckling #Hunterbrothers #backtoschool

"Dad, I gotta go," I say, not really bothering to follow what he's saying anymore. "I'm not coming home this weekend, but I'll be there for the Stoneview ball."

It's not like I have a choice. Dad Sanderson is running for mayor, and we have to play happy family.

Hanging up on him, I call Elijah right away.

"I'm fine, Peach. It's the same as before I left. I'm used to it."

I swallow the reassuring words I was about to throw at him. "Wanna go for brunch? It truly helps one's reputation to hang out with me."

He laughs. *"Sure. My reputation can only get better anyway."*

"That's the spirit. Let's meet at the Acropolis. We can decide where to go exactly then."

I hang up and hurry into the shower. The Acropolis isn't far from here. It's the part of campus where all the cafes, bars, and restaurants that are only accessible to SFU students are located. Our own little town only we can afford.

The residential area, where my friends and I have our houses, is far from classes, but it isn't far from the fun. I just have to walk through Greek row, where all the sorority and fraternity houses are, and I'll be there in less than fifteen minutes.

I'm walking the few steps down our porch when a black SUV parks in front of the neighbors' house. That house belongs to Achilles and Wren, so I'm not surprised when they're the ones who come out of the car.

I tilt my head to the side, noticing they're wearing the same clothes as yesterday.

"Did you guys have a threesome with some girl who lives off campus?"

"What?" Achilles's head rears back in surprise. His silver eyes blink rapidly at me. "How did you come to that conclusion?"

It's not that he wouldn't have a threesome or wouldn't sleep with his best friend. Hell, I know he's had a threesome with two other men before. But he hates when people assume anything about him.

"Same clothes as yesterday, meaning you haven't been home yet." I point at their clothes. Plain gray t-shirt and black jeans for Wren. Black t-shirt with a red skull spray painted on it, leather jacket, and black jeans for Achilles. "Wherever you were, you drove. Meaning you weren't on campus."

I smile mockingly at both of them, playing with a strand of my hair.

"Achilles is a hoe, so you were *definitely* with a girl. And since Wren hasn't fucked anyone in about forever, I'm assuming he'd need someone to show him how to do it. So..." I clap my hands. "How right am I?"

"How right?" Achilles snorts condescendingly. "It's a good thing you study how to save polar bears because the world would be a horrible place if you had chosen crim-inology."

"Environmental Science and Engineering, Achilles." I huff. "You're my best friend and you don't even know what I study."

I say he's my best friend, but in our little group, he's probably the one I clash with the most. He's always had this strange place as our leader, and most of the time, that's a problem with me. Two strong, blunt, mean people are always a problem in a friendship. It doesn't mean we don't love each other, though. Same with Wren. Two dominant personalities doesn't mean we can't be friends.

But it does mean we'll never cross *that* line. You know, the line I would never imagine crossing with Achilles because we're truly nothing more than friends. Why can't my body be numb when I see Wren? When I see Achilles's pitch-black hair that falls below his ears, the way he runs his hand through it all the time and messes it up, all I want to do is scream at him to buy a fucking brush. When his steel eyes narrow on me the same way he does with anyone who dares address themselves to him, I don't fall head over heels like all of the SFU female population. I don't secretly hope to be the special girl he'll finally settle with.

When I see Wren, though? His chestnut hair, short enough that a bit of gel styles it perfectly, his wide frame, strong arms, shoulders worthy to drool over... Fuck. It's painful not to ask over and over again *why don't you have a girlfriend? Why don't you sleep with girls? Is it truly for me?*

His blue eyes catch mine. The kind of blue that's a little too dark to be like the sky during the day, but too light to be the midnight sky. Perfectly in between. His eyes aren't cold like Achilles's. They're welcoming, comforting. But I can't help wondering if they're that way to everyone.

How special am I to you, Wren Hunter?

I notice something where his jaw meets his ear. My curiosity gets the best of me, and I push onto my toes, swiping the red drop with my index finger.

"Is that blood?" I ask as I fall back, flat on my feet. I rub it against my thumb, but there's so little that it almost disappears.

Wren's thick eyebrows furrow, creating a line between them that I usually only see when he's focusing on crushing someone else to make sure he stays on top.

He's not a malicious person by any means. Achilles is a vicious man. Wren is nice, polite, not too wild but not too calm. Quiet enough to make people curious about him but assured in his person enough that he's not a wallflower. He's driven by success and power, but he doesn't need to be loud about it. It's just general knowledge, something everyone has always accepted since Stoneview Prep and all the way to his senior year at Silver Falls University. Wren Hunter dominates everything and everyone. Which is why I love to challenge him.

And that crease... It comes when he focuses at the gym. When he's working on an engineering paper across from me at the library and wants to do better than me. When he's talking about the next lacrosse game. When he's annoyed, done with a conversation.

Or I guess when his friend finds blood on him that she shouldn't have.

"You're looking at me too closely, Peach," he says calmly. The line disappears, and he smiles. "Not that I'm complaining. Maybe I cut myself shaving or something."

"You haven't shaved." I can see it from the beautiful 5 o'clock shadow that appeared overnight.

"Curiosity killed the cat," Achilles adds ominously.

I roll my eyes. "Shut up. I don't care anyway."

"Where are you off to?" Wren asks as I check my phone to make sure my other friend isn't waiting for me.

"Brunch with Elijah. Bye, losers."

I've barely taken a step in the right direction as Wren wraps his gigantic hand around my wrist, making it disappear within his hold. "Elijah?"

His voice always drops when he mentions his brother. They don't get along. And that's putting it nicely.

"Yeah. Cute guy, not very tall, looks nothing like you but shares the same blood. Ever heard of him?"

His upper lip curls in the slightest before he gets his reaction under control.

"Trouble, tell me you're not fucking my brother."

"Whoa," I scoff. "Calm down, will you? I'm going for brunch, not our wedding."

His face softens, but there's still worry in his eyes. "Peach..."

"I'm not," I say.

"Do you promise?" How can he go from stern to vulnerable so quickly?

I roll my eyes, trying to lighten the mood. "Sure."

A smile tugs at the corner of his mouth as I put my hand, palm up, in front of him. He reaches inside his pocket and pulls out a marker. The fucker always carries them around just in case.

"I'll write it," he purrs with a self-satisfaction that should make me change my mind.

"The point is for the one promising to do it on themselves."

"Yeah, but any excuse to touch you." He chuckles.

He uncaps the pen, holds my wrist tightly, and presses the black tip to my forearm to write *I promise*. I'm worried he'll notice the goosebumps while he looks at my skin so closely. I can't control them, though. That's the effect he has on me.

This little ritual has always been our way of keeping our promises and getting the truth out of each other. It came when we were in middle school. I got myself in trouble, and I asked him to promise not to tell any adult. I made him write it on himself so he would remember when he got to his house.

"Happy?" I flatly ask as he puts the marker back in his pocket.

"Yeah. Do you know what's funny? We were actually about to go for brunch too."

"What? Go away, you're not coming."

"We're starving after that threesome," Achilles jumps

in. "And we're going exactly where you are. Let's walk together."

"I don't even know where we're eating, stupid."

"Perfect, we can choose together." Achilles wraps an arm around my shoulders, and Wren still doesn't let go of my wrist as they start walking, dragging me with them.

"Wren," I snap, annoyed. "Seriously, leave your brother alone."

"I will once he leaves you alone." He looks down at me, smiling a full set of white teeth.

"You're not sitting at our table. Fucking bullies," I grunt as I'm forced to keep walking at their insane pace.

He chuckles darkly. "We'll see about that."

Wren's warm skin touching mine is way too electrifying for me to attempt to pull away anymore. But the idea of Elijah seeing us all arrive together feels wrong.

I don't want to be the girl who gets between two brothers. The Hunter family is messy enough as is. And anyone who knows what's good for them would stay away.

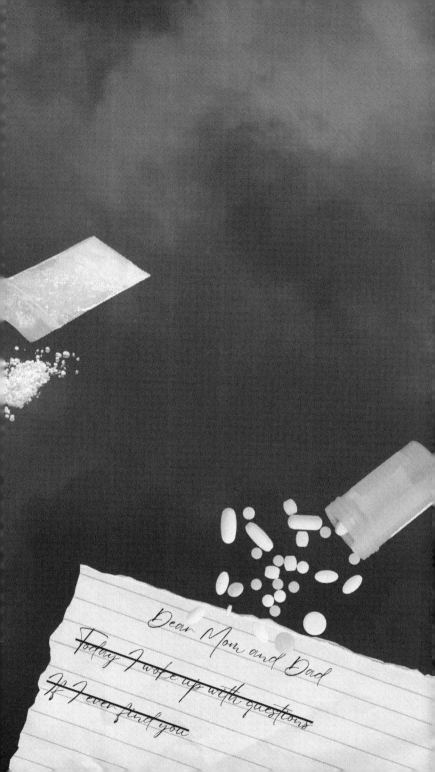

Chapter Three

Peach

Afraid – The Neighbourhood

"Six, seven, eight. All accounted for. Achilles said I couldn't eat eight pancakes, and I'm about to prove that fucker wrong." I take a picture before I look up from my stack of pancakes and smile at Elijah, but his eyes are looking over my shoulders, his jaw clenching.

"You should go eat with them. It would stop the death glares they're sending our way."

I glance behind me, and Wren sends me a knowing smile. He's trying to intimidate his brother to the point I'll give in and move to their table.

He can be such a bully when it comes to Elijah. Even as his best friends, Ella, Alex, and I, never got a real explanation as to why they don't get along. And I don't know if Achilles knows the truth, but if he does, he never told us.

The Hunters are not originally from around here. They're Texas oil billionaires who moved here before Wren and Elijah were born. His family fits the Stoneview clichés. Too rich to care about anything, their dad travels back and forth, and their mom is taken care of and hangs out with the Stoneview wives. They're not worse or better than any of us. But they are very, *very* private. No one goes to their house, no one sees Monty Hunter very often, and their mom stays vague when talking about their business. There's something shady about them, and I have no doubt that's why Wren loathes his family.

"I'm not eating with them," I say as I turn back to Elijah. "And don't tell me what to do."

I dig into my pancakes, but he doesn't touch his food, even when he finally brings his gaze back to me.

"Please, Peach. Go eat with your friends." He sighs, his small shoulders curling on himself as he subconsciously tries to disappear.

When he behaves like this, his skinny body retreating on itself, his eyes down in defeat, the difference between him and Wren becomes so stark they barely look like they're related.

Physically, they don't look alike. Wren's chestnut hair and beautiful blue eyes are nothing like Elijah's dark brown hair and matching chocolate gaze. Elijah has absolutely nothing exceptional about him. He's average looking, borderline invisible. He's a skinny guy with no friends, was never good at school, and often bullied for being quiet and ungifted. In a way, it's what always pulled me to him. Because I might be a bitch, but I'm never a bitch for no reason. And Elijah's shyness or lack of self-esteem shouldn't be a reason to bully him.

Wren is his opposite. Always popular, admired. Men would kill to be him. Women always run after him. He's mastered the mysterious persona without making you feel like you can't approach him. He's a touch sweet, a touch serious, and a touch don't-fuck-with-me. We all love it, don't we? The idea of a man who can melt our hearts but scare us a little. Who can be the sweetest but also know when to put his foot down. The good grades, the great looks, the offers for lacrosse scholarships to colleges all over the country. Wren seems to have balanced it all. He's the perfect man, the perfect boyfriend, and he should be the perfect son.

And yet, he's the hated one in his family. Elijah has always been the favorite. So, I guess that doesn't help their relationship.

"Can you imagine if every time you told me something, I actually did it? Don't be an idiot. I'm eating with my friend right now."

"He hates you hanging out with me."

"Boo hoo, he can cry me a river."

He goes silent long enough to eat some of his food. I'm already halfway through mine, incapable of stopping myself when there's a mix of sweet and savory.

"He likes you, you know? He really likes you. Or he wouldn't follow you to a damn brunch place so he could keep an eye on you while you eat with me."

I roll my eyes. "News flash, everyone likes me."

"I mean, he likes you more than a friend."

"So did I. Everyone wants to be more than my friend. Have you seen me?"

He practically chokes on his food, turning bright red when I wink at him. When he's finally swallowed his tiny bite, he scratches his throat and drinks some of his coffee.

"Don't you like him too?"

I lick maple syrup off my lips, shrugging. "Why does that matter? We're incompatible, and I have countless options. I don't even *think* of Wren."

Not entirely true, but I don't need to let him know that. Especially not now.

"Did you think of him when he went on a date with Ania Livingston?"

It's my turn to choke on my food. I struggle to swallow the bite of pancake that now feels like sand.

Toward the end of our junior year, Wren, who never dates or sleeps with anyone, started seeing Ania Livingston. She was a girl we were friends with at Stoneview Prep and still hung out with from time to time since starting at SFU.

They never got to become serious because Ania died. Everyone knows it wasn't an accident because there's an ongoing investigation. She was murdered. None of the details have been released yet. All we know is that she was found on the south bank of the Silver Snake River early in the morning of our last party of the year. That same river that crosses Silver Falls, where our college is.

"I didn't really care, Elijah," I say with a sigh, hoping he doesn't see the lie in my eyes.

I was so. Fucking. Jealous.

Wren, who never had a girlfriend, and who let the rumors run, spread, *explode*, when they said it was because he wanted me and no one else...was suddenly dating a girl? Anyone in my situation would be jealous.

"Were you jealous of her?"

"Elijah," I snap. "Are you the one into your brother? Because you can't fucking stop talking about him."

"Maybe because he's shooting daggers at me from across the restaurant. All I'm saying is, if you were jealous, it's a pretty good indication that you're into him, and that you should go eat with him. Because I'm not about to get a beating just for eating with the girl he likes."

"Wren and I *aren't. A. Thing.* We'll never be a thing."

He pauses, looks me straight in the eye, and nods. "I'm sorry."

"You two have some serious issues to resolve, but don't put me in the middle of it. And in case you forgot. You and I aren't a thing either."

He blushes again, now staring at his plate like it holds the cure to cancer. "I-I know," he mumbles. "I'd never— I don't think that. I'm not even into you."

I burst into a laugh. "I'm fucking with you."

I know he's into me. Because why wouldn't he be? We'd be practically perfect together.

He finally gets over his awkwardness when I turn around and flip the middle fingers at Wren and Achilles. It makes him laugh and lightens the mood. But something stays with me.

Were you jealous of her?

The poor girl died, and all I imagine when I think of her is how furious I was that she dared to date a man who's known for being into me.

Sweet, kind Ania. A docile girl who would have been Wren's perfect other half. That's probably why he gave in. She asked him out so many times that he finally saw something he liked in her: devotion. She was the exact opposite of me.

"I need the bathroom," I mumble, a stress I can't control starting to stir anger inside me.

I speed walk to the ladies' room at the back, locking myself in a stall and shaking my head as I huff.

She was fucking *murdered*.

I unlock my phone and open the SFU app to scroll down my messages until May. May 29th, to be exact. The night Ania died.

With a trembling finger, I open the conversation with her, biting my inner lip as I watch our last exchange.

> Ania: I'm sorry, Peach. Please, don't be mad at me. I meant what I said to you. I love him.

> Peach: Stay the fuck away from Wren. Or I swear to God…

What the fuck is wrong with me? I never thought of myself as a possessive bitch until she got close enough to take his attention away from me.

The girl was murdered.

I take a deep breath and delete the whole interaction.

"You're fine," I murmur to myself. "You're safe."

Another deep breath, and I school my features, feeling strength coming back to my limbs.

That's until I get a notification. A DM from Hermes on the SFU app.

> Hermes: What starts with an M, has eight letters, and ends with an R? I know what you did, Penelope.

My heart drops to my stomach, crashing so hard it makes me feel sick. The walls of the stall tilt as I look down at the message. Another follows right away.

> Hermes: You and I are going to have a lot of fun this year, little murderer.

-metal IS NOT the same as punk.
-She's still allergic to shellfish and cat hair
-Always leave the green olives to her
-We don't like metal anymore.
-Don't forget the peri-peri powder on her fries
-Bake and shake every first Tuesday of the month.
-No more sugar in her coffee. It makes her feel sick
-DO NOT bother me during girls' night Wren
-Spiced honey on pepperoni pizza
-Check the triangle freckles on her right shoulder
frequently. Dermatologist said to keep an eye.
-New vision results: Right eye -2.75. Left eye -3.25

Chapter Four

Wren

Family Line – Conan Gray

The SUV stops in front of the gates while the driver waits for them to open. Silver Falls University is only a half-hour drive from Stoneview, but it feels so freeing to be over there and not in this suffocating town.

Growing up surrounded by other billionaires took away our sense of reality. When you understand you're invincible, that the rules of the world don't apply to you, it does something to your developing brain. Now we're all grown. We moved to the college only we can access, away from the parental supervision that was already minimal. And we get crazier by the minute.

The whole situation is claustrophobic.

Born in Stoneview, your pampered peers' biggest problem is the Wi-Fi that didn't work on their yacht during the summer break. Attending Stoneview Prep, the important thing is to be the most *something* in a sea of people who believe themselves exceptional. Graduate, get into the best elite college in the country. Move into a beautiful house on SFU campus that costs more per semester than the average citizen's salary. And in exchange for a lavish life and living above everyone else...just do what you're *fucking told*.

It's no wonder I have a need to dominate everything, to be the decision-maker, the one who makes the rules. I'm just catching up on a lifetime of all decisions being taken away from me.

The car snakes all the way up the interminable driveway that's typical to Stoneview mansions. It gives the owners privacy like nowhere else. Especially where my family lives in the hills. No one knows what happens inside our house. Ever.

"Thank you, Henry," I say as our driver stops the car in the circular driveway. Right between the fountain and the front door so there's minimal effort to get inside the house once we're out of the car.

"Of course."

Tension stiffens the muscles in my neck as I look at the front door through the tinted window. I stretch it from side to side, wishing for once in my life I could feel anything else but a dire need for murder when it comes to this house.

"Don't go anywhere," I add. "I won't be long."

It's Elijah sitting next to me who answers. "You don't even know what we're here for. Don't keep the man waiting. It's late."

I close my eyes, begging for patience to take over the fury that makes my blood boil every time my brother opens his mouth.

I don't acknowledge him, locking eyes with our driver through the mirror. "I won't be long," I repeat with a soft smile.

He nods, and I finally open the door. I dust off my black

jeans and take in the grandeur of the Hunter mansion. Such a big house, yet there was never anywhere to hide from my father. No place in there he wouldn't find me.

"My baby," my mom coos as Elijah and I walk in, our butler already grabbing my jacket while she hugs her favorite son.

She turns to me after the overly affectionate hello. "Wren," she says softly, barely enough of a smile left on her face to look welcoming as she squeezes my upper arm.

It's not a cold greeting, necessarily. She's not being mean or detached, but the difference would be painful to anyone who isn't used to it. After twenty-two years of this shit, it barely affects me anymore.

It's not that my mother doesn't love me.

She's scared of me.

"Come, come." She turns back to the entrance hall, her heels clacking against the marble. "Your dad is in his office, but he'll be out in a minute. I had Nicole make your favorite. Roasted pork shoulder and vegetables."

Elijah's favorite.

I run a hand over my face, unsure I can push through the bullshit for an entire dinner.

"Why did Dad ask us to come?" I ask as we walk into the dining room, and I roll my eyes.

Was it really necessary to have a king's banquet served here when we're not even supposed to stay over?

Elijah is already sitting down in his usual spot. "This looks so good, Mom. Thank you so much."

"She didn't make it," I mumble to myself as I stop behind my chair. There's no way I'm sitting down. "I can't stay for dinner. I have a thing."

"What thing?" Elijah asks, the pretense of innocence accentuated by his wide brown eyes as he looks up at me.

"Dinner with friends. You wouldn't know what that's like."

"Wren," my mom scolds. "Be kind."

"Peach didn't mention any dinner with you," he insists.

"No." I chuckle to myself, shaking my head and begging my body to stay calm. "Don't even let her name leave your mouth."

My mom stands next to Elijah's chair as she fills his plate with vegetables, choosing to ignore my threat. "You still like honeyed carrots, don't you, my love?"

"I think I just puked in my mouth," I snort as my brother blushes from our mom's stupid endearment for him.

My love. Like he's still a five-year-old who needs reassurance.

"How's Penelope?" she asks cheerily.

"She's fine."

Time stops as Elijah and I look at each other. We answered at the same time, both assuming if our mom asked about Peach, we would be the best person to update her.

I keep a straight face, swallowing back the need to rearrange my brother's smile, and look at my mom again.

"She's fine," I repeat.

But he can't leave it there. He *has* to insist. "I had brunch with her yesterday, and she's looking forward to presenting her research paper to the head of her department. She worked really hard on it and wants to use it for her postgrad application."

My eyes narrow on him as he starts digging into his food, my hands tightening on the back of the oak chair in front of me.

"She's such a smart young lady. Her dads must be so proud of her. What's her research about?"

Elijah's eyebrows pinch as he bites into his meat.

"Umm..." He chews harder, talking with a mouth full. "Nano-something for the environment? She wants to save trees."

"Environmental science and engineering applications of nanocellulose-based nanocomposites," I answer in one breath, my eyes still on him. Did he really reduce her hard work to *she wants to save trees*? "She's researching ways to create paper, film, and fibers without destroying the environment. It could change everything we mass produce in the world. It could quite literally save the planet."

He pauses his disgusting chewing and swallows thickly. "Alright, Einstein. I knew that. I was trying to make it simple for Mom." Acting disappointed, he shakes his head. "Everything has to be a competition with you, Wren. It's exhausting."

Our mother jumps to his defense right away. "He's not wrong, Wren." She taps Elijah's shoulder, weirdly standing behind him while he eats. "Thank you, my love. I get it. And it's a very noble cause. Good for her."

I bite my inner cheek, smile at my mom, and nod. "So, why are we here?"

"God, is it a crime for a mother to want to see her sons?"

"When you want to see your sons, Elijah is usually enough. So why are we here?"

Struggling to look offended at my remark, she doesn't even deny it.

"Sit down." My father's southern drawl invades the room, putting an end to our conversation. He walks straight to his seat at the head of the table without so much as a hello.

"I'm not staying," I explain calmly, releasing the chair so he doesn't see my unease. "What do you need?"

"Did you not hear me the first time, boy?" he snaps, not

45

even looking at me as he settles his napkin on his lap. "You're going to sit down, spend time with us, and enjoy the dinner your mother made."

"*Had* made," I huff.

"*Sit. Down.* Wren." The flicker of violence in his tone kicks a survival instinct inside me. One Elijah never had to learn.

My jaw tightens as I pull out the chair and sit down. Once I've put a slice of bread on my plate to give myself something to do, I look at him again.

"So, why are we here?"

"Initiations are in two weeks."

I pretend to relax against the back of my chair, but when my gaze crosses with Elijah's excited one, there's absolutely nothing about me that stays relaxed.

My family has been part of an elitist secret society for generations. When powerful people find a way to keep control of everything, they don't let it go. That's what the Silent Circle does. It's a pool of unstoppable billionaires incessantly moving in a circle of favors. Politicians, tech titans, Big Pharma, and all their friends. And of course, the supermajors of the oil industry, including Monty Hunter. For every step they take legally, there are ten others they take on the wrong side of the law.

In two weeks, my brother and I are supposed to initiate into the Silent Circle. But to do so, every prospect has to bring a woman with them. They go through their own rite of passage, and by the end of the night, they get a place within the Circle. Not always the one they hoped for, though.

"I can't initiate." I shrug, playing with the piece of bread on my plate. I was starving before I came here, but seeing my family always makes me lose my appetite.

"You're going to, Wren. You have to."

"I don't have anyone to bring to the initiations."

"Yeah, because she's dead," Elijah snorts.

"That's not my fault, is it?" I grunt, running a hand across my face. "But I know the rules. If I want to become a Shadow in the Silent Circle, I have to bring a woman to the initiations." I smile to let him know he's not affecting me as much as he thinks he is. "I don't have a woman to bring."

"Do you know what's funny," Elijah keeps going. "That you're the only one in this family who's always categorically refused to join the Circle. And just like that, the girl who would have allowed you to become a Shadow, *conveniently* died."

Narrowing my eyes on my brother, I clench my jaw. "I did not kill Ania Livingston."

The men who initiate into the Silent Circle can only become one thing. A Shadow. Initiated Shadows get to keep their lavish lifestyle and more, have access to other members and the favors they can offer. They're also given a position within the Circle. One they can't refuse. They take on a role within the Circle that the board decided for them. My friend, Chris, for example, will be a corporate attorney for them once he graduates. He'll take care of all their big companies, and the mergers they finalize once they swallow smaller ones.

I have no problem with the position they want to give me. But I have a problem doing it for them. I don't have a choice but to join, but as far as I know, not having a woman to bring to initiations is my only way to delay it.

The woman we bring with us can have one of two roles within the Circle. Neither I wish on anyone I love.

I look at both my father and brother, only now realizing

my mother has disappeared. Of course, we wouldn't want her involved in the family business.

"Last time I checked, you didn't have anyone to bring," I tell Elijah. "Did you bring back one of your girls from the South of France?" I can't help the disgust dripping from my voice.

Elijah will be following the exact same steps as my father in the Circle. And their role is worse than the one they're trying to stick me with.

"I've got someone." His smirk truly tempts me to jump over the table and wipe it off his face with my fist. He's clearly bringing someone he likes.

"Who? You do know it doesn't mean she'll be your Hera. Anyone could have her." I lean forward. "Me, for example."

Bringing a woman doesn't mean she's the person we'll end up with once we're initiated. The women have to go through initiations, and they can end up as either a Hera—someone who will, down the line, become the wife of a Shadow. They're stuck with the same man for the rest of their lives, forced to be faithful to a fucker who considers them nothing more than an accessory to their legacy. But they have power in the world. Being a Hera to a Shadow grants you anything you want, as long as your husband allows it.

If they don't become a Hera, then they're an Aphrodite. To put it simply, an Aphrodite is a whore for the Circle. They become toys for the Shadows. Women they can freely cheat on their Hera with. The principle is that Shadows are only allowed to play with them rather than women outside of the Circle. The society is so secretive, they wouldn't want a vengeful woman to have something to hold over a Shadow's head. Having the Aphrodites means the men can enjoy any sick fun they want without worrying about the consequences of the Circle being outed.

There are always more women initiating than men, meaning not everyone can become a Hera. They have to fight for it. And once you come to the initiations, there's no turning back. You become a Hera or an Aphrodite, but you can never leave the Circle. Not alive.

Women still come. They know that, and they try their chances. Money, power, it makes people do crazy, stupid things. Sometimes they do it out of love, tricked by their boyfriend into thinking they'll automatically become their Hera. But more than that, even if they become an Aphrodite, they get one favor from the Circle without having to pay it back. Every single Aphrodite gets her one favor. No matter what it is.

A job you've been dreaming of? Done.

A spot in your dream grad school? You got it.

Killed someone? They'll hide the body.

Want someone killed? They'll take care of it.

Anything. Is. Possible.

And desperation? It makes people do the craziest, most stupid things. Like initiate for the Silent Circle.

"Are you going to initiate just to steal my Hera, Wren?" My brother lets out a loud cackle. "Is that how much you want to humiliate me now? School, social life. Stoneview, Silver Falls. I'm already a pariah at SFU, and classes haven't even started. So, now the Circle too?"

"Me being better than you at everything isn't a personal persecution, Brother. It's just a fact."

"You're better than him at things that don't mean anything." My father's voice isn't loud, simply demeaning enough to shut me up. "Prove yourself within the Circle and you'll matter."

49

I pause for a minute, jaw tight, fist clenched on my lap. My eyes roam over his face. This man hates me. Proving myself won't change anything. It'll just be useful to him and his Shadow friends.

Standing up, I nod at him. "I don't have anyone to bring. I'm not initiating. Next year, maybe. Thanks for dinner."

I wipe my hands of the crumbs, and my dad's eyes dart to my plate with a destroyed piece of bread on it. He stays silent until I'm just about to cross the door, out of the dining room.

"I've got someone. She'll be there. You just have to show up."

Freezing, I barely find the strength to look over my shoulder. "What?"

"You heard me. There's a woman who will initiate for you."

"Who?"

"What, who. You're suddenly so interested." Elijah snorts.

"Shut the fuck up." I point a threatening finger at him as I finally turn around, giving my dad my full attention. "You found some poor woman who needs a favor so badly, she'll do anything, including initiating at the risk of becoming a whore for you and your buddies. Who is she?"

"She might become your Hera, who knows." My father shrugs, biting into his food for the first time tonight. The fucker is so at ease now that he got me riled up.

"If she runs fast enough," Elijah adds.

They both laugh, not caring one bit that someone is about to put their life at risk for their benefit.

"Who is she?" I repeat.

Swallowing, my father waves his fork. "Don't worry about her. Just know she'll be there."

Sounds about as shady as everything I expect from him.

My mom steps back into the dining room, meekly walking to my dad until she drops a kiss on his cheek like the brainwashed little Hera she is.

"It's getting late, Monty. The boys should go back. They have classes tomorrow."

He nods, his chin jutting toward the door. "Get some rest, will you. Work hard. Get ready for initiations. I'll see you in two weeks."

I'm the first one to leave, without a goodbye to anyone. My mother won't care as long as her baby boy gives her a big kiss and a tight hug.

I only talk to Elijah once we're on the highway to Silver Falls.

"Who's the girl you're bringing?" I ask.

"You've become so curious about my life." He chuckles. "You'll see in two weeks."

"Let me rephrase." I turn to him, a condescending smile breaking through the corner of my mouth. "Who could *possibly* want to initiate for you? No one likes you."

"Yeah, you keep making sure of that, don't you?" he snarls, his face turning red quickly. "Is Hermes a good friend of yours? Is that why they posted about me the second I set foot on campus?"

"You're fucking paranoid." I roll my eyes. "I have no idea who Hermes is."

"And yet, isn't it so convenient that everyone at SFU doesn't want to associate with me? Same as Stoneview Prep. Same as any space I have to share with handsome, smart, superior Wren Hunter."

"Glad you know where you stand compared to me."

His face twists with anger, making him even uglier than

usual. Truth is, my brother isn't horrendous to look at. He could easily date pretty girls if his social skills weren't so non-existent.

"You know," he seethes. "There *is* one girl on campus who doesn't look down on me. Who isn't stupid enough to believe the shit you tried to spread about me."

"I'm not spreading anything. Hermes is an anonymous account. They're trying to piss you off—" I stop myself as something finally catches up with me. "Wait."

I take a few seconds to process what he just said, the way he used it in our conversation.

"Tell me it's not Peach."

"You know she's the only one who doesn't buy into the bullshit of 'Wren is the perfect Hunter brother and Elijah is the loser no one should be friends with.'"

"And you know that's not what I fucking meant." His fake innocent smile is getting to me, but I keep a steady voice. "You're not bringing Peach to the initiations..."

Refusing to answer, he blinks at me.

"Are you?" I push out between clenched teeth.

"I thought you and her were best friends. Surely, she would have told you if I was bringing her."

Clarity fights through the hate for my brother, and my shoulders relax.

"You're not." I chuckle, seeing through his lie. "Peach would never agree to that shit. She has two brain cells to rub together. Unlike you."

"Sure, Wren."

I watch as he casually looks ahead, considering the conversation over.

"Look at me," I snap. When he refuses, I can't help myself. I grab him by the collar, pulling him toward me until his seat belt practically chokes him. He brings a hand to my wrist, the other to loosen the seat belt, but there's not much the weak man can do.

"Do. Not. Touch her." His smile doesn't go away in the slightest. "I swear to God, Elijah. Stay away from Peach, or I'll fucking end you."

"Maybe it's Peach. Maybe it's not. The best part is you won't know until initiations because you can't ask her without exposing the Circle. That's a deadly offense, Brother."

"If I show up to initiations and Peach is there, you're a dead man."

"There he is. Wren the big, bad murderer. Are you going to snap?"

My heartbeat accelerates from the accusation. The hint of a flashback narrows my vision before I come back to the present. I crack my neck, attempting to calm myself without success.

"I'm not a murderer," I whisper. If I try to speak louder, I'll sound threatening again, and then he'll be right.

"That's not what the law says." He chuckles. "Come to the initiations, find out who I brought, and we'll see how you react."

I tighten my grip on his shirt, my gaze roaming over his face to gauge if he's bullshitting me. No clues. No indication on whether he's bringing her to become part of a dangerous secret society.

And then I let go.

"Peach wouldn't," I say, trying so hard to convince myself.

"Ah, well. Desperation, Wren. It's a powerful thing."

"She isn't desperate. She's not weak. She wouldn't trust a fucker like you blindly."

He shrugs, but the conversation is cut short by our driver parking in the visitor lot of Silver Falls University.

"Who should I drop first?" he asks, looking into the rearview mirror.

Whereas I live in a campus house, Elijah lives in the dorms. He just came back and has no friends to share a house with.

"Don't worry about me," I say as I open the door. "I need a walk anyway."

Leaving the parking lot, I walk past the red-brick castle and toward the woods of our beautiful campus. They lead to the residences.

The air is cool, calming my heated body.

They always get to me.

I take a deep breath. The earthy smell of the bald cedars surrounding me grounds me.

They always get to me.

They always get to me because they're the ones who created the weaknesses inside me. The monster. The one who shows up when I snap.

And they're desperate to use him for the Circle.

My mind is back in my body, but my heartbeat still hasn't calmed, and I know only one thing will help.

The same thing I had planned before being forced to go to my family's house. The same thing I do most nights of the week. Every fucking night when I need to appease myself.

I finally come out of the woods, excitement brewing in my stomach. My heart quickens once more as I get near my house. It'll ease in a minute, once the rush is gone and I'm sure I'm not getting caught.

When I get to my porch and take a left, I slow down my eager steps, sliding between the two walls that separate mine and Achilles's house from our best friends'. I drag my hand against the wall of the girls' house, until I'm near their backyard and push past the exact spot where their wall meets their hedge. With time, it's become easier and easier, the hole practically the shape of my body. It barely even scratches my skin anymore.

I bend my knees, jumping high enough to catch the bottom of the above balcony, and easily pull myself up. There's a reason I crush everyone in any sport. I work hard. But mainly to be able to do this exact movement with ease. Her balcony is eleven feet above the ground, and I'm six-five. I put the bar in my home gym at exactly eleven feet so I can train every morning to jump that height and pull my weight. I could do this all night long and not break a sweat. I can come and go as I please when it comes to this exact balcony.

I climb over the wooden balustrade and make my way to the French doors, taking out the key I always keep on me. If Peach knew I made a copy the second she moved in and chose her room, she would annihilate me. I make sure to look through the window to check she's sleeping before opening the door discretely and sliding inside her room.

The rush of adrenaline dissipates the second I see her in the flesh. She's breathing heavily, sleeping on her side and hugging her pillow like a teddy protecting her from the bad men who could sneak into her room at night.

I smile to myself. The covers are to her waist, one leg under and one leg out for the most comfortable tempera-ture. Her satin sleeping shorts are black, hiking to the point that her perfect ass is showing underneath the hem.

She sighs, hugging her pillow closer, and my pulse finally goes back to normal. Some nights, I go around looking for things she hides in here and that I don't want her to use. The Adderall she illegally buys from dealers on campus, the weed she smokes too often, the coke she sniffs on nights out. Some nights, I caress her cheek, smell her hair, take in the scent of rose and lychee that follows her everywhere, steal the pen I know she chews on when she's working hard on her research and essays.

But most nights, like tonight, I sit on the floor right beside her bed, my back to the wall, and facing her. She mostly sleeps on her right side. Away from the door, facing the window.

So that's where I sit tonight.

I catch the letter she left on her bedside table.

Dear Mom and Dad...

I stop myself from going any further, my heart fissuring for her. I know where this letter will go. In the box under her bed where she keeps all the other ones she wrote to her biological parents. I read a couple until I felt bad for not respecting her privacy. There's a side of Peach she won't show to anyone. Not even me, and it feels wrong to know about it.

Her insecurities lay deeply in the fact that she was abandoned when she was three, and that, to this day, she has no idea why.

Taking a deep breath, I rest my head against the wall. I look at my best friend, and it finally happens.

Everything. Stops.

The bad thoughts, the fear, the murderous feeling my family puts in me, the anxiety that comes with initiating into the Silent Circle.

It all disappears.

Suddenly, the air is light, the pain nonexistent, and everything quiets.

That's the magical effect Peach has on me.

And if she has to become someone's forever, it would not be my brother's. If she has to initiate, it would be for me.

How easy would everything be if she became my Hera. If she was left without a choice but to be mine.

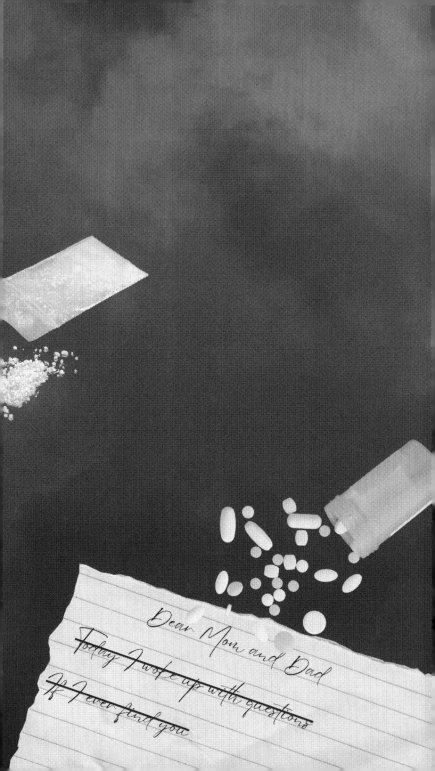

Chapter Five

Peach

OXOX – Dutch Melrose, Lost Boy

I t's been almost a week since the ominous message from Hermes, and I haven't heard from them again. Their last post was outing Miles, some guy from the lacrosse team after he cheated on his studious girlfriend with a cheerleader, and she didn't do anything about it. What did everyone think? That she would fight her? Scream and cry on the lacrosse field to get him back? The girl moved on, good for her.

I'm sitting on a chair outside my professor's office, scrolling through my SFU private messages and looking at the one Hermes sent me over and over again. I had never been sent a private message from them before. They're an account that loves public attention, and if they haven't mentioned my name in relation to that murder, they want something.

I just don't know what yet.

But I won't answer, and I won't play their game. They have nothing against me, nothing that says I was with Ania that night. Or at least no more and no less than the hundreds of other people who were partying at our sorority house.

"Penelope, hi. Please, come in."

I look up at Professor Lopez, putting my phone away and gathering my folder of documents.

Following him inside, I sit down as he points at the chair in front of his desk. He settles behind it, and I put the folder on top of the countless other paperwork he has.

"For you." I smile brightly, the excitement from almost four years of passionate work bubbling in my stomach.

He shakes his head. "I don't need it. I read everything you sent to my assistant."

"Did you? I didn't think he'd even have time to read them."

"Is there anything new in this?" His gaze drops to the folder.

"Only graphs to put some numbers in a simple way, but no new research from what I've sent to Jonathan." His assistant is a PhD student who rarely thinks there's anything good enough to pass on to Professor Lopez. He's a filter if I've ever seen one.

The fact that he didn't get back to me to tell me he'd forwarded my research to our professor should be a good thing. Jonathan hates people who do good. He wants to be the only special person to Professor Lopez. In this class, there are only two students who can get his attention. Me... and Wren. And fuck if we've turned Advanced Innovation in Science Engineering into the most competitive class for ourselves. It's me and him constantly fighting for first spot, and Wren currently holds it. The man majors in bioengineering, and sometimes I think he took this course just to piss me off.

Professor Lopez nods to himself, scratching his salt-and-pepper messy beard. It's short, but so unkept.

"So," I say tentatively as I squirm in my seat. "Do you think it's good enough for my masters application? I know SFU Engineering has very limited spots, especially Environmental sciences. But I don't know, I think I'm onto something here. I just want to be able to do more research, have access to more people. I need more time, but—"

"Grad school?" He chuckles to himself. "This is a one-way ticket right here, no questions asked. But it's not what I'm worried about."

I gulp, hating that there's something *worrying* him. I've been so confident about this paper, have put so much energy into it that it's flawless to me.

"What are you worried about?"

"Well, this is almost perfect. I'm worried about how we're going to improve it to submit it to the E.E.A.J."

The world stops spinning for a second.

"W-what?"

His stoic face breaks into a smile.

"You want to submit my work to the Environmental Engineering American Journal... Are you joking?"

He shakes his head. "Do you need sugar, Penelope? You look pale."

"I think I'm going to faint."

"Take a breather," he says with a soft laugh.

There's a mix of hope, excitement, and complete anxiety running through my veins.

"I can't... It's not ready."

"No, it's not. But we can absolutely work on it, and then submit it. You've done remarkable research on this. It's innovative, interesting, and it would really show Howard Corall who's best."

A laugh bubbles out of me. Corall is from the Harvard postgrad school, and he and Professor Lopez have a long-standing competition on who has the best students.

"You really stuck it to Wren Hunter with this one, didn't you?" His joking tone tells me he's been following Wren and I's competition.

"Could you say this on camera?" I ask, teasing but also dead serious. "That would *really* stick it to him."

"Let's not push it." He tilts his head to the side. "Welcome to the big game. You're about to enter a whole new competitive world."

"I'm ready," I spurt out right away. "I'm going to nail this." I sound like I'm on coke, I'm so fired up, but I'm going to crush this paper. Being published in the E.E.A.J. means being eligible for an environmental engineering award. And an award could one day lead to a Nobel Prize. That's a life-time goal.

"Alright, hold your horses." His eyebrows pinch, and he takes a deep breath. "This isn't only going to be a lot of work. The journal will look into your life"—his eyes dart around my face—"intricately. They'll look into your past, your present, and will decide your future."

I gulp, the first thing coming to my mind being the message from Hermes. Not only that, but all the things they posted publicly about me in the past.

"That sounds scary," I admit.

"It is. The world of science is competitive, invasive, and damn corrupted. You can't just be a scientific genius, but you also have to be a perfect human being with no skeletons in your closet. Or I can promise you, they'll find them and expose them. Anything to stop someone from shaking the people already established in that world."

He pauses, looking pointedly at me. "You've got a reputation on this campus, Penelope."

My mouth drops open. "Professor, I can promise you that whatever you heard wouldn't affect my work."

"Being a"—he searches for the correct words—"*party girl* isn't the end of the world, though it isn't exactly going to lead you to an award." He hesitates. There's clearly worse to come. "But being a near drug addict is most definitely going to stop you from being published. It's *not* a good look on the E.E.A.J."

I can feel the blood draining from my face. "So," I rasp. "Even professors read gossip accounts, I see." I can't hide the disappointment from my voice.

"It's a way to keep up with student safety."

"But Hermes lies. I'm not... This is stupid. I'm not a fucking *drug addict*." I struggle to keep the anger down, correcting myself right away. "I'm sorry. I didn't mean to be so rude. It-it's frustrating. People read that stupid account and believe it blindly. I thought you'd know me better than that."

He puts an appeasing hand on his desk, almost where mine is resting while still making sure he isn't touching me. "I don't believe anything that account says. I'm warning you, the E.E.A.J. board members will use it against you. They might or might not believe it, but it doesn't matter; they will use it. Other people will too. Hell, Professor Corall will be the first one to send them the posts."

I chuckle, rolling my eyes. "Is this the mafia or something?"

"Pretty much." He laughs, eyebrows lifting. "Penelope, I have great plans for you. You're the most splendid student I've had in a very long time. Science flows in your veins. You're destined for a Nobel Prize. I want you to succeed, and for that, I need you to have the most spotless life. You need to work, eat, and breathe Environmental Engineering until we get you exactly where we want you."

It's all I can see now. That message.

You and I are going to have a lot of fun this year, little murderer.

I scratch my throat, making sure I keep pretending everything is fine. "Of course. I'll be leading the perfect scientist's life. You can count on me."

"I trust you."

I force a smile on my face. "I truly appreciate this opportunity, Professor Lopez."

"Good. Enjoy your classes this afternoon. I'll be sending you detailed comments about your work by the end of the day, so you can get started tonight."

"Sure thing." I grab my bag as I stand up, smoothing my burgundy uniform skirt.

With Silver Falls University being the same private institution as Stoneview Preparatory School, where we all went to study, it has the same horrible dress code. It means all undergrad students must still wear a uniform. It was burgundy and midnight blue at Stoneview Prep, and the SFU one is burgundy and black. All it does is reinforce that feeling of the special bubble we live in. The postgrads look like they've at least seen some of the real world since they can dress however they want. We're still looking like the little kids they breed in Stoneview. The ones who don't know shit.

"Have a good day, Professor," I say as I close his office door.

I pull my phone out as I walk through the dark hallway of the science building. It's one of the oldest on campus, and I tend to wear sneakers here because the stone floor is so uneven. Shadows usually creep up the wall when it's empty, but it's full of people right now, and I nod at a lot of familiar faces.

As I head to my class, I send a message to the group with all my best friends.

> Peach: I'm not having drinks with you losers tonight. Lopez loved my work so much he's helping me get it ready for the freaking E.E.A.J.

Texts from them come right away.

> Ella: Oh my god, Peach. Congrats!! You're the best.

> Alex: Congratulations! You're exceptional. All that hard work is paying off.

> Achilles: The polar bears must be so happy. Have a drink with us to celebrate.

> Peach: Shut up, Achilles.

I take a picture of myself with my paper and pull a middle finger before sending it to Wren personally.

> Peach: Lopez said I'm the most SPLENDID student he's had in a while. Eat that, fucker. Next pic you get will be my Nobel Prize.

> Wren: I'm so proud of you.

My heart skips a beat at his instant response. Where's our usual back-and-forth? These words hit differently. It's the thought behind it, the person they come from. They're everything I wanted to hear. And fuck, I think he knows it.

Wren: But he hasn't seen my paper yet...so be prepared to lose his attention.

I let out a small breath, half-relieved, half-wondering why I loved it so much when he was proud of me. I spend the day opening our chat and reading that message again. In class, I'm smiling to myself.

But by the time I get home and it's time to work on my notes for my project, I shut it all down. My focus has to stay on what matters, not how I feel around my best friend.

-metal IS NOT the same as punk.
-She's still allergic to shellfish and cat hair
-Always leave the green olives to her
-We don't like metal anymore.
-Tea tree and peppermint shampoo
-Don't forget the peri-peri powder on her fries
-Bake and shake every first Tuesday of the month.
-No more sugar in her coffee. It makes her feel sick
-DO NOT bother me during girls' night Wren
-Spiced honey on pepperoni pizza
-Check the triangle freckles on her right shoulder
frequently. Dermatologist said to keep an eye.
-New vision results: Right eye -2.75. Left eye -3.25
-If she gets in next September's yearly release of the
EEAJ, the announcement will be in August next year.

Chapter Six

Wren

God Needs The Devil – Jonah Kagen

"Beer, Wren?" Ella asks as she walks into my living room with a few in her hands.

I look down at my phone again, checking if Peach answered my message.

> Wren: Congrats again on your project. Promise you're not going to exhaust yourself working on it, though?

"How about a margarita?" I ask, looking back at Ella as I pretend to relax on the sofa.

"Our margarita queen is busy tonight. She's working on her research project."

She eyes me for longer than necessary, clearly looking for the disappointment on my face. I barely bother to hide it.

I'm dying to see Peach, but I'm not so selfish that I would be annoyed with her for working on her passion instead of spending time with us. That's not what I'm bothered about. I'm worried about the things she does to keep up with the lifestyle she has. No one could stay sane while partying, being an accomplished cheerleader, volunteering at the Silver Falls Women's Shelter, the back-and-forths between here and Stoneview for the family appearances now that her dad is running for mayor. And, of course, the number of hours she spends on her studies.

She's skipping a night out with her friends to work? Great. But I also know she went out all weekend, went to Stoneview, and had cheer practice at seven a.m. this morning. And she also started talking about a "rally girls charity event" where she's gathering a group of girls to take care of the lacrosse players during this season in exchange for the lacrosse league donating to a charity that helps young women who have been sexually assaulted on college campuses. I can't believe she's adding to her already full agenda. She should skip drinks to *sleep*.

Achilles sits next to me, a beer in his hand.

"How does it work? Do you not drink anything if Peach isn't here to tend to you? Do you starve when she's not around too?"

I snort, grabbing a beer from the table and opening it with my teeth. "Any man waiting for Peach to do anything for him would die within forty-eight hours."

Ella runs back to the kitchen as her phone alarm indicates her cookies are finished. At the same time, the doorbell rings, telling us Alex's boyfriend is here, so she leaves the living room too.

"Wren," Achilles says, more seriously the second they're both gone. "I'm going to keep saying this until next Saturday. Peach could be yours. Just bring her to the initiations."

The same wave of hesitation I always get runs through me until I get a hold of myself. I still don't know which woman I'm supposedly bringing. Or who my dad is bringing for me.

"No. We talked about this. If Peach and I end up being a thing, I want it to be because she *chose* me. If I knew she'd choose me over anything else, I'd invite her. But right now, she wouldn't, and if I ask her to initiate, she'll just refuse."

"It's the only way she'll be with you. Make her your Hera."

His condescending way of speaking doesn't get to me like it does others. I've had to learn to keep myself calm and not snap at the smallest things. It's the only way to protect myself and the people around me.

"If I force her to initiate, there's a risk she won't run to *me*. That also means she could be anyone else's Hera. Or everyone's Aphrodite. The only reason I would ever bring Peach into this without her consent is if she needs a favor only the Circle can grant."

Achilles huffs. "Is everyone *that* dumb around here? Your ex-girlfriend died over the summer. The same night Peach drunkenly told you she could fall for you if you weren't...how did she put it?"

"Such a dominating fuck." It comes out naturally because she's called me that many times. "Look, initiations are in a week. I still want to try to do this the right way."

He stares at me like I'm some idiot. "You want to do this the right way? In a week? You've had *sixteen* years, and you think you can turn this around in one week? Are you okay?"

"I was taking it slow. I didn't want to pressure her."

He pinches his lips, so unimpressed I could punch him. "Yeah, that was reaaal slow. Sixteen years slow."

"Fuck you."

"Fuck *her*, please, for the love of God. You're not some kind of sweet dude who doesn't pressure someone. Peach

71

knows that. She probably doesn't give you a chance because you're too nice with her. Give her a fucking challenge."

"You don't know her like I do."

"That's for sure. Never had my fingers deep in her cu—"

My gaze cuts him off, and he moves a little farther back on the couch before carrying on.

"Listen. She disappeared with Ania that night, and you know it. And then the poor girl dies? If you didn't kill her, we both know who did. Here's the favor she's going to need soon. Protection from the law. Only the Circle can help, except it will be too late if she's not already part of it by the time the cops catch up."

"This is how I know you're fucked in the head," I answer calmly. "Because you actually think Peach killed her."

"Did you?" He looks at me pointedly. "Did the perfect boy *snap*? We know what happens when you do."

He runs a hand through his black hair, flashing me his sadistic smile.

"I didn't snap." I huff. "I didn't kill Ania."

"Then your precious Penelope did."

I open my mouth to retort something, but Alex and her boyfriend, Xi, walk into the room.

"Initiate her," Achilles murmurs before smiling at our friends. "You'll thank me later."

I quickly say hi to Xi and leave, pretending to get another beer in the kitchen. Instead, I hang in the hallway between the kitchen and living room, wondering if I should be an asshole like Achilles and simply take what I want. Because it's no secret I'm desperate to have Peach to myself. Hell, the idea of her having no choice but to be devoted to me is something that has been stuck in my mind for months.

But I didn't break all the times Achilles suggested I send her an invite, and I won't break now.

I take a deep breath, check my phone that still doesn't have a message from Peach, and I'm about to head back to the living room, when Xi joins me in the hallway.

"I have something to show you," he says in his toneless voice.

Could be good, could be someone's death. No one ever really knows.

He shows me his phone, and my heart drops right away. It's a message from Peach.

> Peach: Can Addie come to my house tonight? It's just me.

> Xi: You know I don't do this anymore.

> Peach: Who's your friend on campus?

> Xi: Alex would kill me if I told you.

"Come on, Peach," I mutter to myself, running a hand across my face. It was after I messaged her. She's ignoring me but talking to Xi.

"You know what she means by Addie, right?" he double-checks.

Xi isn't from Stoneview like us. Alex met him on the North Shore of Silver Falls. Unlike the South Bank, where SFU is, the North Shore is known for its poverty, gangs, and dangerous criminal activities altogether. It doesn't mean we're better and they're worse, but that they don't have the means to live another kind of life. We do, but we're just greedy. Stoneview and the South Bank of Silver Falls host more dangerous criminals than the local gangs of the North Shore.

Xi happens to be from there, and he used to be a known drug dealer. Everyone knew his name on campus because he could provide them with any drug they needed. And before he stopped for Alex, Peach was a regular customer of his.

"Yeah, I know. She wants Adderall. She's got a huge research paper she's working on. It's a big deal for her career, and she doesn't want to fuck it up."

He shrugs. "Thought you'd want to know."

The second Xi became part of our circle through Alex, I asked him to let me know if Peach ever tried to buy from him. She's not looking after herself, destroying her body for the sake of partying and keeping up with her work. Someone has to keep an eye on that.

"I appreciate it. Thank you." I nod, and we walk back to the living room together.

"Let's play Scrabble!" Ella does a little dance on the spot. "I want to be with Wren."

"Fuck that. I'm always with Wren. You can have Alex's brain," Achilles defends as I sit next to him.

"Alex doesn't play Scrabble religiously, like Wren, our boring boy. She's not good. And Peach isn't here to be his ultimate competition. So I pick Wren."

"Thanks," Alex and I reply in unison from our respective insults.

When we play Scrabble, we always do it as teams. It's just funnier that way. And not only am I a nerd when it comes to this game, but everyone knows I'm also extremely competitive. More often than not, my team wins. And the only times I lose are because Peach made it a point to crush me out of pure combativeness.

"Maybe we should unite against them, Alex," I say with a half-smile.

"And crush all their hopes of winning? Give them a chance."

The cookies, Scrabble, and drinks turn into a walk to the Acropolis. Alex and Ella are drunk, Xi following his girlfriend with a scowl on his face. He'd probably rather be home with their pet bunnies than babysitting her on a campus he shouldn't even be on.

We enter our favorite bar, and Achilles somehow already has a girl on his lap by the time I come back to the table they snatched, bringing a platter of drinks to everyone.

"Wren," the girl calls out, as if she knows me. Does she? "You know my friend Marissa? She's here." She's drunk enough to not care at all about the obvious wink she throws my way.

From the corner of my eye, I can see Alex and Ella elbowing each other, giggling as they attempt to hide behind the drinks I've just handed them.

"Great." I nod.

"I'm going to go get her!"

"No, don't—" It's too late. The girl jumps off Achilles's lap, using Xi as furniture as she goes across him to exit the booth.

He grunts, sending dark looks at Ella and Alex, who both can't stop laughing from across the table.

"Let's switch," Xi tells Achilles, so he's the one against the wall and doesn't have to live through another woman crushing him to get to our campus fuckboy.

Grabbing a stool, I sit at the end of the booth and take a sip of my beer.

"That was Kirsty, by the way," Alex tells us. "Since I'm sure none of you remember her."

"Oh, I remember her," Achilles says with a bright smile. Or the attempt of it. They never quite reach his ears, always making people uncomfortable enough to know he can't be trusted.

"You remembered *her*, but did you remember her name?" Ella asks, cocking an eyebrow at him. She gets way too defensive of girls Achilles has fucked when she drinks. To be fair, they deserve better.

"I'm not the phone book, Els. I can't remember everyone's name," he deadpans.

She rolls her eyes and turns to me. "You remember who Marissa is, right?"

"I do."

"She's *really* into you, Wren. Don't be a dick to her," she warns.

"When was I ever a dick to her?" I take another sip and shake my head at her. "And don't say—"

"When you slept with her freshman year," she cuts me off, knowing exactly where I was going.

"I just slept with her. I didn't lead her on."

"You slept with her *your way*. She told me."

"I slept with her the same way I sleep with everyone else," I defend myself. "I checked if she was okay with—"

"She was a virgin. She got attached after you dominated her because she didn't know any better, and now, she's seeking the same thrill she had with you years ago."

"She didn't tell me. I *checked* with her. She lied," I defend myself, like I always do when Ella brings up this conversation.

"Of course she lied! You're Wren fucking Hunter. Anyone would say anything to be one of the lucky girls you sleep with when you're not desperately waiting for Peach to choose you."

"Can I record this?" Achilles jumps in. "I just want

Murray to see you call women Wren sleeps with *lucky ones.*"

That gets a laugh out of me, and Ella's hand automatically grabs her pendant of a lotus flower she wears around her neck. The Hera necklace. Chris Murray might hate the Silent Circle, but he never complains about Ella being devoted to him. And if there's a guy out there who loves the power he gets to have over his Hera, it's him. Although he didn't wait for her to initiate to assert it, whereas I'm still desperately hanging on to the fact that Peach might realize she loves me one day without me having to force her to do so.

"I didn't— I meant that's the general consensus." Blushing, she takes another sip of her drink to take a break. "Oh, come on. Everyone wants to sleep with you, and you know it." She points an accusatory finger at me.

I chuckle, smiling smugly at her. It's just so fun to rile her up. "What can I do?" I shrug. "Not my fault I'm irresistible, is it?"

"The question is," Achilles adds, eyeing our friends. "Do all the girls want to sleep with him because they know he's so picky and rarely sleeps with anyone, or because he's just that attractive."

"He's *that* attractive," Ella and Alex blurt out at the same time.

That finally brings Xi into the conversation.

"Excuse me?" he grunts.

"I guess it's a bit of both." Ella nods to herself. "I'm not talking for myself, obviously. But I know what the girls around say. See, with Achilles, people want you because they want to be that special person who finally makes you stop being such a moody fuck who sleeps around."

"Why are you coming at me? We're talking about Wren." He raises his hands, portraying innocence.

"Right. I'm just showing the difference. With Wren, well, first of all, you're a challenge. They want to compete with Peach and see if they can finally get your attention away from her, but of course, the fact that you're every girl's wet dream helps."

"It's the shoulders." Alex giggles. "Look at our boy's shoulders."

"Nonsense. It's the eyes."

"Look at what you've done," I tell Achilles. "Now our friends are all over me."

He laughs. "We're used to that."

"Alright, time to go home, Alex." Xi stands up, grabs her drink from her hands, and pulls her out of the booth.

"I'm joking!" she squeals.

"I'm not."

Pouting, she looks up at him and sweetly asks, "Another drink?"

"And risking me hurting your friend who's *every girl's wet dream*? I don't think so. Let's go."

They're out before we can all calm down from our laughing fit.

My eyes cross with Ella right as she freezes with her lips around the rim of her glass.

"What?"

Her baby blues leave mine to look over my shoulder.

"Oh my god. Marissa dyed—" She snorts so badly her margarita spurts from her nose. She coughs, and I tap her back as I move next to her, taking Alex's spot.

When I follow her gaze, I almost choke.

Kirsty is coming back with her friend. Marissa dyed her hair a copper red, and I can only imagine the reason.

"Please, no," I murmur.

Ella finally comes back to reality, and her bright drunken eyes go to Achilles, then back to me. "Be nice," she hisses under her breath.

"Impossible," Achilles mutters back, just as they reach us.

"Hey, guys," Marissa greets brightly. "Hey, Wren," she adds as she puts a hand on my shoulder and flicks her newly red hair.

I flatten my lips, trying to think of the best way to proceed. She doesn't give me time, already talking generally to the group as Kirsty sits next to Achilles and puts her head on his shoulder.

"Is Peach not here?" Marissa asks with too much excitement in her voice.

"No, but since we have her new clone, I'm sure we'll still have a good night," Achilles says with the most serious face anyone could have.

Ella chokes on her drink again, but this time, I'm too shocked by the situation to help her. Kirsty takes over.

"There are no more seats in the booth," she says, putting a hand on Achilles's thigh. "You can just sit on Wren's lap, Marissa."

I eye the stool I was sitting on before I moved next to Ella and that Kirsty decided to ignore. *Great.* Checking the time on my phone, I stand to avoid Marissa's attempt at sitting on me.

"You can just have my seat." I smile politely at her, then tap her shoulder. "It's late, and I've got lacrosse practice early tomorrow morning."

"Aw." She pouts and tilts her head to the side. "I thought practice was on Thursdays? I come watch you sometimes."

If that's not fucking scary, I don't know what is. "And weekends. And many other days of the week," I conclude, taking a step back from the group.

"Well, just so you know, I signed up to Peach's charity event. Fingers crossed, I get to be your rally girl!"

I blink a few times, incapable of finding any word to turn her down nicely. So, I give up.

"Have a good night," I say.

The last thing I hear is Achilles tutting. "Try being a bit meaner next time," he tells Marissa. "That's how Peach keeps him wrapped around her finger."

I roll my eyes as I walk away, and their voices disappear within the general noise of everyone in the bar. In a sense, he's not wrong. Peach always making herself inaccessible to me has become a challenge, and who wouldn't desperately want the one woman they can't have? But that's not why I'm obsessed with her.

It's...*everything*. There isn't one thing she does that makes her unattractive to me. Not one flaw I don't accept. Not one quality I don't want to nurture, and not a weak part of her I don't want to protect with all my being.

It's with those thoughts that I find myself walking to her house again and pulling my body up her balcony.

Check that she's sleeping. Unlock the door. Slide in without a sound.

The light is still on. She fell asleep in a sitting position on her bed, three pillows propped between her and the headboard. She's still got her thick, black glasses on, which she'll swap for her contacts in the morning. Her laptop is on her lap, the screen now black, and there are papers and books all around her.

I huff, finding it easier than usual to make my way to her with the main light on. I take the can of energy drink that's in one of her hands, her relaxed fingers barely holding on to it, and I shake my head when I see the other three on the floor. She must be exhausted if she still fell asleep with four of those in her system.

It's when I'm making my way to throw all her cans in the trash by her desk that I see it. The little packet of white pills barely hidden under a book, the paper weight near it, and the white dust still on the wooden desk.

"Peach...you fucking idiot," I mumble to myself.

I look at the pills, reading the letters engraved on them.

She snorted. Fucking. Ritalin.

I'm silently furious at her for doing this to her body and her brain. I check the time again as I approach the bed. It's barely two a.m. What kind of burned out is she to sleep through all of the shit she took?

"I'm so mad at you," I whisper as I take her laptop and put it next to her on the bed.

I slowly slide her glasses from her face, put them on the bedside table, and pull her down as delicately as I can until she's lying rather than sitting against the pillows. It's a miracle she doesn't wake up.

My heart stops when she starts moving, kicking at the covers until one of her legs is free. Not only her leg... I can see all the way to her ass. And she's not wearing anything but a thong.

I'm too slow to move away as she keeps twisting, and before I know it, she's using my forearm the same way she usually uses her pillow, hugging it and resting her cheek on it.

Oh. Fuck.

My height makes the way I'm leaning down awkward and uncomfortable, and I can't straighten up any more now that she has my arm hostage. Cursing to myself, I end up going on my knees by her bed. I look like I'm about to pray to the lord my soul to keep. Except I'm kneeling for no god... only for the woman I'm already used to worshipping.

I rub my free hand over my face. I still have a perfect view of her perky ass, which ultimately gives me the hard-on of my life.

I'm stuck on my knees by the bed of the only woman who makes my heart palpitate while she's sleeping with a fucking thong. This has got to be some kind of sick joke.

Someone up there is punishing me for being so rude to Marissa earlier.

With her neck against the inside of my forearm, I can feel Peach's heart beating much faster than it should. It's no surprise with the energy drinks and Ritalin mix, and it thickens my blood with worry. Now, it's all I can think about.

"Oh, Peach," I sigh, my breath caressing her cheek. "Why?" I can't help my hand when it goes to brush hair away from her face. "Why are you so harsh on yourself, Trouble?"

Playing with her hair, I notice how split the ends of the strands framing her face are. She's been chewing on them. The more I look at her hair, the more I think of how futile it was for Marissa to dye hers. She'll never match Peach. And it's not because of her hair color, or what she wants in bed, or how mean she is. Marissa can't compete with the way I feel when looking at the woman right in front of me.

She can't compete with the fact that I stay on my knees for Peach until four a.m. when she decides to move in her sleep and release my arm. She can't compete with the fact that I completely forget I have to be up early for practice the whole time I'm here. And she sure as hell can't compete with the fact that I take the Ritalin with me when I leave, because there's no way I'm going to make it easy for that hurricane of a woman to drug herself whenever she feels like it.

Marissa and the other girls can try all they want. Peach is a stake lodged so fucking deep in my heart, every day that goes by could turn me a little more dangerous to her. Because what if she never changes her mind? What if she stays the stubborn girl she is and never becomes mine? It's thoughts like these that make Achilles's voice ring out in my head again.

Initiate her.

She won't have a choice.

Make her your Hera.

Make her yours.

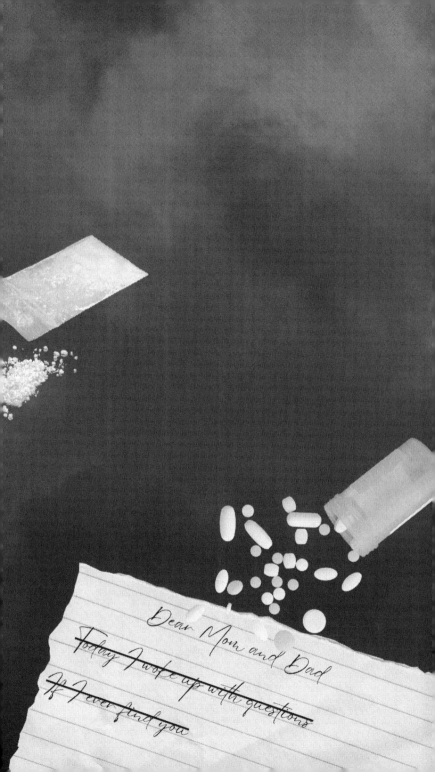

Chapter Seven

Peach

Precious – Omido, Nic Dean

"We already have over fifty women who signed up," I say with a bright smile.

I look down at the notebook on my lap, but the words dance for a second. I scratch my eyes, blink rapidly, and look again.

I'm so exhausted. I fell asleep while working on the notes from Professor Lopez and didn't even get halfway through. I overslept this morning, and when I wanted to take a Ritalin I bought from some kid on the North Shore, it had completely disappeared. I'm ninety-nine percent sure I left it on my desk. And now it's completely gone because I'm losing my fucking mind and have no idea where I hid it. I have a huge day ahead of me, and I need to stay focused. I think I might sleepwalk. It's not the first time I fall asleep and somehow wake up with my mess put away or not remembering where I put some stuff.

"Over fifty?" Coach Gomez repeats. "I have twenty players, Miss Sanderson-Menocci. What am I going to do with fifty rally girls?"

"Menacci," I correct him. "And you're going to pick twenty girls. We have to do a selection. I was thinking to start with if they've volunteered before and then—"

"Shouldn't we just take the prettiest?"

I pause, blinking at him as I bite my inner cheek.

"This remark is the exact reason we're doing this. You've created an environment made of jocks who think they can treat women however they want and the only thing that matters is if they're—"

"Yes, yes, I hear you." He waves a hand. "And you think using those women to get money from us is great?"

My saccharine smile makes him shift in his seat. "What I think, Coach, is that if men, and especially varsity players, are going to objectify women, I might as well make good use out of it. It's a good image for the National College Lacrosse League to donate money to this charity, and your players get rally girls out of it. Where's the issue?"

"More work," he groans.

"I've literally been doing all the work," I snap before I can control myself.

I'm tired and this fucker is making my day longer than it needs to be at seven in the fucking morning.

"I'll select the girls, don't worry. Just make sure the league gets its checkbook ready. The public will also be able to donate, so I'll create a fundraiser page."

Holding my notebook to my chest, I hook my sport bag on my shoulder and leave his office. I'm late to cheer practice, thanks to his slow brain.

I'm hurrying through the hallway, my eyes on my phone as I add some stuff to my to-do list, when I bump into someone big and tall enough to make me stumble back. I try to catch myself on the wall, but I'm too far and start falling before an arm wraps around my waist.

"Whoa," Wren's voice reaches me before I even realize it's him. "Late to practice?"

I look up, my heart skipping a beat when his beautiful gaze crosses mine.

"'Cause you're so early," I say sarcastically, and it settles my heart again.

The tiniest smile pulls at the corner of his mouth, enough for one out of two dimples to show itself.

"Didn't sleep well," he rasps. And I see it.

His eyes are a little puffy, eye bags darkening the skin under them. And his voice sounds like he woke up not too long ago.

"Late night at the Acropolis?"

He licks his lips, his eyes bouncing between mine for a few seconds before he says, "Sure."

"Hey, Wren?"

"Uh-huh?"

"Wanna let go of me so we can both get to practice?"

His first reflex is to bring me closer to him. "Not really, no."

"Come on, idiot," I laugh, and he finally releases me.

"I'll see you on the sideline!" he shouts as he jogs toward the double doors leading to the field.

Number Seven. I can't keep my eyes off him the whole practice. When Wren is on the field, there's no wondering who's the best. He takes hits like they're nothing, catches the ball like he was born with a lacrosse stick in his hands, and scores so hard there's not a chance in the world the goalie can stop it unless he wants a hole through his body.

Everyone's eyes are on him. And mine so much that the second I get in the air, my feet landing on my teammate's shoulder, I lose my focus. It's our last throw of practice, and my eyes went to check if Wren was looking at us. Except it costs me my balance. I tighten my core with all I have, but it's not enough, and a short screech leaves me as I feel myself falling.

Two of them catch me, but they can't stop it completely. I stupidly throw my hand in front of me as I watch the ground get closer.

There's a general gasp, and before I know it, ten heads are looking above me.

"Peach, are you okay?" someone asks.

"Fine," I groan, slightly out of breath.

I push on the floor to sit up and bite my lower lip to stifle a scream. *Holy. Fucking. Shit.* My wrist... The pain shooting up my arm makes me want to roll on the floor and cry, but I don't let anyone see it.

Worried eyes stay on me as I take full breaths, still sitting on the floor with my legs to the side like I just washed up on a beach after escaping a sinking ship.

The crowd is growing around me, creating a tight circle that feels claustrophobic. Too many people are talking at the same time. *Are you alright? Did you hit your head? Do you know your name? What date is it? How many fingers am I holding up?*

"I'm fine," I lie again, with more strength this time. "Everyone, get back to practice." My eyes search for Ella since she's our captain.

"Let her breathe," her voice rings out from behind a few people. "Spread out—"

She's cut off by a stern, "Get out of the way, everyone."

I throw my head back, already knowing who's coming.

"Wren, I'm fi—"

A strangled cry makes people spread away from me, and my stomach bottoms out when I see my best friend's hand fisting Marlon's cheer shirt. Marlon is my base, the man who was throwing me.

"You *dropped her*?" Wren asks calmly, but he's also shaking the poor guy, so his tone doesn't really matter.

Marlon isn't skinny by any means. It takes a lot of strength to be able to send women flying through the air or carry them on the palm of a single hand. But compared to Wren? Any common dog is a puppy next to a beast.

Especially when he's still wearing his shoulder pads and helmet. And *especially* when he's angry.

"I didn't...didn't..."

"It was my fault," I call out. I go to finally stand up, but Wren's gloved hand points a finger my way. He's not even looking at me.

"Stay put."

"Stay put?" I hiss as I do the exact opposite and stand. I feel dizzy for a few seconds, needing to pause before I talk again. "*Stay. Put?* Do you want to die?"

"Peach, calm down, you just injured yourself..." Ella attempts, knowing perfectly well I'm too angry to stop now.

But Wren isn't paying me any attention. He shakes Marlon again.

"If you're too bad at this sport to do your job, maybe you don't need to be part of this team. And since you won't be practicing cheer anymore, it won't matter if I break your legs, will it?"

There are a few sharp gasps in the crowd. Wren isn't exactly known to be a violent man. Within the rules of lacrosse? Sure, because we know he wants to win at all costs. But toward another student? This seems out of character, and the rumors are going to go wild saying that it was because of me.

Holding my right wrist to my chest, I shove him with my left arm. "I told you it was my fault, caveman. Get away from him."

Wren lets go, but only to take his helmet off. Then he grabs Marlon with both hands. He doesn't have to say anything for Marlon to start profusely apologizing to me.

"Peach, I'm sorry—"

"It was me," I cut him off. "I'm sorry, I wasn't focused. Now, Wren, let go."

Marlon's wide eyes keep going from Wren to me with increasing terror.

"Wren, let go, or I swear I'm going to stop talking to you."

It's like I told him I'll kill his entire family. He lets go so quickly, one could think that me not talking to him anymore would be worse than death. He seems to come back to reality and some of the rage dissipates. Marlon takes a few steps back, pulling at his shirt to rearrange it.

"Are you okay?" he asks me, his voice shaking. "I tried to catch you..."

"Take a walk," Wren barks his way before turning to me.

His chestnut hair is a mess from wearing his helmet, sticking to his damp forehead. As his eyes fall on me, they soften, and he looks at me from head to toe, then back up again. When he catches the way I'm holding my wrist to my chest, his eyebrows pull together with worry.

"Your wrist." He takes two long strides toward me, one hand grabbing my arm gently and the other hovering over my wrist before he touches my hand.

"It's fine— Ow!" I hiss.

He tried to roll it softly.

"I'm taking you to the nurse." His words are final.

"Is that really necessary?" I grunt. I take a step back, but he shakes his head.

He lowers his voice, following me as I walk back. "Peach, don't make me force you to get that wrist checked. It'll be embarrassing for you if I have to put you over my shoulder in front of everyone."

"For you, you mean. I'll kick your ass."

He cocks an eyebrow, unimpressed by my light tone. "We're going to the infirmary. This isn't a joke."

I look around, ready to cause a scene, fight him, and then go to the infirmary on my own. But then I catch everyone's gazes on us. More specifically, the heart-shaped eyes from the other cheerleaders watching Number Seven, handsome Wren Hunter, care for me.

"Let's go," I mumble.

"Good g—"

"Don't you let those words out of your fucking mouth if you want your balls attached to your body by the time we get there."

"I love it when you fight me, Trouble." He chuckles, putting an arm around my shoulders as we walk together. "It makes me feel like we're already a couple."

I bite my lip, keeping a whimper in as the doctor twists my wrist for the scan.

"She's hurting," Wren tells him sternly. "Be gentle."

"I'm fine," I rasp. I'm lying on my front on the MRI bed, but only my forearm is in the machine.

"Just stay like this. It'll be a few minutes." He turns to Wren. "Again, you should be out of the room. Radiation—"

"I'll live."

The radiologist huffs and goes to the other side of the window while we stay with my wrist under the scan. Because it started to swell, the nurse insisted we go to the ER to get it checked in case it's broken. We've been waiting for hours, and my stomach has been eating itself from the anxiety. I don't have time for a broken wrist.

There's a pull at my hair, and I only now realize I was chewing on it. Wren pushes the strands behind my ear as I rest on my right cheek.

"It's going to be okay. Take a deep breath for me, will you?"

I shake my head. "No. I'll breathe when it's over and they tell me my wrist isn't broken."

"Peach, maybe this is a sign that you're doing too much. In all those years of cheerleading, I've never seen you fall this badly. Apart from that time you broke your ankle, but you were just starting."

"Oh God, that hurt so much." I look at my wrist and then up at him, standing right next to me.

"How did you even fall today?"

"I wasn't focused," I say without hesitation. "The gaze is everything, and I wasn't looking right ahead."

"What were you looking at?"

Realizing the situation I've just put myself in, I blink up at him. I can't tell him I was looking at him being tackled by two defense players and still coming out unscathed.

"What if it's broken?" I blurt out, hoping we move on.

"Then you'll rest until it's healed."

"I have so much to do."

His eyes stay fixed on me as he lowers to his haunches. "Peach." He caresses my hair, and all my muscles relax except one. Only my heart panics when Wren is a little too close.

"Could you do me a favor and at least acknowledge you take on a lot and that you're going to push yourself past the breaking point?"

I smile, but it's too sweet. "I will never admit such a thing, you naïve boy."

He chuckles and taps my cheek playfully. "You don't have to prove to the entire world how strong you are. We know."

"No, but I have to prove I was the right choice." I freeze the second the words leave my mouth. I don't know if it's the pain or the exhaustion, but they just came out before I could do anything about it.

His eyes search mine, and I do my best to keep avoiding them.

"What's taking so long?" I try to look over my shoulder, but he moves, making sure he's in my line of vision.

"Let the radiologist do his work. What do you mean 'you were the right choice'?"

"Huh? I don't even know."

"Penelope, look at me," he insists when I look down.

"Don't tell me what to do." I keep my gaze exactly how it is, out of pure stubbornness.

"Fine."

There's nothing for a second, then I suddenly feel his hand around the back of my thigh. I'm still wearing my cheer skort, and I squeeze my legs right away.

"Wren!" I scold him as he brings his hand higher.

"That radiologist is about to get the show of his life if you don't start behaving."

"Get your fucking hand off me," I hiss. I want to slap

him in the face, but I can't do anything with my arm in the MRI machine.

Instead of listening, he goes higher, under the first layer, and I feel him where my thigh meets my ass.

"There's been a few times you've loved my hands on you. Why change your mind now?"

Lowering his mouth closer to my ear, he adds, "There's been times I even felt how wet you get against my hand. So don't act all shy."

I refuse to let him see how much those simple words affect me. The mere memories of his hands caressing me lights me on fire.

When I don't move anymore, he finally says, "Can we talk now?"

"Yes," I say through gritted teeth.

"That's what I thought. Now, what is this nonsense about being worth it?"

I try dislodging him, but he won't budge, and I can't move too much, or the scan will take even longer. There's absolutely nowhere for me to fucking go, and suddenly more than ever, I feel the way Wren...*cares*.

It's so powerful, gripping my heart and warming my chest. He puts that weird feeling of giddiness inside me. The one I used to get when I climbed trees as a kid, when I jumped into Stoneview Lake and would barely see the light anymore from underwater. There's excitement and fear, hope...and freedom.

I guess if there's one person I can tell this to, it's Wren, right? Wren cares. Wren doesn't judge. Wren...

"I was picked, wasn't I?" I rasp.

The shock on his face slackens his jaw.

"I was abandoned, and then I was picked. Do you understand? Out of who knows how many other kids?"

He's still speechless.

"The last thing I would want is for my parents to think I wasn't worth it. Because then...then they might leave me behind like the first ones did."

"Penelope..." His disbelief annoys me. Can't he understand? That I wasn't a miracle to anyone. That I wasn't good enough for someone before I was chosen by my dads.

None of my friends can understand that. Because no matter the type of issues they had with their families, they were still the same blood. I was an abandoned kitten gifted as a hope of rekindling a relationship.

"Your dads love you," he finally says. "And even if they were stupid enough for it to be conditional, then you have us."

"I have so many questions for them," I admit. "My biological parents." My eyes sting, and I sniffle when I feel I'm about to let go. "I want to find them and get answers so I can fall asleep at night without having those questions go round and round in my head. Why? Did I do something? Did they just, what, regret having me? Why wasn't I worthy of their love?"

His response is instant. "You're nothing if not worthy of love, Peach. Your friends love you. I—"

"God, what's taking so long? Did that guy go on a coffee break or something?"

In this instant, I'm grateful for the years of friendship Wren and I have piled up. Because he doesn't need to think for even a split second to understand he shouldn't push it anymore. I'm not someone who breaks open the more you probe. If you want to get inside my mind, I'll retreat and put a wall between us.

So he drops it. He lets go of me, and instead, he does exactly what I need. He changes the topic.

"So, about that rally girl thing..."

That gets a laugh out of me, and I'm grateful for his eyes sparkling with mischief.

"Yes?"

My heart skips a beat when he takes a few seconds to appreciate the fact that he made me feel better. It's a very specific feeling when the line between friendship and more starts to blur, but I would be lying if I said I don't like knowing I'm special to him.

"Well," he finally says. "Are you going to be mine?"

My lips part, the sharp inhale making me feel dizzy for a second.

"Yours?"

What would it be like...to be Wren's?

"My rally girl," he clarifies.

The comeback to reality is almost painful.

"Of course not, Wren." My tone tells him I'm sick of his advances, but I'm glad he couldn't read my mind a second ago.

"Oh, come on. I would love to have you bring me cookies and hot towels at rallies."

I shake my head, pressing my lips together to not smile. "Everyone would love that. I'm in high demand. But I'm not sure how we'll pick, to be honest. Probably just draw names."

He opens his mouth, but is cut off by the door opening.

"Nothing's broken," the doctor says. "It's a light sprain, so nothing a bit of rest won't fix. We'll still give you a splint so you don't do any movement that could make it worse. A week should do."

I let out a sigh of relief, but something becomes obvious to me. It was because Wren was here to keep my mind off the stress and the pain that I feel better.

And when he says, "Good, let's get you home so you can rest," something pulls at my chest. And I don't like it one bit.

Before we leave the room, he turns to me one last time.

"I want you to know something."

I tilt my head to the side, waiting for whatever seems to be so important.

"I would choose you. Even if you weren't worth it. And you would have nothing to prove. I would choose you among a million other people. And anyone would be the luckiest person on this planet if you chose them in return."

I'm completely speechless. I can't even open my mouth as I try to digest his words.

"I..." My mouth is dry, my heart changing rhythm so fast I feel like my legs are going to give up.

"You don't have to say anything. However you feel doesn't matter; this is simply how *I* feel." An easy smile spreads on his lips. "Now, let's get you in bed." And the dimples are back. "But promise you won't jump me. I know how handsome I am."

I throw my head back as a laugh bursts out of me.

"Shut up, loser." I hope I sound like he annoys me even though I feel the complete opposite of annoyed.

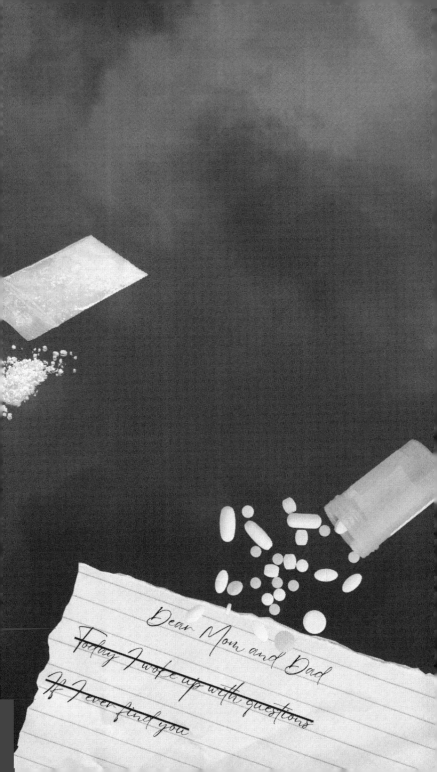

Chapter Eight

Peach

Teeth – 5 Seconds of Summer

I pull at the brace around my wrist, wondering if it's really that useful or if I could take it off. Turning away from my friends, I start to undo the Velcro.

"It's useful," Ella says for the third time tonight. Reading my mind yet again. "Now, will you please leave it alone?"

I pretend I don't hear her over the sound of the piano playing, people chattering and clinking their glasses of champagne, and the loud, snobby men laughing not far from us.

Stoneview ball is always a pleasure.

We're standing near the open bar, where three men are serving spirits while other waitstaff walk around the room with flutes of champagne.

"I know you heard me, Peach. I'm right next to you," Ella insists.

"You say it's useful, but I really don't see how such a flimsy thing helps," I say as I turn back to them.

I pull at it again, and Achilles groans in exasperation. "It restricts your movements, idiot. Now stop." Slapping my hand, he throws me a death stare.

"Alright, Doc. We get it, you study medicine."

He rolls his eyes. "What's wrong with it anyway? Does it not go with your outfit?"

"What's wrong with you? Why do you care if I'm taking it off or not."

"Here's my theory." He leans down a little as he lowers his voice; that way, others won't hear him, but I will.

On my left, Ella mumbles, "Here we go."

"The longer it takes for your wrist to heal, the longer you won't be cheerleading. And the longer you're not being a cute little cheerleader on the sideline for the lacrosse team, the longer Wren doesn't get his bi-weekly look under your skort."

My eyes widen. Did he actually dare to throw this shit at me?

"Do you get where I'm going here? It's all he has, Peach. He's going to be insufferable without it."

"I'm going to punch you in the face," I say in all seriousness.

He smiles brightly at me. "Think about your wrist."

"Think about your teeth next time you want to let that kind of insanity past your lips."

Ella puts a hand on my arm. "Maybe cheer shouldn't be an activity for you anymore. First of all, you don't have time, and I'm worried you're going to have to start selling your soul to the devil in exchange for more hours in a day." Her gaze flicks to Achilles. "Also, we now clearly know of at least one player who looks under your skort regularly, and I'm not sure that's a good thing."

"Ella, please. You've been a cheerleader for a long time.

You're the captain. Don't tell me you think the players look into your eyes when you do your jumps?" Achilles shakes his head at her, and both my friend and I shoot daggers at him.

"First of all, that makes no sense. They couldn't look into our eyes even if they tried because we're moving so much. Secondly, shut up," I simply say before turning back to Els. "I'll be taking a break while this heals anyway. I'm just annoyed. I don't like when something slows me down. That's why I never get ill."

"For the millionth time, you can't decide when you get ill." Achilles gives me his signature unimpressed look.

"I do!" I defend. "That's why it never happens to me."

"Sure."

"Ella, tell him," I order.

"Guys, not this again. Come on."

I down my champagne and look at the crowd. "Alright, time for me to be the perfect daughter. Wish me luck."

"Try to stay sober, at least until midnight," Achilles calls out as I walk away.

All he gets in return is a middle finger. I've had *two* glasses. I'm fine. For now. I walk among my fellow Stoneview residents as I look for my dads. Everyone here is just a mix of the same people I see at SFU, plus their families. It's always the same faces. Grabbing the side of my deep red silk dress, so I don't end up stepping on it, I smile and nod, letting out some polite hellos.

"Penelope," Dad Sanderson's voice calls out from my left, and I join him right away.

"Where's Dad?" I ask as he puts an arm around my shoulders.

He points at a camera I hadn't seen and murmurs, "He

didn't come." Then we both smile and pretend everything is fine as the flash blinds us.

The second the photographer is gone, he takes my hand and pulls me into a corner.

"Red silk, Penelope? This was not part of any of the dresses I had Mabel send you."

"Mabel is the worst stylist you've ever had, and I refuse to let her dress me. Did you see those dresses? I'm not Jackie O. But if I ever become first lady, I'll ask for her advice."

He looks at me with that serious Dad stare.

"Okay." He shakes his head, then his entire body, as if he's warming up for some sort of dance rehearsal, before focusing on me again. "Penny Pickle..." Oh, not the stupid nickname. "Let's start with a history lesson. Jackie O. wasn't first lady when she started getting called Jackie O. So your reference doesn't work."

"I'm a scientist, Dad. History and politics aren't really my forte."

"Don't I know it." Putting a hand on my shoulder, he looks down to my toes and back in my eyes. "Onto a fashion lesson. Well done. You're definitely not looking like Jackie Kennedy tonight, but rather Marilyn Monroe."

"Cool—"

"Not in a good way. I hired Mabel because she was Delacroix's stylist for the entire family when he ran for senator. It's all about appearances, Penny. Please, next time, just do this for me."

"Dad," I sigh. "This sounds so—"

"Stupid? Yes, I know. But I'm a gay man running for mayor of the richest town in the country. If I don't show them we're the perfect American family, they'll use it as an excuse and add it to the list of things they can use against me. Dad didn't show up, and people are already asking questions about divorce."

"Maybe if you stopped cheating on him he'd show up," I mumble.

He pauses as he smiles warmly at someone I'm assuming is walking behind me before focusing on me again.

"I'm not discussing this with you. Unlike Dad, I keep our problems to ourselves. He doesn't want to show up? Fine. My daughter showed up, but she's got on a wrist support like someone's been abusing her and is wearing a dress that screams *sex*. Not fine."

"Does it scream sex, or does it scream independent woman?" I wink at him obviously, but it still doesn't get a laugh out of my fun dad.

Sanderson has always been the chill one. Especially being in his late sixties and having supposedly retired. He used to let me drink with him, didn't care about anything wrong I did, and let me wear whatever I wanted. Menacci is the one who always cared too much about appearances because he's a "famous actor."

"Okay," I huff. "Clearly, *fun* isn't a thing for you anymore, and I shall be the most boring daughter in the world. I'll talk about...hairstyles."

"Too superficial."

"Guns."

"Too sensitive, Penny."

"The environment?"

"I know you. You'll do it from an environmental engineer's point of view and confuse them."

I huff. "My favorite dish at the Stoneview Country Club."

He smiles. "Perfect."

"Ah, country clubs. The American dream."

He chuckles and offers me his arm. Taking it, I walk with him.

"Thank you, Penny Pickle."

"You owe me a whole jar for this stupid soirée."

"Unlimited jars of my little girl's favorite pickles."

I'm perfect all night. Truly. I stay by my dad's side, laugh at his jokes, make people feel at ease every time he subtly mentions his campaign, and proudly nod when he says that my "school project" might end up in a "very serious science journal." I don't even correct him that it's an important research paper that could, many years down the line, lead me to a Nobel Prize. Hell, I even say that Menacci has the flu when people ask where he is. *Not* that he's sick of my dad cheating on him.

Perfect. Daughter.

By the time the older generation leaves, I'm dying for a fucking drink. I couldn't add drinking too much champagne to the *outrageous* red dress.

"Kill me," I sigh as I join my friends again.

Alex hands me a flute, and I down it right away before grabbing another from the passing waiter. Only Ella and Achilles were here earlier, but Alex and Wren have joined them.

Since it's late, we're pretty much surrounded by people around our age now, and this is about to turn into a college party on steroids. Except much, *much* fancier since we're in the Stoneview town hall. The room looks just like the "Beauty and The Beast" ballroom, and we're all dressed in beautiful cocktail dresses, wearing jewelry with prices that would make a millionaire faint, and drinking champagne that costs ten grand a bottle. But that's just what we're used to.

I've downed my second flute when Ella and Alex start cursing at Hermes for their last post, stopping any chance of relaxing. How am I meant to enjoy my night if I'm forced to think about that asshole sending me messages? I'm reaching for a third glass of champagne, when a hand wraps around my healthy wrist, stopping me.

"She's fine." Wren's deep voice resonates next to me as he pulls my hand away from the platter, and I watch the waiter leave with my much-needed alcohol.

"Don't—"

"The night has barely started," he cuts me off. "How about you have reasonable fun before having blackout fun. And aren't you taking pain meds? You shouldn't drink on those."

"Joke's on you. I didn't take them." I flip my hair over my shoulder with my free hand and pull at the one he's holding. "Let go. The night might have just started for you, but I've been chatting up boring old men for two hours."

"How's your dad?" he asks in return instead of actually hearing me out.

"My dad is wondering why you still haven't let go of my arm, Wren," I sing-song.

He chuckles, caressing the inside of my wrist. "Come on." A step closer, and I'm suddenly struggling to breathe.

His next words are barely even audible for me. "Do you even know how delicious you look tonight? With all those men looking at you, someone has to show them you don't belong to any of them."

I narrow my eyes at him, tilting my head up to make sure I can stare him down. "You wouldn't be so foolish as to think that it's because I belong to you, would you?"

The smile pulling at the corner of his lips makes my heart palpitate, but I'm not sure if it's because I want to punch him or kiss him. This is...confusing. Everything is always confusing when it comes to him.

"I wouldn't dare think that, Trouble. I *know*."

And there it is. That fucking dominating smugness I want to crush under my red sole. I subtly lick the matte red lipstick on my lower lip. His eyes catch on it, lighting up as they follow the tip of my tongue.

"God, Wren." A saccharine smile spreads on my face. "Look at yourself. I barely try and you're practically on your knees for my attention. You can't take me, honey. If I were yours, I'd crush your balls so hard in the palm of my hand, your next three generations would feel it."

His mouth drops open, but the challenge is bright in his gaze. He still wants to try to make me his. So I make sure to kill it.

"And keep *Trouble* out of your vocabulary when it comes to me. We're friends, not lovers. You don't get a Wren-only nickname for me."

There. No more confusion.

His beautiful blue eyes stay on me, refusing to back down. That's our entire relationship summed up. Neither of us ever backs down.

"I need to step away. I'm scared I'll get pregnant if I stay anywhere near these two." Ella's voice is the only thing that makes us separate.

He finally lets go of my wrist, and I already miss the heat, miss the adrenaline of us defying each other.

"I'll come with you," I tell Ella.

Alex does too, and we leave Wren and Achilles behind.

"He's still looking at you," Els mumbles.

"Stop looking back," I tell her, even though I'm glad someone checked if he was watching me walk away.

"Oh, Peach..." Alex laughs. "How long are you going to torture that man?"

"I'm not torturing him," I say with a huff. "I'm saving us both the disappointment of sleeping together. We're not compatible."

"Come on, Peach. We're your best friends," Ella says. "Just tell us the truth..."

Alex insists with lifted eyebrows of encouragement.

"I never slept with him," I defend. "It's not my fault you don't want to believe me."

We settle in another corner of the room, and I shove a few canapés in my mouth. They use the moment to ask more questions.

"Okay, let's say you never actually slept together. Something else happened, right? A kiss? Maybe—"

"We've never kissed." I spit crumbs out of my mouth, and Alex offers me a cocktail napkin.

"The sexual energy is so thick, you guys must have done *something*." Ella's excitement is palpable, and I swallow the canapés in one large gulp.

"If you want something to happen with Wren so badly, you do it. You love your men idiotically possessive."

She giggles to herself and shares a look with Alex. "Trust me, if either of us were single, we would absolutely go for him. Definitely our type."

I throw my head back and grab another glass of champagne.

"Sometimes," Alex starts shyly, "you guys disappear together."

"Yes, when I'm angry and he calms me down."

Alex pinches her lips, her cheeks blushing. "How does he calm you down?"

Well, I really fucked myself there, didn't I? When I stay silent, Ella repeats.

"Oh my god, Peach." She practically jumps on the spot. "*How* does he calm you down?"

"Just— We... I don't know. It depends. Sometimes, he scolds me, and we argue. Sometimes, he's sweet. Sometimes..."

"Sometimes?"

"Jesus, you two! Sometimes, he gives me..." I whisper the end of my sentence. "An orgasm. Are you happy?"

"Yes!" they both exclaim, eyes and smiles comically wide.

"You guys are going to get married," Alex concludes.

It's my and Ella's turn to stare at her. "You are so naïve," I tell her with a shake of my head. "It's good you've got Xi, because I worry about what would happen if you were left all alone in this world with that cute head full of dreams."

She smiles sneakily at me. "So, does Wren dominate you when he gives you orgasms?"

I choke on champagne, and it almost comes back out through my nose.

"No! Well..."

I think about the times he was stern with me. But it wasn't dominating. It was what worked for me at the time when I was angry or out of control and might have done something I'd regret.

"No," I repeat. "It's more of a fight for power than him dominating me."

"That sounds hot," Ella says. "And you've never kissed?"

"We've never kissed," I repeat for the hundredth time. "It's just..." I wave my fingers at them, and they both laugh again. "Nothing else ever happened. And even that probably happened, like, three times. It's not my fault I can't get anyone else to give me orgasms."

"Of course not," Alex explains as she grabs a canapé. "He keeps all the guys away from you. And his plan is clearly working. You're going to end up together."

I look at her, deadpan. "We're not."

They disagree. They always do, but I know what I'm talking about. So, instead of listening to them, I drink another flute of champagne and change the topic. We're joined by other people we know as the night goes on. And as we keep drinking and getting more excited, the need for other substances starts tingling under my skin.

It's not an addiction, I'm sure of that. It's just a way to decompress. I'm always so busy, always thinking of the next task on my to-do list. Parties help me forget about the daily pressure I put on myself.

I'm discreet when I catch the eyes of my friend, Conan. He's always got coke on him, and the new SFU dealer screens my messages. I don't doubt Xi told him not to provide for me too often. Dick.

I tilt my head toward the ballroom door, and he smiles at me, nodding.

"Just gonna use the bathroom," I tell Alex before leaving.

It takes Conan about three minutes before he joins me in front of the women's bathroom.

"Not in there," he says, putting his hand on the small of my back. "There's always someone keeping an eye out during balls. Come, the kitchen will be empty at this time."

He catches me up on his summer in the Hamptons as we make our way, his hand never leaving the silk barely covering my exposed back. Conan is a lovely guy. We have some classes together, even though he wants to specialize in civil engineering.

"Imagine my mom's face when she walked in on my sister and the fucking chauffeur. Why are our parents so outraged that their staff are normal people? Do they really think we're better than them? Isn't that weird?"

I roll my eyes. "Different generation. You need to talk to your mom. I had a chat with my dad the time he told off our cook. I can tell you it never happened again."

"Yeah." He nods. "We're still really taking advantage of the privilege, though, aren't we?"

He pulls out the little plastic packet out of his inside tux jacket pocket.

"I'm thinking of just fucking off," he says as he puts powder on the metal kitchen counter. "Traveling to Asia, working as an English teacher, maybe?"

Using his black Amex to cut off the coke, his hand handles all of it like a pro.

"Will you still be using your parents' money?" I ask, cocking an eyebrow at him. "Because I think that would cancel out your *Eat, Pray, Love* experience."

He snorts. "Nah. No one needs that much money, Peach. You know it. You want to use yours to save polar bears."

I roll my eyes. "You spend too much time with Achilles."

He chuckles and points at the table. "Ladies first."

"How kind."

We take turns snorting a line, and I glance at my phone to check the girls aren't looking for me when he puts his head down. Before I know what's happening, Conan is being pulled back, replaced by another man in front of me. One who simply won't leave me alone to do stupid shit.

"Get out of here," Wren tells Conan, his eyes not leaving mine.

"You can't be serious." He snorts. "You're going too far, Hunter. The male population of SFU puts up with enough of your shit."

My head snaps to Conan, and I feel my eyebrows practically touching my hairline. "What shit? What have you been putting up with?"

Conan smirks. "What? You don't know about the warning your boyfriend put out to all the guys? Only the brave ones try to sleep with you, Peach. It's been going on since sophomore year."

It's not the first time I've heard of Wren spreading the word to stay away from me. He used to make jokes about it. But I never realized it's been going on for so long.

"Did you actually tell everyone to stay away from me?" My voice is barely even.

It's hard to not jump him and scratch his face when I understand that I've struggled to get past a few flirty texts with a guy in the last few years because of Wren putting a ban on me.

"I've said this to you many times," he answers casually.

"I thought you were *joking!*" I throw my hands in the air, unable to stay still.

"I wasn't," he deadpans.

"All guys on campus," Conan insists.

I blink up at Wren. He has absolutely no shame, completely unbothered that he's been exposed.

"Only the male population, Wren? So, are you not worried about the women?"

Conan laughs, but Wren's eyes still stay on me when he talks. "Get him out of here."

It's only now that I notice Achilles and his sick smile.

He grabs Conan by both shoulders, dragging him out of the room.

"What the... What the *fuck*. Is Achilles your guard dog now?"

"No. He's my friend, and yours, who knows what's best for you. What are you doing in here, Peach?"

The surprise can't seem to leave my face. "The same thing I always do. What are *you* doing?"

"The same thing I always do. Except this time, instead of picking up *after* your shit, I'm trying to prevent it so I can save myself some time and trouble."

"No one asked you to help. Especially not me."

He smiles, and it pisses me off. The energy within me is thrumming, and it's only being accentuated by the powder I just snorted.

"You don't want my help? Then I better not pick you up off the floor somewhere. I better not stand between you and some dude twice your size you just couldn't help but put back in his place. And I better not get a call from the girls saying they can't wake you up."

I pause while I think for a few seconds.

"Whoever that hypothetical dude is...he deserved it."

It's his turn to not be able to talk, clearly struggling to stay serious when he wants to laugh.

"You're set on getting under my skin for your entire life, aren't you?" The seriousness in his voice is completely unexpected. He keeps getting *too serious* about this.

He closes the space that separates us, making me crane my neck to face him. The silence drags on for so long, it feels like he's sucking my soul right out of my body. Not able to take the intensity, I try to say something.

"I—"

"Give it to me." The perfect blue in his eyes brightens with the hint of a challenge again.

My heart rate explodes, spreading a strange feeling through my stomach and...lower.

"What are you talking about?"

He wraps an arm around my waist, the other starting to roll a strand of my red hair around his index finger.

He can't quite seem to find *it*. What he meant, exactly. But I know, so I push him.

"What you want, Wren, is for me to stop being a woman who thinks rationally. *It* is my strength. That's what you want. For me to hand it to you, so you can crush it. Because that's how you're wired. And I know men like you. They see a strong woman and equate it to the biggest challenge of their lives. You fetishize us like it's an entire kink in itself."

I can feel his whole body buzzing. He could combust any minute.

"But here's the issue." I put a hand on his chest. "I'm not giving *it* to you. In fact"—I push onto my toes. My mouth can't reach his ear, but it still drives my point—"I wouldn't give you anything until you're on your knees, begging for it like a good boy."

His face falls, and he lets go of me as he takes a step back. It's slow, but after a few seconds, I can finally see a pull at the corner of his mouth.

"Huh," is the only thing that comes out.

"Feels weird, doesn't it? When I smack you in the face with how incompatible we are."

He rubs a hand across his face, and the way he then licks his lips tells me he's probably feeling the exact opposite. I've just made it even more enticing.

"Do you really never think about it, Peach?"

He keeps his hands to himself this time, but he might as well be caressing every inch of my skin.

"How it would feel to have that one person with whom you could let down the arms? For once in your life to let someone guide you in the way they can bring you pleasure? Surely, you think about the times you've come on my fingers, about the way I can bring you back down when you lose control. We're attracted to each other. That, at least, you've never pretended to hide when it's just the two of us. And you told me at the last end-of-year party that you could potentially choose me. Drunk you doesn't lie like sober you."

I gulp. Is it the coke or the temperature that's making me sweat? It's because we're in a kitchen. It's so hot in here.

Yes, that must be it.

"Trouble," he purrs, basking in the fact that he's rendered me speechless. "I know all the ways we're incompatible. I've learned them by heart. I've thought about it so many times, for so long, that I've become best friends with them." He shrugs like this is the most ordinary thing to say. "They're not an issue for me."

"They're an issue for *me*, Wren," I finally say with the strength of a kitten.

He processes my words, nodding to himself, pretending he's actually taking in my opinion. And then something I'd never seen flares in his eyes, dilating his pupils and blackening the blue that I usually find so comforting. Something so terrifying I'd never thought it possible on a man like Wren.

"I don't *have* to give you a choice, Peach."

My lungs halt their movement. Did I hear that right? Did my childhood best friend really just say that, or is the alcohol getting to my head, mixing with the coke? Maybe it's the weed I smoked before the ball?

Something isn't right. I fucking know that much.

"Did you just—"

"I can be nice enough to make it seem like I'm giving you a choice, if you'd like." His rasp sends a shiver down my spine. "You know, like Chris did to Ella."

"*What?*" I hiss.

But he ignores it. "Or I could just...take."

I narrow my eyes at him, my right hand tightening into a fist and the tips of my fingers pressing into the splint.

"Peach." He chuckles, almost sweetly. Like some manipulative bastard who gets whatever he wants.

Who the hell is this guy?

He goes to touch my forehead with his thumb, but I slap his arm away.

"Don't tou—" My voice is cut off by my whimper as he grabs me by the hair at the back of my head, keeping me in place.

The shock is what has me stilling, rather than the pain. Something completely unknown reverberates through my body, and my mouth falls slack when he delicately pinches some of the shorter strands of hair that frames my face.

He brings it to his eyeline.

"You really ought to stop stress-chewing on your hair. You'll ruin it." He laughs softly, probably from the fact that I still haven't reacted. "God, I really do love it when you're speechless. The anger is still visible, though. Right"—he caresses my forehead with the tip of his thumb—"here."

And then he presses a little harder to make me realize what it is. That stupid, ugly vein that pops out when I'm furious. I swallow thickly, wondering if whatever he's holding back is about to snap. Cracking his neck slowly, he keeps me in his hold while a thousand thoughts seem to go through his head. Time stops as his eyes become the window to his soul, and I see the torment there. The pros and cons. The weight of consequences.

He inhales, and I barely catch the words he breathes out.

"Fuck it."

His hand in my hair pulls me to him, and his lips press against mine with the strength of a hurricane. And it's on a path to destroy everything. My sanity first. My anger. My reflex to push him away. It's all gone as I melt into him and let him take over my mind. Mainly, he has complete control over the kiss. He angles my head, pushes his tongue inside my mouth, and I lose my mind.

The kiss is almost violent, and for however long my thoughts rest, I enjoy the most passionate moment of my life.

Until I come back down to earth, and I shove him back.

He stops kissing me, but he doesn't release me.

"What the hell is wrong with you?" I pant. "I don't..." Fuck, I can't catch my breath. "I don't want to kiss you."

His wet lips spread into a knowing smile. "Oh yes, you seemed to hate that."

I clench my jaw hard. So hard I'm pretty sure I break a tooth or two. And then the strength finally comes back to me. Before I know what I'm even doing, I've grabbed whatever is on the steel kitchen counter and I'm swinging at him.

I only realize what I'm holding when he fists my wrist, stopping my movement right before I hit his head.

"A meat hook? Ouch." He chuckles. "You'll have to be a little less predictable to hurt me, though. I've known you for sixteen years, and you've been hitting people who piss you off with whatever's near you since kindergarten."

His grip doesn't even hurt, and weirdly I want it to. Because if he could just take it one step further, I could unleash hell on him. Right now...right now, I struggle to think my best friend is creating such chaos within me.

Finally letting go of my hair, he takes the hook from me, and something solidifies in my stomach with the way his eyes light up.

Who. The fuck. Is this psycho?

"Wren..." I say with a warning that sounds more like a plea as I eye the hook.

Slowly, so...slowly that I feel every single one of my cells freezing in fear, he brings it to my neck. He grazes the thin skin with the deadly tip. He looks like he's in a trance as he drags it to the nape of my neck, sending goosebumps down my back.

My eyes flutter shut, fear liquifying into something else. Something indescribable, but that tightens the lower it goes.

I'm pretty sure I'm a split second away from bursting into flames when he places the curve of the hook around the back of my neck, the tip barely pressing into my skin, and pulls me forward.

I slam against his chest, and his lips hover over my ear.

"I think I could get you there, Trouble." Suddenly, that nickname holds a different meaning.

I hate him using it. I hate when he thinks he has something over others, that he's closer to me than our other friends.

But the truth is, he is. He's always been, or it wouldn't have become a running joke. And I've never felt it more than now. In a few minutes, he's made me *desperately* want to be someone he uses a nickname for.

"Get me where?" I murmur against his chest.

"To a state of complete submission."

He releases me before I can fight back. Casually placing

the hook back on the counter, he smiles warmly as he walks backward.

And just like that, he's back to normal, pretending this whole thing that brought me under his spell didn't happen.

"No more drugs, Peach. Don't say I didn't warn you."

I blink at him as he disappears through the doors.

Motherfucker.

I stride after him, but by the time I get back to the ballroom, he's nowhere to be found. I look around to find my girls while my heart threatens to break my ribcage and my lips sting from his kiss.

"Peach!"

My head snaps to the side, and Elijah stops right next to me, observing me as his eyebrows draw together.

"What's wrong?" He searches my face, picking up on all the clues.

"Your brother is a fucking psychopath," I hiss. "That's what's wrong. How you guys are related is beyond me."

His face falls, and worry drips from his voice when he asks, "What did he do?"

"Nothing." I grit my teeth and look at the bar. "Let's get a drink."

-metal IS NOT the same as punk.
-She's still allergic to shellfish and cat hair
-Always leave the green olives to her
-We don't like metal anymore.
-Tea tree and peppermint shampoo
-Don't forget the peri-peri powder on her fries
-Bake and shake every first Tuesday of the month.
-No more sugar in her coffee. It makes her feel sick
-DO NOT bother me during girls' night Wren
-Spiced honey on pepperoni pizza
-Check the triangle freckles on her right shoulder frequently. Dermatologist said to keep an eye.
-New vision results: Right eye -2.75. Left eye -3.25
-If she gets in next September's yearly release of the EEAJ, the announcement will be in August next year.
-Her brace needs to come off in a week

Chapter Nine

Wren

Nightmare - Halsey

Achilles's eyes don't leave me as he takes a pull from a cigarette. He squints through the cloud of smoke, his unimpressed gaze telling me all I need to know before he even opens his mouth.

He saw it all. The way I spoke to Peach. The exact threatening words I used.

I don't have to give you a choice.

And the fucking meat hook around her neck.

"How close were you to snapping?"

I huff, watching my hot breath turning into condensation in the cold night air.

I can still feel her lips against mine.

I'm not wearing my tux jacket anymore, sitting on the staff entrance metal stairs at the back of Stoneview town hall. Achilles stands in front of me, a few steps down.

When I don't answer, my best friend gives me another minute.

She was so compliant in my hold.

He drags slowly on his cigarette, then exhales. And again, his eyes never leave mine, despite his face being partially hidden by the cloud of smoke forming around us. I hate the smell of cigarettes, but he doesn't really give a shit.

"How close?" he repeats before his lips wrap around his death stick again.

I rub a hand over my face before undoing the bow around my neck. It's been choking me all fucking night. I let it hang there, looking at Achilles's knees, slowly back up.

"So close," I rasp when my gaze reaches his. "I was so fucking close."

He throws his cigarette, and I roll my eyes internally. I would usually give him a lesson about littering, but I don't say anything when we're talking about the fact that I almost snapped and killed someone tonight.

"Peach?" he asks.

"I'd never hurt Peach. Don't be an idiot."

He snorts, pulling another cigarette out of his pack.

"Tell that to the guy you turn into when we lose you, Wren." He must catch my look at his hand and then the glare I throw him, because his eyebrows raise, and he puts the cigarette back.

"Alright." He nods to himself, putting the pack in the pocket of his tux pants.

"I would never hurt Peach," I repeat to myself.

I know it so deep in my soul; it's almost part of me at this point. The same way my blood flows through my veins as my heart beats, it's a natural instinct to protect her. Achilles could never understand. He's never felt that way about anyone. To me, it's what makes her different from the rest of the world.

I could switch at any point, and whoever's in my way could get their neck snapped. Except her.

"So it was Conan who got you so close to the edge. Because he gave her drugs?"

Running my tongue across my teeth, I nod.

"Poor guy doesn't know how close he was to death tonight." My friend chuckles. But a split second later, his focus is back, his sharp eyes on me, and humor leaves him completely. "Except you weren't back when you talked to Peach. You weren't the Wren she knows. *I don't have to give you a choice?* That kind of shit will get you in trouble. It'll get *us* in trouble."

"I know."

"You can't allow yourself slipups."

"*I know.*" I feel my molars clashing as my jaw grinds. "I didn't hurt Conan, even though I should have, but most importantly, I didn't hurt her." I stand, now towering over my friend. I'm already the tallest guy around, but I'm also a couple of steps above him. "And that's all I care about."

He stares up at me, not a care in the world that in a split second, I could push him hard enough for him to tumble down the stairs and probably break his spine. Or hit his head. Something bad enough to kill him.

He knows I'm fully capable of it, that I could switch just like that.

But he isn't scared of me. Never has been, never will be. He's got his own twisted mind, and unlike me, is in full control of it. It makes us the perfect team, the best of friends.

"If by not giving her a choice, you meant initiating her, I still think you should. However, be more discreet about it." He leans forward. "Because Peach is smart, really fucking smart, much more than you. She'll see something coming and won't be tricked."

My silence brings a smile to his face. Because silence is not a categorical *no* like he's used to hearing from me.

"You know..." I chuckle to myself, shaking my head at how stupid I've been. "I've always had this stupid idea in my head that one day she'd initiate for me. When we were in high school, and I still had time. I really thought I would make her mine, and that by the time initiations came around, she wouldn't hesitate one second and would do it with me."

"Oh yeah?" Nodding to himself, he looks like he's imagining what that would be like. "Well. Initiations are tomorrow, so I think that ship has sailed, Brother." He shrugs. "So, like you said, don't give her a choice. Who cares, anyway? Once she's yours, what is she going to do? Anything she tries against you will get her punished by the Circle. She'll get sick of rebelling real soon, believe me."

I give myself exactly ten seconds to enjoy that idea. Any more and I would get hard in front of my best friend.

"We should go back inside," I finally say.

"Yeah, your girlfriend is probably causing some sort of chaos while we're out here."

I don't correct him when he calls her my girlfriend. I never do.

He's not wrong about the chaos. By the time we walk back into the ballroom, we find Peach toe-to-toe with some prick I know from lacrosse. It was only a matter of time before they ended up in an argument. The man is about as sexist as they come, and because I always put him back in his place with a quick glare when he tries to turn our locker room into misogynist central, he's too scared to ever say anything too bad in front of me.

I don't think he was too scared of that with Peach. He should have been.

While they're toe-to-toe, they're not really face-to-face since he's got about a head on her, but her shoulders are squared, and she's looking up at him like she's ready to punch him as he keeps talking.

"I'm just saying"—he shrugs, a smug smile settling on his face—"you girls wanted equality, didn't you? He slapped her a couple times and she ran to your little shelter? What do you women fucking want? I'm confused."

I'm surprised there's no fire coming out of her flared nostrils when she exhales.

"First of all, we're talking about more than a couple slaps. And even if it was 'just'"—she uses air quotes—"a couple slaps, I would have encouraged her to leave anyway. Secondly, are you seriously comparing a woman escaping her abusive husband to women fighting for equality? Maybe someone should punch you a few times and see how you react."

He cackles in her face before standing straighter with pride. "I play lacrosse, Peach. I've had my fair share of being hit in the face, and I never ran crying to my friends like a little bitch."

Her voice drips with sarcasm. "My God, Caleb, you play lacrosse. You're so cool!" Then her face drops. "Does that also mean I get to hit you in the head off the field?"

"Try and see what happens."

She pushes on her toes to be closer to his face as she smirks. "So, what you're telling me is, there's a time and place you choose to be hit and you wouldn't want that to happen to you without your consent. Like, let's say, at home when you're just chilling with your partner?" She pauses when his eyebrows pull together with confusion. "Do you see what I'm getting at here? I do try to talk in terms you can understand since you decided to compare domestic abuse to a fucking sport."

With how tightly she's holding her flute of champagne, I wonder how long we have before it breaks.

"You know what?" Caleb snorts. "If that bitch was as annoying as you, it's no surprise her husband hit her. Maybe it was the only way to shut her up."

That does it. The flute breaks. Not because Peach was holding it too tightly, but because she smashes it on Caleb's head, and it's followed right away by a punch to his cheekbone. The idiot probably hurt her hand more than she hurt him.

People gasp, but a lot of the women who were watching cheer Peach on.

Caleb is disorientated for a few seconds, taking a couple of steps back as he wipes glass from his hair. But as soon as he comes back to reality, his face twists with anger as a drop of blood appears at his hairline.

"You're right, asshole," Peach seethes as she shakes the hand she punched him with. Amazing, it was the wrist she sprained. "Maybe it really is the only way to shut someone up. Seems to work with you."

I'm moving closer now, Achilles right behind me as we make our way through the people who gathered around them. Just another Friday night being Peach's best friend.

Caleb shoves his hand into Peach's chest, signing his death warrant, and she stumbles back. She looks back up at him, and I push someone out of the way, now knowing I don't have much time left.

"What's wrong?" Caleb taunts. "You think I'm not going to hit back because you're a woman?"

The challenge on her face is not something he should ignore. Before he knows it, she's tackling him.

"Peach!" Alex screams next to her as both Caleb and her fall to the floor.

Pushing one last curious student out of the way, I wrap an arm around my best friend's waist as she starts straddling Caleb to punch him again. I lift her up back to her feet and away from him.

"Let go!" She fights me, but I doubt she could do much damage when I think she's also using me to stand up.

"You've drank too much for this," I tell her calmly.

"I'm sober enough to kick his ass," she hisses back.

It's easy to stay calm as long as she's the one I'm talking to, but when Caleb stands back up and strides toward Peach with his fist closed, I can't quite see straight anymore.

I push my friend to one side, keeping her at arm's length before turning to Caleb on the other side.

"What the fuck do you think you're doing?" I say to him, my voice lowering.

"What? She thinks she can fight me. Let her try."

I keep Peach away when she tries to get past me and stay focused on Caleb. "I believe I can also fight you. Should we test that theory?"

He takes a small step closer, and I look down into his eyes. He might be a head taller than Peach, but I'm one taller than him. The cut from where Peach got him with the glass is now bleeding enough that a droplet rolls down the side of his face.

"Should we?" I insist, feeling a zap of electricity course along my spine. I could kill him before he even blinks.

I stare him down until he finally steps back, and I nod, showing he made the right call.

"Go back to the party, Caleb." I turn to someone in the crowd, grabbing their drink from their hand. I stay there for a second, keeping my calm before I turn back around. "Here. Enjoy the rest of your night."

In a sense, I want him to say something, anything, just so I can knock him out right here and now. But I'm a patient man. I can wait until it's just me and him.

He nods, taking the drink and downing it. "Whatever."

"Come on," I tell Peach as I look to her. "Let's get you home."

"I'm going to fuck him up. I swear he's dead," she rages, but she's addressing herself to me rather than Caleb.

Everyone can see how riled up she is. Her long hair is a mess, strands flying everywhere. Her right hand is limp, and her tense face shows she's not done with Caleb.

But what I see is the hurt shining in her eyes, and I can tell he truly touched a nerve.

"Did you hear what he said?" she insists.

"I did. And he deserves to get his ass kicked. Just not by my friend who could get herself in danger by doing it."

I glance away for a split second, looking for Achilles to let him know I'm leaving with Peach. That's all it takes for her to attempt to get back to Caleb.

"Wren!" Alex calls out.

I'm barely quick enough to grab her by the back of the neck and pull her to me. "Peach, come on," I grit out as I bring her closer. "Let's go."

"I'm so angry." And I can feel it in the way her body shakes against mine as we make our way through the small crowd and out of the ballroom.

"I know." I kiss the top of her head, attempting to soothe her, and I sense the way her nervous system glitches. There it is. That weird effect we have on each other. Her trembling eases, settling into a calmer energy.

She smells of alcohol mixed with her usual scent of rose

and lychee, and she doesn't walk straight. I'm annoyed, but now isn't the time to bring it up, so I stay cool when I say, "You put yourself in a state again."

"That's not true," she fights back as I open the back door to my SUV.

My driver says a polite *good evening, Mr. Hunter,* and I'm about to reply when Peach misses the step to get in and falls back onto me.

I catch her at the waist and lift her onto the seat.

"What was that?" I tell her, barely able to hold back a laugh.

I settle next to her and pull the strand of hair she's nervously biting out of her mouth. "You drank too much."

"And you care too much," she whispers, looking down at the seatbelt I just fastened around her.

It's not the first time we've ended up in a situation like this. My friends always count on me to deescalate Peach, no matter how right or wrong she is. Our aim is simply for her to not get hurt or in more trouble than she can handle.

"Caleb is a real asshole, you know?" she carries on, playing with the seatbelt. With a hiccup, she throws her head back against the seat. "I hate him."

"He's an asshole who wouldn't hesitate to punch a woman. I don't want that woman to be you."

"If he's capable of that, he needs to fucking die," she throws back.

I nod, but I stay quiet. I couldn't agree more, but it's not like I'm going to get into it with her.

"You kissed me, Wren." She sighs, but in her state, I can't quite catch if it's of pleasure or annoyance. "That's bad. Very bad."

Caressing her cheek, I tilt my head to the side as I observe her.

"Why is it so bad?"

"Don't you get it?" she huffs, rolling her head from side to side. "What if I end up falling for you?"

An uncontrollable smile spreads on my face, chest warming ever-so-slightly.

"What if?" I whisper.

She's too gone to answer. She doesn't even realize where I'm taking her. Too drunk and high to notice much. I don't have time to drive back all the way to SFU. I need to get back to the ball before it ends. So my driver brings us to my parents' place. I hate it here, but I won't see them at this time.

She's barely awake when I carry her out of the car. I make sure to gently deposit her on my bed and get rid of her shoes. Pushing the sleeves of her dress off her shoulders, I put a t-shirt of mine on her and slowly pull at the dress until it's off. I knew she wasn't wearing a bra, and I didn't want to have her half naked in front of me when I took the dress off. The t-shirt technique *before* removing the dress works wonders. Placing the covers on her, I give her a soft kiss on the forehead. I could watch her sleep all night. It's my favorite thing to do. But I have something to do for her.

"I agree with you, Trouble," I whisper. "I think Caleb should die."

And with that, I grab a few letters from my Scrabble game, put them in my pocket, and I leave to do exactly what Peach would have wanted me to if she was awake.

-metal IS NOT the same as punk.
-She's still allergic to shellfish and cat hair
-Always leave the green olives to her
-We don't like metal anymore.
-Tea tree and peppermint shampoo
-Don't forget the peri-peri powder on her fries
-Bake and shake every first Tuesday of the month.
-No more sugar in her coffee. It makes her feel sick
-DO NOT bother me during girls' night Wren
-Spiced honey on pepperoni pizza
-Check the triangle freckles on her right shoulder
frequently. Dermatologist said to keep an eye.
-New vision results: Right eye -2.75. Left eye -3.25
-If she gets in next September's yearly release of the
EEAJ, the announcement will be in August next year.
-Her brace needs to come off in a week

Chapter Ten

Wren

Demons - MISSIO

I yawn, wiping my hand across my face as I wait for the last people leaving the ball to clear the parking lot. Leaning against my car, I cross my arms over my chest and keep looking for Caleb. I returned here on my own. No need for a driver.

There's a knock on the window from the inside of the car, and I glance over my shoulder to check what Achilles wants.

He rolls down the window. "Snapped yet? I want to sleep, and Kirsty is inviting me over. Are we done soon?"

I run my tongue across my teeth. "Want to sleep, or want to sleep with Kirsty? Pick one."

"Either way, I don't really want to be here. So, back to my question. Snapped yet?"

"Shut up, Achilles."

A knowing smile spreads on his lips, and his steel eyes sparkle.

"What?"

"You sound like Peach."

A very specific voice steals my attention away, and I look ahead of me again.

"He's here," I say, excitement burning through my veins.

"I changed my mind about sleep. Even I get excited when you're about to lose it. I'm a giddy fan girl right now."

My non-committal *humph* doesn't tame his joy.

I raise my hand, calling for Caleb as he reaches the bottom of the stairs that lead to the town hall. I'm not parked in a spot, rather taking the space in front of the fountain roundabout, where drivers usually drop the guests. It's only two a.m. and most people are on their way to Marissa's after party. I know, because she didn't hesitate to message me about it five times today. And again when I left with Peach. No scruple, truly.

"Caleb!" I call out again since he was too drunk to notice me the first time.

"Ooh, it's happening." Achilles giggles behind me.

"You're a child," I mutter as Caleb runs toward us.

"Whatsup," he slurs. "Here to gimme a scolding 'cause I teased your girlfriend?"

I shake my head, laughing softly. "Nah. Once I put her to bed and she's not a nuisance anymore, I get to really have fun."

"Nuisance is the word alright. So is ball breaker."

He stumbles to the side, and I put a hand on his shoulder. A calm settles over me. Complete peace.

"I was going to offer to drive you to Marissa's. We're just leaving."

"Nice." He nods. "You're a fuckin' great guy. I know you are. I know you don't actually believe in all that feminist bullshit Peach spurts out. We're about to be brothers. Real brothers, once we initiate."

I look around to make sure no one is catching the part about the initiations.

"For sure, brother. Get in."

He slips in the back of the car as best as he can, and I get back in the driver's seat.

As soon as I start the car, Achilles says quietly, "You slipped something in his drink earlier, didn't you?"

"Of course I slipped something in his drink," I mumble.

"Oh, I've got chills. Literal chills. I'm so excited."

I don't answer as I drive away. It's such a peaceful drive, I almost want to whistle, but I stick to tapping my fingers on the steering wheel. I wouldn't want to give anything away with something as obvious as whistling. Although I think with the state Caleb's in, he doesn't notice much.

I guess most people would assume someone becomes a violent murderer when they "snap," like Achilles calls it. I don't. There's a change in my body, for sure. But it's more of a relaxing feeling.

The violence comes a bit later. First, it's like everything in me slows to a steady hum. All the bad thoughts, all the anger. And I've only got one thing in mind: getting rid of any inconvenience. Like Caleb.

He doesn't notice we're not heading toward Marissa's. He talks some nonsense about how Peach would be ten times hotter if she just learned to stand there and be pretty. I inhale deeply, a poised smile settling on my face. This feels really, really good. This feels like an afternoon by the lake. Like the sun kissing your skin on a cold winter day. Like a hug from Peach. Scratch that. Nothing compares to a hug from Peach.

I park at the edge of the Stoneview forest. In this part of town, we're not far from the lake, but mainly, once we'll advance through the woods, they're practically never ending. They stretch all the way to the city of Silver Falls, meaning the man can run...but he won't get anywhere.

"Alright. Get out of the car."

He stumbles out, following Achilles and me.

"Marissa's backyard has changed," he slurs. "It's cool."

I wrap an arm around his shoulders. "Dude, you drank too much. Are you okay?"

He nods, but his chin falls heavily against his chest, and he struggles to bring it back up.

"Whoa, stay with me," I say, pretending worry like an Oscar-winning actor.

I help him lift his head up as I bring him near a tree, but it falls back down again.

"I said *stay with me*," I repeat calmly as I pull at his hair and force his head up.

"The fuck, bro." He struggles against me, but his movements are slow and lethargic, and I don't even need to use any strength to keep him in place.

"I'm not going to lie, it's a bit boring when they don't struggle," I admit to Achilles standing behind me. "The drugging wasn't the best idea."

"You're sick, my friend." He laughs softly.

"And you're in no place to judge."

His palms facing me, he raises his hands in front of him. "I'm in complete control. Absolutely aware of what I do."

"Me too."

"You're on a high and won't remember this tomorrow."

He thinks he gets it, and he's very close, but that's not exactly it.

"See, you're wrong," I explain, keeping a tight hold on Caleb's head. "I'll remember up till here. When everything feels so perfect."

I feel my friend shift behind me as I put my free hand in

my pocket and count the three Scrabble tiles I have there. All good.

"You're so terrifying," he says with interest in his voice. Passion even. And I hear him clearer than Caleb's futile protests asking to let him go, even though he's not sure what the fuck I'm doing.

Achilles has always had interests in everything different and freaky. He loves psychopaths, true crime, and all the sadistic things that make him feel alive. We're best friends, but I'm also an amazing case for his sick obsessions. Fucking weirdo.

"I really do think I'll remember everything until..." I readjust my grip on Caleb, placing him right in front of the tree.

I don't know why I picked a tree tonight. I don't have a favorite way to do things, and I don't have some kind of secret coded way of getting rid of people. I just do what feels right in the moment.

"Until now," I finally say.

I crack my neck, feeling a surge of strength within me. My ears are ringing, my blood feels thicker to pump, and my voice lowers when I talk to the man I'm holding.

"Caleb," I purr. "Say what you said about Peach earlier."

"Bro, you sound really fucking weird. Let me go."

"Say it," I repeat, a smile spreading on my face. My cheeks feel numb, like I've been to the dentist, and I can't control my expressions anymore.

"I don't know. I agreed that she was a nuisance."

I breathe in deeply, almost able to smell the panic wafting off him.

"And?"

"And...and she's a ball breaker. But you agree, don't you?"

I roll my shoulders, unable to contain the energy within me.

"Who does Peach belong to?"

"What?"

In a lightning-fast movement, I press his cheek against the bark of the tree.

"It's an easy question, truly. The word has been passed around for a few years now. Who. Does. Peach. Belong. To?" I articulate.

"Y-you, bro," he stutters. "What the f—"

"Say it in a full sentence, Caleb."

"She belongs to you!" he squeaks as I press his entire mouth against the trunk.

"Good." I nod. "Good." I pull him back and whisper in his ear. "Then why would you say that about the woman who belongs to me? Have you never learned respect?"

"I...I..."

"I. I." I repeat in a whiny voice. "Who does she belong to?"

"You— Stop!"

I smash his face so hard against the tree, blood spurts out of both his eyebrows. "Who does she belong to?" I hiss as I pull him back.

"You," he cries out. "Fuck, Wren...please."

"Again."

"She belongs to...to you..."

I smash his head again. Blood splashes everywhere, including my clothes.

"Again, Caleb. You'll be saying those words until you can't say anything anymore. I want your last breath to be you trying desperately to scream that Peach belongs to me. I want you to die knowing that it's because you disrespected her, upset her, and that because of you, I have to be here ending your life instead of in bed with her."

My heart explodes with joy as I keep hitting his head against the trunk of the tree, and he keeps babbling that he's sorry and that she's mine. He doesn't last long. The thunder of my own pulse in my ears accentuates the fact that his has stopped.

He falls to the forest ground as I let him go, his blood covering the moss, mixing with the soil under him. I roll him onto his back and squat next to his face. Pulling his mouth open, I take the pieces of plastic out of my pocket.

"This is fucking sick." Achilles chuckles behind me as I push the pieces down his throat. It's disgusting to go too far, so only one goes down, the second at the back of his throat, and the third stays in his mouth.

I observe his face, or whatever is left of it, tilting my head to the side.

"Did you hear what he said?" I look over my shoulder and smile brightly at my friend. "Peach belongs to me."

Achilles runs a hand through his hair.

"Wren...my brother, you are one delusional son of a bitch."

I shrug, standing back up. "Just saying, he agreed with me."

I remove a butterfly knife out of the inside of my suit jacket and give it to my friend. "Do me a favor, put it on the Circle. We don't want the police asking too many questions."

I shudder from the cold as I start walking. "I'll wait for you in the car. It's too cold."

Settling in the driver's seat, I rest my head as I close my eyes.

Isn't the world just so much better when I know there's one less man in it who made Peach feel terrible?

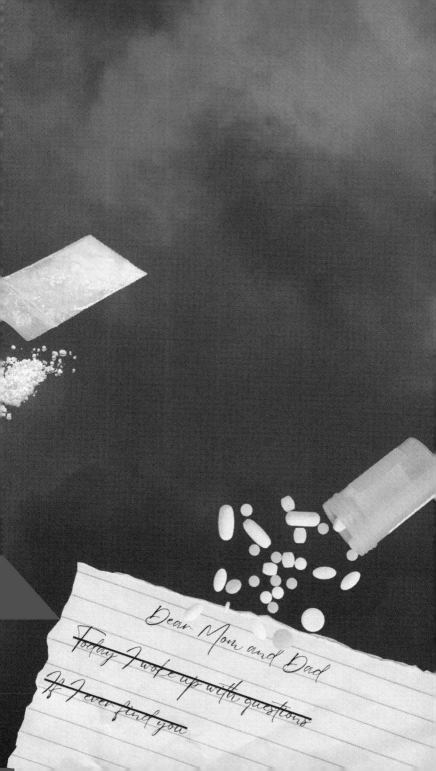

Dear Mom and Dad

~~Today I woke up with questions~~

~~If I ever find you~~

Chapter Eleven

Peach

Scream My Name – Thomas LaRosa

My favorite smell is the one of trees after the rain has fallen. They're suddenly so pure, so alive. The line of red cedars behind our school are the gates to the Stoneview forest, and after a storm, I love to come and climb them. If I manage to get high enough, the smell is a perfect blend of earth and sky. Like freedom.

"Penny, please. I'm scared."

"You're fine," I throw back at my friend Alexandra.

"You're going to fall."

I look down at her. She's biting her fingers, her wide eyes looking everywhere around us.

Sometimes Alex isn't fun. She's always scared of everything. Even climbing trees.

"My daddy says little girls shouldn't play around in the mud." She looks down at her shining black shoes now covered in mud. I told her, first to get to the big branch that looks like a snake wins. But she said no.

Pushing on my foot, I grab a thick piece of the trunk

sticking count. If I can just reach the lower branch, I'll sit there for a while and breathe in the tree.

"Don't tell your daddy about this, then!"

"But my daddy says I shouldn't lie." I look down at her again, and her lips are trembling as she twists the skirt of her uniform. That's what she does before she cries. Alex cries a lot.

"Alex, we're not in kindergarten anymore. We're second graders now. We're not babies, and we don't have to tell our dads everything. Right, Ella?"

When my other best friend doesn't reply, I look down again. "Ella?"

I'm just about to grab on the branch when Alex says, "She went to get the boys."

"No!" I tell her off. "They suck!"

"You can't say that word," Alex cries out. "Please, come down. I'm scared."

"I'm almost there—" My foot slips against the trunk and my leg scrapes along the bark as I fall. It happens in a split second, a shriek leaving my mouth.

I squeeze my eyes shut, bracing for the impact as Alex screams. But there's something weird. It doesn't hurt that much. It's a soft landing, like when Daddy used to throw me in the air and catch me. Except this time, there's also a big grunt and then another fall.

"Ow," I moan as I roll onto my back in the mud and look above me. There are clouds in the sky, but they're mostly hidden by the branches of the trees.

"Are you okay?" That's Ella.

"She's hurt." And that's Alex crying. "She's bleeding! Oh, no, Penelope..."

Something moves next to me, and then my friend Wren's face is above me. He's scowling like my daddies when I do *something bad.*

I didn't do anything bad.

But my wrist and knee hurt.

"Are you trying to get us killed?" he says.

"Us?"

"Who do you think caught you?"

It's only now that I realize he's sitting on the ground next to me, his uniform muddy. He caught me.

"You're always getting yourself in trouble." So grumpy. "And now you're covered in mud." Boys suck.

I close my fist in the gooey soil next to me, staying on my back as I slap mud on his face.

"Now you're covered in mud too." I giggle.

"Penelope, stop!" Wren groans as he wipes it off his cheek. "I just saved you."

"Yeah." I blow on strands of hair falling in front of my face as I sit up. "That's why I can keep getting in trouble. You're always here to save me."

He helps me up and wipes the blood off my knee and shin. "Your dads aren't going to be happy."

But I don't care about the mud and the knee. Right now, I care about the pain throbbing in my wrist.

"It hurts," I whine, showing my limp hand to Wren. "My wrist...it really hurts." I try to keep the tears at bay, not wanting my friends to see me cry. But...

Fuck. My wrist really fucking hurts. The first thing I know is that it was another blackout.

I keep my eyes closed, trying to put the night back together while I fight my horrible headache. I can only remember up until the drink I had with Elijah. There was some bright light at some point. Like some sort of flash. I think I laid down too? Fuck, I don't even know how I got home.

I twist in bed, and something hits me. It smells good, like cedar trees and earthy citrus. It smells like Wren. For a few seconds, I let myself bask in it. His scent is the most reassuring thing in this world, and I love having it all around me. I roll onto my side, rubbing my cheek against the sheet. And that's when it hits me a little clearer...

It smells like Wren.

My eyes snap open at the same time as I sit up. I haven't been in this room in forever, but I would never forget Wren's room. It's so impersonal. The walls are painted a sand color, the furniture a rich, earthy brown. It's a large but simple room. A lot of space but not a lot of life in it because Wren has always refused to accept this house as his home.

I know the two doors lead to a black marble bathroom and a walk-in closet. The third is the way out of here, which I should seriously consider using.

I check my clothes, noticing I'm wearing one of my friend's t-shirts. How do I not remember getting here or getting changed at all? I don't see Wren, but I assume he's in the shower I hear running in the bathroom. I throw the covers to the side, getting out of bed as quickly as I can. Holy shit, I slept with contacts in. That's bad.

My wrist feels so much worse than yesterday afternoon. I try to move my fingers as much as I can with the brace restricting my movement, but the pain it sends up my arm stops me from trying again.

I need to check the time. It's Saturday, and I have to be at the women's shelter on the North Shore of Silver Falls before ten a.m. I spot my dress and handbag on the floor across the room, and I'm about to grab my stuff, when something catches my eye. Wren's clothes are piled in a corner, and the shirt of his tux has drops of red splattered on it. Surely, that can't be blood, right?

Curiosity gets the best of me. I abandon my initial goal to go to the corner and instead pick up what was a crisp white button-down yesterday, squinting my eyes at it. Not so clean looking anymore with splatters of what is *definitely* blood.

"What are you doing?"

My heart jumps out of my chest as I snap around to face Wren. I didn't hear him come out.

"You scared me," I huff.

Droplets of water drip from his light-brown hair, rolling down his forehead and getting lost in his dark eyebrows. As my eyes travel lower, I notice he's only wearing a towel around his waist, and his damp six-pack is doing things to my body I'm not sure I should allow. Just like I shouldn't allow the way my tongue darts out to lick my lip when I stare at his Adonis belt.

"Peach." Startled, I look back into his eyes. "My shirt."

His waiting hand prompts me to give him his shirt, and I finally come back to reality.

"Is that blood on it?" But he's already throwing it to the side.

"How's your wrist?" he asks, softly grabbing my forearm to look at the bandage.

"*Is that blood on it?*" I repeat through clenched teeth. Does he think I'm stupid?

"Obviously, it is. Now answer my question."

"Whose blood, Wren?" I'm talking slowly now, making sure he can't pretend he doesn't get what I'm asking.

My friend has always been a private person, not one to share a lot about his family, his childhood, or whatever goes on in this house. But lately, he feels more mysterious than he's ever been, and I remember the drop of blood I found on his face a couple of weeks ago. The way he and Achilles refused to tell me where they'd been all night.

He pauses, his thumb subconsciously drawing smoothing circles on my inner arm. As his gorgeous blue eyes dart between mine, his face softens.

"Probably mine. I cut myself when I picked up the pieces of that glass you smashed against Caleb's head."

That sentence triggers a flashback of last night, and I can feel my headache coming back tenfold.

"Wait..." I step back, forcing him to let go of my arm. "Caleb...he was being an asshole."

"Don't worry about it. You put him back in his place. I got you out of the situation as usual. It's all done."

I rub my temples with the tips of my fingers. "Fuck." Yeah, I remember now. "I swear I didn't drink that much. And I only did that one line—"

"Save it, Peach."

"But it's true!"

"I'm sure you can't remember punching a guy in the face because you were completely sober, yes."

That's why my wrist is so much worse than yesterday. I punched Caleb. Narrowing my eyes at Wren, I attempt to cross my arms, but the pain rings out again. "I wasn't sober, but I didn't drink enough to black out."

He doesn't believe me, I can tell. I'm not really sure I believe myself anyway.

Putting his hand in front of me, palm up, he cocks an eyebrow. I hesitate for a few seconds. He cares, he wants to make sure I'm okay, and I probably put him in a shit situation yesterday. Sometimes I know when to stop being so stubborn. So I put my hand in his and let him undo the brace.

"You complained about not wanting to take a break from cheer, yet you still put yourself in a situation where you injured yourself. Make it make sense."

I roll my eyes, attempting at the same time to not stare at his shirtless form. I look to the left and at the Scrabble pieces on his desk. With my left hand, I put together a few letters. I notice a ripped piece of paper on there, *Caleb Mitchel* written on it, but I ignore it to finish aligning the letters.

"I don't need a life lesson right now," I say before pointing at the desk.

His gaze follows, and I feel him hold back a laugh when he reads the plastic squares I put together.

FUK U

Licking his lips, he goes back to being serious. "You always need a life lesson, Peach."

He checks my wrist, moving it and asking how it hurts before nodding to himself and putting the splint back on. His hands land on my hips, and I gasp when he turns me around and presses me against the desk, my back to his chest. His deep voice is in my ear before I can say anything.

"Did you like our kiss yesterday?"

My breath gets stuck in my throat, my muscles tightening with need. I'm ready to lie, but I can't get myself to. I can't push the truth out of my mouth either. So, I stay silent.

"Tell me, Penelope." His lips skim the skin below my ear, and he presses a kiss on my pulse. "How many times are we going to play this game before you truly give in?"

I take in a trembling breath, my head falling to the side.

"You and me...it's not going to happen, Wren. Giving in isn't exactly in my nature."

One hand goes up to my hair while the other slides

149

down the t-shirt I'm wearing until he can wrap his palm around my thigh.

"Okay," he says against my skin. "I'll speak your language. Did you *hate* our kiss yesterday?"

I shake my head, incapable of thinking straight now that he's pulling my hair, his skin so hot against mine.

"No. I didn't think so," he purrs. "And do you hate it when I'm there to clean up the messes you make?"

My head is moving again, telling him a silent "no."

"What do you think this is, huh?" Pulling at my hair, he forces my head back, dragging a harsh exhale out of me. "That I'm your little puppy at your beck and call every time you need help? That I'm always taking care of you because I'm a *good guy*?" He growls the last words, bringing his hand from my thigh to between my legs.

His fingers test the wetness there, and I bite my lip to keep myself from moaning.

"I'm not a good guy. You know that. I'm good *to you*. Only you, Peach, can be my weakness and my strength. In sixteen years, you've put the biggest smiles on my face, and were the cause of the little tears I shed. Do you have fun doing it? Giving me hope and crushing it in the palm of your hand?"

One of his fingers pushes inside me, and I can't control the moan that falls from my lips. Fuck, he feels too good.

"Answer."

"Yes," I pant. Because it's the truth. I *love* having him wrapped around my finger. It makes me feel powerful, and I love power.

Until Wren takes it away.

"You love being special to me, don't you?" he purrs, moving his finger in and out of me. "You love watching me

turn down other women, knowing that it's because of you."
As he pushes a second inside me, my knees buckle.

"*Yes*," I whimper. "Fuck."

"Bend over the desk."

"What?" I gasp, moving my hips to the rhythm of his fingers.

Until they disappear.

"Bend. Over. The. Desk."

I try to turn around, understanding he's taking it further than we ever have when he presses his rock-hard cock into the small of my back.

"Wren—"

The pull on my hair hurts in the best way possible.

"You've been taking and taking from me. It's time to give back."

He pushes me forward, and I plant my forearms on the desk so I don't crash onto its surface.

"Spread your legs."

When I don't, he slaps my pussy with a strength that makes me cry out.

"Fuck!" I spread my legs at the same time as I breathe through the pain.

"Tell me you don't want this," he murmurs softly as I hear the towel drop. "Tell me that all the time we spend together is just friendship." He pulls the t-shirt all the way to the middle of my back. "That every time you wake up in my bed after a night out is a mistake. That the times you've allowed me to touch you were to fuck with me."

I feel his tip at my wet entrance, and I struggle to not push back against him.

"Tell me that I'm just your foolish best friend with too much hope, Penelope. I want to hear it cross your lips."

"I can't," I moan, nearly shivering with need.

"That's what I thought," he growls.

He presses forward, and I freeze, a flash of clarity pushing through the fog.

"Condom!"

When I try to lift up, he holds my head hard against the desk, and I blindly slap his body behind me.

"Peach, baby, it's no secret I don't fuck anyone else." He laughs proudly before adding, "And I know you haven't been fucking anyone because my word is law at SFU. And the law says stay away from what belongs to Wren Hunter."

I can't even find it in me to reply, too lost to the desire clouding my mind. He pushes slightly farther in, and the movement makes my eyes roll to the back.

"I want you to stay still and let me use you exactly how I want. Do you understand?"

There's only one thing in me that tells me not to do it, and it's a tiny voice in my brain that I shut down right away.

I want to enjoy. I want to let go. And I want Wren Hunter to fuck the living hell out of me.

"Yes."

The second the word is out of my mouth, he surges deeply inside me. My jaw drops open, and my breath catches until he pulls back and slams back in.

"Fuck," I pant, clenching around him. "Fuck, you're big and...really deep right now."

He presses harder against the back of my head to keep me in position.

"And you're going to take it like the strong girl you always say you are."

I lose myself completely when he thrusts again, forcing my hips to hit the edge of the desk as I pant breaths. Pushing onto my toes, I try to meet his movements as wave after wave of pleasure wash over me with every drag of his length.

I can't formulate a single thought when he slows down and rasps, "Fuck yourself on my dick. Show me you want this just as badly as I do."

I push back with all my strength, but it's nothing compared to the way he was destroying me a second ago. The difference makes me needy, and despite putting everything into it, a hopeless whine escapes me.

"More," I pant as I writhe my hips. "Wren..."

"You don't get what you want out of me when I have my dick inside you, Trouble. You take what you're given."

"Fuck you," I whimper. "Shit..."

He leans over me, kisses my shoulder, and just as he bites into it, he thrusts into me again.

Every movement is a statement to how big he is, and how I adapt to every inch of his cock like we were made for each other.

"Your little cunt is desperate for me. Almost as much as I'm desperate for you."

He accelerates, so powerfully that the desk bangs against the wall in a repetitive telltale sound. The building of pleasure makes me sweat, and I can feel my muscles stiffening as I'm driven closer to the edge.

"Wren..." I moan.

"That's it, Trouble. Call my name when you come. And get fucking used to it."

"Fuck, *Wren!*" I scream as I explode around him, stars blurring my vision as my entire body pulses with sweet relief. He doesn't give me a break as his fingers come to caress my clit slowly in a drastic comparison to his thrusts.

"W-wait," I sigh, the sensations too much, too good.

Like he already knows my body by heart, he delicately strokes me again, and pushes deeper inside me.

"Oh God...oh God..."

"Wait to come again before you call me your god. Wait"—he presses his whole body against mine, and the edge of the desk pushes against my lower stomach—"until I show you"—he presses some more, stroking my clit at the same slow pace —"what I can make your body do for me."

With his dick deep inside me and angled just right, the wood pressing at my front, his fingers bring a pleasure like I've never experienced before. And that's when I feel it leaking out of me uncontrollably.

"Fuck," I whimper. "I can't stop..."

"I know, baby. Keep going. Squirt all over yourself for me. Soak my dick like a good girl."

His voice wavers, and I feel him climaxing inside me as he shortens his thrusts.

Absolutely nothing feels real anymore when he pulls out of me. Right away, his cum spills down my thighs, and I can't even seem to care about it.

"Don't move," he says softly. "I'll get you something."

"As if I could move," I whisper, my eyes closed as he walks away.

I'm barely awake when he comes back, and I feel a warm, wet cloth at my entrance.

"Let me," I say as I try to grab it, but he softly pushes my hand away before caressing my lower back.

"Just stay still."

"This is weirdly...intimate," I mumble, my cheek still against his desk. I think I'm resting on a few Scrabble tiles.

"You just squirted all over me, but yeah, me taking care of you is where you should draw the line."

"Ah. Ha," I deadpan as he finishes and delicately helps me stand on shaky legs.

We end up facing each other, his t-shirt still on me and now back into place, and his towel back around his waist. Our eyes cross, and my heart plummets to my feet.

Oh. God. *This* is where I draw the line for intimacy. That look in his eyes that tells me this was just the beginning is terrifying. That dimple on his cheek that barely holds back his pride at finally getting me. And the way he bites his lower lip, announcing he's already hungry for more.

"Um..." I scratch my throat.

I'm not ready for this. Not ready to know what Wren is like when he fully unleashes on me.

"Do you want to have a shower here?"

I shake my head. "You won't have the right shampoo for my hair."

He arches an eyebrow at me. "I have your shampoo. The tea tree and peppermint one. Of course, I have it."

"Okay, uh, weird," I admit. "And I changed shampoo last year. I use one with coconut oil in it now because my hair is longer than it used to be."

"Oh...you changed? Well, you didn't tell me." He sounds accusing, like I'm the one who did something wrong by not keeping him in touch about which shampoo I use. He grabs his phone that's on his desk and starts typing on it.

"I didn't tell you because you *shouldn't* keep my shampoo at your house. You don't even live here."

"I keep it everywhere, just in case," he mumbles as he keeps on typing. "Your hair is beautiful, and I know you like to take good care of it. It's important to you. So it's important to me."

This is too bizarre for me to process when I'm still throbbing inside from his dick pounding into me a minute ago. I'm about to ask what he's writing on his phone when a sound in the hallway startles us both. A door opening and closing. Something shifts in him. It's instant, like a mask that settles on his face as his features harden.

"Let's get you home."

I jump on the chance to change the topic.

"Why did you bring me here?" I ask as he grabs my dress and gives it to me. "You hate this place." I don't know why I feel the need to remind him. I haven't been here in forever because Wren rarely comes anyway.

"I just had some stuff to deal with. Get dressed. I want to leave sooner rather than later."

It's annoying to walk through Wren's house in yesterday's clothes. Like I'm some sort of girl he brought home for the night and he's now kicking out. He's so serious suddenly, and I want to snap at him that if he's going to be so cold, he shouldn't have brought me here. He shouldn't have fucked me the way he did. I hate this vulnerability building within me. I feel raw and open, and as much as I was scared of intimacy, I also can't take the unexpected coldness.

"Come on, Peach. Don't you have to be on the North Shore before ten?"

His words make me realize I stopped on the last step of the grand marble stairs.

"Uh, yeah." I shake my head. "What time is it?"

"Seven." He looks around as he presses a hand on my lower back and urges me forward.

"Seven?" I look up at him, feeling the sweet warmth of anger pulsing up my neck. "You're kicking me out of your house at seven in the fucking morning? What am I, some random Wren Hunter groupie you picked up at the Stoneview ball?"

He swallows, his Adam's apple bobbing before he presses his full lips together. Still, it doesn't stop the smug smile from tipping the corner of his mouth.

"I'm just trying to get us out of here before anyone wakes up. But you're spoiling me, Trouble." His gravelly voice sends electricity down my spine. "First, you sleep in my bed. Then, you finally let me sink my cock into you. And now you get all needy on me?"

His hand slips through my hair, pressing on the muscles at the back of my neck. Dear God, his hand is too strong for a girl to stay sane.

"If the next step is being clingy for the rest of the day, just know it'll be a perfect day for me."

He drops a kiss to the top of my head, then steps back, and I can finally breathe. Slapping his shoulder, I start walking again.

"Me? Clingy with you? You can keep dreaming." Fuck, I want to be clingy.

"I sure will." He chuckles.

Their butler is about to open the front door for us, when a voice stops us short.

"What the fuck?"

Wren throws his head back, huffing at the same time as I turn around. Elijah stands right behind us, wearing a black robe over black silk pajamas, and holding a cup of steaming coffee in his hand.

"Oh, hey," I say, trying to act natural. Like me sleeping over at the Hunter mansion is a weekly occurrence. "How was the rest of your night?"

Elijah doesn't reply. He can't since he's cut off by Monty Hunter coming out of a hallway I've never been through. He's wearing a dark gray suit with a bolo tie around the collar of his white shirt. There's a lightning bolt striking a mountain engraved on the silver clasp, and I could swear I've seen that emblem somewhere.

"Penelope, to what do we owe the...pleasure." Replace pleasure with "unwanted presence," and you get exactly what he meant.

The constant scowl on Monty's face doesn't waver, and his unwelcoming energy makes me straighten up to show I'm not bothered by his behavior.

I can't help it. Men exist, and I feel the need to challenge them for their audacity of breathing the same air as me.

"Good morning, Mr. Hunter." I plaster a fake smile on my face. "Oh, you know, just sleeping in your son's bed after punching another student in the face. Same old, same old."

Elijah's death stare is so lethal I sense it before even turning my gaze toward him. He doesn't say anything, doesn't even see me. He's too focused on his older brother.

"What about you? How have you been?" I turn back to Monty. "Any environmental devastation from your company lately?"

He scoffs, his head rearing back slightly at my nerve. "You've always been a very interesting character, Penelope. I'll give you that." He juts his chin toward Wren. "Enjoy her while you can."

I open my mouth to ask what he means by that, but Monty dismisses me by walking to Elijah, who's still awkwardly silent. "Come, we've got a lot to work on today."

Work on? Since when does he work with his dad?

"Environmental disaster?" Wren huffs as soon as we're outside the house. "Really, Peach?"

"What?" I shrug. "It's a genuine question. His work impacts mine."

My friend shakes his head, unimpressed as he guides me to his car. We don't use their driver today, but rather one of Wren's many toys.

"It's red. I'm assuming this is a Ferrari?" I say as I sit down in the passenger seat. Those things are way too low. It's annoying.

"This is a Ferrari 12Cilindri. It can hit sixty-two miles per hour in under three seconds."

I snort. "And I'm sure the planet will thank you for it."

I'm pushed against the seat when he speeds out of his driveway, and we're on the highway before I bring up something that can't leave my mind.

"Wren?"

He comes out of the comfortable silence with a knowing, "Yes?"

That's all I need to understand he's been thinking about the same thing as me.

"What did your dad mean?"

This time, his silence is palpable, and his fake ignorance makes me uncomfortable.

"What did your dad mean when he said *enjoy her while you can*?"

"My dad is an idiot, Peach. You know that." His eyes stay on the road, and I'm dying to force him to look at me.

"Do you know who's not an idiot? Me. Now tell me what he meant."

I observe him while he doesn't observe me, and it's unusual. I know that wherever we are, Wren's eyes are always on me. But his focus on the road is a good excuse for him to avoid staring into my eyes.

"Wren," I insist. "What the hell? You're hiding shit

from me. And until today, I didn't think they were things about *me*."

"I'm not—"

"Don't disrespect me," I snap. "You and Achilles have been acting weird since last year, but it's getting worse. Whatever you're hiding, come clean, because I'm struggling to reconcile your recent behavior with my best friend."

"Your best friend." He snorts. "It's a fucking curse to be your best friend, you know that?"

"For you? Or for me? Because I haven't changed. But you... I'm finding blood on you, on your clothes. You keep things from me and the girls."

He grinds his teeth to dust, swallowing back whatever the truth is. But then as if he can't keep it all to himself, he continues.

"What my dad meant is that I soon won't have the option to choose you over everyone else like I always do." He looks to the left, out of his window, hiding his expression from me. I know there's something else he wants to say. "Unless—"

Both our phones ring at the same time, cutting him off. It's that specific sound we recognize so well, and it puts an end to our strange conversation. It doesn't matter that I need answers. Hermes news always takes over everything.

"I'll check." I huff when his eyes keep going to his phone in the central console.

I unlock the SFU app, my heart pounding in my ears. There's that nagging fear within me when Hermes is involved. Especially since the message I received about Ania.

It's not about me...but it's bad.

One of you has access to seriously secret information...and I thank you for it.
Someone won't make it to the post Stoneview ball brunch... R.I.P.

#murdererontheloose #youhearditherefirst

The picture posted is a police report that clearly shouldn't be out yet. It's written by hand and doesn't say much but how they found him. The weirdest part is that the whole thing is crossed out with another type of pen, different from the one originally used, and instead a small circle was drawn at the bottom of the page with the letters S.C. next to it. I still manage to read a few lines. A body was found in the large forest that separates Silver Falls from Stoneview at four this morning.

Hematomas to the face. Skull crushed in.

Lacerations to the chest.

Square plastic pieces (possibly from a Scrabble board game) found in his trachea and mouth.

Male body currently identified as Caleb Mitchel (ID found on him).

I read whatever I can of the report three times before I can finally process the words. My chest is so tight I can barely inhale enough air to survive.

"What is it?" Wren asks as he passes the gates of the SFU campus. The red-brick castle comes into view as we drive up the winding road that leads to it and the rest of the campus.

I read the line about the plastic pieces again. *Possibly from a Scrabble board game.* They were found in his mouth and throat. Did he...choke on them?

Someone murdered Caleb last night. Someone smashed

his head in and shoved letters from a Scrabble game down his throat.

Wren stops, letting some students cross the road, and looks at me. "What is it?"

"Caleb." I gulp. "He's dead."

I search for anything I can find on his face. Because my instinct is telling me something, but my brain promises me it's impossible. Wren, *my* Wren, my best friend I've known for sixteen years, is not a violent murderer. He's stubborn and commanding, and he lives for the win. But he's not someone who would *murder* another human being.

Something pierces through my stomach, my gut screaming at me when I focus on his features.

There's nothing. No surprise, no attempts to justify anything, no innocence but no confirmation of guilt either.

He barely even blinks.

When he drives forward again, I feel something I never have around him. Fear.

I can still feel him inside me from earlier in his room, and now I fear him like I've never feared anything else in my life.

"What is it you want to say so badly, Trouble?" He pushes me to talk through my crazy thoughts. But are they *that* crazy when the proof is right there on my phone screen?

I try keeping my voice under control in any way I can. "They found Scrabble letters down his throat."

Letting out a dry laugh, he finally parks in front of both our houses. My entire body tightens as he turns to face me.

"Isn't it fucking crazy?" he says slowly, like he sounds as surprised as I am. "The things I do because some guy upset you?"

"This isn't funny." I attempt to sound strong, like I can

fight the unhinged energy pouring out of him right now. But my voice is trembling, and my mouth is dry.

"No. It's not. A man is dead." He reaches out toward me, attempting to pinch a strand of my hair, but I slap his hand away out of pure instinct.

"Don't touch me," I gasp. "Wren." I squeeze my eyes shut and open them again. "Please, just please tell me you didn't..."

He just stares. He stares at me with death in his eyes as he says, "I'm sick of hiding who I really am from you."

I don't wait to make sense of it. My survival instinct kicks in. I pull at the car handle, jumping out before he can catch me.

I run to the house without looking back. Everything seems out of proportion if I think too hard, but thinking won't save my life. I slam my front door shut, lock it, and take a few steps back.

He didn't follow me. He's not on the other side of the door, trying to break it down. I'm panting, struggling to catch my breath, let alone think coherently. I stay here for a few seconds...and they turn into a minute.

Nothing happens.

And here it comes...the feeling of utter stupidity. How could I think for one second that my best friend could do this. What the hell is wrong with me?

My shoulders slump, and I rub my hands over my face.

"What the fuck, Wren," I huff to myself.

That was the worst joke ever. And I'm too fucking mad at him to go back out. I walk upstairs, checking for my best friends in their bedrooms. They're both probably at their boyfriends' houses. And I'm here, going fucking crazy, thinking Wren would kill someone because they upset me.

That's the kind of shit Xi and Chris would do for Alex

and Ella. The kind of act they consider romantic and never understood is, in fact, absolutely insane. I always tried to give them a reality check when it comes to these things. Men shouldn't be as possessive and obsessed as their boyfriends are. They shouldn't kill for you, even out of protection. God, just live a normal life and understand that shit is toxic.

Taking a deep breath, I try to calm myself as I walk into my room. I need to get ready to go to the shelter. I need to think of how I'm literally going to crush Wren's balls into dust for that stupid jok—

A hand slams on my mouth from behind me, making my heart drop as it pulls me into a hard body. I freeze for a split second before fighting back, attempting to scream behind it and bite the palm to release me.

"Peach, baby. Why would you run away from me? You know I'd never hurt you."

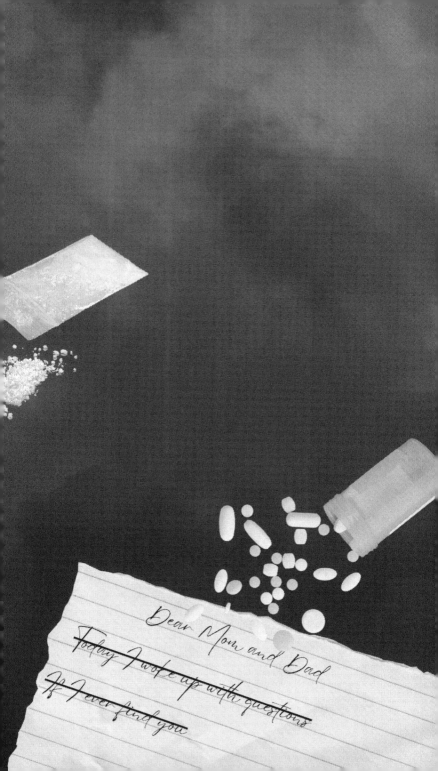

Chapter Twelve

Peach

Can you love me? Croixx

Recognizing Wren's voice in my ear is a mind-fuck. Hearing it makes me think I'm safe, and so does smelling his cologne. My body could almost believe in the illusion of safety. But then everything hits again, and I attempt to scream with all my might.

"Calm down. Shh. Calm down, Peach."

I. Don't. Fucking. Calm. Down.

I throw my elbow back, hitting him in the stomach, but that doesn't change anything. The man is made of steel. I pull my weight down and move from side to side like a crazy woman, but he doesn't let me go.

Bringing both hands to his arm around my face, I grip on to him tightly, feeling his muscles and how strongly he's holding me, and I lift my leg to crush my foot onto his toes.

"Fuck! Peach!" he hisses. I use the moment to try to destabilize him some more.

Hoping to slam him into the wall behind us, I push back

into him. Nothing works. He doesn't even move an inch. He doesn't give a shit about his toes, and I'm still stuck with my back to him and his hand on my mouth.

And I tire...very quickly.

He stays immovable for another minute before I completely give up and a whimper gets stuck in my throat. I knew Wren was strong. Anyone who looks at him knows that, but I thought I was too. I'm so strong-willed that I thought myself invincible, even when faced with a man his size. We've play-fought before, and nothing has ever felt like the strength he's using today.

"Are you done?" he purrs behind me.

I mumble a "fuck you" that can't be heard, but I think he knows because he chuckles.

"I don't want to hurt you, and the longer you fight, the more likely it is to happen. Promise you won't scream if I let you go?" How can he ask this so casually, like he would ask if I want to go on a walk.

I don't move. I don't say anything. What kind of promise is that? He's holding me fucking hostage in my bedroom.

He killed a man. He killed a man. He killed a man.

"Please, Peach. I really want to let you go. But I need you to promise you'll be a good girl."

My lack of a response triggers something in him. He brings his other hand to the back of my head, pulling my hair until I'm craning my head so far back, I can see his head above mine.

His voice doesn't hold the same reassuring tone when he says, "I'm going to let go, and you're going to keep quiet if you don't want to find out exactly what happens when you don't behave. Now, nod."

There it is again. That lack of anything in his eyes. How

have I never seen this before? The pain in my skull becomes unbearable, and I nod before I can even tell my brain to resist. Something relaxes in him, and he lets go of me completely.

The first thing I do is snap around to face him.

"Thank you," he sighs, running a hand across his face as if easing some tension. "Thank you," he repeats. And he truly sounds grateful.

"What the fuck, Wren?" I rasp, taking a few steps back. "What the—"

"I'm sorry. I never meant for it to come to this, okay?"

I take another step back when he takes one forward.

"Please...don't be scared of me." The plea comes right from the depths of his heart.

My response is as automatic as a reflex. "I'm not scared of you." Even though I know that's not true. Saying it is just how I'm wired.

He pinches his lips and nods slowly. "Listen, Hermes published that police report, and I didn't expect it. This isn't how I wanted you to find out."

"Find out what?" I bark, raising my voice when I didn't intend to. "Find out you're a *murderer*?"

He shakes his head. "I'm not— I mean, yes, I probably killed Caleb." He's talking to himself now.

"*Probably?* Did you?"

"I think I took him out of the equation, yes. I believe it was me. But he upset you, so..." Looking right at me, he taps the side of his head with the tip of his index finger. "It makes sense."

I feel my eyes round, and I open my mouth to tell him it makes no sense whatsoever. Except no words come out.

I'm too terrified by the manic look in his eyes, by the smirk on his face. "Do you understand now?"

I shake my head, but the next step back makes me trip on something, and my ass ends up on the floor. He doesn't stop advancing, though, so I crawl backward.

"Do you understand, Peach? The things I'm capable of doing for you?"

He chuckles to himself. "I tried, you know? I tried to show you only the good side. I pretended for *years* that all I was, was your good friend. I swallowed rage when you flirted with other guys, and I punched walls when I wanted to punch their faces. And when I hurt them, I did it behind your back. Like a good person."

Oh. Fuck.

"I pretended I cared for things like college, our friends, parties, sports. I put on the mask of the perfect fucking human being so you wouldn't see there's absolutely *nothing* behind it. I did all of that in the hope that when the time came, you'd finally be mine." He snorts. "Years of pretending not to be *crazily* obsessed so I could slowly lead you to this exact date, and you'd tell me you'd choose me. And we were doing so well this morning, weren't we? We finally took it a step further. So, what? So Hermes can fuck it all up for me?"

He stops above me, a foot by each of my hips as my insides tremble.

He tilts his head to the side, discovering something he never had before. "You look delectable under me."

My heart is beating so harshly in my ears, I can barely hear him. When I try to move backward some more, I realize I've reached the wall.

"Wren, what are you talking about?" I pant. "Choosing you today? Of all days? What do you even mean?"

"You didn't receive an invite, did you?"

"An invite to what?" I snap. "What are you saying?"

He shakes his head. "So no one has their eyes on you. Only me. Really, all the chances were on my side. The only thing I don't have is your willingness." He runs a hand through his hair. "Achilles was right. I should have just done it."

"Done *what*?" I attempt to use the wall to stand up, but he moves closer, pinning me there just as I reach a position on my knees. "Move back, for fuck's sake!" I bark.

"I would really rather not. I quite like you there. Let me enjoy it while I can, yeah?"

Wrapping a hand under my chin, he grips to make sure I keep looking at him. "Tell me something."

He licks his lips, his eyes sparking. "If I told you that tonight, you could be mine. Forever. What would you say? That there would be nothing that would ever get between us, but that you'd also never have a chance to leave me. And that, if you refuse, we will never, *ever* have a chance to be together. You and me, it's now or never, Trouble."

Wondering if he's officially lost all sense of reality, I blink up at him. But the anxiety he's pulling out of me is very real.

"I know all the reasons you shouldn't want this. I heard you the many times you told me. I thought about them over and over again. What I'm asking you right now is to think of the reasons you *should* want it. You know we have feelings for each other. Our clashes of personalities, our need to dominate, put that to the side, please. Just *feel* what we mean to each other."

My heart threatens to leap from my chest and run away. The fear, the confusion...the feelings he mentioned, it's all too much.

"You've fucking lost it," I rasp. "I have no idea what you're talking about, so let me go."

Instead of doing just that, his grip tightens. "Choose, Penelope. Us, tonight and forever. No way out, no safe word. Or nothing. Ever."

For a moment, I think of what I truly feel for Wren. How he's always been different from the others. How I feel the closest to him. I used to look for him the second I walked into our school when we were kids, and I still do every time I step into a party or the classes we share. How my eyes search for his number seven on the lacrosse field. How he's the first person I go to for good and bad news, for advice and reassurance. How my heart warms when he talks to me, and my stomach tightens when he touches me.

Wren and I have something special and undeniable, but I've always put our friendship first. I've always put reason before passion when it comes to him, because he's too important to me to lose him.

Him and me? One day. Maybe. But, for whatever reasons he won't explain, choosing him tonight and forever? No way out? That's just not who I am. That's not how I've ever acted with a man. Giving him that kind of power over me is not an option. I don't put myself second just to feel how much someone can complete me. I won't ever hope for a knight in shining armor or a villain in a dark cloak to steal me away and give me the world. I want to build my own world and relish my success with pride. I want to bask in everything I've achieved and know that I didn't have to sacrifice anything for a man. Especially one I've now learned can go to extents I didn't think him capable.

"Tonight and forever, or nothing?" His voice resonates in every single corner of my mind as he repeats the choice he's offering.

I look straight into his eyes, and he knows me enough to hear it before I say it.

"Nothing."

His jaw clenches as his eyes flutter shut. I feel his pain so deeply inside me, it could almost make me change my mind. It doesn't.

My stomach flips when he opens his eyes, and his free hand comes to the back of my head. Something changes in his expression as he forces my head forward and presses it against his groin. Panic overtakes me, and I whimper as I try to push back against his thighs. It brings the purest form of fear. If he's capable of murder, I'm not that special that he would spare me.

"Wren, stop..."

He presses harder, and all I manage to do is move my head so my cheek is against the coarse material of his jeans rather than my mouth. Our difference in size and strength is so obvious it hurts. In fact, it scares me to the bone. Because all I have right now is hope that my friend isn't going to do something stupid. I can't stop him if he wants to. I can only ask him not to and trust that he won't.

My world falls apart when I realize he's hard. I can feel it so clearly. It turns him on to make me submit.

"Stop," I grunt as I struggle some more, the blood freezing in my veins.

He lets me go so suddenly I fall back against the wall and attempt to stand up in messy movements as he takes a few steps back.

He looks at me with heartbreak in his eyes and anger in his features.

"I regret giving you a choice."

That's all he says before storming out of my bedroom.

My best friend, who I always thought was a safe haven, the man I've always had conflicted feelings for and who *killed* for me...regrets giving me a choice.

And as I catch my breath while staring at my bedroom door, I wonder exactly how dangerous Wren Hunter is. Could he really do it? Take my choice away?

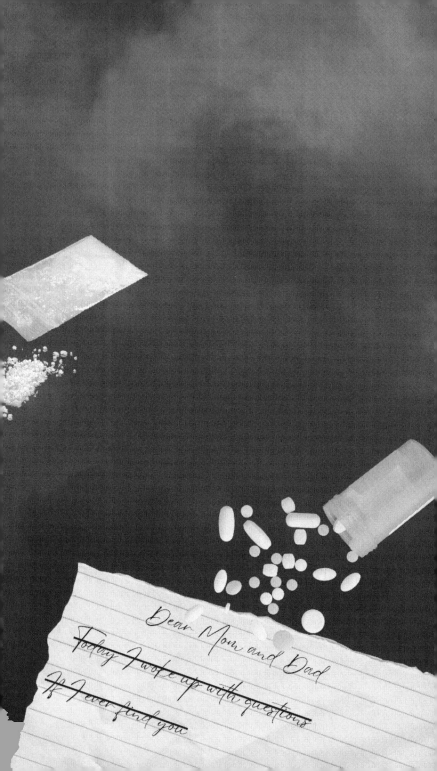

Chapter Thirteen

Peach

In The Woods Somewhere - Hozier

I exit the rundown building, waving at Cathy as she shouts to get home safe.

"Always!" I throw back, carefully closing the glass door behind me.

The window on the door is a mosaic of broken glass that looks like it'll shatter in a million pieces if someone blows on it. We added a protective film to prevent that, but it's not the first time a man vandalizes the shelter because we helped his ex-wife escape an abusive relationship.

I get into my expensive car, always avoiding looking at all the other ones parked here. It makes the difference between them and me too stark, and I hate it. With anticipation making me tense, I check my messages as soon as I'm sitting behind the wheel. Alex, Ella, the different groups. Three missed calls from Elijah.

Nothing from Wren.

My stomach twists, and I'm not sure if it's from stress,

the need to hear from him, or the wish that what happened this morning was just some nightmare I made up.

Something has changed, and there's a hole inside me. Like the man he was held such a special place in my heart that I'm missing him. I don't want to lose him, yet I can't help the fear that consumes me when I think of that report from the police.

Caleb's skull was crushed in. How violent does someone have to be for that to happen?

I call back Elijah as I start driving away from the shelter, and I already hate myself for the reason I do it. I don't care about what he has to say, and I don't want to talk to him. But I want to see if he talks about Wren.

"*I haven't heard from you today,*" he says instead of a hello.

"It's Saturday. I was volunteering at the women's shelter."

I turn onto the main street on the North Shore of Silver Falls and double check the car is locked. Anything can happen on this side of town, and I know my car screams *I have enough money, please come rob me.*

"*Of course. It's just...you know... You were with Wren this morning, slept in his room and all. I wasn't sure if you spent the day with him or something.*"

Just hearing his name makes my whole body tighten with anxiety. Yet I want nothing more but to hear about him.

"Yeah, I was just too drunk last night. He took care of me."

"*You know you can always come to me if you're not feeling well, at a party or anything.*"

Yeah. Except I don't want him to ravage my body like his brother did.

"What happened with Caleb? You had an argument?"

God, this really doesn't look good.

"And now he's dead. Is that where your question is going?"

"Peach, I know you didn't kill Caleb. I just want to make sure you're okay."

Of course I didn't kill him...your brother did.

"Have you heard from Wren today at all?" I ask, unable to help myself.

"Not since I saw him with you. Look, I can't talk for long, I just wanted to check on you."

I nod, even though he can't see me. "Thanks. I'm fine." I hesitate for a moment, then decide I need to clear my mind. "Are you doing something tonight? We could grab dinner and watch a movie at my house or something?"

"Uh...I can't, actually. I'm busy tonight."

"Elijah Hunter," I gasp jokingly. "Are you finally making friends other than me on this campus?"

He chuckles awkwardly. *"Yeah, no. It's a family thing. I probably won't be on my phone either, just so you know if you don't hear from me."*

"Oh...okay."

I'm dying to ask if Wren is going to be there, but he would clock that something is wrong. He and I never talk about his brother, and I already mentioned him once in the conversation.

"Well, have fun with your family. I'll see you tomorrow or something."

I hang up as I'm crossing the bridge back to the South Bank of Silver Falls. Everything seems newer here, the contrast with the poorer side of town too shocking to ignore. Yet it doesn't seem to bother anyone who grows up in the richer part, let alone us kids who were raised in billionaire town half an hour or so from here.

The second I get out of my car, I notice a package on the porch. It's a good indication that the girls still haven't been home today. Surprised to see my name on it, I pick up the black box and envelope, wondering if my dads had a gift delivered for me since I told them about the paper I'm working on for the engineering journal only yesterday.

Walking in, I still scream Ella's and Alex's names in case they're here, but since no one has replied by the time I get to my bedroom, I know for sure I'm not seeing them until probably tonight or tomorrow.

I drop the box on my bed, my bag on the floor, and open the envelope as I kick my shoes off.

Penelope Sanderson-Menacci,
After careful consideration, I have decided to personally invite you to the Dionysian Mysteries.
Under my command, you are to present yourself at the structure designed by Daedalus tonight before sundown.
You will drink Circe's wine and turn into who you truly are.
Find a husband, and you will become the patron goddess of lawful marriage.
Get caught by a god, and you will serve us as a goddess of lust.
You may not be late.
Yours,
Hyperion

"What the fuck?" I mutter to myself.

I take a picture of the letter and send it to the group chat with the girls only.

Peach: I think Xi Ep is having a stroke.

Not thinking much about it, I put my phone to the side so I can take off my clothes and get in the shower. That letter and package can only come from Xi Ep, the sorority I'm part of. I barely participate in anything anymore, especially since both Ella and Alex left. There're a couple girls from cheerleading I still talk to in there, and I go to their parties from time to time, but not much else. They'll kick me out before the end of the year, I have no doubt. Especially because I don't plan to play along with whatever the fuck this new thing they have going on is.

I'm standing in front of my bed in my towel, water dripping from my hair when I decide to open the box. It's clearly going to be clothes of some sort. It's the exact package for it.

My eyes widen as I pull out a see-through dress.

I snort. "Fucking hell."

It's a dress that looks like what women would wear in ancient Greece. The kind we see on sculptures and vases, representing the goddesses of Greek mythology.

I grab my phone again to tell my friends, but realize I have a few missed calls from Ella. I call her back right away.

"*Peach.*" She's panting, sounding like she's running. "*No matter what happens. Do not go.*"

"What?"

"*I'll explain everything as soon as I get home. I'll be there in a minute.*"

I check the time on my phone before putting it back against my ear. "Don't you teach dance classes at this time on Saturdays?"

"*Chris is calling. I'm going to take it. See you in a*

minute. You will not be going to the initiations tonight. Promise me."

"What initiations? Is that what that letter is?"

"Promise me."

"What the fuck. I promise."

She hangs up, and I look at the letter again. *Dionysian Mysteries.* What the hell is this thing?

I'm glad I got dressed by the time Ella comes in because she isn't alone. Her boyfriend, Chris, is with her, towering over the both of us with his 6'4" frame.

She wouldn't bring him for no reason, and it doesn't help with the state of anxiety I put myself in while I was waiting. Something serious is happening, and I need to know what.

"Peach, when did you receive this?" he asks as he approaches my bed.

I realize I'm cracking every single one of my knuckles one by one as I answer, betraying my stress. "It was on the porch when I got home from the shelter. What is it?"

They eye each other, and Ella sits on my bed, tapping next to her. "You should sit down."

I do, my gaze on Chris walking anxiously around the room as he massages the back of his neck.

"Did your dads ever mention something called the Silent Circle to you?" he asks as he finally stops right in front of me.

I shake my head, this situation becoming more confusing by the minute. "No."

"I didn't think so," he agrees. "As far as I know, they're not part of it. Anyone else? A family member? A friend?"

"What are you on about? You know my family is just me and my dads. Who else would talk to me about this... thing. What even is it?"

"It's a secret society," Ella explains calmly next to me, but it doesn't hide the slight tremble in her voice. "And what you received today is an invite to initiate."

"However," Chris jumps in. "They're very secretive. Only members and their families know about it. And receiving an invitation usually means someone trusted you enough to talk to you about it and invite you to join them. They had to get you approved by the board too. So, I'm sorry, but I have to ask you again; has *anyone* ever mentioned the Silent Circle to you? A boyfriend, maybe? That's usually how it works."

I roll my eyes. "Yes, because I'm known around here for my long-term relationship with my boyfriend, who's part of a secret society. Don't be ridiculous. I'm telling you, no one ever told me about this. It must be a mistake."

"A mistake with your name on it," Ella says, putting a hand on my thigh. "It's for you. Someone wants you to initiate, and you must not go."

"Okay, I'm going to stop you right there. I'm learning just now that you're part of a secret society, Ella Baker." I push her hand away. "How long have you been keeping this from me? Does Alex know?"

She shakes her head. "She doesn't. And you can't tell her. They're dangerous, Peach. Anyone who knows about them and shouldn't is dealt with."

"Dealt with." I snort. Making fun of this is easier than accepting the fear that is thickening my blood. "What, do they kill people? Are they some sort of Illuminati or something? Is Beyoncé part of it?"

Ella's face scrunches with anxiety. It's only when she brings her hand to her collarbone, scratching and turning her skin red with stress, that the seriousness of the situation hits me.

"Els," I say with a calmer tone. "Don't scratch. I'm joking."

"It's not a joke," she rasps, her voice barely audible.

Chris grabs her hand delicately, pulling it away from her skin. The damage is done; she scratched herself to the point tiny drops of blood are appearing on her red skin.

"I'm sorry I kept this from you. I didn't..." Her eyes dart to Chris. "...I didn't have a choice. They don't give you one."

And with that statement, everything hits me.

I regret giving you a choice.

"Wait." I put together the words from Wren and his behavior this morning. "Wait," I repeat. "Wren...is he?"

She shakes her head, refusing to answer rather than it meaning *no*.

"He said something to me this morning, about...about choosing him tonight and forever? It was weird and he—"

I stop myself short. Do I say something about Caleb's murder? Ella is my best friend, my confidant. I've never hidden anything from her. Chris, however, I don't trust. Even less now.

"Did Wren say anything about asking you to initiate into a society called the Silent Circle?"

"Of course not," I snap. "Because it's fucking ridiculous, and because if he did, I wouldn't be so clueless. But he did ask if I'd received an invite. He just... He didn't invite me."

"Then there's nothing we can tell you about who is or isn't part of it," Chris concludes, keeping the secret to himself, even though it's clear as day that Wren is part of it.

Ella takes the letter from my bed and gives it to Chris. "Who's Hyperion?"

"Well, he won't say that in front of me, will he?" I say as a challenge to Chris.

His eyebrows pull together as he reads it again. "I have

no idea. But in Greek Mythology, Hyperion was a titan. I'm going to guess it's someone important, a board member, probably." He pauses. "Which makes no sense, really."

"None of this makes sense, Christopher." I release a frustrated breath. "But please, tell me why this *titanic* board member of a secret society inviting me makes even less sense."

"Because invites are usually sent by members who are about to initiate. They send them to their girlfriends or whoever they want to initiate with. They have to bring a woman to the initiations. An established Shadow inviting someone is always with the wrong intentions."

When I blink up at him, he explains in more detail. "A man who wants to initiate into—"

"Of course, only men would be allowed to initiate for that kind of bullshit. We're just brought along as prizes, aren't we?"

Ella grabs my hand on her thigh before looking at me with imploring eyes. "Please, try to stay calm for more than a minute."

"How about he tries not to piss me off." I bite my inner cheek, swallowing back the rest of my rant. "Fine."

I turn back to Chris, waiting for the rest. "You may talk."

He nods. "A man who wants to initiate into the Silent Circle has to bring a woman with him. She'll have to be successful in her initiation to become part of the society as his Hera, or his future wife. If she fails, she becomes an Aphrodite. Men who are already members, or as we call them, Shadows, already have a Hera. If they invite a woman to initiate, it's very likely she'll become an Aphrodite."

I take it all in. I'm not stupid; his words technically make sense, but the whole thing sounds completely made up. I catch myself biting on a strand of hair I hadn't even realized I'd brought to my mouth, then pull it out and tie my hair in a ponytail.

"I'm going to pretend this whole thing doesn't sound like it's coming out of a conspiracy sub-Reddit and go along with it." I huff. "If a Hera is a Shadow's wife, what's an Aphrodite?"

His hesitant gaze darts to Ella.

"What's an Aphrodite?" I insist.

"In simple terms, any man from the Circle can access her whenever they want, and she has to be available for them at all times," she murmurs.

"What the fuck?" I spit, jolting to stand. With fire in my eyes, I turn to face my best friend. "When you say *access,* I'm guessing you mean she's a fucking sex toy for them?"

"Yes," Ella whispers as shame coats her cheeks a deep red.

Weirdly, it doesn't sound made up anymore. Because any occasion those disgusting bastards have to use women's bodies, I know they will. Reality, if I've ever seen it.

I turn to Chris. "You're part of this? *You* had her initiate, didn't you?"

Ella jumps to his defense. "Don't be mad. It's more complicated than that."

"You're letting it happen?" I hiss at her.

"I don't have a choice."

"What are you?" I ask my friend. My head keeps on turning from him to her and her to him, and I'm getting whiplash. "His devoted wife, or every man's whore?"

"Peach." Chris's stern voice cuts through my anger, but he must think he's talking to someone else if he believes a telling-off will stop me.

"Ella." I grab her arm, shaking her slightly as if needing

to wake her up. "Please, *please*, tell me you did not follow this man into a secret society that would take most of your consent away."

"That's enough." Taking hold of my wrist, he forces me to let go of her. "It was complicated."

I shrug him off, pointing an accusing finger at him. "Oh, please. *Complicated* coming from a manipulator like you means it took you a while to trap her, but you finally did. I told her you were poison for her life. But here we are. You're still here, and she's forced to stay with you now. Isn't she?"

"Peach, please," Ella pleads. "It's not like that. Not anymore."

The anger that comes with watching someone lose their freedom boils my insides.

"Not *anymore*? Are you fucking brainwashed? Who else is part of this? That's what Wren meant this morning, isn't it? He wanted me to initiate, and now he's sending me this fucking...fucking bullshit invitation."

Chris shakes his head. "I'm not at liberty to share any information about members. If you don't know who invited you, or anyone who told you they were part of the Circle, then I can't share any more details."

"Fuck you, Chris. Seriously, *fuck you*."

"No one had a choice in this, Peach," he adds calmly. "I know you're angry. I was angry too. But the difference between you and us is that no one is forcing you to attend. You caught a member's eye. He wants access to you. You don't have to go. In fact, I'm telling you not to go. Your best friend is begging you not to go."

Tilting my head to the side, I smile at him. "Your condescending tone is infuriating. So much so, it almost makes me want to go."

"God, Peach," Ella huffs out.

"I might be infuriating, but your stubbornness could kill you. Just let that sink in."

Chris is always calm. He's not the kind of guy to shout or get into a fight. He's dangerous alright, but not the kind of danger you tell yourself to stay away from. That's how he got Ella. Mind games, scheming, manipulation. He's good at it, and the fact that he never snaps shows a control I could only dream of having.

But I see it today. The way his jaw clenches when he mentions that secret society called the Silent Circle. The anger flashing in his eyes when he talks about the *Shadows*. And the undertone of fear when he tells me not to initiate.

"I have to go," he murmurs as he checks the time. "I won't be home tonight, Sweets. Maybe you should stay here."

I want to scream that *home* is here, in the house she shares with her best friends. But I know that's not true. First, it was Alex, when she moved half of her stuff into her boyfriend's house on the North Shore of Silver Falls, far from campus and our sheltered life. She splits her time between here and there. Then it happened to Ella.

Chris might be a manipulative fucker, but everything he does is for her. He encourages her to do whatever she loves, he got her back into SFU after she got expelled for sleeping with a professor, he helped with her crippling anxiety, her eating disorder, got her to see a therapist again when she had all but given up. He pays for everything now that her family has fallen from grace and lost it all. He takes care of her mom, keeps her in Stoneview when everyone knows she can't afford it anymore. And in the summer, he bought Ella her dream house by Stoneview Lake. She didn't even have to ask because he *knows* that's what she dreamed about. It's peaceful, relaxing, and she's always wanted to live by the water. And so, she splits her nights between here and there too.

Sometimes, I end up all alone in this huge SFU mansion, not really knowing what to do with myself, but what kind of friend would I be if I told them? They found happiness, and there's absolutely no chance in hell I'd get in the way of that. Even if their boyfriends are obsessive, possessive, unhinged people. I fucking hate men, but I love my friends.

Ella goes onto her toes, wrapping her arms around Chris's neck. His big hands grab her waist, practically snapping her in two.

"I'll stay here."

He nods, stepping away. "Send me a picture of what you have for dinner because I know it'll look good." Smiling softly, he brushes strands of hair behind her ear.

A flash of jealousy courses through me. Not because I want Chris. But the way he cares is so beautiful and subtle. He doesn't tell her to eat, to make sure she's fueling herself. He knows her issues, but he doesn't make them obvious or remind her. He's smart about it, and I know how much it helps a girl like Ella.

Fuck, I hate moments that make me wonder what it's like to not be the only one taking care of yourself.

The second he closes my bedroom door, my best friend turns to me.

"I know you were never the biggest fan of Chris—"

"And even less now," I cut her off without being able to control it.

She takes a deep breath. "I *know*, Peach. I'm not asking you to love him or even trust him. But I'm asking you to trust me. I didn't have a choice. My family was indebted to the Circle. Joining was the only way to help them. Chris never had a choice either."

"It's funny, but I have a feeling he had way more of a choice than you did. Because he's a man. Because that's just how the world works, and that secret society works the same."

"And that's why I'm telling you not to join." Her stern voice surprises me, but it shouldn't. Ella always becomes much stronger when it comes to protecting her friends rather than herself.

"Of course I'm not going to join, Els," I tell her more calmly. "Why...*why* would I ever?"

She digs her baby blue eyes into my green ones. "Because they're good. And if someone from the Silent Circle wants you, they'll do everything in their power to have you. And they have a lot of power, Peach. More than you can imagine. Forget about the money your family has, the help cops could get you, the power you think your dad holds from being a local politician. Forget about how strong you think you are as a human being. They have control over *everything*."

"You're scaring me." I don't feel ashamed to admit it to my best friend.

"Good. If anything else happens, you need to tell me, okay? Because the only person who could help you is someone from the inside. That's Chris."

I nod, my eyes playing ping-pong between hers. "I won't go to those initiations. No matter what. Promise."

As I take her into a tight hug, I can feel her heartbeat racing against my chest. "I love you, Els," I murmur against her head.

She pulls away. "I love you too."

She's about to leave, but stops after taking a step backward. Her lower lip trembles when she says, "They killed his dad."

"Chris's?"

It has to be him. His father died in November last year.

She nods, silent until she finally admits what happened. "He was part of the Circle, and he betrayed them. Chris joined to save him and failed. Every day of his life, he's part of something he hates. Every day, he talks about revenge. But a single man against the most powerful society that ever existed isn't much, is it? We're stuck, but you don't have to be."

Suddenly feeling the guilt from snapping at Chris earlier, I gulp. "I won't be."

She smiles. "I'm going to have a bath. I need to relax."

"Of course. And Els...thank you for the warning."

She waves a hand as she leaves. "That's what best friends are for."

What a fucking mess. I still struggle to believe anything they told me, but reality often feels stranger than fiction, doesn't it? And things start to make more sense now. I believe strongly that Wren was talking about the Silent Circle this morning. I have no way to prove it, but what else would he be talking about?

I don't have time to process anything Ella just said when my phone pings. I swipe it open right away. My legs can barely carry me when I see the message.

It's a picture from May.

A picture of me laughing as I stand right next to Ania on the bank or the Silver Snake River. Right where she died.

The message is what makes me crash to the floor.

Lola King

Hermes: Did you receive your invite, little murderer? You will go to the initiations, or I'll post the picture. And not a peep to your little friends.

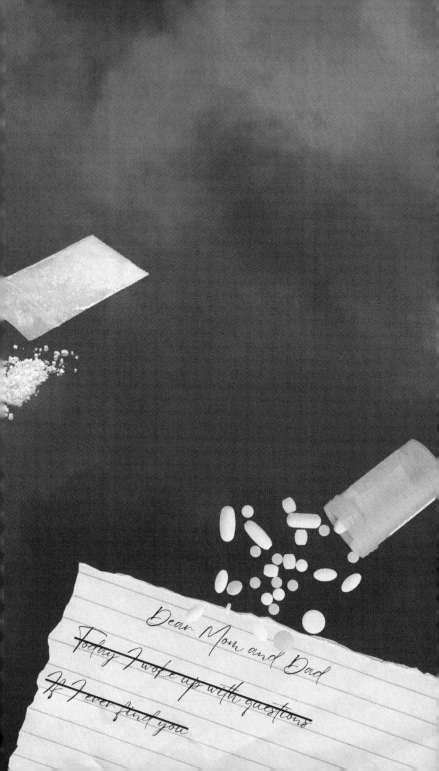

Dear Mom and Dad

Today I woke up with questions

If I ever find you

Chapter Fourteen

Peach

Poison – David Kushner

The dress hides nothing. Absolutely. Nothing. I had kept my underwear under it, but the second I walked into this place and saw how the other women were dressed, I knew to take them off.

It wasn't hard to figure out where to go. Daedalus built a labyrinth, and the Stoneview Country Club has a maze as their logo, even though I don't believe they have one. When I showed up with the invite and the dress under my trench coat, I was taken to this building, separated from the main club. The resemblance to a Greek temple told me I was in the right place, and as soon as I passed the Doric columns, someone opened the door for me. I'd never been here, never seen it, and mainly, had no idea of the kinds of things happening here.

Half an hour later, I'm surrounded by a couple dozen women who are dressed exactly like me, holding invites, most of them not even wearing shoes. There's a mix of excitement and anxiety moving thickly through the air, created by giggles, stressed huffs, and awkward smiles. It's clear some of us wanted nothing more than to be here, some aren't sure it's a good idea, and I wonder how many are like me, forced to attend or else...

The paintings of different scenes from the *Iliad* and *The Odyssey* cover the maroon walls, and in-between each painting, there's a statue of a Greek god or goddess. It feels like I've been looking at them forever when someone guides us through another room. A man at the door asks for our invitations and he stares at mine for a moment longer.

Looking at me again, he says, "Hyperion, huh? You better run fast, girl." Is that pity I hear in his voice? He looks all the way to my feet and mumbles, "Take off your shoes." Then he coughs to hide it some more before showing me inside with his right hand.

I move along, taking off my shoes before crossing a long room and following the other women through double doors that lead to a garden.

In front of us, trimmed grass extends farther than I can see, the rest of it being hidden by the night. As everyone walks forward and toward the blackness that feels like a void, men in black suits walk between us. Every time they see a woman with her shoes on, they order her to take them off and drag them to the back of the cortege. The grass is soft, almost like walking on a cushion, but the anxiety makes my entire body tighten, and my jaw aches from gritting my teeth.

I'm stuck. Stuck and scared.

I replied to Hermes before leaving the house. I asked them what they wanted. I angrily typed I would find out who they are and out them to the entire college. And I got nothing in response. This is their game, and they're playing it by their rules, whenever they want. No answer from them meant the threat was hanging over my head.

Little murderer.

I weighed everything as I watched the clock. Would I really be in trouble if someone found that picture? Could Hermes go that far? Am I truly willing to put my life in the hands of the Silent Circle when my very own best friend told me not to go to the initiations under any circumstance? But what else? Prison? At least if this society is as powerful as Ella mentioned, then they could protect me from the law, from Hermes.

We stop in front of the walls of a maze. They're so gigantic they make the entrance look as small as the door to Wonderland. My eyes observe the many men all dressed in black suits lining up with chalices in their hands, and I wonder...what does their protection cost?

And why does Hermes want me here so badly?

I pull the strands of hair I realize I'm chewing on out of my mouth and look around. This is it. There's no going back, is there?

I struggle to tell myself tonight might be the night I become a sex toy for rich men or forced to...marry? Date? I don't know, and the ignorance is the worst. How many women here were told the truth about what is meant to happen and the consequences?

All I want is to see a familiar face, someone who can explain something to me, but mainly reassure me that this is all a big, unserious joke.

I'm given exactly what I want when my eyes cross Chris's. I feel a wave of strength taking over me, and I'm about to take a step forward when he shakes his head subtly. He's wearing an all-black suit, his face set into a scowl, and he's holding a chalice. Like all the other men around here, he's got a signet ring around his pinky finger, and I understand it's because they've all initiated.

Which begs the question...where are all the men initiating? The ones the women around me are here for.

Men like Wren. Because I know that's what he was talking about earlier, and if I see him here, he better give me a fucking explanation.

It's a struggle to listen to Chris's silent warning telling me to stay where I am, but I have no choice when a man I've known since I was a little girl steps forward.

Eugene Duval. Achilles's father.

Betrayal slices through my gut. They all know, are all in on it. I have no doubt that if Eugene is here, Achilles knows about this society. Chris is a member.

And Wren... Where the *fuck* is Wren?

The only thing cutting through the highway of my thoughts going a hundred miles per hour is Eugene's calm voice.

"Ladies." His welcoming smile holds something terrifying, making me feel like a lamb being readied for the slaughter. "I am honored to welcome you to the yearly initiation into our community. Within this circle, you may call me Zeus, as I am your president. There's no higher authority than me."

I swallow thickly, wondering what kind of power he holds to wield it with so much pride. If this society is truly that powerful...does that make Achilles's dad a god? The Duvals have always had power within our community, especially with Eugene being the state attorney.

They're a well-respected family, going back so far that I'm pretty sure they founded Stoneview. I already had a problem with that kind of privilege, but president of a secret society? That certainly goes too far.

"Tonight," Eugene carries on, "some of you will become Heras, and some of you Aphrodites." This sentence sends a wave of murmurs through the crowd. "Show us what you truly want and who you truly are, and we will allow you to be whatever you wish."

With a show of hand, he presents the Shadows holding the cups. "You will now all be given a chalice filled with Circe's poison, then you will enter Daedalus's labyrinth. The bachelors who are being initiated as Shadows are waiting for you in the center. Your eagerness to be a wife to a Shadow must shine through the darkness of the labyrinth. Get to the center, be the first to grab a Shadow's hand, and you shall become his Hera. You will become a goddess highly respected in the Circle. You will carry our children and ensure our legacy."

Could this become more of a nightmare? I feel sick to my stomach.

Duval's smile turns predatory as he keeps us waiting for the rest of his speech.

"Five minutes after you enter the labyrinth, the Shadows who are already established members of the Silent Circle will come chasing after you. If one catches you before you become a Hera and brings you to the center of the maze, you shall become a goddess of lust, a servant to our needs...an Aphrodite. Your bodies will be ours, and we will forever cherish them."

He brings his hands together, almost like a prayer. "Ladies, it's time."

Old man gets a hard-on thinking about chasing and fucking younger women. Not really different from everyday life, is it?

The men approach us, each picking a woman to give their chalice to. It all happens too quickly as Chris comes toward me with slow but intense strides. He doesn't stop where I am, forcing me to step backward into the crowd as he takes hold of my upper arm.

"Keep going," he murmurs, looking above my head, to make sure I'm not hitting anyone, I guess.

Once we're far enough from the entrance, lost in a sea of women and away from prying ears, he gives me the chalice.

"Don't drink it. It's drugged." His voice is so quiet, I'm not sure I heard anything at all. So he adds louder, "You heard that right."

I feel my eyes widening, and he finally looks down at me.

"I don't have enough time to ask why you're here when Ella and I told you not to come. You're here and it's too late to go back. So all I can advise is run for your life, get to the center, and grab Wren."

"Wren?" I choke out.

"Pretend to drink. Now. Get rid of the wine."

I look around me, all the other girls are almost finished with their drinks. I look back down at my cup and pretend to bring it to my lips, then spill it to the side.

"So it *was* Wren, wasn't it? He sent me that invite?"

His eyes flick around again, taking in everything around us while all I do is focus on him. None of this feels real.

"He's not Hyperion, if that's your question, but I don't *know* if he invited you. It wouldn't be the first time someone invites a woman under a fake name."

He pauses, puts a hand on my shoulder, and my first reflex is to take a step to the side. Nodding, he pulls back.

"It's about to start. Run. Get to Wren. Then we'll talk."

"I won't go to Wren. I can't. He tricked me into this." I barely have the strength to say those words, let alone show him the fury I truly feel. But it's there.

Wren is a murderer. He betrayed me, our friendship, and our trust. He's the last person I want to run to tonight. I lost something I had always felt around him. Safety.

"Peach." Chris massages the back of his neck. "We don't have time for this. Ella would *kill me* if I didn't help you get to someone safe. I trust Wren."

"And I don't trust either of you."

He shakes his head, at a complete loss. He's not used to having someone so stubborn in front of him.

At the front of the crowd, Eugene Duval shouts, "On your marks..."

Everything becomes a rush. The women trying to be first in line to get inside the maze, the crowd tightening, and Chris's movement as he drags me closer to the front.

"Get ready..." Eugene continues.

Chris's words accelerate too.

"Please. You don't trust me, but you trust Ella. And Ella chose me because she knows I'm safe. I'm trying to do the same for you. Go to Wren, Peach, I'm begging you."

He stops at the front line, letting go of me.

"Let the Dionysian Mysteries *begin!*"

A shot resonates, startling me and sending my heartbeat into a frenzy. Before I know it, women are pushing around me to get to the small entrance of the maze.

Chris urges me forward, hissing low, *"Run."*

So I do.

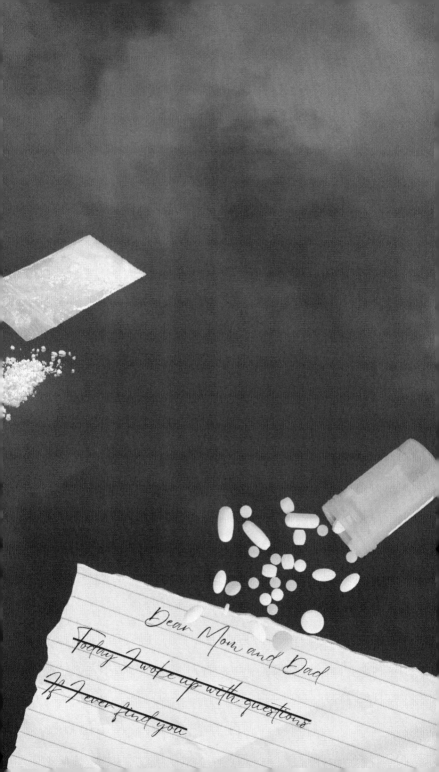

Chapter Fifteen

Peach

.Goetia. – Peter Gundry

A scream resonates somewhere around me, but there's no way of getting to the woman who needs help. I have no idea where she is, lost in the corridors of Daedalus's labyrinth, and all I can do is keep running to find my way to the center. A minute or so ago, they sent the Shadows after us, and one tried to catch me so harshly he ripped a piece of my dress.

I tried to help another woman when I saw her crying in front of a statue of the Minotaur. They're all drugged from the roofied wine, and she thought he was real. But when I touched her shoulder to tell her it was just made of stone, she slapped me and ran away. Everyone is terrified for their lives, letting their survival instincts drive them.

I should do the same, especially when I hear steps coming after me again. But my way to the center is a sure solution, and I can't panic and run around.

"Penelope," a voice sing-songs.

I whirl around to find Josh Addington turning a corner to

face me. I can't believe my own eyes. This guy is in most of my classes. He's my age. How could I have ever guessed that he's a member of a secret society. Is everyone at SFU hiding secrets?

"Peach, I knew you'd initiate for Wren," he says knowingly as he approaches me.

"Don't come near me," I blurt out.

"No? But I'm dying to make you an Aphrodite." He stops in front of me and his hand shoots to my hair.

"Get off me!" I scream as he drags me violently. Digging my heels in the muddy ground, I grab his forearm with both hands as I try to stop him, but it's hard to have much control with one of my wrists wrapped in a splint.

"I can't wait to push my cock into that sassy mouth of yours." He snickers. "No more fiery Peach, who shuts men up on campus. You're going to become our little toy, aren't you?"

As if he just got himself too excited to carry on, he stops walking, pushing me against the hedge of the maze. "I'm going to have you now."

He presses his disgusting lips against mine, biting me until I bleed. I scream against him, hitting him anywhere I can reach and hurting myself in the process.

When he pulls away for a split second, I spit blood in his face.

"Go fuck yourself," I rage.

It doesn't stop him, one hand wrapping around my throat and cutting off my air as the other goes under my dress.

I slap him, my nail scratching at his face, but my vision is also narrowing by the second. His hand is on my upper thigh when a voice calls out behind him.

"Addington, move along."

I'm unsure who it is until Josh steps back and Monty Hunter appears in front of me. Dizzy from adrenaline, I stride away from them, facing them to make sure neither jumps me. As I try to catch my breath, I witness as Josh doesn't even attempt to debate Monty's order. He glares at me, wipes my blood off his face, and disappears around a corner.

My racing heart doesn't calm in the slightest when Monty approaches me.

Every single cell in my body tells me to run. But something else, something stronger, makes me face him. Suicidal tendencies, maybe.

I cross my arms over my chest, narrowing my gaze at Monty as I stand my ground. He approaches slowly with a canine smile. There's something familiar to it, but I can't quite place it. Not just that, but there's something in his eyes that I've seen before.

"You do remember what happens to you if I catch you and bring you to the center of the maze, right?" he threatens, clearly not liking the fact that I'm not shaking with fear at the mere sight of him.

Every step he takes feels like the ground is trembling. It's him, the Minotaur, half-human, half-bull, who's going to turn my bones to dust. When I still don't move, he stops right in front of me.

"You'd become a whore for the Silent Circle." He observes me from head to toe. "Accessible by any member. Anytime." He brings a hand to my shoulder and delicately pushes my hair behind it.

I step to the side, my lip still throbbing from Josh's bite. But I keep a steady voice.

"Believe me, Mr. Hunter, I would die a hundred times

over before I'd let you turn me into a whore for you and your friends."

Despite my words, he tries again, bringing his knuckles to my face like I'm a challenge he loves. So I slap his hand away this time, and he looks at me like I just drove over his dog.

"Didn't I just tell you?" I say, my voice lowering to a dangerous octave. "Don't touch me. It's not a plea, it's a warning."

"Is that how you thank me for saving you from Addington?"

"You saved *him* from *me*," I snarl.

Unimpressed, he carries on. "I'm extremely tempted to turn you into a slut for my friends and me, Penelope. But that's not the plan I have for you. Now, run before I change my mind."

Plans? For me?

I don't want to play his game, and I don't want to run when he tells me to. But you have to pick your battles, don't you? And I won't become an Aphrodite tonight.

I take a few steps back, my eyes still on him, and I hiss, "Don't ever come near me again," before turning and sprinting into the next corner.

It's not an easy task to find my way to the center. The ominous music in the maze drives me insane, and it takes me forever. Not because I'm lost, but because from the moment I entered, I decided to use the left-hand rule. I've been mentally keeping my hand on the left wall—actually doing it when I could and wasn't fighting for my life—since I ran inside. It might take me all night, but it's a foolproof way to get to the end of the maze, or the center in this case.

I don't run into any other man, but I do hear noises that make me feel sick. Like the sound of a woman's whimper while a man grunts. And the choked sound of a call for help. The hardest thing isn't being here, it's being unable to save them from this torment.

There's no relief when I finally see the center. Men are drinking around a firepit, some a little farther from it and some closer to the corridor where we're all arriving from. They're chatting, laughing loudly. Some of them are holding women's hands, some consoling them, telling them they did so well.

A few of the women aren't so lucky to be protected by a newly initiated Shadow. No, they sport a bloody lip, a ripped dress. They're wrapping their arms around their shaking bodies, surrounded by older men who are cackling about how excited they are to have them as Aphrodites.

I stay in the darkness for a few seconds, looking for Wren. I can't see him, but I can see Chris. He's standing near a hedge, as far as possible from the other established Shadows playing with their new toys. He's alone, observing the scene with his hands in the pockets of his pants, maybe looking for me.

It's too hard to distinguish every single person, too many people around. More women arrive, sprinting to their boyfriends, the man who invited them. Some of them, I think, are just throwing themselves at the first Shadow they see. As long as they can escape the men left in that maze.

As I watch two people hugging, my eyes finally fall on someone familiar behind them, and for the first time tonight, hope flourishes in my chest. Finally, I see a way out, a solution.

Someone who won't hurt me.

My feet move before I can think any further. This is it.

"Elijah!" I call out, relief finally lighting up my chest.

He looks up, his face lifting with surprise as his eyes

widen. I'm shaking as I start to jog through the crowd of men. I won't become an Aphrodite, and I certainly won't become Wren's personal puppet, or worst...next victim. He wanted me here? Well, wherever he is, he can watch me run to his brother rather than his murdering, psychopathic ass. He betrayed me once today; it won't happen twice.

My trust and faith in Wren are completely lost, and my friendship and love for Elijah is all I can hold on to. He might not have told me about the Circle, but he didn't try to get me to join. He starts hurrying toward me too, pushing people out of the way.

"I'm coming!" he shouts. "Don't let anyone grab you."

I want to cry from his soothing voice. He's everything I need right now. Calm reassurance. He's my comfort in this nightmare.

He reaches me, his hands hovering over my shoulders and arms, as if to protect me.

"Peach," he pants. "What are you doing here? What if I hadn't seen you? Anyone could have—"

His face falls at the same time I feel cold fingers wrapping around my wrist. My entire being freezes, and my heart plummets to my toes.

"Grabbed her?"

Wren's voice sounds nothing like the man I've always known. It sends a shiver down my spine, and his grip on me becomes an inescapable shackle.

I try to pull away. Once...twice.

"Let me go," I grunt. "I was already with Elijah. I chose to go to *him*."

The man who used to be my best friend looks down at me, and something comes back. That predatory smile, the death in his eyes...that's who Monty reminded me of earlier. His son. They might hate each other, but they have the same terrifying look about them when they put away their social masks. One that tells you they take what they want, and no one gets in the way of that.

Maybe that's why they can't stand each other. Two psychopaths in the same house leads to trouble.

"Wren, let her go. She was clearly with me." But Elijah's order is weaker than mine, fear of his brother dulling his eyes.

Instead of letting me go, Wren brings me closer to him, and I crash against his side. "The rules are the rules, Brother. You weren't holding her, now I am. And believe me"—he leans closer to Elijah—"I'm not letting her go."

-metal IS NOT the same as punk.
-She's still allergic to shellfish and cat hair
-Always leave the green olives to her
-We don't like metal anymore.
-~~Tea tree and peppermint shampoo~~
-Don't forget the peri-peri powder on her fries
-Bake and shake every first Tuesday of the month.
-No more sugar in her coffee. It makes her feel sick
-DO NOT bother me during girls' night Wren
-Spiced honey on pepperoni pizza
-Check the triangle freckles on her right shoulder
frequently. Dermatologist said to keep an eye.
-New vision results: Right eye -2.75. Left eye -3.25
-If she gets in next September's yearly release of the
EEAJ, the announcement will be in August next year.
-Her brace needs to come off in a week
-New shampoo: coconut oil in it

Chapter Sixteen

Wren

Hayloft – Mother Mother

"You're shaking, let me." I take my suit jacket off and try to put it around Peach's shoulders.

"*Don't,*" she hisses as she accelerates.

"You're cold—"

"I'm not cold. In fact, I'd say I'm fucking fuming."

She keeps walking ahead of me as we cross the secret gardens of the country club. We're out of the maze, but I'm not out of trouble when it comes to Peach. That I know.

Surrounded by other newly initiated Shadows and their soon-to-be Heras, there's nothing I can discuss now. But surely, Peach knows I never would have let her choose Elijah. Not in this life or any other she intends to live. I still hadn't come to terms with having to choose a Hera for myself. I hadn't come to terms with the fact that I would be forced to spend the rest of my life with someone who isn't her, so surely, *surely*, no one expected me to let any other Shadow snatch her from under my nose if I saw her here?

What the hell was she even doing at initiations?

"Can you slow down?" I call out as she all but sprints ahead of me. "You're hurt. Who was it?"

She freezes, forcing me to come to a stop right behind her. The fury in her eyes when she turns around could make a weaker man crumble.

"Who was it?" she asks. "It was Josh Addington thinking I'm now up for grabs. So, if you don't mind, I'm in a rush to get back to my life, my home, *safety*. You know, anywhere there are no men running after me in the hopes of turning me into their personal whore."

"You're not going home. Initiation night isn't over. And believe me, Trouble, you can forget about going back to your life. Safety? Yes. Your safety is me now. Back to normal? Try again. I'll take care of Josh. Don't worry."

"Are you out of your fucking mind, Wren Hunter? This whole thing... *Fuck this whole thing.*"

I pause for a few seconds because I could melt from how beautiful she looks when she's angry. It's hard to focus when she calls me by my full name, and I see that little vein popping on her forehead. Shit, it takes all of me not to lean down and kiss it. I'm dying to feel it throbbing against my lips.

My eyes dart to her bleeding lip. Josh is a dead man; I hope he enjoys his last night. I wonder if he's the one who invited her, but I'd rather not ask Peach about that. She's already going through a lot, and I'll check directly with the Circle.

She shakes her head in disbelief when I take too long to react. Even *that's* cute. Does she do it on purpose? I forget what we're even talking about, because every time I'm facing her, all my brain can process is how much I want to wrap her in my arms and keep her to myself.

"...this is betrayal like I've never seen, Wren. Too far.

Too deep. Our relationship will never be the same. You— I don't feel safe around you anymore."

Those words bring me back like only a bucket of iced water would.

She huffs to herself, and my heart sinks when tears shine in her eyes.

"No, no, no," I panic, putting my palms on her cheeks. "Please, don't cry. I'm here. Don't—"

Bringing her hands to my chest, she pushes hard, only managing to move herself backward rather than push me away. It doesn't matter. The effect is the same. We're farther apart.

"Don't touch me!" she roars. "I'm not crying. I'm disgusted by your behavior. I don't know who you are. You..." She looks around, making sure no one hears her. "You killed a man."

I blink at her, watching her pant from anger. I could observe her reactions all day long. Poke, trigger, learn, repeat. It's my favorite pastime.

Something hits me. Something that hadn't a minute ago. I can do that now. Any time I want. Forever. I can observe her, learn more and more about her.

A smile tickles my chest, all the way up my throat, and no matter how much I attempt to keep it down, it tips the corner of my lips.

"You're smiling." Death darkens her voice. "You're... *smiling*?"

God, any man in the world could die happy knowing they've been killed by Penelope's lethal gaze.

"You're finally mine, Peach. Why wouldn't I be smiling?"

This is cruel. I'm aware of it. In the last twenty-four hours, the woman has learned that I've killed one person— it's probably too soon to tell her about the other ones—that there's a secret society in the town she grew up in, that her closest friends knew about it, and now she's stuck with a man she's probably terrified of. It's a lot, and I shouldn't add the smugness of finally making her mine to that list. But fuck, I've waited so long for this; can I really be blamed for it?

According to the woman of my dreams, that's a yes.

"Who are you?" she rasps.

Oh, she's going to hate me.

"Someone dangerous, but not someone you should fear."

Her jaw squares, and she gives me another few seconds to correct my behavior. I bet she thinks it'll happen, because that's what she's used to. When I don't, she puts a stop to the madness.

"Goodbye, Wren," she says, disappointment slipping from her lips, gliding with the words she believes are true.

She turns her back to me, but she doesn't take two steps before I grab her by the arm, forcing her to face me again.

"Where do you think you're going?"

"*Home!*" she screams.

"You're my Hera, Peach. You're not going anywhere until you've pledged your loyalty to me."

"Go fuck yourself," she snarls, her green gaze searing into me. "Real deep. You had my loyalty as my best friend. Now you have *nothing.*"

She keeps vacillating between being furious and being scared. This is good. This means no matter how much her brain knows I'm a murderer she should be scared of, her body knows me as someone she can snap at safely. I haven't completely lost her.

"Fine," is all I say, and her eyebrows shoot up. "Have it your stubborn way."

She doesn't understand what I'm doing when I lower

myself to wrap my arm around her thighs and press my shoulder against her hip. It only hits her when I straighten back up and flip her over my shoulder.

"What the fuck do you think you're doing?" she shrieks and tries to wiggle from my grip. "Wren!"

"I really hate to force you to do things, Trouble. Or I would have had sex with you a long time ago."

Her screaming "Put me down" to cut me off doesn't really bother me.

"But we're about to promise the Silent Circle our union forever, so I have to be a little drastic, if you don't mind."

Her fists hit my lower back as she kicks her feet. "I mind! I fucking mind, asshole!"

We had time a few minutes ago, but we're now running late to the rest of the initiation, and the last thing I need is to bring attention to myself. Especially with my dad watching my every move.

We've almost reached the building by the time she gives up trying to get me to let her go. I'm a fool to think she's done, because when I put her down in front of the doors, her slap is harder than some punches I've gotten to the face.

My head whips to the side, and I rub my cheek when I look back at her.

"I deserved that, but it could get you in a lot of trouble around here, so I'd suggest attempting to keep your violence down for once."

"I'm not going in there," she says with confidence. As if she didn't just run through a maze, chased by powerful men. As if I didn't just carry her here without a care about her opinion.

As if she has a *choice.*

"Listen, I'll run you through the rules when we have more time. I have a feeling it's going to take you a while to assimilate." My smug smile is probably pissing her off even more, but I can't help it. "For now, all you have to worry about is doing exactly what you're told in there."

She opens her mouth, but I'm quicker, wrapping a hand around her jaw and forcing her to stay still.

"I'm trying to protect you here. So keep that mouth closed and those ears open."

All she can do is narrow her eyes and circle a hand around my wrist, but she knows I won't let her go until I want to.

"The men in there are dangerous, Peach. You want to go home tonight? Unscathed? Then follow my lead, do as you're told, and you'll be home before you know it." I lower my voice so she understands how important this is. "But be a sassy little brat and you'll not only learn how much power the men of the Circle have over you, but how mean I can get." Bringing my face closer to hers, I say, "Even to you."

The way she goes completely still is the only indication that she's finally taking this seriously. I never wanted her to find out about the murders. But maybe it's not such a bad thing. Maybe her knowing what I'm capable of will keep her in check for once.

I have her.

God, I have her and I'm never letting her go.

Metaphorically speaking. Because I have to let go of her jaw to grab her hand.

"Some Shadows," I explain, as someone opens the main door for us, and we walk in, "forbid their Hera to speak completely when they enter the temple. This is the temple, by the way. It was based off ancient Greece temples, where—"

"Your mansplaining is already getting on my nerves," she mumbles. "I can *act* docile, but don't insult my intelligence."

I lick my lips, internally cursing myself as I feel blood flowing to my dick. There's just something about her sass.

"As I was saying," I carry on as I walk her through the hallways leading us to the ballroom. "Some men don't allow their Heras to speak. But you won't give me trouble, will you? I really don't want to have to teach you a lesson in front of everyone on your first day."

She tries to pull her hand away from mine, but there's absolutely no way in hell I'm letting go.

"Funny, because you sound like this is exactly what you want to do."

I chuckle, stopping in front of the doors leading to the ballroom. "Then don't tempt me even further, alright?"

I'm about to open when I stop myself. "Oh, and by the way. You normally would have had a chance to shower and get dressed in a ballgown. But since you wasted both our time out there, your see-through dress will have to do for the ceremony."

"The what—"

She doesn't get a chance to ask any further questions. We're entering the room, and even though I was prepared for this, it's a lot to take in, so I can't imagine what it's like for someone who had no idea this society existed twenty-four hours ago.

I keep her hand in mine, making sure she follows as I walk to the line of initiating Shadows. I settle along the wall, guiding her to stand before me.

The ceremony isn't supposed to be long for Heras. Unlike Aphrodites, who will be down in the chambers, having sex with men they don't know all night, Heras vow their loyalty to their Shadows, put a signet ring on our finger, a necklace around their necks, then we have a quick dance. They are pretty much good to go after that, unless they wish to stay and party.

But nothing is simple when it comes to making Peach do something. Especially when she doesn't want to. Hell, it's hard enough for her to do something she's told, even when she *intended* to do it in the first place.

We're third to last in line, and I feel her eyes widen the more she watches other Heras pledge loyalty on their knees to their Shadows. Her agitation is palpable, and I'm worried she'll run away before it comes to us. Because the way every single woman answers Duval's questions with all their faith is not something she was prepared for. She now knows from witnessing the others that she's about to have to kneel in front of me, bow to the point her head touches my foot, and promise her loyalty before asking me to accept her as my Hera.

This is not going to go well, is it?

Duval comes to a stand between us, and he smiles coldly at Peach.

"Penelope, it's a pleasure to have you here." His eyes dart down to her sheer dress and her nipples showing underneath.

I scratch my throat, nodding to encourage him to get on with it. Duval knows me, what I'm capable of, so hopefully, he understands the threat in my gaze. The one that silently says to not look at what doesn't belong to him.

He taps my shoulder and looks at Peach again.

"To complete your initiation to the Silent Circle, you need to answer 'I do' to the following questions."

"You forgot to specify I'd have to do that on my knees." She can barely articulate her words from how tight her jaw is.

"You saw the other women," Duval answers casually. "Get down."

Her small form stares at him with unblinking green eyes, and it only hits me now that I must have been truly stupid if I thought Peach would complete her initiation without giving us all a hard time.

I feel something shift in her before she even makes a movement, but before any of us can react, she's sprinting out of the room. I only catch my father's disappointed stare as I run after her. But I'm not the only one. Security guards follow her out and into the hallway.

I have to catch her before they do.

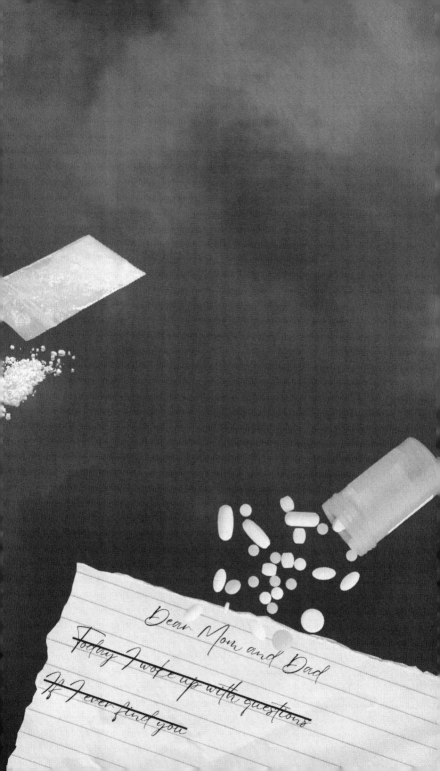

Chapter Seventeen

Peach

Burn – Davis Kushner

My feet hurt from slapping against the marble. They didn't give me back my shoes, and the disadvantage is striking. I don't get very far before someone pushes me to the side and slams me against a wall.

There are two of them. Fuck.

It's crazy how I'd never realized two men big enough to be hired as security guards can look deadly threatening when they're cornering you against a wall. I'd like to say my survival instinct drives me to cower and admit defeat. But what I actually do is throw my leg up to kick one of them in the balls. And I succeed, which earns me the other one slapping my face so hard it connects with the wall.

The bang resonates in my skull, and my legs wobble as I attempt to look forward again. For a few seconds, I see four of them as dizziness submerges me, and I blink a few times before being able to see straight again. But I can't think, and I can't move.

"Looks to me like she still wants to run." One of them chuckles.

I try to shake my head, but the pain is still resonating, ringing in my ears and stiffening my neck.

"No," I mumble, tasting blood in my mouth for the second time tonight. "Am not runnin'..."

The second strike brings me to the floor, a whimper bursting out of my mouth at the same time as my lip cuts open again.

"There you go. Now she's not going anywhere."

They laugh together, both taking a step closer, making sure I don't get it in my head to stand up, to defend myself, to even let the thought of running cross my mind.

I hear steps. People arriving behind them. My stomach twists at my vulnerable position, never mind the fact that I'm wearing next to nothing.

There are more of them. Guards, Shadows—new and old ones—but there's only one face I'm searching for.

They all part for him, and my heart drops as he appears. Tall as a god, wide as a beast, and evil in his eyes.

"I have a joke," I mumble, tasting blood so clearly on my tongue. "The devil walks into a room..."

"Stand up," Wren says sternly.

"...and he's very hot. Get it? Because we're in hell. And because you're the hottest man who ever walked this planet."

Shit, I can't think straight. Did I say that out loud?

I can hardly breathe. It's one thing to learn all those new facts about my best friend, but it hits different to feel the physical pain from the betrayal. The throbbing in my jaw, the stinging sensation in my cheek, the cut on my inner cheek and lip.

And it hurts some more when Wren repeats, with a freezing cold voice, "Stand up, Penelope."

I am not weak. And my strength lies in my mental fight. Because men are too weak to take us on.

So I make sure I channel all my hate for these men in my gaze and aim it at Wren as I use the wall to help me stand up.

When I'm finally on my two feet again, the guards step away so he can get closer to me. Nothing. There's nothing I find in him that could show a hint of reassurance. That he's putting on a mask in front of those men, maybe?

No. The truth is, I'm the one who was fooled for years. The mask he was wearing was the one of a caring friend. It's fallen off now. This is Wren Hunter in his purest form. It's clear as day.

There's no violence in his movement when he wraps a hand at the back of my neck, sending a chill down my spine. The knot in my throat is getting harder and harder to swallow, but I school my features and stand tall.

"Unbreakable little thing," he murmurs, only for me to hear as he starts walking, inevitably having me follow along.

I only feel slightly better being away from the men who cornered me. It doesn't last, anyway. How can it when Wren walks me down another hallway and opens a door to a room empty of anyone else.

It's a simple room with a few red velvet sofas, wood flooring rather than the cold marble in the hallways, and dark green walls covered with paintings of scenes from ancient Greece. Oh, and there's a murderer in it.

I don't sit down. Wren doesn't make me, and he stays standing too.

He observes my face for a second, his as impassive as I've ever seen on anyone. His only gesture is to push my hair over both my shoulders. Just with one hand, over one shoulder, then the other.

"Did you learn your lesson?" he asks with more coldness I can't take.

I don't want to talk. I don't even want to breathe, my chest too tight to take a full breath.

"There's no escaping the Circle, Peach. Not for me, not for you. Not for anyone. You came to the initiations, you're aware of their existence, and they do not let anyone walk away once there's a risk they could talk. You've now proven to them you're strong-headed, disagree with their practices, and could expose them to the outside world."

I just want to hear a hint of emotion in his voice. Any. Anger if it has to be, but he needs to give me something.

He doesn't.

"Now that you understand that, I need you to get it in that stubborn head of yours that you are my Hera, and you must obey me."

I close my shaking hands into fists, or as much as I can with my splint, then take a shallow breath, and exhale, "I can't."

He doesn't miss a beat. "I can make you. Now tell me you'll obey."

Feeling strength coming back the more he insists, I shake my head. "I'll take the violence. I'll take a beating. Torture me. But I will not obey a secret society who uses women as objects."

His jaw ticks, but I don't miss the impressed glint in his eyes.

"I would never hit you. Don't ever insinuate that again." He takes a step back, and I know what's coming next is worse than a hit. "But I can still make you, Peach. I don't want to be horrible to you. I don't want to blackmail the woman I spent most of my life chasing."

"How kind of you," I snarl.

"Give up. You're part of this now. Duval is waiting for us in his office. You'll complete your initiation, and the worst of this will be over. Please, don't make me pull out my last card. This is not the example I want to set for our relationship."

"Then don't!"

"You're not giving me a choice. You won't do what you're told." He shakes his head. "Peach, you *have* to let go of your pride and accept this."

I'm shaking. Shaking with rage and fear. Shaking with the need to fight back harder than this. But I'm in pain, and I'm stuck. So I stick to one word. "No."

He pauses for so long, it's like he's waiting for me to change my mind. Like he doesn't know who I truly am deep down.

He gives up with a dejected sigh. "If you initiate...I'll find your biological parents for you."

My heart stops. My brain stops. The *whole. World. Stops.*

A sickness like never before digs into my stomach and slithers through my senses. I stumble back a few steps before my ass falls onto one of the sofas.

"I—I—" Nothing comes out. I keep being cut off by the feeling that my heart is going to be expelled out of my body through my mouth. It's stuck in my throat, stopping me from breathing.

The room is spinning, and I don't even see Wren move. He's just suddenly on his haunches in front of me.

"You're okay. Breathe."

"I told you about this in confidence. Because I trusted

you," I pant. "You can't...can you? You can't find them...right? You're just messing with my head."

Putting a hand on my cheek, he rubs his thumb against my forehead.

"It's not just what you told me at the ER the other day, Peach. I already knew."

"How?" The word feels like swallowing a knife.

"I know a lot of things about you. That you help at the women's shelter on the North Shore because you somehow found out that it's where you were dropped before being sent to an orphanage. But that when you asked them about your parents, they weren't allowed to give you any information. And I know you made no progress with finding them since that."

"How?" I hear myself repeat, but nothing feels real anymore. The colors in the room have dulled, and a vertigo has taken over me, making my head spin like I'm falling backward down an infinite well. "Wren, how do you know all that?"

"Because I might follow you to the shelter from time to time. I might ask people about you and they don't ring the alarm because I'm just your charming best friend." How can he look into my eyes while saying these things? "Maybe... maybe because I sometimes slip into your room and see those letters you write to them."

"Oh my god," I gasp, letting my head hit the back of the couch. "No. No, fuck no." I squeeze my eyes shut.

Those letters are my most vulnerable thoughts.

"Look, it doesn't even matter how I know all that. What matters is if you initiate with me, I will use the Circle's resources to find your biological parents. You have my word."

His voice is barely audible when he admits, "With

their help, I can find them, Peach. And yes, the most selfish part of me has waited for this opportunity my entire life, but if it can also bring you anything good, then let's do it. But you *have* to initiate with me. Or I won't be a Shadow."

"Reality." Pain burns my throat as I swallow thickly. "Reality is painful."

He nods, agreeing fully. "It is, but I know there's nothing you want more in the world than to find answers. And there's nothing I want more than for you to be mine. This is the deal I'm offering you."

His face hardens again. "So tell me you'll obey."

I squeeze my eyes shut. It's the only thing I can do to stop the tears from falling.

"We've known each other since we were kids," I rasp.

"I know."

"You're my best friend."

"I am."

"Please," I plead as I open my eyes again and lock onto his. "Wren, please, don't do this to me. Don't use my past... my...my weaknesses against me." My head drops forward, knowing there's nothing else I can do.

I feel his fingers on my chin, and he pulls my head up.

"Tell me you'll obey."

I inhale a shaking breath, and it comes out as a sob. "I hate you."

"And I understand why. Now say it."

"Do you promise? To find my parents?"

He shifts, letting go of me to pull out the marker from his pocket. I hate him for keeping it on him at all times like he truly cares about our friendship. He clearly doesn't.

He uncaps it and writes on his own arm. *I promise.*

Putting the pen back in his pocket, he says, "Now *say it.*"

I hate myself more for the tears that flow down my face, than for the words that come out.

"I'll obey."

That agreeance is as dead as the soul in my being. But the hope of finally finding some answers, finally knowing why they didn't want me. What happened to them? What did I do? It's everything I've ever wanted to feel complete. To have some closure.

"Let's get this bullshit over with," I finally say. "I'll hold my part of the deal, so you have no choice but to hold yours."

"Let's." His voice is different now. He's finally giving me something. There's an excitement in it that's barely restrained. "Kneel." And the order is so softly spoken, it barely feels like one.

"You've got to be joking." I sniffle as I wipe the tears off my face.

He repeats, "Kneel. Like you'll have to in front of others to finish your initiation."

"Remember one thing," I say, my heart accelerating. "No one who's forced to kneel can ever be truly loyal."

"Oh, Peach, baby." He chuckles. "This isn't about loyalty. It's about submission. Now show me how pretty you are looking up at me on your knees. And get used to the position."

I'm trembling as I slide down from the sofa until my knees hit the wooden floor.

"Atta girl," he whispers, his hand threading into my hair and grabbing it softly. "Look up."

Trembling from an anger I can't control, I do. I've never felt so stuck in my life. He has nothing to truly hold against me, but he has something to offer, and that's more tempting than any threat I've ever heard.

He smiles fondly, appreciating the moment until I see a line creasing between his eyebrows.

"Now that this is out of the way. Tell me, which one was it?"

I lick my lips, struggling to swallow with my neck craning back.

"W-what?"

"Of those two men who cornered you in the hallway, which one hit you? Hudson is the one with the ponytail. And Lane is the brunet with the short hair."

I blink, my eyes feeling swollen from the tears. It's with sudden clarity that the pain in my cheek and mouth come back, along with the taste of blood. Is it visible on my face? How did he notice? Because he wasn't there when they hit me.

"Both?" he insists.

"No. It was—the—I'm not sure. It happened too quickly."

"Huh," he says to himself. "That's rather unfortunate for one of them."

I want to ask what he means, but I've taken too many hits tonight. My brain can't process one more bit of information.

Wren leans down, pressing his lips on my forehead, and I want to tear out my own heart and stomp on it for its stupid reaction. How can it suddenly beat to a calm rhythm? How can my body relax when the man kissing my forehead just blackmailed me into getting on my knees for him?

He helps me up, his hands settling on my waist as he looks down at me. His beautiful blues search for something in my eyes, and I cut the moment short.

"You won't find it," I say with a strength he didn't expect. "The submission you want so badly."

His eyebrows raise with surprise.

"Don't tempt me to show you exactly how I can make it happen. You only know the nice side of me, Penelope baby."

I narrow my eyes at him. "This deal," I purr, "is the worst decision you've ever made. I will make your life a living hell, and you know I'm capable of it."

A smile pulls at the corner of his mouth, so light I could have missed it if we weren't so close. With his hands still on my waist, he turns me around, and with one knee, pushes the back of my legs until I'm kneeling on the sofa, my back to him.

He brings a hand between my shoulders blades and pushes until my arms fly to the back of the sofa. Making sure I'm not straightening up again, he keeps his hand there.

"Don't–"

His free hand is already pulling up my dress.

"I have no doubt you can make my life a living hell, Peach. I strongly believe that's what you've been doing for sixteen years, but that I was too lovesick to realize that."

Pausing, he pushes my knees apart with his hand.

"Mm, how gorgeous."

"If you think I'm going to have sex with you after what you did...think again." But I'm already hot, my pulse pounding in my stomach and my core liquifying.

"What I think," he explains slowly, "is that we just signed a deal, and I believe you obeying was your half of it. How unfortunate would it be to not start by setting an example?"

My thighs shake as I sense his hand approaching.

"See, your first mistake was sleeping with me. Because now you know how well we fit together. Your body remembers. Your body"—a thick finger drags along my seam, making me realize I'm already wet—"recognizes who it belongs to."

"Someone could come in," I panic, tensing.

"Good, I hope they see you bent over and coming on my cock."

"I won't come on your co– Aah..."

The man has no mercy, pushing two fingers inside me. And my body does nothing but betray me, welcoming him easily.

My eyelids fall, my heart sinking as the pleasure spreads through my veins. As I try to stay in the position he put me in, my arms feel weak.

"From now on, there's no more refusing me anything. Do you understand that?" He thrusts in and out quickly, cutting my breath as I try to keep up. "I have complete control over you. And you're smart enough to know that if you want me to hold my part of the deal, you're going to behave."

When my moans are my only answer, he pulls his fingers out and slaps my clit. "Answer. Do you understand?"

"Yes," I squeak. "Fuck...yes."

I hear him unzip behind me, and he presses at my entrance, making me whimper as he stretches me.

"This is the cock you're going to worship for the rest of your life. Now, hold on tightly to the back of the sofa, Penelope baby."

He thrusts so hard, my fingers tighten around the soft material of the sofa out of necessity. My wrist should hurt, my lips should sting, but all I feel is the pleasure spreading to my toes. The heat in my being. The spark that's lighting me up.

He holds my hips in a bruising grip, making me hiss from his strength.

"I'm going to take so much pleasure destroying that friendship you tried so hard to preserve." *Thrust.* "I'm going to fuck you so hard, put you at my mercy, have a hold on you so tight, that the word *friend* will never cross your mind again when you think of me."

And with that, he proves his words truthful by pushing in and out of me so fiercely, I feel lightheaded when I come around him with an aching cry. I lose sense of anything that happened tonight as he finishes inside me and caresses my hair as he pulls out.

He barely gives me a minute before holding me by the waist and putting me back on my feet.

"Breathe, baby. You look flushed."

Do I, fucker?

I don't even have the strength to snap back at him.

He presses a chaste kiss to my mouth before looking down at my dress.

And with my head still spinning, I hear him say, "Let's go. I want you to feel my cum running down your legs when you officially become my Hera."

-metal IS NOT the same as punk.
-She's still allergic to shellfish and cat hair
-Always leave the green olives to her
-We don't like metal anymore.
-Tea tree and peppermint shampoo
-Don't forget the peri-peri powder on her fries
-Bake and shake every first Tuesday of the month.
-No more sugar in her coffee. It makes her feel sick
-DO NOT bother me during girls' night Wren
-Spiced honey on pepperoni pizza
-Check the triangle freckles on her right shoulder
frequently. Dermatologist said to keep an eye.
-New vision results: Right eye -2.75. Left eye -3.25
-If she gets in next September's yearly release of the
EEAJ, the announcement will be in August next year.
-Her brace needs to come off in a week
-New shampoo: coconut oil in it

Chapter Eighteen

Wren

Angel - Camylio

She's so still as we wait to enter Zeus's office, that I press my thumb against her inner wrist to make sure she's still alive. Her heartbeat is fast, but you wouldn't notice from her cold exterior. Although her pale cheeks are still pink from the orgasm.

"This night is almost over, I promise," I murmur, just as the door opens. "I'll take you home right after this."

I say *this* casually, as if it's not going to be the hardest part for her.

Eugene Duval's personal bodyguard lets us in, and I'm not surprised to see my dad in the room with him. His Stetson hat is sitting on the desk as he stands next to Duval in his chair.

"Penelope," my father purrs. "You made it."

His eyes dart to the cut on her lip, and she licks it, like she had forgotten it was there.

I can barely hold on to reality when I stare at the cut. It knocks at my chest, the need to hurt. I want to feel bones cracking within my grip. I want to hear them beg. Beg me for mercy, beg her for forgiveness.

Cracking my neck, I focus on Peach's hand in mine. It grounds me to feel her skin touching my skin. She's magical like that.

"You gave us quite a show down there," Duval finally says. "How did that work out for you?"

She refuses to answer, so I take over and cut it short. "She's here. Let's just get this over with."

"Sit down. Both of you."

The chairs on this side of the desk are too far apart to keep holding her. She sits down right away, but it takes me a few seconds to let her go. It makes it even more difficult to stay in the present, and my father notices.

"He's going to snap." He's so sure of himself, thinks he knows me so well, that it pumps more anger into my veins.

"Are you?" Duval asks with fascination.

I wave a hand dismissively as everyone's attention zeroes in on me. Sitting down, I offer Duval an easy smile.

"No," I lie. "I'm fine."

I turn to Peach to see her inquiring, angry eyes, but she doesn't speak the hundred questions swirling in them.

"Do you need a minute?" my dad asks. It's not out of care, and it doesn't sound like it whatsoever. He's mocking me, calling me weak in his own way.

"I'm perfectly fine," I repeat, a high-pitch sound now ringing in my ears.

It brings a calm over me that I know is lethal, and I smile again.

Duval looks disappointed. He wanted the freakshow my dad promised him, and I'm not delivering the entertainment.

"Anyway." Getting back to business, he leans back in his

chair to look at me. "You should not be allowed to initiate privately in my office. Your Hera should be pledging in front of everyone else. And she certainly shouldn't be running away from you. You're in luck, though, because I have an urgent assignment for you. We can only ask fully initiated Shadows to execute the mission they were chosen for, so let's get it done."

He looks at Penelope, his upper lip curling with repulsion. "I never liked you."

It's not me snapping I'm scared of anymore, it's Peach's reaction.

But she says nothing.

"Every time Achilles had his friends over to our house, I thought, Penelope Sanderson-Menacci talks too much. She tries to accomplish too much. And you always stood your ground against my son, bickering like your opinion mattered in some way."

Placing his palms on the desk, he leans forward. She stays still as a statue.

"Your opinion does not matter, Penelope. Now more than ever. You belong to the Circle, to your Shadow, and I hope your little chase through the hallways taught you a good lesson."

He stands up, rounds the desk, and I twitch when the knuckle of his index finger caresses the bruise starting to show right where her cheek meets her mouth. I crack my neck again, trying to fight back the uneasiness in my body, the tickling in my limbs.

Peach keeps staring ahead, refusing to acknowledge Duval, and his hand drops by his side again.

"You'll see. A woman's place is under our protection and care. They thrive under our will, and the tighter the leash, the happier they are. You'll come to like it. Hell..." He chuckles to himself. "You should see how wet my wife gets when I order her around. It's in the simplest things. She gets so turned on by cooking me a meal, I had to fire my kitchen staff."

He laughs louder now, turning to my dad and back to Peach. "She likes serving it to me, and she can't eat until I've shoved my cock deep in her cunt to satisfy that starving before she feeds herself."

A pained huff leaves me, and I throw my head back, feeling sweat rolling down my spine. My dad is right; I'm going to snap, and Duval will be my first target.

"You don't seem surprised that I know what a woman wants," Eugene insists, his fingers now playing with a strand of Peach's lush hair. "I'd think a raging feminist like you would have something to say about that."

With a bright, polite voice, she answers, "Oh, Mr. Duval, I'm not surprised at all that you think you know anything when it comes to women. After all, there's not a person in the world more confident than a man who has no idea what he's talking about."

A laugh bursts past my lips as Duval's face falls. I put a hand in front of my mouth, coughing to hide it. Just like that, with a witty remark from my best friend, that strange feeling inside me retreats. The tension is gone, my shoulders relax, and my father's death stare doesn't affect me.

"Get on your knees." Duval's cold order has Peach's head snapping toward me.

In a room full of men she doesn't trust, I'm her anchor, and my heart skips a beat at the idea. Even if I'm part of all the people she hates.

I stand up, putting a hand on her shoulder as I look at Duval. The way he spoke to her is the same way many men have before when she's hurt their pride. He sees her as a challenge, and he's not asking her to kneel so we can finally finish this godforsaken initiation. He wants to prove he has power over her.

"You're not asking her to kneel for you, are you?" I ask in a low voice. I don't need to shout at someone to show not to fuck with my patience. "You can't use my Hera, Zeus. Not without my permission. Don't bend the rules to soothe your burnt ego."

His angry eyes ping-pong between mine, and he must have heard stories from my dad—things I do when I'm not myself—because he nods, a forced smile spreading on his lips. He knows there's something within me to be scared about. *I'm* scared of it.

"I'm telling her to kneel to finish the initiation." His lie is obvious, and I don't want to know what he actually wanted to do to her.

I squeeze Peach's shoulder reassuringly, but my voice is cold. "Do as you're told. It's been a long night, and you need to go home and rest."

Her green eyes dig into mine, and with a barely audible voice, she says, "Do you promise? You'll find them?"

"I promise," I murmur back at her.

And there she is, the woman I've always been obsessed with, finally kneeling in front of me. The only thing ruining it is Duval starting his usual speech to link a Hera to a Shadow.

He says the Circle will protect us if we protect it, reminds us we are sworn to secrecy, and I watch Peach tense when he explains that a Hera is so I can procreate within the sanctity of the Circle. A visceral need courses through my entire being. She's about to be mine. I've waited for this my entire life. Penelope will be linked to me, unable to go anywhere, and down the line, she'll have no choice but to marry me and give me the family I dream of having with her.

And I must be a worse motherfucker than I thought, because I struggle to hold on to any remorse.

"Penelope Sanderson-Menacci," Duval says. "Do you pledge your allegiance to the Silent Circle?"

She swallows thickly, eyes shining with tears. She saw how it went downstairs. She doesn't need to be told again. "I do."

"Do you promise loyalty to your Shadow?"

"I do."

"And do you accept that you will serve your Shadow faithfully and in any way he sees fit?"

Her chest shakes, and I want to breathe air into her lungs. I want to scream that it'll be okay, but staying silent means it'll be over quicker.

"I do," she says weakly.

Duval grabs her limp arm and shoves the Silent Circle signet ring in her palm. I offer her my hand, and she puts it around my pinky finger.

It's with immense satisfaction that Duval purrs, "Show your devotion to your Shadow."

"Do you need me to give you the words?" I whisper.

She shakes her head, her eyes dropping to my polished shoes. She takes a deep breath, and I pray with all I have that she doesn't let her pride get the best of her.

But she's an intelligent woman. She knows this is it, and she knows when fighting is pointless. With her palms on the floor on either side of me, she bows tightly and presses her forehead to the tip of my shoe.

"Shadow," she says. "I am bowing to you as a show of loyalty and devotion. From this moment on, I am yours, and I...and I..." The lie is a squeak past her throat. "I submit to you willfully, in all ways you deem necessary." She rushes through the last part. "Do you accept me as your Hera?"

I hate myself for enjoying her misery so much. I'm selfish, and I know it. But I've never felt more exhilarated in my entire life.

I put the lotus flower necklace around her neck. The same one all the Heras wear as opposite to the seashell necklace the Aphrodites are given.

"I do. Get up. Come on. Let's go home," I say in a hurry.

Before she can even try, I help her up, wrapping my arms around her waist. I carry her toward the door, and to my surprise, she lets me, clasping her legs around my waist.

"Wren," Duval calls out.

He hands me a book as I turn back to him. "Your assignment."

Nodding, I grab it. This isn't important. I can figure it out later. Right now, I need to get Peach home safely. I feel her impatience as she buries her head in my neck.

My heart accelerates, and I press my lips against her hair.

You are mine, Trouble. Finally. All. Mine.

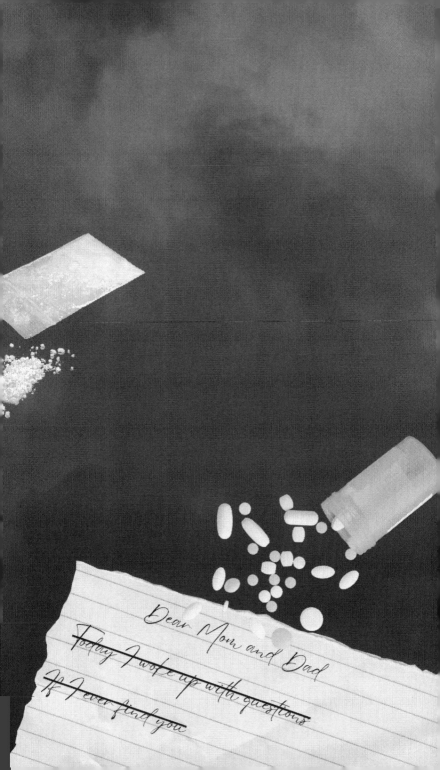

Chapter Nineteen

Peach

Bottom Of The Deep Blue Sea - MISSIO

"Your friend, you know he's an asshole, right?"

"Achilles is the worst," I say with a sorry face. "He straight up doesn't give a shit what anyone thinks of him. Are you alright? Did he hurt you?"

The girl shakes her head, dumbfounded by my reaction. "I'm talking about Wren."

"Wren?" I repeat. "Oh, he's all bark, no bite. He seems a bit off-putting sometimes because he's strong -headed. I get it. I don't like his dominant side either. He wouldn't hurt a fly, though."

She hops on one foot as she pulls her boot up her calf, and I sit up on the sofa. That party was a bit wild. I fell asleep on whoever's sofa this is, but apparently, I wasn't the only one who stayed over.

"I don't mind a dominant guy," she says, throwing her red hair over her shoulder. Hers is a little lighter than mine. "Pull my hair all you want, shove my head in the pillow until I can't breathe. Cool."

My eyes widen slightly, but she doesn't seem to notice. She slept with Wren.

He slept with someone.

"But I mind a guy who calls you a different name while he's fucking you from behind. And I mind when he doesn't let me pull away from the pillow because he doesn't want to see I'm not actually whoever the fuck Peach is."

My heart stops.

He slept with someone and called her my name.

"And do you know what I fucking mind?" She huffs as she pulls her hair into a ponytail and fans herself. Yeah, I get the hangover heat too. "That when I corrected him, he kicked me out of the bed. That's not even his bed!"

I pinch my lips, incapable of stopping the onslaught of happiness.

Why the fuck do I care? I don't want Wren. I would hate *having sex with Wren.*

Right?

...

Right?

I shift on the spot, thinking of what it would feel like to have Wren pull my hair and push my head against a pillow. At least it would be the right name he calls—

No.

I'm not into this. And I'm not getting wet purely from this girl describing two sentences of her night with him.

"I need the bathroom," *I murmur.*

We're just senior high schoolers who showed up at a college party, but I should leave before she realizes I'm the Peach she's mad at.

Mainly, I need to leave so I stop feeling that zap from my lower stomach to my chest.

. . .

I'm still wet. I can feel it the second I wake up. Wet from dreaming about the memory of hearing for the first time how Wren likes to have sex.

I blink my eyes open, staring at the ceiling in my bedroom. Or maybe I'm wet because he ruined my life while simultaneously giving me an orgasm yesterday, yet still found a way to reassure me on our way home. Because he messed with my brain in a way that shifted something within me.

He's going to find my parents.

He's going to give me all the answers I've ever wanted to feel whole. All I have to do in exchange is give him all of me.

The man made me kneel at his feet but carried me to the car like I was his most prized possession.

You don't have to worry about anything anymore, Peach. I'm here.

I will keep my promise. My word is everything.

I held on to those like a lifeline.

Sitting up, I bring my wrist to my lap. It's sore, but the brace doesn't feel necessary, and I'm dying to take it off, but the worst thing would be to make the injury worse. Swinging my legs over the bed, I let out a deep breath. At least with Wren not around, I can think straight again. I don't have to battle wanting to kill him and wanting to stay on my knees in front of him...just to see what else he can do with all the power he now has.

He's taunted me with the idea of us for so long, and I've resisted for so long, that being forced to give in to it has snapped my resistance. I should have never had sex with him. He's right. That was my first mistake.

I stand up, round the bed, and jump back as my eyes catch a form on the floor.

"What the fuck," I gasp, my hand coming to my chest.

Wren is sleeping in front of my bed. Topless, lying on his belly, his back muscles tensed, like he's not fully relaxed despite being asleep. His breathing is slow, and he used his black button-down from yesterday as a pillow. Because he's resting his cheek on one forearm, his shoulder is flexed. Do his shoulders have to be so big? Do the muscles have to be so defined? He has no right being so hot, not after being such an asshole.

His other hand is by his side, fisting what looks like a piece of paper. Curiosity gets the best of me, and I silently step near him. I'm dying to slide my fingers through his chestnut hair. It looks so soft compared to the rest of him. Instead, I delicately touch his hand, and when it doesn't wake him up, I take the ripped piece of paper out of his sleepy grip.

My jaw drops. It's got blood smeared on it, and two names are written in a black marker.

Hudson

Lane

It's written the exact same way *Caleb Mitchel* was on the piece of paper I found on his desk yesterday morning.

And he admitted he killed Caleb.

I slowly step away from Wren's sleeping form, my eyes now on his hand. His *bloody* hand. The knuckles are split open. He beat up someone. Two people, I'm guessing.

Swallowing, I try to keep my cool as I process something. I'm stuck with a man who's a murderer. Not stuck in this room, not stuck for a few days. I'm stuck with him for life.

Another step back, and I call out his name calmly. He

wakes up right away. It seems like I could have whispered it, and he would have still heard my voice in his sleep.

Looking around my room, he looks as confused as I am. So, he didn't expect to wake up here either.

"Peach," he says, his voice hoarse with sleep as he stands up.

He takes a step toward me, but I put a hand up.

"Don't get closer. Why are you sleeping on my floor?"

He stretches his arms above his head, his abs tensing. Fucking hell. I have eyes, I'm human, and there's no way in hell someone can stay sane while watching Wren Hunter topless.

"You said you didn't want me to sleep in your bed," he explains simply.

I look at him, unimpressed. "I kicked you out of the house. You left."

He opens his mouth, but I cut him off. "You know what? I don't want to know how you got back in here. I don't want to know why you're covered in blood. I don't want to know why...why you asked which of those men hit me and now they're on this piece of paper."

"One of them hit you, and I wasn't sure which one," he answers with blunt truth.

I raise my hand higher, pressing the tip of my thumb to all my other fingers, indicating for him to shut up.

"I said *I don't want to know.*" I drop the piece of paper to the floor. "What I want is for you to pick this up and leave my house. I'm going to go to class and pretend my life is normal."

His head tilts to the side like a confused puppy. "But your life isn't normal anymore."

"I don't care!" I hiss. "I want to *pretend* it is. Slow much?"

He shrugs, putting his wrinkled shirt on and buttoning

it. "You can pretend all you want. Facts are facts. I'd like you to wear those really cute pink lace underwear with the red hearts under your uniform skirt while you're in class."

"Keep dreaming." I snort. "Wait...how do you know about those?"

His small smile is telling enough. He's been through my stuff. Of course he has. He knows about my letters to my parents.

"See, this is something you're just going to have to get used to, Trouble. My word is law now. So when I tell you to wear something for me, you do it."

I take a step back when he's close enough that I have to crane my neck, but after a few, I'm stuck against the wall. And the fucker won't back down.

"We have a deal, remember? I can make it seem like you have a choice, though. Should we try again?" He brings his palm to my cheek, his skin soft against mine, but his hand smells of the coppery scent of blood.

"Penelope baby, could you wear those pretty underwear for me?" he asks, and his tone could make him sound like Prince Charming.

I swallow thickly, my eyes digging into his as my jaw tightens.

"N—"

His hand gripping my hair stops my denial; it's so tight, I whimper as he presses me harshly against the wall.

"Peach, don't be like that. Because when you act like a brat, I want to fuck it out of you. And I'm trying really hard to give you the time you need to adapt." He keeps his body flush with mine, and I feel his hard-on against my lower belly. "But since you can't play nice, wear them, and I'll check if you did. Say 'no' again, and you'll be forbidden to wear any underwear for the rest of the day."

I can't breathe for a few seconds. And for once, it's not because of anger. There's something in the way he holds me, something in the passion in his voice that keeps the oxygen stuck in my lungs. Worse. There's something uncoiling in my lower stomach.

He brings his other hand to my face, holding the pad of his thumb against my lips but not trying to enter my mouth.

"I'm not such a dick that I'll make you say 'yes, sir' when you've barely gotten over last night. But some sort of acknowledgment would be greatly appreciated. So, will you wear them?"

I gulp loudly, my lips only parting slightly when I finally manage to spill out some sound.

"Y—yes," I rasp against his thumb.

"Good girl. Don't work too hard today, please. You're already exhausted."

He kisses my forehead and steps away.

I still can't breathe as he slips the piece of paper in his pocket and goes through my bedroom door. I can only, *finally*, function again when I hear the front door closing downstairs.

What the fuck is happening to me?

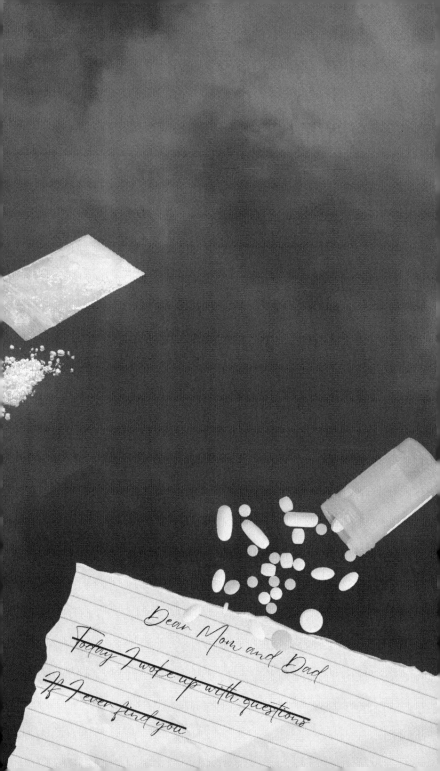

Chapter Twenty

Peach

Make Me Wanna Die - The Pretty Reckless

I tap my pen repeatedly on my notebook. I can't focus. I can't focus. I can't focus. All I can focus on is the fact that I can't focus.

Two days. It's been two days since I've initiated, and all that's happened so far is that Wren is having the time of his life telling me what to wear under my uniform. He's been busy going back and forth between the temple and campus, so I haven't even seen him since we were both in my room.

This morning, I got a text from him while I was getting ready.

> Wren: I watched you sleep last night, with one leg hooked around your covers. Those shorts you wear make it hard not to touch you. Black looks so good on you. Wear that black lace thong today.

I could hear the lustful rasp in his voice as I read it, yet I couldn't get myself to realize how creepy it was.

He breaks into your fucking room, Penelope.

He watches you sleep.

Definitely creepy.

"Peach."

I startle, looking up at Ella and Alex.

"Can you not?" Ella says tightly as her eyes go to my pen. "We're all trying to work here."

She's annoyed with me. Not because I'm stopping her from focusing too, but because her boyfriend told her I went to the initiations. Because I have a bruise on my cheek, right at the corner of my mouth, and a cut on my lower lip. Both of which we can't explain to Alex. Both of which made her worry to death.

The only thing that reassured her is the fact that Wren is my Shadow. *Wren*. What a joke.

I haven't told her about the murders. If I say too much, she'll ask more questions. I still haven't told her why I went to the initiations. What Hermes has on me. That's why she's so mad. She knows I'm keeping things from her.

Alex observes me silently. "I still can't believe you got so drunk you walked into a wall."

I offer her half a smile, the best I can do. "Yeah. The hangover felt as bad as I look."

Her brow furrows, and she shakes her head as she looks down at her notebook. "Sure."

Alex, too, knows I'm lying to her. Because why wouldn't she? The three of us have been best friends since kindergarten. First, there was Wren. Then, Alex. They're the first people I met when my dads brought me home from the orphanage. It was just before I turned six, and after spending three months with only my dads, I met Wren and Alex on the first day of kindergarten. Ella was a year older, so we became close later.

It breaks my heart to keep them at a distance, but it also feels overwhelming to share everything that's happened. So, I stay in this limbo and hate myself in the process.

Ella's eyes stay on the lotus flower necklace around my neck. She wears the same, and we both acted surprised when Alex pointed it out. I hide mine under my uniform shirt and look back down at my notebook.

I'm dying to ask her a million questions, information I'd rather get out of her than Wren, but she's no help. The second I asked her about what happens to Heras on a daily basis, she shrugged.

I wouldn't know. Chris doesn't treat me like one and doesn't include me in anything regarding the Circle. It didn't change anything in our relationship; we just didn't have a choice but to initiate me as his Hera if we wanted to be together.

I look at the notes I'm working on following Professor Lopez's feedback. I need to at least finish a third today, but everyone's concentration takes a hit again when all our phones vibrate.

"Oh no," Ella murmurs.

"Who wants to look?" Alex asks.

"I will," I say in a rush. I'm terrified of what Hermes could put out. I listened, so they have no excuse to air out my dirty laundry, but I've still been on edge.

It's not about me. But it's somehow linked to me anyway. The picture is of police cars parked by the library building. Reading the caption, I'm assuming that was last night.

Another body discovered on campus...
One of you is thirsty for blood and isn't scared to leave traces.

Josh Addington's body was found behind the library last night, and if campus security hides it from you...I WON'T. Do we think he forgot to return a book he borrowed? We all know how strict Mrs. Davis is.

#byebyeJosh #murdereronthe loose #SFUishidingthings-fromyou

"What the hell?" Alex says. "That's horrible. Peach, wasn't he in a lot of your classes?"

"Yes," I rasp.

He also assaulted me during the initiations. And two other men have already died for that. It's just that no one knows about them.

"That's the second student from SFU who shows up dead," Ella murmurs.

My heart palpitates. This one doesn't say he was found with Scrabble tiles down his throat, but I know he was. After all, Caleb died because he upset me. Josh *hurt me.*

When I look up, Achilles and Wren are standing right behind Ella, books in their hands, clearly ready to join us.

"Did you guys see what happened?" Ella asks.

Wren's knowing eyes don't leave me. Beside him, Achilles gives me a smile, and I don't need more to understand that Wren got him up to date.

My cheeks burn from the idea. I don't like that Achilles now has an image of me kneeling at Wren's feet to prove my devotion. Nor do I like the fact that he knows his best friend is offing people whenever he feels like it.

Achilles sits down at the end of the table. "The campus and the police are bound to say something at this point. That's two students."

"Exactly what I was thinking," Ella agrees. "We'll at least hear from SFU."

I feel myself pale. If the police get involved, what does that mean? How protected are we now that Wren and I are part of the Circle?

Wren sits next to me, and the first thing he does is press his lips to my cheek before putting a possessive hand at the back of my neck. I stiffen as Alex's eyes widen.

"What the hell?" she squeaks, barely holding back her excitement. "Is it happening? Are you guys...together?"

Well, she quickly forgot about Addington.

Her eyes lighten with happiness, and I stand up so violently my chair falls back, earning more eyes on us. Fuck. I'm. On. Edge.

I shake my head. "We're not."

"We're not?" Wren chuckles. "Want to try that again?"

I narrow my gaze at him and push the words past my gritted teeth. "We're not."

Ella watches me with shock slackening her face, and Achilles mumbles to himself. "Someone is going to be in trouble."

"Shut up, Achilles." I ignore Alex's confused face as I slap my books shut. "I've got a headache. I'm going home."

I stride out of the library, hugging my books to my chest and ignoring people's gazes—more specifically, Mrs. Davis's, our librarian.

I'm in the dimly lit hallway of the library building when I realize Wren's following me. I press on, refusing to look back. I'm wearing high-heeled Mary Janes, and I hate the way the click against the stone floor picks up. I hate even more that I accelerate, as if I'm scared of him.

"Peach, you're going to make this worse on yourself," I hear him call out calmly.

I'm *not* scared of him. This building is just creepy in general, and there's a murderer behind me. Plus, I'm mad at him, and for once, I don't want to confront him about it. I just want him to leave me alone.

But I must be seriously stupid if I think I can get out of here without him catching me. I can see the old wooden double doors leading out of the building when he grabs me by the elbow. He pulls me back so harshly, I drop all my stuff, and I'm between him and the cold stone wall before I can even catch my breath.

The walls in here are so old, I feel stone dust fall in my hair when he puts his forearm above my head. His other hand is still holding my arm, and all I have left to defend myself is to glare up at him.

Smiling like this is his favorite game, he tilts his head. "Come on. I thought chasing after you was a thing of the past now."

"Let me go before someone finds us like this."

"Change your tone with me before someone finds you on your knees with my dick so far down your throat you can't breathe."

My mouth drops open, his words tugging something in my stomach. Actually, lower. Way lower.

I swallow thickly, and he arches an eyebrow, waiting to see if I have a retort. Waiting to see if he can put his threat into action. I've seen Wren with people he doesn't like. People he doesn't treat like me. He only warns you once.

"I—" I take a deep breath, softening my voice. "I don't want people to think we're together."

He snorts. "You bowed to me and promised loyalty and obedience, Trouble. We're past 'being together.' You quite literally belong to me."

"In the eyes of the Circle," I correct him. "Not...not for real."

His face falls. "For *real*?"

I turn my head to the side, desperately holding on to the illusion that the Silent Circle isn't real life.

"Hey, hey." His hand leaves my arm for my face, grabbing my jaw and turning me back to look at him. "There's nothing more real than the Circle, do you understand? I'm not saying this about us, I'm saying this about life. There's nothing above them. No law, no politician, *no god.* For your own good, never forget that."

"Fine," I snarl. "We're together. Happy? I can say any words you want to appease you. But God knows, you're going to be the most frustrated boyfriend who ever walked this planet. Your dick is going to feel so fucking lonely, Wren."

"Interesting of you to say that," he says proudly. "Because my cock doesn't feel so lonely when you come hard around it."

His eyes shine with delight, and I don't have a foot to stand on if we're going to stay on the topic of his cock. I *did* have sex with him twice now.

"Well, I'm telling you, on this campus, I don't want anyone to know about us. So step back."

"You're a funny one, Peach. There are dozens of women at SFU who would die to be in your place. Even you've admitted reciprocating the attraction. But you just want to stick to your idea of independence, don't you?"

My heart stops, and I look right into his eyes. "It's all I have."

His breath is the only indication that he's still present with me. His chest is so close to mine they're almost touching.

"In this place, it's all I have. We're from a town where people want to stick a label on you. Everyone reduces everyone else to a few words, so we can all fit into a box in their narrow minds. Alex is reduced to a goody-two-shoes, Ella the queen bee. Achilles is the devil. You're the best at everything." I take a trembling breath. "And I'm the independent, strong headed girl who insists she can survive this place all on her own."

When he just keeps searching my eyes, I hate myself for it, but I insist, "Please. My freedom is all I have."

"You mean being the girl who pushed me away for as long as everyone can remember is all you have. The reputation of turning me down, the rumors that you're the only thing I can't get, that's what you love. That's what you call your freedom."

He's right. Somewhere along the way, I associated refusing to give in to him with my entire personality. I lost track of whether I liked Wren or not, because I was too focused on turning him down at every turn. Because it was more important to me to show everyone else that I stuck to my decision than be the girl who gave in. Even if that could have meant being with the only man who's special to me.

I think he's right. I think I'm the most stubborn woman I've ever met.

"Yes." My admission surprises him. "Maybe that's it. Still, it's mine. After everything that happened at the initiations, this is all I ask for. To not admit to the entire college...hell, the entirety of Stoneview—because word will spread, and you know it—that I *gave in*. Because then I won't be Peach, the strong girl, anymore. I'll be Wren Hunter's girlfriend. Just more proof that you get anything you want."

He tightens his grip on my jaw, and for a second, I think he'll never give up. For a second, I think there's nothing remaining of the Wren I once knew, the friend who would have done anything for me, and that all I have in my presence is Wren the Shadow. But then his grip softens, and he does this thing again. He kisses my forehead. I noticed that's what he does when we argue.

He's done it a lot over the last few days.

"It breaks my heart that you see yourself so one-dimensionally," he rasps. "You're more than a reputation or a label. You're human, Peach. My favorite one, as it just so happens. Don't do this to yourself."

I pretend the declaration flies right over my head, even though my heart feels like it's melting in my chest.

It doesn't matter.

This isn't what I want to hear, and he sees it, because he says, "I won't tell anyone, and I won't act differently on campus." His gaze hardens before he adds, "But one wrong move, and you can kiss your independence goodbye."

I nod. Fake freedom will do until I get the real one back. I can deal with that.

"Wren," I say shakily. "Did you... Josh?" My heart pounds harder, anticipating his answer.

He shrugs. "Probably."

I knew it. He doesn't remember when it happens. I understood it the first time he admitted he *thought* he killed Caleb.

"You don't remember, do you?" I insist.

"I have my ways to know."

"That's what those little pieces of paper are for. So you can remember."

Smiling at me, he kisses the top of my head. "Such a smart, pretty girl."

The fact that I didn't fuck up calms me, but he's done with the topic. And he flips me around, my cheek now pressed against the wall.

259

"Pull up your skirt. I want to see if you listened," he growls.

He leaves a small space between us, so he can look down, I'm sure, and he doesn't pull my skirt up himself. No, he wants me to show I can do what I'm told. And now that he accepted my request, I need to execute, don't I?

My stomach tightens, knowing that anyone could catch us. If someone walks out of the library, they'll see me showing my black lace underwear to Wren Hunter.

Fisting the hem of my skirt with one hand, I pull it up to my lower back.

"What a good girl," he purrs in my ear. "Mm, the way your ass looks in those is better than I could have imagined. Keep your skirt up and bring your other hand between your legs."

For a few seconds, my brain tries to convince me I didn't hear him right. I hesitate for too long, and his grip on my hips tightens.

"You heard me. I do you a favor, you do me one. Put your hand in your pretty thong and feel if you're wet for me."

My heart palpitates, my thoughts stuck on the fact that anyone could walk by at any time.

"You can't order me around all day every day, Wren," I whisper, hoping he'll see reason.

"It looks like that's exactly what I'm doing. One of us has to be in control in this relationship. And you know me, I never relinquish control. You...well." He laughs softly. "You already have, baby. Now, tick-tock."

Technically, even if someone was walking past us, they would only see me against the wall, not really what I'm doing...

I slide my hand beneath my underwear and almost

startle when I feel how wet I am. Is it because he manhandled me? The control? The mix of those things and the soft kiss on my forehead? I don't think I understand myself anymore.

"I want you to taste yourself," he murmurs.

My cheek burns hot even though it's still pressed against the cold stone wall. He can't be serious? But then again, a part of me would be disappointed if he wasn't.

"Bring your fingers to your mouth, taste how I'm making you feel, and I'll let you go."

Slowly, I bring my hand up, and before I can think it through, my trembling fingers are moving past my parted lips. I close my mouth and swirl my tongue around my middle and index fingers. My eyes shut tightly, not used to the way I taste, but Wren's thumb caressing my hip relaxes me.

Especially when he adds, "There's something about you, Penelope, that drives me crazy. I've spent years trying to pinpoint what it is, and to this day, I still fail. All I know is *you* make me lose my sanity, baby."

He breathes me in and finally releases me. The first thing I do is take my fingers out of my mouth. I let my skirt drop back into place, and he helps me turn back around slowly.

Just like that, I'm free to go. He picks my books up off the floor and hands them back to me.

"I have to travel for a week. The Circle is sending me away. Me not being on campus doesn't mean you can do whatever the hell you want. Behave and you won't get in trouble when I come back."

I can't hide my surprise. He's leaving? For a week? That's a long time away when he just flipped my life upside down. No one can understand what I'm going through anymore, and that's his fault. How can he just leave me?

I keep the disappointment in my chest and ask something else instead. "What is it for?"

"Why do you sound disappointed? I thought you'd like a bit of time away from me."

Scratch that, I didn't hide the disappointment that well. This man reads me like an open book.

I shake my head. "I like it," I lie.

He licks his lips, his gaze dropping to my mouth. It's like he's wondering if he could taste me too. He's going to kiss me. I can see he wants it so badly he can barely hold himself back.

My heart accelerates all over again, feeling stuck between panic and anticipation. I can't breathe.

And then he pulls away.

"When I come back, I'll take you on a date so we can have some quality time together. In the meantime, behave," he says before walking back toward the library. There's dejection in his voice. Like he didn't get whatever he wanted. But I didn't move, didn't stop him. He could have kissed me.

Fuck. I think I wanted him to kiss me. That man drags me through misery and then says the most honest words I've ever heard. He says I'm his *favorite human*. I want to be someone's favorite.

I want to be *Wren's* favorite.

My brain is in overdrive as I step outside the building. Rushing down the few long steps, I cut across the grass. I want to get home and away from everyone as fast as I can.

I bump harshly into someone, stumbling back, and a voice calls out my name.

"Peach, are you okay?"

Elijah's voice grounds me. I look up, and the weight of everything that's happened becomes unbearable. I want him to take some of it. Eyes filling with tears, I swallow thickly.

"I—" I'm cut off by a sob sticking to the back of my throat.

I'm about to pour my heart out when I notice the woman next to him. Camila Diaz is holding his hand. She's a few years older than us and went to Stoneview Prep too. Her mother is a famous celebrity defense attorney, but she's mainly known for defending rich criminals. And her father is the biggest developer on the East Coast. She's a postgrad now, who used to be the President of Xi Epsilon, the sorority I'm somehow still part of despite never showing up to anything. She left when she started her Master's in Architecture.

"I've been trying to call you all day," Elijah insists.

I shake my head, blinking at Camila. "Uh...are you two..." That's when I catch the necklace around her throat, the one with a lotus flower pendant. My eyes automatically go to Elijah's hand. He's wearing the signet ring.

"Fuck," I huff. "You're everywhere," I murmur as I look back up at his face.

Camila pulls my necklace from under my shirt. "*We're* everywhere, honey."

"Peach," Elijah repeats. He's clearly attempting to keep me in the present as my ears start ringing. "I tried calling you. Many times. Why aren't you picking up?"

"You didn't," I mumble, feeling like my soul is starting to detach from the situation.

Reality is too harsh right now.

I unlock my phone and show him my phone log. His name is nowhere to be seen.

"What the hell?" he says as he grabs it. "I fucking knew

it." He taps on the screen then shows it back to me. "Your Shadow blocked my number."

I snatch my phone back, unblocking Elijah's number right away.

"Motherf—" I let out a short shriek, losing my mind and unable to keep it together. "He doesn't even have my password!"

"He's obsessed, Peach. He can guess it easily."

"I'm not stupid. It's hard to guess," I defend.

Elijah cocks an eyebrow at me, insinuating my naivety. "He knows you inside out. The man has no other hobby than studying you. What's your password?"

"The date my dads picked me up from the orpha— Yes, okay, I see it."

"Fucking psycho," Elijah murmurs to himself, but we all hear it.

"I have to go." I take a step back, needing to breathe from everyone connected to Wren or the Circle.

"Wait, wait. We need to talk about everything. Your face. Did he hurt you? I need to know you're okay."

"I'm *not* okay," I spit out before striding away.

I can't do this.

I rush home, throwing my stuff on the floor before diving into my bed and under the covers. I already have a few texts from Elijah, telling me we need to talk, asking me to spend time with him, that he's here for me. Only the last one gives me hope.

> Elijah: Camila is having a party tonight at her house. She's a few doors down from you. Lots of people are going to be there. Come and we'll talk. Nothing can happen to you in front of so many people. Not even Wren will risk it.

I need to spend time with someone I trust. If I want explanations about all this, shouldn't I go to the man who didn't trick me into going to the initiations? Who didn't blackmail me into being his Hera? Who, on the night, was about to help me, not *force* me.

I'm going to that party. Because Elijah's right. What's the worst thing Wren can do?

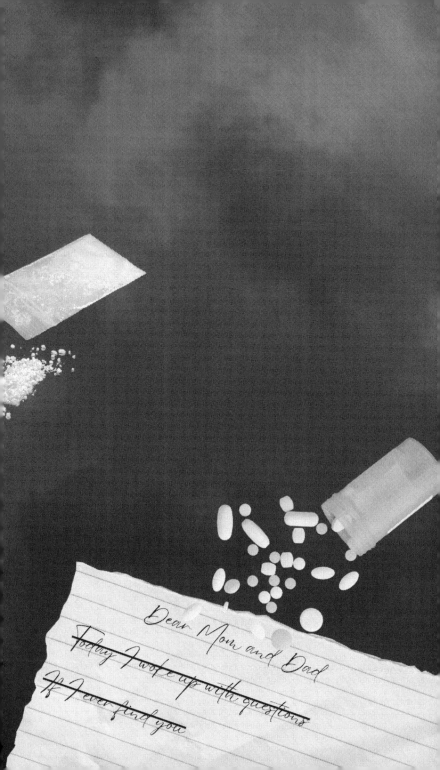

Chapter Twenty-One

Peach

SEX LOVE DRUGS - Dutch Melrose, Lost Boy

"Not yet," Elijah mumbles as he hands me the drink he just got me. God, my impatience must be written all over my face. "People aren't anywhere near drunk enough to start talking about topics no one should hear."

I roll my eyes. "Let's just go talk somewhere else, then."

He shakes his head, silently refusing me. "We'll speak during the party, don't worry."

It's barely past eight, but people are already pouring in through the front door. And I'm drunk. Not only that, but I took a pill. I needed something to take the edge off. It's nothing crazy, just ecstasy, and all I'm feeling is a little lighter. I've got a new energy buzzing inside me, and this mouse wants to play while the cat is away.

Elijah's eyes flick to the bruise at the corner of my mouth.

"It wasn't Wren," I explain as I struggle to stay in place.

"It doesn't make him any less dangerous. You know that, right? That he's extremely dangerous."

He's clearly aware of the murders and checking if I know too.

"I know."

"Have you seen it? When he snaps?" he insists.

I hesitate, biting my inner cheek. I keep hearing that word around him. *Snap.* Like he's some sort of beast who can't control his killing urges.

Of course I'm terrified of Wren in that sense, but I also know deep down that he would never truly hurt me. I'm not worried about my life; I'm worried about living said life *freely.*

"I haven't," I admit. "I don't think so. And I want to know what that means exactly but—"

"That's why our family has problems with him. He's uncontrollable. Dangerous."

I pinch my lower lip a little too hard, wondering why I'm suddenly annoyed at the criticism. He's not a circus freak.

"Yes, *dangerous.* That's the third time you've said it. I get it." Looking around, I add, "I thought you said now isn't the time to talk. But if it is, I would rather know how to get out of the Circle than talk about Wren."

The house fills up with people around us, the music getting louder. When Elijah catches up with everything, his eyes light up. "So, this is what SFU parties are like?"

"No, they get way worse. Busier, rowdier, and people will start fucking everywhere. Welcome to your new social life. You can thank Camila later."

He laughs, and it's nice to have a relaxing, genuine moment with him. The pill probably helps.

"Is it nice?" I ask. "To have someone? Do you even like her?"

He shrugs, putting his hand on my shoulder. "I would rather have saved you from Wren."

My gaze drops, and I wonder for a second if I would have liked that. To be stuck with Elijah instead of Wren.

Elijah is kind, a good friend. He's never crossed any line, never looks for trouble. People don't hang out with him because they look up to his older brother like he's some king, and it just so happens that Wren banished him from his kingdom. I've always hated that.

I love Elijah.

I just don't love him like I love Wren. I don't yearn for his hands on me. And maybe that's the difference between real friendship and...whatever is between Wren and me.

No, I wouldn't have liked to be Elijah's Hera. The truth is, he doesn't know me deeply like Wren does. He couldn't even understand the connection Wren and I have. But it doesn't mean I want to be Wren's Hera. No matter what I feel toward him, he took my choice away from me, and I can't forgive that.

"Thank you," I finally say. "For trying, at least."

He smiles shyly, just as my phone vibrates in the back pocket of my jeans. My vision is a little blurry, and for a second, I can't believe the text I received.

> Wren: Consider this a general rule. No hanging out with my brother anymore.

I blink at it. How the hell does he know where I am? He said he was leaving for a week.

> Wren: That includes his fucking hand on your shoulder.

"What the hell?" I murmur as I look up and around the room.

Either this pill is hitting harder than I thought, or Wren didn't leave. I take a step back, forcing Elijah to let go of me.

"What's wrong?" he asks.

I'm not sure what to say until my eyes cross with Achilles. My friend is holding his phone as if he's just about to text someone.

"Motherfucker," I hiss.

Striding to Achilles, I snatch his phone from his hands and barely hold myself back from slapping him when he smiles at me.

I look down, and without surprise, he sent a picture of me and Elijah to Wren.

"This is none of your business," I tell him. "Stay out of it."

I press call, and the second Wren picks up, I'm snapping at him.

"Who the fuck do you think you are?"

"The man who owns you," he replies as casually as one would talk about the weather, and not at all surprised that it's my voice through Achilles's phone.

Oh, I bet he thinks I'm so predictable.

"Now listen, you can stay and enjoy your party. Or you can be a good girl and go home. But I just want you to know something. If you so much as talk to Elijah again, I promise you the second I'm back in Silver Falls, his head is going to meet my fist so many times he won't have a functioning mouth to talk with anymore."

I inhale through my nostrils, attempting with all my might to keep my calm.

"Is that clear, Penelope baby?"

"Crystal," I push past gritted teeth.

"Atta girl. We'll speak tomorrow."

Achilles is still smiling by the time I hang up. "Want me to walk you home?"

"Go fuck yourself."

I'm forced to ignore Elijah when I walk past him again, but I don't miss his hurt expression. His shoulders slump, but I keep moving. I might not be able to talk to him, but I'm going to be at this party until the sun rises, I can promise that.

───────

I wake up with a mean hangover, the knowledge that I blacked out at yet another party, and the memories of those weird flashes I sometimes get.

Oh, and of course, a message from Wren.

> Wren: No more drugs. This is the one and only warning.

I put a pillow above my face, screaming into it before I answer. Is this what my life is going to be from now on? Him giving me orders without reason and me having to do whatever he says?

> Peach: I'll just add it to the list. It's called: Everything I hate about Wren Hunter.

> Wren: You should rename it the Good Girl List.

> Peach: Fuck you

Wren: Funny you say that, because all I can think about is fucking you. Do you think about my dick inside you, Trouble? Because I can't forget the way you feel.

Peach: I hate you

Wren: Makes it sweeter to know that you come for me even when you hate me.

I choose to ignore him. What I can't ignore, though, is that feeling between my legs. And it stays all week. Every time I get a new text, something that tells me what to do or not to do, I get angrier and hornier. He makes up new rules every day. Sometimes he's caring, and sometimes he's borderline insane. All I know is, his control is giving me whiplash.

Don't skip lunch again.

How was your day?

You stayed too late at the library last night.

I miss you.

No talking to Camila. She's Elijah's Hera.

I want to sleep next to you.

Never. Take. The. Necklace. Off.

I put it back on the second I got home, and that was yesterday. Now I'm on my way back from the hospital with Achilles driving me, because today was the day they took my splint off. He's been following me everywhere, and I'm starting to get fucking claustrophobic.

"What do you want now, Achilles?" I huff as he follows me inside my house. I've got another text from Wren. This one saying to not go back to cheer practice until he can see with his own eyes that I'm better. I'm going to lose my mind.

"Why are you mad at me? I'm just being a good friend."

"To *him*," I snap as I turn around. "I can't stand your face anymore, always somewhere around, sending him pictures, snitching to him, telling him what I eat, and how long I stay up, and where I am. *Back. Off.*"

"Do you know what I haven't told him about? Your little secret meetings with Elijah at the back section of the library."

I freeze, eyes narrowing on his. "If you keep your mouth shut, I won't have to shut it myself," I threaten.

"Do you kiss or something back there? Do you even know how Wren would react? You don't care because Wren is a puppy for you, but you're definitely putting Elijah's life at risk."

"We're just friends," I defend. "And Wren doesn't get to decide who I'm friends with. How would you feel if Wren had said I couldn't hang out with *you*."

He thinks for a second, smiling to himself. "One less unbearable person in my life?"

I don't even grace him with an answer, and he follows me as I head for the living room.

"Do you want a picture of me getting changed into my cheer outfit?" I snarl.

I'm still looking at him as I turn into the living room.

"Wren said not to—"

"I don't care! He's no doctor. I have the all-clear from a real doctor telling me I can practice. So, if he wants to be a little bitch about it, he can say it to my face. He can come back and be all *Shadow* about it." I imitate Wren's stern voice. "*Penelope baby, I'm going to put you on your knees and make you beg for forgiveness if you go to cheer practice—*"

"Penelope baby, I'm going to put you on your knees and

make you beg for forgiveness if you go to cheer practice when I said not to."

I jump in surprise at Wren's voice ringing out from behind me.

He's standing right there, in my living room, with a hand in the pocket of a black suit and a folder in the other. All six-five of him. His square shoulders, his defined arms stretching his black shirt. His perfectly brushed and gelled chestnut hair, and his annoyingly captivating eyes. Yeah. All of him is back.

"Fuck," I whisper, finding no strength in my voice. There's no way he didn't hear that conversation about Elijah. "You scared me."

Cocking his head to the side, he purrs, "I think you're nowhere near scared enough when it comes to me." His eyes go to Achilles. "Thank you for looking after her. I owe you."

"He didn't look *after* me," I mutter bitterly. "He just looked *at* me. He looked at me for six whole days, and it's creepy."

Achilles chuckles behind me, and I feel surrounded by crazies again.

"I don't think anyone can complain when they're being tasked to look at you. You're back early," he tells Wren.

Wren's eyes bore into me, up and down they go, analyzing my entire body and setting me on fire. "Yeah," he finally says. "I missed being home."

"Let me guess." Achilles snorts. "Home is Peach."

Wren's tongue darts to his lower lip, his beautiful eyes not leaving mine as he makes me melt entirely.

"Home is Peach," he confirms.

"In that case, I think what you missed is *fucking* home."

I snap around. "Get out of here!"

He laughs to himself as he leaves, muttering a last *tell*

me I'm wrong, though. And I'm left all alone with the man who has been obsessively occupying my thoughts.

He doesn't move for a minute, observing me from afar. Every movement of his eyes as they roam over my body makes my heartbeat accelerate. Why is it so hard to breathe in his presence? And why do I always lose myself in the idea—scratch that, the *reality*—that Wren only has eyes for me. It's so...special.

That's what he makes me feel. *Special.* Like I'm his favorite, his everything. And who wouldn't want to feel that way? I just wish the man who makes me feel it had at least an ounce of morals or laws he could live by. Something like, *Don't force a girl into a relationship with you.*

My knees almost buckle as he approaches me. He doesn't utter a word until he's right in front of me, and I feel his minty breath on my skin as he talks.

"I missed you." His low voice holds the truth. I can hear it reverberating with undertones of longing.

He did miss me.

His hand comes out of his pocket, and he brings it to my throat, caressing my skin with the knuckle of his index finger. I gulp, and I can tell he feels it because the corner of his mouth lifts in the sexiest yet most annoying way.

"Did you miss me, Trouble?" he carries on.

The truth is, with him taking over my every move with something as simple as *texts*, all my thoughts have been focused on him. I have no doubt he did that on purpose. He turned my life upside down and left me alone for six days, forced to think of him and how to navigate our new dynamic with no help whatsoever, and no way to adapt. Did I miss him? I don't know if I missed the man who played on my vulnerabilities to get me to become his Hera. But did I miss Wren? My Wren? Of course. I always miss him when he's not around, but I can't admit that. That would make it too easy for him. So, I focus on his part of the deal instead.

"Did you find my biological parents?"

His eyebrows raise. "Are you too scared if you admit that you missed me, you'll be making things too easy for me? Do you think you're punishing me by not telling me the truth?"

It's my turn to smile. "Oh, Wren, honey. I *know* I'm punishing you by doing that. So, did you find my parents?"

He takes a step back, and I cross my arms over my chest, tempted to tap angrily with my foot.

"I can't just *find your parents*. It's a bit more complicated than that."

"Well, are you getting anywhere? Because I've been here playing the docile little Hera and obeying every order you dare throw my way, so you better hold your end of the fucking deal, find something, *anything*, or even the Silent Circle won't be able to protect you from me."

He smiles smugly. "I do have something." He waves the folder in my face. "I didn't find them, but I have some information."

Something takes over me, and I can't control myself anymore. My hand swiftly reaches out for the folder, desperation pouring out of me, but he's too quick and lifts it way above his head. Somewhere he's sure I can't reach.

"That's not funny," I snap, my gaze searing. "Give it to me!"

"Why don't you calm down and take a seat first?" His attention flicks to one of the three couches in the living room. It's the one facing the giant screen.

Shivers of anxiety make my lower back tremble. This is big. Whatever he has, I want it. The hole in my stomach that grows every time I think of my biological parents is contracting, twisting, making me emptier than ever.

"Wren, give it to me," I rasp.

"Sit." His strict demand deepens my vulnerability, and I feel myself losing composure.

Slowly, I round the sofa, my ribcage feeling bruised from my heart beating out of control. When I sit, he stays behind, and I keep my gaze ahead until he drops the folder next to me. My hand shoots out, but he grabs my wrist, followed quickly by the back of my neck as he pushes me forward so my nose practically touches my knee.

"Here's the issue, Trouble." Grabbing my other hand, he pulls it behind my back. "You haven't held up your end of the deal, have you?"

I feel something between my wrists, the texture coarse against my skin.

"I did," I squeak in panic. "What is that?"

"Rope."

He tightens it, and my wrists crash against each other.

"See..." Continuing, he wraps more of it around my now bound wrists. "An obedient Hera would have done what she's told when I said to stay away from Elijah, not see him at the back of the library, hoping no one catches you. What is he, your secret, forbidden lover? Because whatever you have with him is just him being a pathetic boy trying to get to me. Do you understand?"

"He's my friend," I say as he brings me back to a sitting position. My eyes dart to the folder again. It's right there, so close yet so far, and Wren is going to make me suffer for what I did.

"He's whatever I decide he is. And that is *nothing*."

He rounds the sofa, standing tall in front of me. "Now I have to punish you. Isn't it such a shame?" It's purred with the voice of someone who's looking forward to said punishment.

"I want to know what's in the folder. Let me see." I pull at my wrists, claustrophobic. "Let me see, Wren. Fuck, let me see!"

Shaking his head, he brings a hand to my cheek. "Not yet. First, you're going to suffer, and then you get your reward."

I release a deep groan, a ball forming in my throat and making my voice waver. "How can you do this to me? Hold my most wanted wish over my head like it means nothing to you."

"Do you think I like punishing you?" he asks seriously. "I want you compliant to the point I'd barely have to think of something for you to execute. That's the opposite of enjoying punishment." He caresses my jaw, my collarbone, and finally, his fingers undo the top buttons of my uniform shirt.

"You're not leaving me with a choice, Peach. How can I have an obedient perfect version of you if I don't train you? Training is always hard. The quicker you get used to it, the easier it'll get."

I suck in a trembling breath. "I hate you," I exhale.

"You made a deal with me. Be a big girl about it."

My upper lip curls as I watch him take the folder and put it on the far end of the couch.

"I won't hurt you. You have my word." Sitting next to me, he takes the remote for the TV. "We'll just watch a movie."

I can't think straight as he goes on a streaming platform and selects my favorite movie, *Death Proof*.

"I don't want to watch a movie," I say quietly. "I want—"

"I know what you want," he says as he wraps an arm around my shoulders and presses play.

This feels creepy. I have this horrible impression that I'm being held hostage by a psychopath in my own home. I'm stiff as a board, my wrists burning from the ropes as he relaxes next to me.

"Oh, I almost forgot."

He pulls something I can't quite see out of his pocket and flips my skirt up. My eyes round when he pulls at the waistband of my underwear. Not to remove them, but like he's about to look under. Only, he doesn't look, just brings his other hand holding the object closer.

"What is it?" I try to squirm away.

"Don't move."

I hate his orders. I hate them and love them, and they make me feel every emotion and sensation possible under the sun. It's because they hold that specific tone he had never used on me before this shift in our relationship. It scares me and turns me on. It makes me furious and docile. It melts everything inside me, yet sets me on fire.

I stay perfectly still as he slips what I now see is a bullet vibrator into my panties. He presses it right against my clit, puts the waistband back in place, and pushes my legs closed. Out of nowhere, the toy starts vibrating, startling me.

"Fuck," I pant, my breathing picking up as the film keeps playing. I notice the remote control in his hand. He presses again, and the vibrations slow down but don't stop.

Kissing my cheek, he says, "Only one rule. You cannot come before the end of the movie."

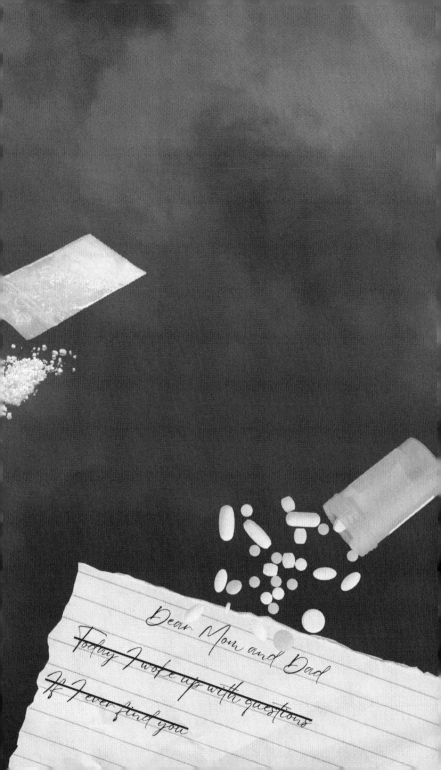

Chapter Twenty-Two

Peach

THE RIDE - Omido, Kae

"Wren," I moan, sweat coating the back of my neck as I writhe on the couch. "Please..."

All he's been doing for the last half hour is turning the toy on and off, on and off. Sometimes, the vibrations are quick enough to bring me right to the edge, and sometimes, they're a slow, unbearable buildup that keeps me completely hopeless.

I pull at the ropes, to no avail, and when his massive hand wraps around my upper thigh, I moan. The simple act of his skin touching mine is setting every single cell of my body on fire.

"You're redeeming yourself wonderfully, Trouble. Keep being good for me."

"I can't," I gasp. "Fuck, I need to come, please."

"I know that, baby. But I need you to understand I'm the one who controls your body now, and I decide when you get to come, or not. So hold it."

"Please. Please, please...I can't."

The vibrations stop, and I whimper, folding onto myself.

"If you can't control yourself, I'll teach you how."

He presses on the remote, and my back arches from the need coursing through me.

"Spread your legs."

I'm quick to open, need burning everything inside me. I've become a puppet, and Wren Hunter is holding my strings.

"Good girl," he purrs. "You're doing so well."

My eyes are trained on the screen, and I've watched this movie enough times to know we're nowhere near the end.

Slowly unbuttoning the rest of my shirt, his hand caresses me down to my stomach, leaving a trail of goose-bumps on my hot skin. He skims my skirt until he's sliding his hand under my underwear.

I'm full of hope until he removes the toy and throws it to the side.

"God, no. Wren," I whimper.

"I think now is the time you might want to apologize for disobeying."

"I'm sorry!" It flies out of my mouth, showing the lack of control I have over myself. It's all gone. He stole it. "I'm sorry for not..." My hips shift forward, the need to be filled and touched so strong I want to die. "I'm sorry for not listening. Please."

"I believe you, Penelope baby. But the punishment stays the same."

His fingers are on my clit now, and I throw my head back as he caresses it slowly.

I shake my head, feeling an onslaught of emotions rising to my throat. "B-but...I can't."

He keeps stroking. "Do *not* come."

I don't know what's happening anymore, and I feel tears breaching past my eyelids. My chest is heaving, and all I can focus on is the exact milliseconds he caresses my clit, then disappears, then comes back...and again...and again... Pressure builds in my entire body, and my legs start to shake.

"I can't."

He stops.

And he pulls his hand out of my panties.

"Breathe, baby." His other hand caresses my hairline as I try to catch my breath. "Do you like when I edge you?"

Squeezing my eyes shut, I shake my head.

"Maybe you should take my orders more seriously next time, huh? Because you're mine forever, Penelope. And this could be your life if you don't start behaving. Do you understand who's in control?"

I nod, sniffling as more tears fall down my face. "Yes. You."

"Good. Get on your knees between my legs, facing the TV."

"Please, let me come."

"The movie isn't over." He snaps his fingers and points at the floor. "Don't make me repeat myself."

It's hard enough to move with my trembling legs, but having my arms tied behind my back isn't helping. I struggle, finally making it between his legs, my back to him and the sofa. He undoes the rope and fists my hair, pulling my head back until it's resting between his thighs on the sofa, and he bends to look down at me.

"You keep your hands behind your back. Show me you can listen."

I look ahead again and, without the rope forcing me, I spend the rest of the movie on the floor while he sits on the sofa, my hands behind my back. He's not touching me, bar the hand caressing my hair, and there's no friction on my clit anymore, yet all I can think about is the throbbing need between my legs.

"You picked a movie I know on purpose," I whisper. "So I can tell how much suffering I have left."

"Of course, I did," he purrs. "Knowing you by heart has its advantages."

We must have ten minutes before the end when he softly says, "Lay down on the couch with your hands above your head."

I slowly stand up, my knees and ankles hurting from the position I was in. I lie down as he ordered, and he settles between my legs.

"I love your fire, Peach," he says as he pulls my panties down my legs. "But I'll have to admit, taming it feels like nothing else I've experienced before."

He lowers himself, and his mouth is so close to touching my pussy, I whimper.

"The movie isn't finished. Don't come until you see the credits on the screen." His breath so close to my molten core forces a whine out of me, my hips thrusting forward.

And then he's licking me. He avoids my clit on purpose, cleaning the mess I made from his torture without touching anywhere that could set me off.

"What a wet little slut," he growls against me as his fingers come to spread my outer lips.

He presses his tongue at my entrance, and my body shudders as he pushes in.

Something clicks inside him because he becomes a man obsessed. Worse than usual. I don't understand what happens anymore as he buries his tongue inside me, pulling it back out and licking all the way to my clit.

"*Fuck*," he growls. His hands grab the back of my thighs,

and he holds them wide open, my knees to my shoulders. "Don't you fucking move."

I don't even recognize him as his tongue starts playing with my clit. Over and over again, he strokes it with a force he can't seem to control.

I'm panting, tears trailing down my cheeks from the overwhelming pleasure. "Please, Wren. Fuck, I need to come."

He accelerates, slows, takes a breath, and says, "Look at the TV. Wait for the credits."

My eyes can barely keep open as I moan languidly, so close to coming I can't breathe.

He doesn't answer anymore, too busy ravaging me with his mouth.

The screen goes black, the room silent apart from my pants and the embarrassing sound of how wet I am.

Music starts.

The first name of the credits comes on screen.

And I explode like never before.

The orgasm makes me shake harshly, my legs pushing back against his grip as it rips me from the inside.

My voice is hoarse from all the screaming as he lets go of me to sit up. Once I've stopped shuddering, my breaths back to normal, he helps me up too, pushing strands of my hair away from my sweaty forehead.

"What do you say when I give you a reward for taking your punishment so well?"

My mouth drops open, and he arches an eyebrow at me. "What do you say, Penelope?"

"Th-thank you?"

"Atta girl."

My eyes drop to his crotch, and the hard-on is almost

painful to look at. "Let me help with that," I say as I bring my hand to his belt, but he grabs it and pushes it off.

"Oh no." He chuckles softly. "You don't get my cock."

I could swear I feel cold sweat down my spine. "What?"

"My cock is a reward for when you behave. Do you feel like you deserve it?"

I'm suddenly painfully aware of how empty I feel. How one orgasm was bliss, but I need to be filled and slammed into, and to have Wren holding me down as he thrusts into me.

I blink at him.

"Answer."

"Ye— No. I don't know," I say meekly. *What the hell is he doing to me?*

"Don't get me wrong, Trouble. All I've thought about while being away was how much I want to sink my cock into you until you're screaming my name. All I want is to feel you break apart as I give you what you need. But the answer is no. You don't deserve it. And I can be patient." He smiles. "After all, didn't I wait all my life to finally have you?"

His hand goes to his side, and the folder is on my lap next. My heart skips a beat. I forgot that's what I wanted. Wren took over my entire mind, and now my chest tightens at the thought that I let this man make me forget that this was my ultimate goal.

"You may open it."

I want to scream, *I don't need your permission!*

But the truth is, every single thing I do now is dictated by whether Wren allows it, isn't it? Hell, breathing feels difficult when he's not around to tell me to do it.

"Did you look?" I ask.

"Yes. And I want you to know, it's something, but it's not everything. I'll explain why."

God, all I wanted an hour or so ago was to read whatever is in here. It's thin, light, probably only a piece of paper. I realize that it's a brown string envelope rather than an easy folder to open.

I undo the string slowly, my chest feeling hollower at every turn. Do I even have a heart in my ribcage anymore? All I can do is feel it in my ears.

Time slows as I pull out the piece of paper. It's a birth certificate.

My eyes scan it quickly.

"It's mine," I rasp. "It's my birth certificate." I don't recognize my own voice, so small and full of hope.

Saoirse Anderson née O'Malley and *Keith Anderson*

"Oh my god. Wren... These are my parents." A sob bursts out of me as I shoot up, running for my bag I left behind the couch. I reach for my phone inside it, and I go straight to my search engine.

"Peach, wait."

I start with my mom.

"Saoirse Anderson," I mumble as I type.

Nothing comes up right away, so I scroll and scroll some more. Moving on quickly, I type Saoirse O'Malley instead.

"Saoirse O'Malley. That's Irish, isn't it? Am I Irish?" I giggle as I look up at Wren and then back at my phone. "That's crazy!"

There's not much at all except a woman's social page, but she looks to be in her twenties.

Whatever, I'll get back to that. I type Keith Anderson. But all that comes up is an explanation for the Anderson last name. That one's Scottish, it seems.

I scroll down, page one, page two. Nothing.

A shadow of disappointment creeps over me. Is this it?

"I don't get it," I say, trying to keep the hope I had a second ago. "Did you find anything else? I can't find them online."

Wren stands right by me now, and I'm cross-legged on the floor.

"That's the thing," he says. "There's nothing."

"What do you mean? Where did you get the certificate?"

"Someone I trust in the Circle has a family member who works at the Maryland Vital Records Office. He was able to find it for me."

He sits down next to me, looking so childish now that he's crossing his legs too. I'm back in my bedroom when we were kids and talking about our biggest dreams while eating candies and chocolates one of my dads would have brought up for us. Except we were so happy back then, and his smile would never leave his face while he would spend time with me. Why is it twisted with so much pity now? Where is the reassuring Wren I know?

"There's nothing else about them, Trouble."

"Thanks for doing a half-assed job. There's literally an address on here. Did you check records of people who lived there and where they could have gone? Hell, they might still be there."

He shakes his head, putting his hand on my knee. "They don't live there anymore, and there's no record of them ever living there." As he squeezes my knee, I can feel he knows the exact kind of support I need. Nothing overwhelming, nothing that is *too much* or feels fake. Just enough to let me know he's here. And yet, for once, it's not enough.

"Those people are your biological parents, baby. But for whatever reasons, they don't want to be found. In fact, they've made themselves completely untraceable."

"But..." I look down at the certificate again.

Penelope Anderson.

They gave me their name. It's not like they wrapped me in a blanket and put me in front of the orphanage as a newborn. They declared me as theirs. Until when? At what point did they realize they didn't want me anymore?

"They just don't want to be found?" I ask, emotions crashing through me in waves of despair. There's a sack of rocks in my heart, and every time I have thought of my biological parents in my life, another pebble has been added to it. I'm twenty-two now. A lifetime of pebbles is getting heavy. So heavy I can't breathe.

Wren nods. "It looks like they went through a lot of trouble not to be."

"But why?" I croak as I look up into his eyes. I can feel the tears starting to fall. God, my throat, it's so tight.

"I don't know," he whispers as he wipes a tear from my cheek.

"Was it...me? Did I...was I...because I wasn't what they wanted?"

His face falls. "No, of course not. Please don't think that." He wraps me in his arms, and my head falls onto his shoulder. "Don't you ever think that again."

"My heart," I cry, the sob in my throat falling lower, choking me and making me unable to breathe. "It hurts."

"I'm here, baby." He strokes my hair, hugs me tighter, and somehow the tightness of his hug releases the pressure inside me. "I'll always be here."

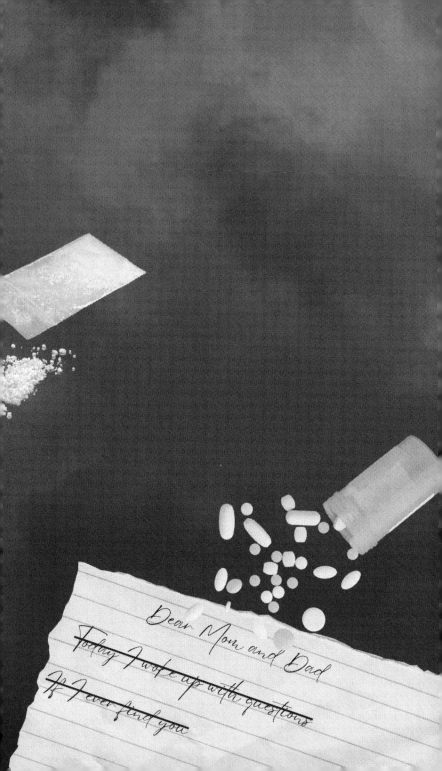

Dear Mom and Dad

Today I woke up with questions

If I ever find you

Chapter Twenty-Three

Peach

EXTRA EXTRA – Chandler Leighton

Three days in a row, I wake up in Wren's bed with swollen eyes and a need to sleep forever. My head feels heavy, my brain foggy. My body doesn't feel anything anymore. I'm completely detached, and I've refused to utter a single word. Wren has been attempting to feed me, but all I've accepted is water and toast.

"Please," he murmurs as I shake my head when I see the platter with a plate of fries and a bowl of ice cream.

I go deeper under the covers, pulling them above my head.

"I put peri-peri powder on the fries," I hear from the other side of the covers. The side that isn't the safety of the bed. Out there, my parents made themselves untraceable so I would never find them. That's how badly they *didn't* want me.

The covers disappear. "Please, Trouble. It's unlike you not to eat anything. Especially if it involves both sweet and savory."

"I don't like peri-peri on the fries anymore when I put them in my ice cream."

"Alright, then I'll get you something else."

I peek from under the covers. Putting the tray on the bedside table, he sits next to me. He's dressed in his uniform, and I realize he feels cold. He smells of fall too. He's been outside.

"Have you been out?" I croak.

"Yes, to classes."

I feel my eyes widen, and I look at the clock on my phone. It's 1:03 p.m. I slept all morning.

"You missed Lopez's class," he carries on. "He asked about you. Don't you have an appointment with him in a few days?"

I nod. Sometimes, one piece of bad news will ruin everything you worked so hard for. It's unfair.

It's unfair that all my dreams mean nothing just because of *rejection*. This is how I am, and it's always been my incurable curse. My perspective on things changes all the time to point out where I'm being rejected. It follows a schedule of moods and the *feeling loved* label I put on different parts of my life. I remember when we were in high school, and I would get the best grades possible in all science subjects. In my head, the *feeling loved* label was focused on getting into SFU so I could start my journey to a Nobel Prize. I thought that, then, I would feel loved. But then, Ella would get all the boys' attention, and my *feeling loved* label would be ripped off my work and slapped right onto the *feeling beautiful* box.

Now we're years later, my ideas shifted, my personality changed, yet here I am again, feeling the rejection like it's a nasty part of me that gets awoken at the snap of someone's fingers. And I feel it so deeply. I'm hollow, only alive when filled with someone's need for me. I want my biological parents to want me. That's where my *feeling loved* label is. I want them to tell me this was all a mistake. But the truth is, the only mistake they ever made was...me.

"I can catch up on Lopez's work whenever," I mumble, my eyelids heavy.

"What about his notes for your paper?"

"I'm still feeling tired. And I can easily catch up on that too once I've rested." I turn to face away from him, but his hand is on my shoulder, stopping me.

"If by catching up, you mean snorting Adderall to pull three all-nighters in a row, you can kiss that idea goodbye."

When I don't respond, he caresses my hairline and lies down with me. "Trouble, if this was like you, I would lie down and spend days in bed with you. But you're not being yourself, and I can't let you do this."

"Maybe it's like me. The new me. You don't know."

He stays silent for a moment, and I struggle to read him. Sometimes, he's an open book. Lately, everything feels different.

"Lopez fired some questions at us during the class. You would have loved it. Especially the ones I couldn't answer."

Now he's got my attention.

Shifting to face him properly, I cock an eyebrow. "You couldn't answer Lopez's weekly rapid-fire questions? Are you okay, loser? They're so easy. What did he ask?"

Challenge tightens his lips while raising my heartbeat.

"Alright," he says. "Well, if you're so good, why don't you answer them for me."

"Go ahead. Someone has to teach you the answers."

"Name a common air pollutant regulated by the EPA."

I snort. "Easy. PM2.5. Next?"

"Okay," he says, impressed. "What does an anaerobic digester produce?"

Energy coming back to my body, I sit up a little. "Biogas. Are you planning on making this difficult, or what?"

He thinks harder about it, eyebrows pinching together. "What's a typical removal method for NOx in flue gas?"

"Selective Catalytic Reduction. Wow, Wren. You really need to get your shit together if you didn't know any of these."

I'm fully sat against the headboard now, the covers down and excitement about my favorite class buzzing through me.

"I love Professor Lopez," I say. "He always allows me to show you how much smarter I am than you." I wink at him, and it makes him laugh beautifully.

"Eager to go back to his class, then?"

"Yeah." I smile. "Don't feel bad, though. After all, environmental engineering is my major, not yours—" I cut myself off. "Wait."

"Hm?" he asks, but his innocent act isn't fooling me.

"You love environmental engineering. You work hard on it because you want to challenge me in class like an idiot."

He raises his eyebrows. "Do I?"

"Wren," I say, tone stern. "You knew the answers to those questions. You did this to get me back to class. Do you think I'm dumb?"

"Quite the opposite, baby. Trust me."

"I don't want to go to classes," I throw back firmly. "I want to stay here. I want to rest."

I put my back to him again, but this time, I hear him shift. I don't move until I feel him poke at my ribs with something. I turn around, and he's holding a marker.

"If you promise to go to classes today, I promise I will

find them. Not find any information I can about them. I will find them, and you will meet them and talk to them."

My chest constricts, and I sit up, wiping the tears I hadn't realized were falling again. "But they're impossible to find."

"I'll find them," he insists. "But now that you remember that classes actually make you excited, I want you to get out of bed, go to class, and work on your paper for the journal."

I snatch the pen, writing on my forearm, *I promise*, then give it to him.

"Do it," I say in a hurry.

"Peach, baby." He huffs, pausing with the tip of his pen above his skin. "I will, but please, I need you to understand, this doesn't define you. You are... Fuck, you are the most intelligent, beautiful, and unbearably, perfectly stubborn woman I know. For whatever reasons, your parents couldn't keep you, but that reason *isn't* you. You were just a kid."

"A three-year-old kid. They had time to get to know me. I might not remember anything, but I know they should have had time to get attached."

"Baby, please," he insists. He presses his lips on my forehead. "No one in their right mind would let you go. Ever. The proof is your dads love you and they *chose* you."

"*Write it, Wren*," I hiss. "Do it."

My eyes are stuck on the tip as he writes it down on his arm.

I promise.

And finally, a weight falls off my shoulders.

Wren has flaws I'm struggling to get past, but if one person will do anything in their power to make me feel better, it's him.

"Why do you do this?" I ask, a strange hope warming my stomach.

"Do what?"

"*This. All* this. You take care of me, and you encourage me to get back to class. You know me, and you trick me into feeling better. It's... How and why?"

"How?"

"How do you know me so well?"

He smiles proudly. Full-teeth-dimples-out kind of smile.

"According to my calculations," he answers with a playful lilt. "It's twenty percent observation over sixteen years. One percent, you opening up from time to time. And seventy-nine percent"—he hesitates, licking his lips—"that's just who I am with you. It comes naturally. Like it's meant to be."

I look down at my lap, twisting the cover around my index finger. "But...how do you know it's meant to be?"

It seems he struggles to put words to it as he pauses. And then it comes with a simplicity I never expected from either of our complicated brains.

"You're my home."

He continues as if my heart didn't just suddenly stutter and accelerate. As if the room isn't spinning around me.

"My house and my family have never felt like a home. I think I started feeling that very early for many different reasons. And then we met. And grew up together. My feelings were always confusing me, but I always wanted to get back to you. I lived in a huge mansion in Stoneview, yet I wanted nothing but to be near you. In a tiny fort in your bedroom. In the back of my car when we'd have lunch at the top of the Stoneview hills. A seat next to you in class. *Those* felt like home."

I swallow thickly, my skin buzzing with the need to touch him.

"And that's when I understood." He looks at me, smiling

shyly now. "Home is a small place. It's the tiniest place. It fits in my heart. It's you. I hope I can be that for you someday too."

Words aren't something I can utilize in this moment. They would feel so little compared to his declaration.

So, I place a hand on his cheek and give in to this closeness. The warmth of his skin fills me with a hundred dancing butterflies.

Wren Hunter. What are you doing to me?

Thankfully, I don't need to talk. He takes my hand, kisses my inner wrist, and I know he understands that everything he said is now safeguarded in a special place in my heart.

"Now, please go shower. I bought your moisturizer and sunscreen. It's in the bathroom."

I give him half a smile and jump out of bed.

"SPF50?"

"50," he confirms.

"You know too much about me." I look over my shoulder just before I enter the bathroom and his silent staring tells me, *You have no idea how much.*

And my heart skips a beat. As I turn on the shower, I let my thoughts run wild, and a feeling sinks into my bones. I truly think this man would do anything for me. And that if someone could fill the emptiness inside me, it's him.

We're about to walk into the science building when his hand tries to grab mine.

"What are you doing?" I ask as I take a step away from him. Something tugs at my heart, like separating physically only reminds me of the invisible magnets trying to bring us back together.

We keep walking together, but someone could get between us now.

"Taking your hand?" he points out, as if I'm the one who's lost her mind.

"We're on campus. You promised, remember? We're not together on campus."

His jaw settles in that tightness he always wears when someone refuses him something.

"You said you would give me time, Wren," I remind him as he follows me to where my next class is. His is nowhere near this part of the building.

"You've had over a week," he answers casually. "You've been in my bed for three days. Hell, you've come with my tongue inside you."

"Shut up." I keep looking around, making sure no one is near enough to hear us. "You left me alone for days while I was trying to figure this out. I need time."

He runs his tongue across his teeth, looks away, then back at me. "Fine."

"Good. And I want to know where you were for a week."

He cocks an eyebrow. "You seem to be throwing a lot of orders around."

I smile brightly. "Of course I am. You forced me into this, remember?"

Putting a hand on my cheek, he licks his lips. "I still don't regret anything."

I push his hand away. "You made me your Hera, left me for a week, and came back with horrible news. I will make you regret a lot if you don't start answering some questions."

"I'll take you to dinner tonight. You haven't eaten properly in days. Feed yourself, and I'll answer any questions you have."

"Any questions?"

"Any questions, Trouble."

I pat his cheek condescendingly. "Good boy."

He chuckles but calls out after me as I turn my back to him. "I'm going to make you regret that."

"Try," I throw back, my body weirdly buzzing with excitement.

I'm invigorated when I walk out of my class. I don't know how I could let myself feel down for so long when I know moving forward has always been the way for me to get over something. And Wren will find my biological parents. He can do anything. I know it.

I stop in front of a paper that's been taped to the announcement board. It wasn't there when I went to class. The campus security and local police are working together to try to find a witness to Josh Addinton's murder. They put a date and time and added short notes, not giving anything else away.

If you were at the library or around that part of campus at the date and time above and heard or saw anything, we urge you to come forward and call the line below.

Shit, they opened a special line for the murder. This and the email we received earlier from the dean, urging us to be careful as the murderer hasn't been caught, send a shiver down my spine. This isn't good.

I'm passing the men's bathroom when someone pulls me by the arm. The door closes, and I'm dragged into a stall before I can even fight back. When I do, the slap leaves me without any control.

"Ow! Peach!"

"Elijah, what the fuck?"

He stands in front of me, a hand rubbing his cheek. "You tell me what the fuck. You disappeared for three days. I thought Wren found out about our library talks and hurt you or something."

I shake my head. "He would never hurt me."

There's a long silence, during which Elijah's glare tells me the opposite. That he knows his brother better than I do, and that I'm not safe with him.

The problem is, I *feel* safe with him. That prevails any warning he could give me.

"I was so worried," he says.

"Wren took care of me. I was feeling...down."

My gaze drops, and I suddenly find the black bows on my shoes incredibly interesting.

"Hey, are you okay?" His hand comes to my upper arm, squeezing in a caring way.

It feels strange to hide something from Elijah. After all, it's no secret that I'm adopted. Everyone knows. And I trust him with everything.

"To be honest," I rasp as I look back up, "Wren has been looking for my biological parents. And uh, he came to a pretty big bump in the road."

He tilts his head to the side, eyebrows scrunched together. "What kind of bump in the road?"

"They don't want to be found," I admit as shame creeps up my neck.

The surprise on his face is undeniable, and he lets go of me to cross his arms over his chest.

Looking away from me, he says, "He'd never hurt you, huh?"

"What?" My heart palpitates, already feeling like my world is about to fall apart yet again.

"Tell me, Peach." He looks at me again. "Did it hurt you that he couldn't find your parents?"

"Of course."

His expression tightens, nostrils flaring. "Then I can tell you Wren has already purposefully caused you pain."

"No." I shake my head in panic, my voice dying in my throat before I can try again. "No, he tried. He found my birth certificate, but he couldn't find *them*. He said he'll keep trying."

He snorts, but his eyes tell me how pathetic I am. "He's a liar and you shouldn't ever put your trust in him. Anyone in the Circle could find someone untraceable. We're the most powerful secret society on the damn planet. Do you really think anyone can hide from us?"

"I-I don't know... He said he couldn't find them. He promised to keep looking."

"And I bet there'll be other surprising bumps in the road..." He chuckles, and my stomach sinks. "Peach, listen to me. If Wren has used the Circle and couldn't find your parents, it's because he's the one getting in the way."

"You're wrong. Why would he do that? What would he gain out of it?" I say it with so much certainty, I can see the challenge lighting up in his eyes.

"What would *I* gain out of telling you the truth?"

We pause, stuck. My thoughts are running a thousand miles an hour, and I almost feel dizzy from it.

"Okay. Fine. You know what? I don't know why he would do that either," he says calmly. "So, I can't expect you to blindly believe Wren is a liar who has put a mask on in front of all of you for years." He pinches his lips, breathing harshly through his nose. "But here's what I'm offering you.

I'll look for them. Give me two weeks. If I don't have anything more than he does, then he means no harm. If I do...then you'll finally know the truth about him."

I swallow thickly. "He wouldn't do this to me. But fine. Maybe it'll erase some of that paranoia you have toward him if you realize it's truly difficult to find them even with the Circle's help."

"Okay," he says as he takes me into a hug. "I just want you to be safe."

"I know."

"And don't say anything to him. He'll only try to get in my way."

My heart skips a beat, but I nod against Elijah's shoulder. Wren kept the Circle from me for years. He kept the fact that he was a murderer to himself too. I can keep this from him for a couple of weeks.

-metal IS NOT the same as punk.
-She's still allergic to shellfish and cat hair
-Always leave the green olives to her
-We don't like metal anymore.
-~~Tea tree and peppermint shampoo~~
-~~Don't forget the peri-peri powder on her fries~~
-Bake and shake every first Tuesday of the month.
-No more sugar in her coffee. It makes her feel sick
-DO NOT bother me during girls' night Wren
-Spiced honey on pepperoni pizza
-Check the triangle freckles on her right shoulder
frequently. Dermatologist said to keep an eye.
-New vision results: Right eye -2.75. Left eye -3.25
-If she gets in next September's yearly release of the
EEAJ, the announcement will be in August next year.
-~~Her brace needs to come off in a week~~
-New shampoo: coconut oil in it
-No more peri-peri on her fries

Chapter Twenty-Four

Wren

The Darker The Weather // The Better The Man - MISSIO

The reaper. That's what the Circle insists on calling me. It's not a nickname; it's a job title. And when the Silent Circle gives you a job, you take it.

Sitting on a bench in the Stoneview park, I watch a woman jog toward me. She stops not too far, using the trunk of a tree to do some stretches. Bending over, she looks back at me and gives me a smile. I offer nothing in return. I can't, her teeth are too straight. Peach's bottom canines are both a little crooked. It's so beautiful, how could I smile back at Miss Perfect Teeth.

Instead, I look down at the book on my lap. The one Eugene Duval gave to me the second I came back from my trip. He hasn't been wasting any time since I initiated. First, sending me away to find two members that had put the Circle at risk. They're gone. Now this.

I open the book to the page that's been dog-eared and, for the tenth time since yesterday, I look at the words and single letters that have been underlined with a pencil.

Evening.
J.
Ford.
St.
Park.
Sunday.

I knew that's what it was going to be from now on. I didn't choose the Circle. It chose me and didn't leave me a choice. I asked them for a favor once as a teen. I wasn't a Shadow then, and a favor is a debt. The Circle always collects their debts. Now I'm part of their little privileged club and took on the role they gave me.

There's no explanation I'm given, no questions I should ask. Who knows what Jared Ford—whom I know well since he used to work for my father—has done to the Circle to deserve his cruel fate. Is he a member who betrayed them? A random man who was at the wrong place at the wrong time? An old employee who saw too much?

Poor guy is a dead man walking, that's all I know. The woman throws me one last look as she goes back to her jog, and I wait, book on my lap. When I finally see him, the sun is setting. Jared. He's walking his dog, squatting to undo the leash, and the long-haired Dachshund starts running toward me.

It's almost too easy.

The little sausage yaps at me as it attempts to jump on my lap. This thing is really bad at being a dog, it's kind of funny. Jared follows, apologizing as he grabs his pet away from me. He sits down next to me and puts him on his lap, but the thing keeps trying to come back to me.

"You're Monty's son, aren't you? Elijah?"

"Wren," I correct, a little too harshly.

"Right, right. The eldest. The superstar."

"That's right." I smile brightly, showing my best inno-cent face. If only he knew what my dad truly thinks of me. My entire family, in fact.

Sausage yaps again, trying to jump on my lap, and Jared struggles some more. He's probably in his mid-forties, but he looks like he's truly been through life.

"She used to be my daughter's," he explains, patting the dog's head. "But then my wife met a younger guy, she left, took our kid with her to Chicago, and apparently, her new husband wasn't a big fan of the dog. So, she gets my daugh-ter. I get...her."

He taps his pet on the head again.

I nod. This is going to be much harder than I thought. The Circle sees me as someone they can use to do their dirty business of eliminating people. Hell, my own father is so scared of me that he spent most of his life beating the shit out of me to make sure I couldn't hurt him.

The Circle relies on what they think is a total lack of empathy or regret. And I do have that. But not when I feel like myself. It only happens when I *snap*.

The problem is, I don't feel anywhere near snapping, and it's not something I can control. Usually, when I kill, there's a whole process, and mostly, I don't remember what happens. I don't remember killing Hudson and Lane last week. I just remember being angry at what they did to Peach. I remember leaving Peach's room when she fell asleep and going back to the temple. But after that, it's a complete blackout. Addington? Fuck, I remember *nothing*. Not even how I found him. Not even what I did to him. But I was sloppy because, apparently, I left the body on campus. There was no worst place to leave it.

That lack of a memory is dangerous, and that's why my technique works. I shove three Scrabble tiles down their throat. Always an I, an L, and a U. Because the truth is, people tend to die because of my love for Peach. It's a sad reality. For them. So, I leave her a message. I love you. Not that she knows.

Then, I write their name on a piece of paper and I hold it in my fist, because I know that when I come to, I'll want to be aware of what I did.

These jobs the Circle gives me don't work. It makes things more complicated. The issue is, I don't have a choice.

I scratch the back of my neck and huff. There's only one proven way to make me snap.

"Do you know Penelope Sanderson-Menacci?"

He looks at me, his incredulous face making me sad for him.

"I've heard of her, seen her from afar a few times. She's Sanderson's daughter, right? He's running for mayor."

"Yeah."

My long pause must make him think I'm completely crazy, but he doesn't ask anything, still petting his dog.

"So, what do you know about her? What do you think?"

He shrugs. "All I heard is she has a big mouth she can't seem to close. Most men complain about her at the country club behind her fathers' backs."

"That's only because she's smarter than most of them and puts them back in their place," I explain.

"Probably." He chuckles. "Is she your girlfriend?"

Now I truly can't stop the smile spreading on my face. "She is," I say proudly. "All mine."

"Congratulations. I'm sure you make a great couple."

I nod, because we do. It might be against her will, but we make a great couple, nonetheless.

"Is there *anything* you don't like about her? You can tell me," I encourage him.

He stares at me, completely dumbfounded. "Um...is there anything you don't like about her that you'd like to share?"

I feel my face fall.

"I love everything about Peach." My answer is quick and violent, and he moves back a bit, so I smile again and speak more calmly. "But you know, she does that thing when she's losing an argument and has nothing else to say. She'll just flip her hair and go, *shut up, Wren.*" I laugh a little. "Like it'll get her out of trouble, you know?"

"Right..."

"I mean, I'm sure *you* must find that really annoying?"

"I've never spoken to her."

"Yeah, but in principle."

He blinks at me. "Sure."

For fuck's sake, this isn't doing it at all. There's a long silence, the dog hopping off his lap and starting to run around my ankles when, finally, he speaks again.

"I once heard she slapped the country club owner because he commented on her ass." He turns to me. "I mean, that's a bit much, isn't it?"

"Not really. I was there, and he made a really rude comment about it."

I remember that night. We were in high school. The man was a sixty-year-old commenting about a seventeen-year-old's ass. He almost died, only lucky because when I went home and my dad saw me close to snapping, he got the reason out of me. He didn't want his friend to die, so he used me as a punching bag to make sure I didn't go back out to kill the man.

"If she doesn't want anyone to comment on her ass, maybe she should stop letting everyone call her Peach."

I tilt my head to the side. It's working. My blood's starting to boil.

"Her nickname was a joke between her closest friends. Her deciding to embrace it doesn't give anyone the right to comment on my body." I blink a few times, realizing what I said. "Her body, I mean."

"I've seen that ass, Wren, and believe me, I understand why you like the girl. But slapping, really? Come on, the man was just appreciating what was right in front of him."

I pause and let the tingling sensation spread to my limbs. Once it's taken over, I feel so serene my soul is lifting and bouncing on the clouds.

"Great," I say calmly. "That will do."

"What will do?"

I slip out my folding knife too fast for him to react, and it's already in his carotid by the time he thinks of pulling away.

"I don't think you should ever talk about my woman's ass, Mr. Ford." Time stops as he looks deep into my eyes, unmoving, as I see the realization in his. He knows he's going to die tonight.

One less person who wrongly talks about Peach. I'm truly doing everyone a favor.

Pulling the knife out, blood spurts everywhere. I'm quick, standing up and stepping away as he falls to the ground, two hands pressing to his neck.

I almost step on something.

Woof!

"Ah, shit," I groan.

Woof!

"I swear to God, sausage roll, don't make this hard on me."

She stands still at my feet, her head tilted to the side as

we both wait for her owner to die. The dog has no pity on him. Neither do I. I remember why she won't leave me alone and pull out the dog treats I had put in my pocket.

"You're an accomplice to this murder," I murmur. "So keep your mouth shut."

When I'm sure Jared Ford is gone, I approach him again and drop to my haunches. Taking the Scrabble tiles from my back pocket, I already know this is going to get me in trouble with Duval, but I do it anyway. Because no kill is perfect without a message to Peach.

I push in the I first, then the L, and finally the U. The U always stays on the tongue.

I'm in my own bed when I come to my senses. I wasn't asleep, so I wonder how long I've been staring at the ceiling. My fingers hurt from how tightly I'm holding the piece of paper in my hand. I close my eyes, swallow, and sit up.

Alright, let's see the damage.

Please, let it be the man I was supposed to kill and not some random fucker who bothered Peach.

When I see Jared Ford written, a sigh of relief leaves me. I'm not happy I took a life, but I'm happy I won't get caught. The Circle will take care of protecting me, especially if it protects them. It's when I kill people like Josh Addington and don't cover my tracks that I get myself in trouble. Achilles was involved when it came to Caleb, and he left his mark on him. Protection is the only reason I brought my friend with me that night. Having Zeus as your father has many advantages. Like if you leave your signature on a body, your dad will take care of it with the police. That's why there was a circle drawn on that police report

Lola King

and 'S.C.' written next to it. That cop was in the Circle's pocket. It was never meant to get out, and I have no idea how Hermes found it, but I know neither Achilles nor I will get in trouble for Caleb because that's how I always used to get away with things. Josh, though...how could I be so careless?

I check the clock, realizing it's almost six p.m., and I have to be ready to pick up Peach next door. I texted her earlier that I booked us a table at her favorite tapas restaurant in Silver Falls. I told her which dress to wear and when to be ready, and the simple fact that I know she'll be the voice I hear tonight is making everything else insignificant.

I hop in the shower, put on a simple white shirt and dark denim jeans, and grab the book and piece of paper before rushing downstairs.

Achilles is reading sheets of music on the couch, his eyes flicking to me as he sees me approach the fireplace. He lit up a fire, which coincidentally saves me time.

"Who was it?" he inquires as I throw the piece of paper and the book in the fireplace.

"Doesn't matter," I mumble, watching the flames dance. They swallow the proof of my crime.

"Was it at least Jared Ford? Or did someone accidentally graze Peach's pinky finger?"

I turn around, my back now to the fire. "You haven't initiated, my friend. You shouldn't know about Jared Ford."

His eyes drop to the music sheet in front of him, and he chuckles. "Just like I should never be at the temple, shouldn't know what happened at the initiations, shouldn't hear anything from my dad or be protected by the Circle debt-free. But it turns out being Zeus's son has its advantages, huh?"

"Yeah, like not being forced to initiate at any point."

He shrugs. "I'm sure his patience will run out, and he'll find a way to make me. But that's beside the point. You're getting sloppy, Wren."

I run a hand through my hair and look away, somehow trying to find an excuse, but I have none. "It won't happen again."

"What did Josh do?" he asks with sincere curiosity.

My mouth twists, and that same anger I felt after the initiations comes back. "He assaulted her in Daedalus's labyrinth. What was I meant to do?"

As he takes a minute to think, my friend's piercing on stay on me. "Alright. He hurt her, and we know that gets someone in trouble with you. But leaving a body on campus? Are you insane? After Ania, *and then* Hermes leaking that Caleb was found with Scrabble ties down his throat? The cops are starting to look for someone."

I feel my head rearing back. "I didn't kill Ania."

"Oh, of course. Because you'd remember, right?" he says, sarcasm thickly coating every word.

"Members of the public don't know I left tiles in Josh's throat."

"The fucking *cops* know, idiot. Just because they're tactically not revealing it for now doesn't mean they're not starting to link the murders. That's what happens when you don't bring me along, or at *least* leave the same mark I do so the Circle covers you."

Jaw tightening, I ignore him as I make my way to the closet by the entrance.

"Listen," he calls out. "When you do things behind the Circle's back, they don't protect you. Especially if you kill one of theirs. If you don't invite me to murder parties, at least hide your fucking bodies, will you?"

"Got it," I mumble. "I'm off to dinner with Peach."

He looks up again, confused this time. "Are you sure she's aware? Alex and Ella stopped by earlier, annoyed because Peach was going to the Acropolis with the druggies."

I stop mid-putting my coat on. "What?"

The "druggies" as Achilles calls them, are her cheerleader and sorority friends that have a drug for every occasion. Ecstasy and coke for the parties. Adderall or Ritalin for their afternoons at the library. Xanax for the anxious days that come after taking too much cocaine on a night out. When Peach hangs out with them, it ends in a blackout.

"She's at—"

"I heard you."

"Didn't seem like it," he deadpans.

"I told her no more drugs."

My friend rubs his jaw. "Wren. You told *Peach* not to do something." He throws me a disappointed look. "You don't tell her not to do anything. You *make her* or you kneel in front of her like all the other little boys she controls."

I run my tongue across my teeth, my brain struggling to accept she completely defied me. Bringing out my phone, I pull out the SFU app and check some of those girls' stories. One of them is panning and filming the bar she's at. The video shows Peach sitting in a booth, her eyes shining while she chats with Camila Diaz. Who I know is Elijah's Hera. Meaning, my brother has to be there.

"Do you know what your problem is, Wren?" Achilles jumps in again. "You've always been too easy on her. She's your obsession and your weakness. Everybody knows you as the man who will do anything to get what he wants. People give up on competing with you before the competition even starts. And yet, the thing you want the most...you never truly got."

"She's my Hera," I say with a tight jaw. "I've *got* her."

"Brother, you ran after your Hera like a lost puppy when she left the library the other day. All you have to do is be yourself instead of that pathetic version of you who's still begging for her to give you crumbs of attention."

He must see something change on my face because a smile spreads on his. "There he is. Now go get your Hera."

She wants to take drugs instead of going to dinner with me?

I warned her, didn't I? One wrong move...

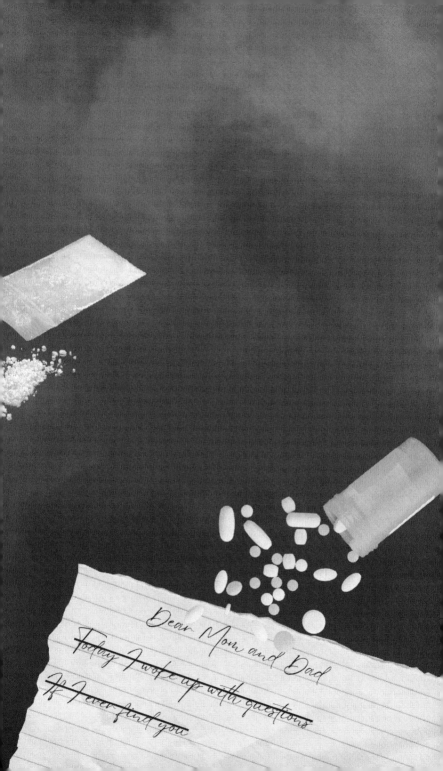

Chapter Twenty-Five

Peach

I love it - Croixx

I accidentally spill some of the drink Elijah got me as I throw my head back laughing and bump into whoever is behind me at the bar. My friend is still waiting for his, so I'm standing right next to him.

"Sorry," I mumble before turning back to my friend. This bar is always so busy, full of only SFU students.

"How about sorry to me?" Elijah laughs. "I've got beer all over me."

"Oops. Don't make me laugh so hard next time."

"I like to make sure the little time you can escape and be with me is time you enjoy."

I roll my eyes, taking a few large gulps of my drink. "Come on, you talk about him like he kidnapped me or something. He's not *that* bad."

His mouth twists, and he shrugs. "As I said before, we don't get the same version of him. The problem is, I think the one he uses on you is purely to manipulate you into thinking he's not dangerous." He puts a hand on my shoulder. His platonic version of a protective gesture.

"I know he's dangerous. I just know he's not dangerous to me." I look down at my phone, and my brain freezes for a second.

"Shit," I hiss, wiping my mouth. "It's past six. Wren was meant to pick me up from my house."

For a second, he looks like the mere mention of his brother's name scares him, but as his eyes widen and his hand drops, I understand what's happening.

My jaw tightens. "He walked in, didn't he—" I don't have time to finish my sentence.

Right here, in front of everyone, Wren slips a hand in my hair, pulls, and forces me to turn around. I don't get a second to complain because his lips crash against mine, his tongue forcing its way inside my mouth.

I whimper when he bites my lower lip, my back curving as I go onto my toes to alleviate the tension on my hair. All it does is give him more access. He holds me in place as he ravages my mouth, and I'm helpless to do anything about it.

Worse. I'm enjoying it.

I can feel it in my chest, the weight lifting as my muscles relax. The tightness against my skull is almost like a relief, canceling any thoughts that attempt to form in my brain. I'm putty in his hands when he grips my waist to bring me even closer.

All I can feel is him. His tongue caressing mine, his hard chest against my body, his hands owning me. All I can smell is his scent that has been following me around all my life. And just like that, my entire resolve turns off as I give in to him.

It wasn't supposed to feel this good to give him exactly what he wants.

But I'm not actually giving anything, am I? He's *taking*. *Taking all my sanity*.

So much so that I'm dizzy when he finally lets me go. I blink up at him, swaying on the spot, and he keeps a hand on my waist to make sure I don't lose my balance.

I only come back down from my Wren cloud when I hear someone whistling, someone else claps like a fucking idiot, and some guys I recognize from the lacrosse team start shouting toward us.

Finally!

It's happening, guys.

He got her.

"No." I shake my head. My lips are tingling from the kiss as I realized what just happened. "You said you wouldn't," I murmur. "Not in front of everyone."

The corner of his mouth tips up smugly, and he pulls me closer. He presses his lips to the side of my head, right above my ear.

"I also said to do what you're told. You didn't. Your actions have consequences."

He lets me go, but not for me. Not to give me time to process anything. Taking a step past me, he forces me to turn around in his direction to see what he's doing.

"Wren..." I call out in warning as he approaches his trembling brother, who had taken a few steps back during our kiss, it seems.

Towering over him, he says, "Do you understand who she belongs to?"

Elijah only answers with the tiniest nod.

"Who?" Wren asks.

"That's enough," I hiss and grab him by the arm. "Leave him alone."

Instead of letting me pull him away, he slaps him condescendingly. It's not hard. More like a harsh tap, as if to wake him up. But it's humiliating, showing Elijah couldn't take a real fight with his bigger, stronger, older brother.

"Who, Elijah?" he insists.

He gulps, looking all around at the people watching the interaction, laughing at him, until his shoulders scrunch together and his eyes drop. "You."

"That's right. So, keep your fucking hands off her if you don't want to lose them."

Not waiting another second, he grabs my wrist and pulls me through the crowd. People are still talking about what they just saw, and my glares don't even stop them.

Fucking harpies feeding on everyone's drama, as long as it's not theirs.

"I can't believe you." I'm panting as he strides across the Acropolis, struggling to follow with his long legs. "I can't... You couldn't keep your word. All I asked was for you to keep this private—"

He stops so suddenly, I bump into him. And there he is again, on me, his hands wrapping around my waist, so tightly I can't think straight.

"Look at me." I do without a second thought. My body doesn't feel like mine when he's holding it. "I'm done. Done taking it easy on you. I warned you, and you didn't want to listen. That's it."

"What is it?" I ask tentatively, hating how I've gone from ripping pissed to hesitant.

It's back, that feral smile he hid until this year. That side of him that makes it seem like he could lose control at any second.

"You've lived a life of privilege because I was so desperate to have you. I was too nice. Too caring. Too scared of pushing you away and blowing up my chances." His head tilts to the side. "I have you now. I don't need to be so nice anymore. I could *fucking ruin you.*"

There's something in his voice that stirs anticipation within me. This is worrying.

Because I think there's something I'm enjoying more than the men I can control and put into submission. And that's the only man who can fight back.

"If you force me to do anything with you," I rasp, "you will lose me forever."

His chilling smile sends goosebumps down my spine as he shakes his head. "Oh no. That's not my kind of thing at all."

"What's your thing?" I find myself asking the question before I can even form the thought in my mind.

"You've seen what I like, Peach. You experienced it first-hand. What is it?"

One of his hands comes to my face, his fingertips caressing my cheekbone and then the corner of my eye before he pushes a strand of hair behind my ear.

"Control," I answer, swallowing roughly.

"You learn so quickly. I'm never going to force anything on you, Peach. See, I'm going to have so much control over you, you're going to be begging for me to touch you. You're going to beg me to sink my cock deep inside you and ruin you." His fingers go to my neck, tracing a new line all the way to my collarbone.

"You're going to be so desperate, you won't only ask how high when I say jump, but also how low it is I want you to bow when you're at my feet. And, believe me"—his soft caresses turn into a hand around my throat—"after every-thing you put me through for all these years, after all the yearning to have you while you were having fun turning me down, I will make you go through every. Single. Hoop. Before I give you any sort of release."

His hand doesn't stop me from breathing, but it stops the blood flowing to my head, and the second he releases me, the lightheadedness mixes with a need he created deep in my core.

Speechless, I blink up at him, completely lost, and he taps the top of my head like I'm a puppy who just did a trick.

"Atta girl. Let's go to dinner now."

What is it?

What is it he saw, or I did, that satisfied him so much?

I'm wearing a dress, but not the dress he wanted, and he sure doesn't miss that detail once we're walking side-by-side.

"Are you color blind?" he asks as he looks down at my dress. "Because I could swear that's a mini black dress you're wearing, and not the lavender one I texted you about."

"Are you dumb?" I bounce back without hesitation. "Because I could swear you just picked me up from a bar instead of my house, so it should tell you how much I care about doing what you tell me."

I cross my arms over my chest, the cold evening making me shiver. Or maybe it's the anger. Or the excitement of still feeling my lips tingling from his claiming. The hand I can still feel around my throat. Maybe it's all of it.

His coat is on my shoulders before I can finish my thought. I'm not alone in my head; Wren is there too, reading everything like all my thoughts are breaking news, worthy of stopping his own.

"Is there a reason you went out in an outfit to catch

pneumonia?" he asks, wrapping an arm around my shoulders.

"Yes, to piss you off. So you'd have to give me your coat and freeze to death."

"Knew it," he whispers playfully.

He winks at me, smiling, and his dimples make me want to smile back. It's a conscious effort to keep my mouth in a straight line. That's until I realize where we're heading.

"Wait...why aren't we leaving the Acropolis?"

His arm tightens around me, as if making sure I won't bolt. "We were supposed to go to that tapas place you love, but someone made us miss our reservation."

I try to slow down, but his momentum forces me to keep walking. "Wait, wait. I'll call. I don't want to go to a campus restaurant."

"Is that so?" he says knowingly.

"Don't do that. I don't want to be on a date with you where all the other students can see us."

"I guess you should have thought of that before being a brat, huh?"

"I'll call them," I plead. "Drop my dad's name. They'll give us a table right away."

He shakes his head, looking ahead to show he doesn't care about what I'm saying. "The issue isn't that we can't get another table. The issue is, when you're training someone to listen to orders, you have to force them to put up with the consequences of their actions. That's the only way you'll learn."

My ears burn as my blood boils. "I'm not a fucking puppy. Stop saying you're training me."

He keeps walking as he brings his free hand to mess with my hair. His eyes are shining with arrogance.

"You're no puppy, Trouble. If anything, you're a mean,

full-grown rottweiler. But you *are* my new little pet, aren't you? So, when you misbehave, I punish you. And when you behave, you'll get a little treat." He pats the top of my head. "That's how I plan on *training* you."

I know he's exaggerating, mockery dripping from his tone, but I want to kill him, nonetheless.

"You should be careful. I could easily kill you in your sleep."

"And I would love nothing else but to see you try." His arm slides off my shoulders, and he grabs my wrist. "I imagine you'd straddle me, bring a knife to my throat. But I'd wake up just before and take hold of your wrist." He tightens his grip. "And then I'd flip you around, pin you to the bed, and—"

"When in this little fantasy do you go back to looking for my parents?"

My cold tone doesn't only bring him back to earth, but it also helps me keep sane before I let myself fantasize some more about Wren Hunter pinning me to a bed.

He scratches his throat, but his grip on my wrist doesn't relent. "I want to be discreet about it. Going further into searching for them is going to take time."

"Why?" I snap, remembering Elijah's words. "Just get everyone on it. If the Circle has access to so much, then everyone should know, and everyone should help, and then we'll find them quicker. I want to talk to them. I have *questions* for them."

My face is burning by the time I finish my rant, and Wren's eyes are on me. "Breathe."

It's not a calm query. If anything, it's a strict order. But I understand why when I let air into my lungs and realize I was in apnea.

I'm panting now, trying to catch up with my own stupidity of not knowing how to breathe.

"You're looking at this as if the Circle is our ally. They're not. They're selfish, and they'll hold everything over our heads, ready to drop the guillotine at any point. Knowledge is power, and the less the Circle knows, the better."

Is this true? Or is that an excuse? If Elijah is able to find my parents quickly with the Circle's help, why would Wren want to keep this to himself?

"Peach," he insists. "I have to go about this carefully, ask the right people. I don't want anyone, least of all my dad or Duval, to know what we truly want."

I look at him, and I should have things to say. But only one word registered. "We?"

"Yes, *we*. I'm here, in your corner, wanting nothing but for you to get the answers you so desperately need. You and I have always been a 'we,' Trouble. We're just changing the dynamics of it."

I'm losing count of the times my heart somersaults when Wren shows me how much he truly cares. Why do I like this idea so much? That feeling of safety and fulfillment is back, but I shove it down.

"Without my consent," I add, trying to surface that resentment I have toward him. It's so faint, though. Like it never even existed in the first place, and I'm just trying to force it out of me.

Because the truth is, I liked that kiss. And I like when he takes care of me. And I *love* that everyone saw how he can't keep his lips off me.

So what am I even fighting against?

"That's the fun part." He winks and finally grabs my hand rather than my wrist. "We're here."

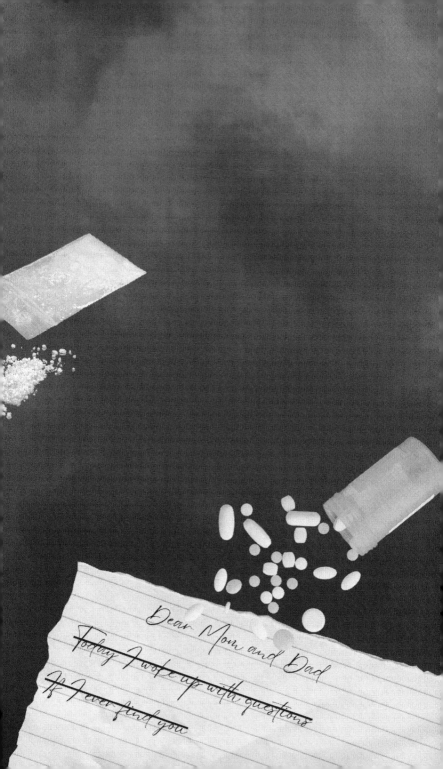

Chapter Twenty-Six

Peach

Paradise - Henry Morris

"Very funny," I say as we enter the restaurant. "Hilarious, asshole."

We get a table at the pizza place beloved by so many students on campus. They're meant to serve real Italian pizza, but they've been so Americanized that I'm not sure the concept applies anymore.

The waiter shows us to a space for two. A small, square table covered with a red checkered tablecloth and surrounded by two dark wooden chairs. Wren pulls one out for me, making sure I'm sat comfortably before taking the space across me.

I go to open the menu, but he takes it from me and places it on his side instead.

"What are you doing?" I try to grab it back, but he pulls it closer to him.

"Put your hands flat on the table, Penelope."

My heart skips a beat. A *long* beat. There's something

when he calls me by my real name that tugs in my lower stomach and sends a current all the way up my spine.

Sensing my hesitation, he insists, "I don't want to have to remind you of our deal or what it means to be my Hera every single time you refuse to listen."

That's warning enough. I press my palms to the table.

"Good. You asked me what my thing was. I'm giving you a taste of what I like *all the time*. Not just during sex or when I punished you a few days ago, and not just by text while I'm away. All. The. Time." His deep voice resonates through my entire being, shifting cells in all the right places.

"So, is that what it's like? Control? I'm not allowed to pick my own food?" I barely manage to put any edge into my voice.

"It's part of it. So is you sitting still and holding the exact position I'm telling you while I choose your food for you."

Refusing to acknowledge the heat spreading to my cheeks, I focus on what I can still control.

"I'm allergic to—"

"Shellfish. And cat hair. Not that the second matters in this case."

Running my tongue against my teeth, I narrow my eyes at him, but he ignores me, his on the menu.

The waiter comes back, and I don't dare move when Wren talks to him. I notice his eyes dropping to my cleavage as he pulls out his pad and pen.

"She'll have the pepperoni, and please, could you bring hot honey on the side. And I'll have the mortadella pizza."

Of course he knows exactly what I like.

The waiter's eyes come back to the exact point where my dress meets my boobs.

"Eyes up here, buddy." Wren's voice is so glacial, I

shiver. "We wouldn't want them out of their sockets by the end of the night, would we?"

His gaze drops to his pad, and he scratches his throat. "Uh, any...any drinks?"

"Water's fine," Wren concludes before handing him the menus. That's unlike him. He loves sodas. It's one of the only things that he knows is terrible for him and yet he keeps having them.

When he looks back at me, there's an excitement like I've never seen before in his eyes. A satisfied smile pulls at the corner of his mouth.

"You didn't move."

I have nothing to say. Because it wasn't that hard not to move. In fact, I started to feel myself relax before he talked to me again. I didn't have to put a man back in his place for his wandering eyes. Wren did it for me. And it weirdly felt really good.

The waiter comes back with the glasses and leaves them quickly before he can get told off again. Wren pours me a glass and puts it in front of me.

"Drink."

I do, and it's refreshing after the beers I had.

"I said no more drugs, Peach," he finally says. I get the *water only* now.

"I—" I clear my throat, struggling to talk. "I didn't take drugs. I promise."

"Your pupils are telling me otherwise."

"I didn't take drugs, Wren. I feel fine. I had two beers."

He looks deeply into my eyes. "You better not be lying to me."

"I'm not," I defend. "I'm not an addict. Why would I lie about drugs?"

He doesn't answer that question, and it's clear it's because he disagrees. He believes I'm an addict.

"Are you enjoying it?" he asks with sincere curiosity, his gorgeous blue eyes attempting to dig the truth out of mine. "Being told what to do?"

"I hate it," I lie.

He licks his lips, seeing right through me. "Take off your underwear."

My face drops so fast I probably look like I'm having a stroke. I certainly feel like I am.

"Are you out of your mind, Wren Hunter?"

He attempts to wipe the smile forming on his face, but it comes back tenfold. "It's funny, because I hate my last name. But it turns me on when you call me by my full name."

"Shut up," I snarl. "I'm not—"

His smile fades. "Do as you're told."

And we're back to the exact same problem. I'm his Hera, and we have a deal.

Narrowing my eyes at him, I look around. We're strategically placed, in some sort of alcove. My back is to the wall, his big body hiding most of our table while his back is to the rest of the room. And there's the tablecloth.

No one is going to see anything.

Plus, there's that voice in the back of my mind. The eagerness that screams at me to keep discovering the other side of what I usually do. For as long as I could, I've used men in bed. I put them on their knees, and I made them treat me like their queen. But it always felt like I was putting on a show.

There's something about discovering what happens when I let Wren take over. I want to let go, and I don't have a choice but to do exactly that with him.

I slip a hand under my dress, hooking my thumb in the

elastic band of my black thong, and pull until it's sliding down. Adjusting myself on the seat, I pull farther down, until it's around my ankles.

Once it's off, I feel Wren's hand under the table.

"Give it to me."

"You're a perv, I hope you know that."

"Only for you, and I love it. Sit back."

I do as I'm told. The exchange is so quick, I barely feel like it's happening.

"Good. Now I want you to take your napkin and sit on it. Don't unfold it."

I pause for so long, I don't think my brain is functioning anymore.

"What?" I finally drop.

"You heard me."

He hands me the checkered cloth napkin, and I blink at it for a few seconds.

"Sit on it."

I swallow thickly, my heart racing as I grab it. I lift my ass so I can put the fabric under me and sit back down on it.

"There you go," he purrs. "I like the flush on your cheeks when you do what you're told. It's very sexy."

Does he have to point out every single thing he likes or dislikes? It's unnerving.

I don't get to retort anything, with the waiter now back with our pizzas. He puts everything in front of us and leaves again, without a look at me this time.

Wren makes a point to stare at me as he unfolds his napkin on his lap.

"Don't worry. I'll share mine, should you need it."

I don't say anything, deciding to focus on my food instead. I reach for the sauce cup with honey in it, but he snatches it a split second before I get it.

Shaking his head, he tuts. "Control, remember? Keep your hands on your lap until I tell you that you can eat."

"Are you for real?" I scoff.

"I want your brain off when you're with me, Trouble," he explains calmly. "Only then can I really have fun with you."

He pours the honey on my pizza, and I salivate. I love a mix of sweet and savory, and hot honey on pepperoni is a perfect combination. But I don't think that's what is making me salivate. It's purely watching his huge hand holding the small cup. A bit of honey drips on his finger. After putting the container down, he licks the side of his finger, and I practically choke on my own breath.

What. Is. Wrong. With. Me.

He offers me a small smile and says softly, "Eat."

I only hesitate for a split second this time, and all I can think about is the fact that every time he orders something new, it takes me less time to execute. And that the quicker I do what I'm told, the more turned on I get.

I take a shaky breath, barely able to take a bite of my pizza. The salty pepperoni hits me first, followed by the sweetness and kick of the spicy honey, and I practically moan as I chew it.

"Alright," he says as he takes a huge bite of his slice. He takes his time to chew and swallow, dabs the corner of his mouth, and nods at me.

"Tonight, you can ask me anything you want about"—he looks around to make sure no one is close enough to hear —"the Circle. But only tonight. You won't be involved in anything. I'll give you updates on your parents whenever I decide. And you will *never* come to the temple unless it's an official event that requires Shadows to bring their Heras. Other than that, I don't want you to approach the Circle, and especially not the Shadows. Is that clear?"

I swallow, dig my eyes into his, and say, "I'll do whatever the fuck I want is what I think."

"Sure. I don't care. You're my Hera now, and you can't get rid of me. The Circle would be the ones to punish you for that, and you've had a taste of what they're capable of. So if you're not a good girl, I guess all that'll happen is..." He tilts his head to the side. "...Oh, I know. I won't look for your progenitors anymore."

"You didn't used to be such an asshole, you know?"

"I used to think being nice to you was the way to your heart. Then I realized you were too stubborn to ever give in to our attraction. I'm trying a different technique. You like a challenge, and so do I. I think that's what's going to work for us."

Our staring contest only lasts long enough for my biggest insecurities to resurface, tickle my throat, and press against the back of my eyes: the empty hole in my heart that was created when I was abandoned, and that keeps getting bigger every day.

"We keep circling back to the same thing, so let me help you here." He puts his hand on mine on the table. "If I have to mention our deal again, it's over."

My stomach squeezes so hard the pizza threatens to come back up.

"What?" One word, but my desperation is loud.

"If you fight back again, badly enough that I have to remind you about our deal and why you accepted it, then it is off. You won't be able to leave me, but you won't find your parents either. Now, to be clear, you accepted being my Hera in exchange for my help. Being my Hera includes obeying me without questioning it."

"Wren..." I rasp. "I need time."

"And I will take it easy on you. But I need to see you try.

And so far, you've barely tried. I told you not to see Elijah, and I told you no drugs."

"I didn't—"

"You will behave, Peach. Is that clear?"

I look at anything but his face. I can't process the soft tone, the threatening words, and the lust in his eyes. They don't go well together.

"Got it," I whisper.

"Are you sure?" he insists.

"I'm not fucking stu—" I cut myself off, pinching my lips and closing my eyes to calm down. "I'm sure."

"Good. You'll see. It's hard at first, but you'll get the hang of it. Start from the principle that my word is law. Everything will be easier after that."

I nod, blinking away the tears I refuse to show him.

When I lift my hand to grab the carafe of water on the table, he shakes his head.

"Let me." He pours me more water as he keeps talking, his beautiful eyes focused on my glass. "Before you ask anything, I have one for you. It's been going around in my head since the initiations, and with being away, and then... you not feeling well, I never got to ask."

I nod again, my eyes stuck on the glass as he keeps it to himself.

"Who invited you to the initiations? I've been asking people at the temple and no one is giving me an answer. So, either they don't know, or they're refusing to tell me the truth."

My gaze snaps to his, and the anxiety comes back tenfold, beating in my ears. "It wasn't you?"

How can he keep such a blank face? How am I meant to understand what's the truth?

"It wasn't me. I offered you forever, and you declined it.

334

I wasn't going to invite you. Obviously, since you were there, the result is different than what I anticipated. But we have an issue with whoever *did* invite you. So..." His voice is steady, but I'm starting to notice the clench in his jaw. "What was the name on the invite?"

There's a part of me that's scared to tell him. There's no other way to put this; Wren is a dangerous serial killer who doesn't even remember when he murders someone. Am I signing someone's death sentence by telling him?

But then again...whoever that was, they fucked up my life. Signed *my* death sentence.

"Hyperion."

He can't keep a straight face now, his eyebrows pushed together by the anger betraying him.

"What?" I ask. "Who's that?"

He massages his temple with one hand, pressing against the side of his head. "My dad," he finally says.

"Your dad?" I squeak. And a moment from the labyrinth comes back to me. "Wait. He said he had plans for me. Oh my god."

"He what?"

My chest tightens, and I shake my head, trying to keep myself sane. "In the maze, he almost caught me, but he let me go because he said he had plans for me."

When Wren doesn't say anything for a few seconds, the fear increases.

"Should I be worried?" I'm already past worried.

He shakes his head, but I can't relax now.

"Is that a no? How can you be so sure? What does your dad want with me?"

Taking a deep breath, he runs a hand across his face and smiles softly at me.

"I don't know what he wants with you. But if there's one

thing I am sure of, and that's from experience, it's that anyone who becomes a threat to you shortens their lifespan significantly. *That's* how I know you've got nothing to worry about. Stay away from my dad. That's general advice, anyway. But don't worry about him. I'll find out what he wants. Nothing happens to you on my watch, Trouble, so take a breath."

I nod numbly, and he finally gives me the glass of water. Yeah, I need that.

"So, your questions."

"Uh..." I take the glass, bringing it to my lips so I can swallow the sand in my throat.

It's hard to think straight now that more pieces have been added to the puzzle of my new life. But this is my chance, and I have to focus on anything I can get out of him.

"The Circle. You mentioned you had to do a job for them. What do you..." I bite the inside of my lip, trying to take my time and calm my nervous system. "What do you do for them?"

He stays silent for this, refusing to put it into words, yet also refusing to keep the secret from me. Instead, he drags the side of his finger across his neck. I feel my blood draining from my face, even though I know now what he's capable of.

Still, my reflex is to pull my chair away, but he cuts off my movement with a hard tone.

"Keep your chair exactly where it is." He nods when I stop my momentum. "Good girl. Are you scared?"

"I don't know." It slips from my lips quickly, but barely audibly.

"It's okay not to know. It's a lot. But I want to make it clear again that I would never hurt you. Keep eating. You need the energy."

Before I do, I ask, "Is that why they sent you away? You just travel around, committing murders?"

He nods.

"How often will that happen?"

"Too often."

My head is swimming. He's too calm about this, making my heartbeat rise to the point my legs shake under the table. "How many times has it been since you initiated? When... when was the last time?"

"Three. And this afternoon. Let's stop with those questions. It's making you panic. Keep eating."

God, he sounds like those psychopaths who are interviewed from prison in true crime shows. I take another slice, and he eats at the same time as me, in silence while I try to gather my thoughts.

When I stop, he stops too.

Another gulp of water, and I'm back.

"Does every Shadow have a job for the Circle?"

This answer is easier to listen to.

"Yes. Most of us are legacies, so the Circle has known us since we were kids. They know our strengths and weaknesses, and they decide in advance what they want us for. Not every legacy is offered to initiate. They pick who they need to keep the society as powerful as it can be without burdening themselves with useless people. Not everyone *has to* initiate if they're offered to, but it's strongly encouraged."

"And they chose you because you *snap*, right? That's useful to them."

"Where did you hear the word 'snap' when it comes to me?" He asks the question in a way that tells me he knows the answer. It's more of an encouraging tone to tell him the truth, rather than an inquiry.

337

"You, once. But also, your dad, in Duval's office. He kept asking if you were going to snap. And Elijah, he said you were dangerous when you snapped."

"Huh." He puts an elbow on the table, the pad of his thumb resting just under his chin and his index finger caressing his upper lip. He stays in his thoughts, keeping me in limbo, letting me wonder if he has any control over being the grim reaper.

Finally coming back to me, he says, "I won't get into what happens when I *snap*." He says the word with deep disgust, cracking his neck right after. "You know enough. That I struggle to remember, and that I need to write their names down so I do—"

"And the Scrabble tiles. What are those for?"

He smiles, but he doesn't tell me what I want to hear. "I don't feel like sharing any more. But know that's why the Circle wanted me. To kill. I'm only good for one thing when it comes to them."

And he believes that. I can see it.

"You're good at so many things," I correct him. "Why would you join the Circle and reduce yourself to a...killer?" I whisper the last word, even though there isn't any chance of anyone hearing me.

Sure of himself, his shoulders square, and he takes a sip of his water, keeping a softness to his voice that he only saves for me.

"I'm only good at many things because I wanted to convince myself I was more than what the Circle wanted me to be. But it turns out, Trouble, that there's nothing I'm better at than killing without a second thought."

The exchange accelerates because I refuse to believe it. Wren is *perfect* in every discipline. He's more than a mindless killer.

"But why... Why did you join them? You could have just—"

"I didn't have a choice."

"What do you mean by that?"

He sighs. "No more questions about why I joined, about me snapping, or why, or what happens when I do it."

"So, you being forced into the Circle is related to something you did when you snapped."

He's speechless, his jaw slack, when he realizes how well I can read him. How quickly I catch up with his thoughts. The same way he does with me. There's something about us, something stronger than friendship, that has always linked our souls.

"Next question."

"Our relationship is never going to be fair anymore, is it? If you decide everything, even the small freedoms you give me will always feel controlled."

"Bingo."

"Fine. What does Elijah do?"

"Oh, Penelope." He shakes his head. His nostrils flare as his jaw tightens, and I understand I shouldn't have mentioned his brother. It's detestable that Wren looks so handsome when he gets angry. All I want to do is rub my thumb between his eyebrows. "What do you want from me? To see how mean I can get?"

My heart skips a beat, and my pussy wakes up. The bitch wants to play, and it wants to play with the mean side of Wren Hunter. The napkin between my thighs is suddenly *so* present, its material feeling close to my skin as I grow wetter.

"It's a genuine question," I defend, trying to focus on the conversation, rather than how he makes me feel.

"I'm not at liberty to share that. Rules are rules, and only

339

a Shadow can decide if they want to share their role. What I'll tell you, though, is that you're going to stay away from him from now on, and do not disobey me on that again."

"He and I have been friends for almost as long as you and me. It's not that easy to just *stop* being friends."

"Relationships change over time. Look at us. We used to be best friends, and now you belong to me. Well, you used to be friends with Elijah. Now you'll be nothing."

"It's not fair."

He takes a bite of his food, drinks some water, and finally says, "I have a feeling you're going to think a lot of things aren't fair moving forward. I'm afraid you're just going to have to learn to live with that feeling until you get used to stop thinking and instead simply do what I tell you."

I rip a bite out of a new slice of pizza. My anger is palpable, but I turn it to my food instead of him. It's the only way I won't get in trouble. I chew angrily, and it makes him chuckle like I'm some sort of show.

"Spread your legs a little. Not too much."

I gulp down my bite, the pepperoni nearly going down the wrong tube.

She died eating what she loved, killed because her body couldn't handle anger and lust simultaneously.

I uncross my legs, spread them slightly, and he checks I've done it by extending one leg between mine. He taps his knee to my inner right thigh, then the left, checking the distance.

"Good girl."

"I will puke if you keep using that on me."

Cocking an eyebrow, he answers casually. "Well, I do prefer using 'good little slut,' but I had a feeling it would be moving too quickly for you."

That takes my breath away. Worse, my muscles

contract. I feel more wetness pooling between my legs as my lower belly tightens. My legs automatically try to close, partly to uselessly attempt to stop myself from dampening the napkin, but mostly to feel pressure on my clit.

He feels my movement, and a carnal smile spreads on his face as he relaxes back in his chair.

"Tsk, tsk." His ankle hits the side of my right calf, and he pushes my legs back open. "Keep them open."

"Wren." My exhale is deep, needy, and he catches that. I see it in the way his eyes darken. The blue is almost entirely swallowed by the black of his pupils.

"I'm looking forward to you opening your legs wide for me while you beg, Trouble. I'm counting the days until you're lying down and planting your palms on your knees to spread them open for me while whining because you can't wait anymore."

He tilts his head to the side as my breathing accelerates. "I know you're not the most patient girl, but you're going to be so...*so* patient for me. Aren't you?"

I'm getting so wet the napkin must be soaked. My entire body is hotter than the sun, and I need a bucket of ice water to be dropped on me so I can think straight again.

As I shift in my seat, his smile widens.

"Put your hands flat on the table." I've barely done it as his voice hardens. "I said *flat*, Penelope."

My eyes drop, and I notice my fists are tightly closed. So, I try again, flattening my hands.

"Atta girl, straighten your spine."

My shallow breath passes through my parted lips as I do what I'm told, but I feel like I'm suffocating. I'm going to burst into flames any second now. The new position pushes my chest forward, and it makes my panting obvious, my boobs moving up and down too quickly for it to look natural.

Still smiling, Wren bites his lower lip, and I barely catch the whimper that wants to force its way out of my mouth. He looks *irresistible*. I signed a deal with the devil, and he loves playing with his new toy.

"I'll ask again," he says in a deeper raspy voice that translates his own lust. "Do you enjoy being told what to do? Do you enjoy being controlled, Peach?"

I can't talk, not trusting my own voice. I don't trust my entire body. All I do is shake my head, lying shamelessly like the stubborn girl he always accuses me of being.

"I see." He nods, and I'm surprised by his acceptance of my response. Is something wrong with him? "You should go use the bathroom. I'll settle the bill."

I don't question anything. I *need* to run to the bathroom to do something about the wetness now coating my inner thighs.

I wince when I attempt to get up, feeling like I'm going to cry from the fact that I'm so wet the fabric of the napkin is sticking to my skin. I hover awkwardly over my seat, discreetly sliding my hand between my legs to dislodge it.

Wren's eyes don't leave me, following my every movement knowingly. My ears are burning by the time I reach the bathroom, and I release a much-needed exhale. I check the two stalls. No one's here, and I release a heavy breath as I arrange my hair, checking myself in the mirror. I then press my palms on either side of the sink. My eyes are shining, my cheeks red against my porcelain skin, but I don't have time to process a single thought when the door opens, and Wren appears behind me.

I watch my own eyes widening in the mirror, and I move to turn around, but he's quicker.

"Don't move. Keep your hands exactly where they are."

"Give me a break," I plead. "I need a minute from you."

"You'll get it. As soon as you learn not to lie to me."

"What—"

"Open your mouth, Penelope baby."

There's a long pause as my eyes dart to what he's holding in his right hand. The napkin.

My lips part but only to allow me to breathe.

"Wren..."

"Keep doing what you're told."

I keep my eyes on his through the mirror as I slowly open my mouth. It feels like it's taking me hours, my body suffering waves of heat as I do so. It's almost as wide as I can reach when he says, "That'll do."

He settles behind me, gathers my hair with one hand, and wraps it twice around his fist. My head pulls back, and I lower my eyes to keep my gaze on him.

Slowly, without an ounce of violence, he brings the napkin to my mouth. I close my eyes, unable to take the embarrassment of what's coming.

He pushes the damp fabric into my mouth, not too far, but far enough for my own taste to spread on my tongue.

"Bite," he growls in my ear, and I've gone too far to turn back, so I do exactly that. "Open your eyes."

I don't know the people facing me. Not the flushed woman held by her hair, and not the stern man behind her, holding her prisoner, using nothing but a hand and her own pleasure.

"Tell me, does this taste like you hate when I control you?"

I barely have enough movement to shake my head, but I give him what he wants. The truth. Still, it's not enough.

"Say it."

343

"No," I mumble behind the cloth in my mouth.

He reaches his hand across my hip, down my leg. And so, *so* slowly, back under my dress. I moan when he cups my pussy. The delicate gesture makes me combust inside. My thoughts turn to ashes and my body takes over. I push against his hand, but he doesn't move it. With the pressure of his palm, my lips are sealed shut, and I can't get any friction on my clit. I know I'm wetting his fingers, and I don't care in the slightest. I need more, and I need it now.

Pulling his hand away, he laughs softly at my desperate whimper being muffled by the napkin.

"Look at me."

My eyes are stuck on his when he pushes his middle and ring fingers into his mouth, tasting me.

"Fuck," he growls. "I hate you a little for depriving me of this for so long."

The back of my head is fully resting on his chest now, and he looks down at me with his head above mine, making sure to drive his point as deep into my brain as he can. I feel like I'm floating, my eyes hooded and my breaths slow and steady now. I've never been so turned on in my life. But there's no pride or performance, no point to make. No, this is pure lust, and I'm incapable of controlling it. Any movement or word pulls at my soul, at the very base of what makes me human, and my reactions are purely instinctive.

"Now bend over."

I've completely lost myself, and when he pushes behind my head, I bring my torso to the sink, my hands going to either side of it.

He's quick to undo his jeans, and I moan the second his cock presses at my entrance. He enters me ever-so-slowly, lighting up every single one of my nerve endings in the process.

"Listen," he murmurs, forcing me to focus on his voice. "I want you to tell me when you're about to come. I want to learn what you feel like when you're on the brink of falling. Do you understand?"

I feel his hard dick retreating gradually, tearing a whimper out of my trembling lungs.

I nod, and he pulls at my hair a little harder. "Try 'yes, sir.' Just for me."

His words come with a new push forward, giving me back pleasure.

"Y-yes," I pant behind the cloth. "Yes, sir."

And that only makes me wetter. He fucks me languidly, deeply, in no rush whatsoever. As if we're not in a public place. As if this isn't the sweetest form of torture that ever existed. If I try to push back, he pulls at my hair and adds a harsh "stay still" that feels like a slap to the face.

I need his mercy, and I need it now. But every micro-movement coming from me, every whimper that begs for more falls onto deaf ears.

"You're doing really well, Trouble. Just keep taking me." He thrusts a little harsher, and my entire body threatens to crumble to the floor.

Zaps of electricity build every time he slides back in, sharpening my need.

"Fuck," I moan as I clench around him. "I'm gonna— I'm gonna come..."

"Are you sure?" he purrs. "Are you close?"

"Yes!" I'm struggling to stay still, my body *begging me* to give it what it needs.

He pulls back, and my breathing stops when I don't feel him pushing back in.

I try to lift up, but a simple *no* keeps me in place.

"Stay like this. Look at me." My eyes do exactly that, looking at him through the mirror.

"Beg me, Penelope."

I don't care what I look like. I don't even inhale to talk. "Please."

His smirk shouldn't look so hot, but I'm desperate, and I'll eat any fucking crumb he feeds me.

He snatches the napkin out of my mouth. "Try again. Spread your legs this time. Show me your beautiful cunt. I want to see how desperate you are."

I catch the way he's stroking his dick behind me, and I curve my back, spreading my legs farther.

"Please, Wren," I whimper. "I need you."

His hand accelerates, and panic takes hold of me as my core aches and pulses to be filled again. He's going to make himself come.

"Please, please. I need you inside me. Fuck."

"Is this pretty pussy desperate?"

"Yes... Please, sir. Please, will you make me come?"

My last words do it for him.

"No," he growls.

I feel his cum spilling on my ass as he throws his head back, and my own falls forward, ready to cry.

Pulling my dress lower, he makes sure it doesn't wipe his fucking masterpiece as he puts it back into place.

There's a beat when all that can be heard is my pathetic panting. I'm twisted. Because there's a fucked-up part of me that's even more turned on by the fact that he didn't let me come.

He helps me straighten up, his hand still in my hair, and his mouth is against my ear in the next beat.

"Did you learn your lesson about not lying to me, Trouble?"

"Yes," I breathe out. I sound like I'm in pain. And I am. I need to come so badly.

"Good." He tugs my head farther back. "Little." And again, pulling a moan out of me. "Slut."

Slowly, he releases my hair, and my knees buckle when I stand straight again, so he catches me by the waist.

"Take a deep breath. Come back slowly," he murmurs in my ear.

I still feel pleasure zapping through me, but my head also feels like it's underwater, and I struggle to formulate a sentence.

"Wh-what's happening?" I mumble.

"Nothing bad, don't worry." He caresses my hair, kisses the side of my face, and I slowly feel myself come back, but the need deep inside me is left unsated. "You're just feeling a little bit of a sub-drop."

With two palms on the side of my head, he gives me a chaste kiss on the lips. When he pulls back, his eyes dig into mine.

"There she is." Brushing my cheeks with his thumbs, he says, "Let's get you home. I think that was enough for one night."

He holds my hand, and I try to take a step, but my knees buckle again.

"Wren..." My tongue feels heavy in my mouth. "Something's wrong. I...I don't feel good."

All I remember is him asking me to look into his eyes, and I do try, but my body doesn't feel like mine anymore. The rest is a complete blackout.

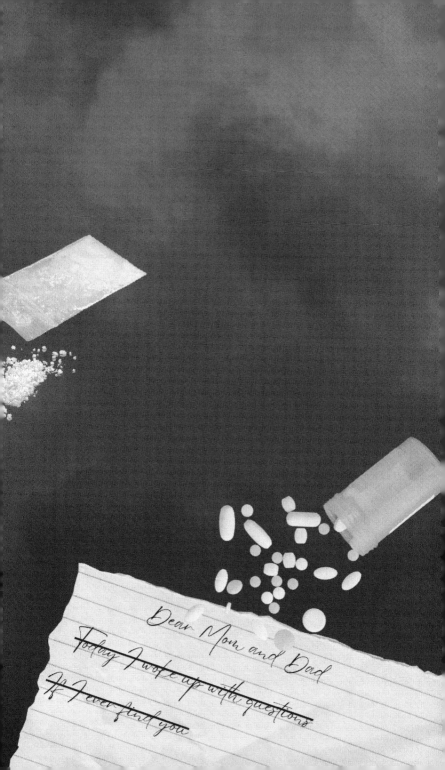

Chapter Twenty-Seven

Peach

Yours - Conan Gray

My head pounds. My mind is slow. My eyes are heavy.

"Fuck," I groan as I turn onto my side.

My heart palpitates from how unwell I still feel.

Another day waking up in sheets that smell like my best friend. I inhale a deep breath because it's the only good news right now.

"No drugs, huh?"

I startle at Wren's clear voice resonating from somewhere beside me. I finally open my eyes to see him standing right by the bed, already in his SFU uniform, his arms crossed over his chest. His face is tense, jaw clenching, and the rest of his body is stiff as a board. His shoulders are flexing so hard I wonder how they haven't ripped through his shirt yet.

Sitting up, I place my feet flat on the floor to face him. My head is hurting badly enough that my vision blurs for a few seconds.

"I didn't—" I croak, but he's too mad to let me speak.

"If you weren't feeling like shit, I'd put you on your front, tie your hands behind your back, and spank you until your ass is raw."

I gulp as that same feeling of excitement and fear courses through me again. Except today, it's making me feel sick.

"You lied to me."

"I didn't lie to you," I try again, frustrated. "I didn't take anything."

He leans forward until his eyes are right in front of mine. "I knew your pupils were dilated during dinner. I don't know why I believed you."

"But—"

"Shower. You're not missing classes because you can't control yourself."

He rips the covers away, and I shiver. Another wave of sickness washes over me as the cold and bad hangover mix. I stand up in a rush, running to the bathroom before emptying whatever is left from last night's dinner.

I wash my face, brush my teeth, and the second I look back into the mirror, I notice Wren leaning on the bathroom door frame. The scowl on his face is there to stay, and his arms are still crossed, shoulders tensed. I've always taken our arguments as a challenge, but this feels different. My gut is twisted at the idea of him being disappointed with me.

"Wren," I huff, desperate to make things right. I hate that look on his face, hate that it's aimed at me. "Please, can you at least listen to me?"

"So you can lie some more?" He shakes his head. "You're my Hera, Peach. Lying to your Shadow gets some women killed within the Circle."

My heart drops, and I remember his words from yesterday about him canceling our deal. I flip around so quickly I have to put a hand on the sink to stay standing.

"Wait, wait," I blurt out in a panic. "Don't throw our deal away. I heard your warning. I'm not fighting back. I'm not."

"See, my problem is that I'm too naïve when it comes to you. I'm blindly in love, wanting to believe anything that makes me hope we're heading toward something great, something I've yearned for my entire life. But you..." He rubs a hand over his face, clearly looking for the right thing to say. "You'll do *anything* to keep me at a distance."

He stays silent, biting his inner cheek. I see it in the dent it makes against his perfect skin. His square jaw has never seemed so tense.

I take a step toward him, but a sharp shake of his head makes me freeze.

"You're in love with me?" I croak, my vocal cords hurting from the acid that went up my throat.

It's both his hands that go to his face this time, rubbing like a man losing hope in being understood.

"God, Peach," he groans, the words swallowed by his palms against his mouth. He looks up. "How? How can you not know that?"

"You never said it," I whisper as my stomach swoops. "That's how."

"No," he says tightly. "You never *heard it*, that's the difference. Because how could someone who believes so strongly, they're not deserving of love ever see how desperately in love with you I am. For heaven's sake, I've followed you around my entire life. I'm a lost puppy, always eagerly waiting for a drop of your attention."

"You're my best friend, of course you're around," I defend.

He throws his head back in exasperation.

"Stop," he huffs. "Fuck. Just stop. Stop ignoring what has always been there. You're special. You're my favorite. You've *always* been my favorite. Just spend a second with your own thoughts for once and think of the differences I've always made between you, and Alex and Ella. I don't take care of them. I don't let them sleep in my bed when they take too many drugs and drink too much. I don't look for them when I walk into a room. They're not the first people I call to talk to about something. I don't text them to make sure they're not exhausting themselves with work. Shit, I didn't *force them* to be my Hera."

He takes a step toward me, but he doesn't touch me. His words though...they pierce through my heart.

"You want to ignore the signs? The proofs? Be my guest, but don't deny my love for you. *Never* deny my love for you," he says through clenched teeth.

"Because there has never been anyone else in my heart but you, Peach. You take all the space in there with your attitude and sassy mouth. You left no one else a chance because no one has your eyes full of challenge, your soft hair, your perfect skin. No one has two crooked lower canines like you, three freckles that make an equilateral triangle on their right shoulder. No one makes my heart *beat*. And I don't mean they make my heart skip a beat, or make my heart palpitate. I mean that when I'm not around you, I don't feel my fucking pulse, do you understand that? I feel dead unless I can hear your voice that's always a little too loud and opinionated, unless I can see that little vein on your forehead when someone angers you."

I can't breathe. Fuck. I can't breathe. My heartbeat is racing, the room swimming.

"I'm crazy when it comes to you. But I accepted that a

long time ago. Because why wouldn't I be crazy? When you've been through one-sided love for so long, no wonder you start breaking into their fucking room at night and killing for them. You shove Scrabble tiles down people's throat when they hurt your obsession. I.L.U. I love you. Because *fuck*, I love you."

Breathe, Penelope. Breathe. Breathe. Breathe.

I'm panting, but he's worse. His face is red from the long speech. And I don't think I can take a breath until he does the same.

"And you," he finally says. "You lie. To me and to yourself. Because you're an addict. A functioning addict, so well done. But those fucking pills, and coke, and alcohol, it will always come before anyone else in your life."

As I blink, tears fall from my eyelashes onto my cheeks.

"No," I try to say, but my throat is so tight it comes as a squeak. "No, Wren, please, I didn't mean to lie. I don't remember. You have to believe me."

The beautiful blue in his eyes has never looked so mournful.

"Maybe I-I did take something. Maybe I had more beers than I thought. I don't know. Just, please don't be mad at me."

I try to grab his hand, but he steps back. It's so clear to me, clearer than anything else in my life, that Wren has put up with so much when it comes to me, that it would kill me to lose him. I can't.

He chuckles sadly. "The most heartbreaking thing is that I'm *not* mad at you. I can't be. I try to find your flaws and sear them into my brain. I try to hate them and you. I try to tell myself that you've hurt me enough times that I must be angry enough to fucking leave you behind. But I can't. Just like no matter what you do, our deal won't be off, because I'm not looking for your parents to hold something over you. I'm doing it because I'm full of hope that maybe, *maybe* then you'll finally be whole and happy and understand that being abandoned doesn't. Fucking. Define. How worthy of love you are. And maybe...maybe once you learn that you're worthy of love, you'll be able to accept mine."

He runs his tongue across his teeth. He's so full of sorrow it crashes into me in unstoppable waves.

"So no, I'm not mad at you, Peach. But fuck am I disappointed and...and *sad*."

The truth of such a simple, common word rips through my entire chest. It's a massacre. Painful and deadly, leaving me with internal bleeding.

"Because you're mine. You're my Hera. You'll always be by my side, willingly or not. But me? I'm not yours. And I might never be yours." He swallows thickly, his words barely audible as his eyes shine with unshed tears. "And that hurts."

He's right. It does hurt.

I look at Xi wrapping a hand around Alex's face as he pulls her in for a kiss and toss my head back, rolling my eyes. I've barely calmed down from what happened this morning with Wren, and these two are reminding me of how delicious it feels to have someone holding you possessively. Something that Wren would do if I hadn't fucked it up so badly.

It wasn't the first time in my life that he had a go at me about the kind of states I put myself in. More than once, he's lectured me about not hanging out with my sorority sisters. It's the role I've always allowed him to have. He keeps me in line with his brand of strictness, and that worked in our friendship.

It threatens my sanity in our new dynamic.

Especially when it comes with knowing he does it out of pure love for me.

"Xi," I groan. "Is it me, or are you on this campus *a lot?*"

"Peach," Alex tells me off quickly. "You can't say things like that. It's rude." We're all sitting on a bench in the middle of the Acropolis, cold, but enjoying a sunny fall day while we eat our lunch.

"What? I love him," I add. "I'm just saying, you know, he's not a student. This is basically trespassing."

Xi's face stays impassive as he turns to me. "Yeah, because I've always cared a lot about respecting the law."

"Ooh, you're so bad," I mock.

"Well, he did set a car on fire because someone bothered me once," Alex mumbles to herself.

"Yeah, so what? I've set a car on fire once. You didn't fall in love with me afterward, for all I know."

"You did it because that man had parked in a disabled spot," she explains. "Not for me."

"Yeah, whatever."

I turn to look the other way on the bench, only to find Chris's arm wrapped around Ella's shoulders as they murmur in each other's ears and start giggling like two lovesick teenagers.

Why did I sit between two couples? All this does is remind me that I might have blown my chances with the only man I've ever felt strongly about.

For fuck's sake, even in my own thoughts, I refuse to use *being in love* as a term when it comes to Wren. The vulnerability it would come with could tear me to pieces.

"Alright," I declare as I stand up. "That's enough PDA

for me for the day. Actually, for the week." Throwing away the paper bag that had my burger in it, I pick up my books I had left in the grass.

"You didn't seem to mind PDA when this happened." Alex laughs as she shows me the last Hermes post again.

I've seen this shit too many times. Someone took a picture of Wren kissing me at the bar. Elijah is in the background, looking so distraught, everyone is having the time of their lives tearing him apart in the comments.

Hermes only wrote one sentence.

She gave in to one Hunter brother. But the other is not giving up.

#threesomeincoming #Wren1Elijah0 #WrenHunterisFI-NALLYtakingabiteofthePeach

I huff. "Alex. You're my friend, and I say we are not talking to Wren at the moment."

I might be starting to vaguely put names on my feelings for him, but I'm not going to pretend to forgive him for not keeping his word about showing everyone else we're together.

We're not together, anyway. This was *forced*. I never agreed to being with him out of my own free will.

Except, I want to be with him.

But that's beside the point.

"You're both my friends, and I will keep being Wren's friend," Alex assures me. "Especially if you won't tell me why I shouldn't be talking to him. And you didn't look like you minded that kiss. I'm just saying."

"I minded," I snap. "I minded a lot. You're *my* friend," I repeat, pointing at myself. "Mine."

"Fucking hell, she's possessive," Xi comments.

"You're one to talk." I glare at him before I turn my back to them. "I'm off to cheer practice."

"But practice starts in half an hour," Ella calls out.

"Didn't you hear the part where I said I was done with PDA? And I have to see Coach Gomez so we can draw the rally girls."

"I'm so glad I didn't participate in that," Ella mumbles.

I wonder if she even had a choice on whether she could participate or not. She's Chris's Hera after all, and their dynamic must be similar to the one I now have with Wren.

"Yeah, sure," I conclude as I start making my way to the sports complex.

It's a ten-minute walk of absolute disaster in my head. How am I ever going to think straight again when I know Wren Hunter is in love with me?

Why the hell is he even in love with me? He's clearly hurting from it.

Making a deal with him was the tip of the iceberg. He admitted to stalking me, breaking into my house at night. He's been waiting for this forever. He's *murdered* people. And the only thing I manage to focus on is that someone out there is in love with me. My best friend is in love with me.

I make my way through the hallways, drop my bag and books in the women's locker room, and get changed in my cheer uniform. Checking my phone again, I read the messages I sent to Wren while I was in class. I asked him how he is. I apologized for *accidentally* lying about how much I drank last night. I justified myself, telling him I felt fine at dinner and didn't realize how drunk I was. But the truth is, I don't even remember us leaving the bathroom of the restaurant and going home. It's by reading the text again that I realize how pathetic I sound. Like a real addict. No wonder he didn't reply. It's been years I've tried to ignore the thoughts in my head by using substances. So I don't have to deal with vulnerability and the things that hurt me. I smoke, I drink, I snort, and I write letters to my biological parents to tell them that it's all their fault.

I'm pathetic.

I'm about to enter Gomez's office, when Wren comes out of it.

My heart squeezes, my brain going numb. It's only been a few hours, but I missed him.

He's not in his full lacrosse kit yet, only wearing his jersey and a pair of gray sweatpants that leave absolutely nothing to the imagination. I'm practically salivating when he calls my name.

"Peach, you should really try to hide how badly you want me. You're so obvious it makes it hard for me to resist you."

He tries to make it sound lighthearted, like the same advances he's always thrown my way, but he's angry. I can hear it. I know him. This isn't the same and it makes my chest heavy.

"You didn't answer any of my texts?" Why am I making it sound like a question. It's a fact.

"I was in class," he explains. His lips pinch, and he rolls them inwardly as he thinks. "Trying to focus on one thing at a time so I can keep you out of my mind."

"Wren," I murmur desperately, every feeling I have for him rushing to the surface. "I don't want to lose you because I've always been too stubborn to see how much you mean to me."

Refusing to hear me, he looks away. "You won't lose me. We were promised to each other in front of the Circle.

You're stuck with me forever. A fact you were pretty angry about until recently."

Swallowing my nerves, I put a hand on his cheek, forcing him to look back at me. "You know that's not what I meant. You. I don't want to lose *you*. I don't want to be with you as your Hera. I want to be with you as the girl who finally opened her eyes to the kind of relationship we've always had. I know I'm stubborn, but if there is one person who's always made me feel safe enough to be vulnerable, it's you. That's the man I don't want to lose."

He snorts, unable to keep his beautiful eyes on mine, and it breaks my heart.

"You're just scared of losing the man you're used to having around. Not *me*. You can't deal with all of me. All the bad that comes with it. I don't..." He huffs. "I can't do this right now, Peach."

My face falls. "You sound like you're giving up on me," I say in a barely audible voice.

I fucked it. This is what I do. I fuck everything up and people give up because I couldn't open up. Because...I couldn't believe someone was capable of truly loving me.

"Were you on your way to see Coach? You should get going before practice starts."

"Please, don't give up on me," I squeak.

"Are you in love with me, Penelope?" he blurts out.

"I–" My heart gallops, but the words don't come out. Why do they feel so impossible to say?

"I can control all of you," he says calmly, the words ringing their truth in the empty hallway. "But I can't control your heart." A mask transforms his face, the one he shows everyone on campus. "Now let's get to practice."

With a hand in the pocket on his sweatpants, he brings

the other to my face, squeezing my cheeks together in one grip and making my lips pout.

"But before you talk to Coach Gomez, I want you to remember that this conversation doesn't mean you're free of me. And it certainly doesn't mean you get to go around doing whatever you want."

"Wren," I groan, attempting to step away with no result. I don't think I'm *really* trying. The back-and-forth used to feel real, but now it just feels like foreplay.

I grab his wrist, but he shakes his head. "Keep your hands by your sides."

"We're in public," I try to articulate behind his grip as I drop my hand.

"That we are. Better listen, then. I want you to be my rally girl. I won't accept anyone else, but mainly, you won't be bringing cookies and showing up with glittery signs for another player. Nod, pretty girl."

When I don't, his eyebrows pull together.

"Don't you think you've angered me enough today? Last night in the restaurant didn't teach you anything, huh?"

It's come to a point where any attention from him feels like a gift, even his control.

"We're picking at random."

The words are barely articulated, but he gets it.

"Peach, I apologize if I made it sound like I care how you do it. Just make it happen. Try again with the nodding, will you?"

The condescending tone doesn't even make me mad. It just turns me on. I nod, trying my best at the same time to calm my heartbeat. He's too close. His smell is overwhelming, always surrounding me with his presence. And his skin electrifies mine to the point that I can't stop the tingling from going all the way to my lower stomach.

He releases me, and I look around to make sure no one saw us. Observing me from head to toe, he seems hesitant to say something. In the end, it clearly pains him to say it, but I think we both need to hear it.

"You shouldn't have come to the initiations," he whispers, his deep voice cracking from the hurt. "Then we would have both been free of this torture."

By the time I come out of Gomez's office, I have a list of players' names and their affiliated rally girls. Of course, my name is right next to Wren's. Gomez was paying so little attention, it wasn't hard to make it happen.

At the end of practice, all the players and cheerleaders gather around me. Wren stands at the back, his helmet at his feet and arms crossed over his chest. His hard gaze is on me, and all I want is for him to kiss me and soften his features. Instead, I focus on the sheet in my hand. I address myself to everyone, while inside, his words from before practice still bounce against my skull.

Is that how he really feels? That this is torture?

"Alright, I'm going to give you each player's name and their rally girl. Please, remember this isn't just so you can have a pretty girl supporting you for the rest of the semester. You have to actively participate in raising funds for the Silver Falls North Shore Women's Shelter. So, post you and your rally girl on socials and share the link to the funding page everywhere. Talk to people after games and all that. Girls, same for you. Share what you do for your player, ask for suggestions of what people want to see, show up to all the games, even those of you who aren't cheerleaders. And keep asking for donations."

I'm met with a completely disinterested group, bar Ella and Wren. I'm about to whistle and snap at them, call them out on their over-privileged lives, when Wren slaps the back of the lacrosse captain's head.

"Get your team in order," he says, voice low.

If Wren wanted, he would be captain. Jordan knows perfectly well he would not have a chance at keeping his spot if Wren fought for it. He simply doesn't want it. But the hierarchy stays the same everywhere on campus. Wren Hunter is at the top of the chain, and if he says something, everybody listens.

Jordan is suddenly in a rush to get everyone to shut up. And less than a minute later, I've got everyone's attention. I repeat my little speech and give every rally girl the name of her player.

"Any questions?" I ask, looking at all of them.

Marissa, who was one of the first girls to sign up for this, despite not being a cheerleader, raises her hand, and I nod at her.

"Are you sure the names were picked randomly?"

"I'm sure," I lie without hesitation. "Anyone else?"

"I just think it's weird you got the exact guy you wanted," she insists.

I offer her a smile, so falsely sweet it would probably taste of aspartame on my lips.

"Believe me, I didn't want him." Another lie. I'm really on fire.

I catch Wren arching an eyebrow at me, and I'm thankful for the fact that he's standing at the back of the group when he silently mouths "liar."

"If you don't want him, can I have you?" Miles, the other attacker, asks.

A couple of gasps mix with a few laughs. Apparently, not everyone is that scared to upset Wren today.

"You can have her," Wren says calmly. "As long as you don't mind living with two shattered knees."

The laughs double, making me roll my eyes. Wren slaps Miles a little too violently on the shoulder as he makes his way between his teammates.

"I think they understood what they have to do," he tells me as he approaches.

My heart accelerates when I understand he's done with sharing my attention. I barely have time to shake my head to attempt to stop him as his hand clamps at the back of my neck.

"Go get changed. I'll meet you outside."

I watch him walk away with the rest of the players and cheerleaders. And I stand on the lacrosse field all alone, wondering if I missed my one and only chance at being happy. Is this what it's going to be forever? Us stuck together and suffering?

"I know this is a risky thing to ask Peach Sanderson-Menacci, but penny for your thoughts?" Ella's voice rings out beside me as she bumps her shoulder into mine. Everyone's gone, and it's just the two of us here.

I want to joke back, but there's so much truth in her words that it deepens my hurt. That's what people expect of me, that I'll snap when they ask what's going on inside my head.

"I really am an idiot, aren't I?"

She puts an arm around my shoulders. "Everyone's an idiot when it comes to love."

I turn to her, my lower lip trembling. I bite hard on it to make sure my best friend doesn't notice. "Am I in love with him?"

She laughs softly, her baby-blue eyes lighting up with a mix of amusement and pity. "No one can answer that for you. I can tell you what I *think*, but I can't force you to look inside yourself and acknowledge what's there. That has to come from you, even if it's a terrifying thing to do."

My nostrils flare from how much I'm trying to hold back the pain I'm starting to feel.

"He didn't invite me to the initiations, Did you know?" I tell her.

She shakes her head, waiting for the rest of my explanation.

"That morning, he offered me forever or nothing. He said we were meant for each other and that he wanted me to be his. I refused. And he left me alone. He didn't invite me; he accepted that my freedom was more important than anything else. He let me go. *That's* how much he loves me and knows me. The truth is, he's my Shadow because I was there, and he didn't want anyone else to get their hands on me. Not because he wanted to force me."

I swallow thickly. "And now he feels stuck with me, thinking I'll never love him the way he loves me."

"Do you, Peach?" Ella asks in her soft voice. "Do you love him the way he loves you?"

"I–" I lick my lips. "He's always been there for me. Always put me first."

"Do you love that he loves you, or do you love *him*?"

"I don't want to lose him," I insist, a knot tightening my throat. It's worse than that. It's a noose around my neck.

"I understand that being vulnerable is hard for you. We all have things that scare us, and opening up is not something you do easily. There is *nothing* that will make you more vulnerable than loving someone. You at least have the reassurance to know that Wren Hunter would die for your love."

I nod, but I still can't seem to calm down. So she pulls the strands of hair I've been unconsciously chewing on outside of my mouth and whispers, "Say it. Just try to see how it feels."

I look at the floor and push past the tightness in my chest. "I love him."

Ella smiles when I look back at her, and I understand why. She must see it on my face, everything I feel. Lighter. Like the world is suddenly brighter. The pain in my stomach is gone, and my shoulders don't feel so heavy anymore.

It's not the fact that I'm in love with him; it's admitting the truth.

"Oh God," I groan. "What did you just do to me?" I tell Ella.

"Nothing," she giggles. "I just guided you through what you already felt. I do expect to be your Maid of Honor at the wedding, though."

I nod, feeling so many emotions rising up that my head is spinning.

"I think you should go find Wren," my friend says, letting go of me. "It's about time you guys get your happily ever after."

I think I'm going to find Wren in the men's locker room, or maybe outside the building, but no, he's in the hallways. He's down on one knee, a carefree laugh bursting out of him as he plays with an excited dog. And the owner of said dog is no other than Marissa. Where the hell did she hide it when we were talking about the rally girls?

She laughs as the dog tries to lick Wren's face. Wren

calmly orders the dog to sit, and Marissa's eyes sparkle with excitement.

Oh, please.

"There's something about a man who's good with dogs," she says, smiling down at my boyfriend.

"Why?" I bark as I stop by them. "It reassures you that he can treat a bitch right?"

Her mouth drops open, just as Wren's eyes come to me. He does that thing where he wipes a hand against his mouth so I can't see him smile. Too late. Caught him.

"Peach," he says as he stands up. "Don't be mean."

"I'm not being mean," I say with fire bursting from my lips, and probably smoke coming out of my ears. "I'm saving her from further disappointment." I take a step toward Marissa, and she takes one back, the leash forcing her labrador to follow. "He's not into you. Do you know why? Because he's in love with me. It's always been me, and it'll always be me."

Marissa looks at Wren, waiting for a denial or approval.

"Hey, I'm talking to you." I snap my fingers, grabbing her attention back. "There are some things that science still struggles to explain to this day. Dark matter, consciousness, the Methane Puzzle." Her eyes widen, clearly having no idea where I'm getting at. "And Wren's obsession with me. Today, we're also adding being unable to explain me being a complete idiot and not realizing that all those years I've been in love with my best friend." I can't look at him, too scared to see his reaction, but I feel him shift. "So, really, it's not your fault," I finally tell her. "You're into someone who will always choose me. And if you had a chance before, it's over. Because I now also know I will choose him."

Her wide eyes go to Wren again, and she huffs. "Wren?"

"Bitch, I just *told you* you stand no chance. Why are you turning to him and not walking away."

"Because you can't make decisions for others," she snaps back without even looking at me. "So...Wren?"

His eyes are on me when he answers, "It will always be her. Her over anyone else."

"You two are ridiculous." She huffs, then she's walking away, but our eyes are stuck on each other.

I've never felt so scared in my life, but the light in Wren's blue eyes and the pink tint on his cheeks are calming my heartbeat.

"Jealousy is so pretty on you," he finally says to cut the silence.

"This wasn't jealousy," I assure him. "It was me finally being in touch with myself. It was me finally understanding that you didn't have to stick by me all those years. You chose to. Because you love me. And all that hope you had? It was because your soul knew it was linked to mine. You were just facing a seriously stupid girl."

He winces, almost like I slapped him. "Don't call yourself stupid. We all carry pain within us that builds who we are. It just so happened that your pain made you feel like you weren't worthy of love."

"I don't care if I'm worthy of love," I admit. "As long as I can have yours. Because..." I lick my lips, but this time I'm not so nervous to admit the truth. "I love you, Wren Hunter."

The smile that spreads on his face is more breathtaking than I've ever seen before.

"I think," I add right away, panic suddenly rebounding and coursing through me before I can stop it.

He laughs softly, shaking his head. "You were doing so good."

But he knows that was just my stupid fear of being rejected, because he puts a hand on my waist, one at the back of my head, and pulls me to him.

I go onto my toes and press my lips against his. The softness of our kiss takes me by surprise, but deep down, nothing crazy happens. Because those feelings were there from a long time ago. I'm just finally putting a name on them.

My heartbeat picks up the same way it always has. And my nervous system relaxes because that's the effect he has on me.

This is beautiful...because our relationship has always been one of two people in love.

He pulls away, a small, smug smile lifting the corner of his mouth. "I really do always get what I want."

"Oh, shut up," I cackle.

"One last thing." His serious gaze sears into mine.

"No drugs, no alcohol. And if you struggle, I will help you. I will always help you in any way you need, but please, no lying."

I nod quickly. "You have my word. I love you." It feels so good to say.

The smile on his face makes my belly tingle. "I don't know how to get used to this," he admits.

I shrug playfully. "Well, do. Because I love you."

"I need to shower. Wait for me. I want to take you home," he says, cupping my cheek before he steps away.

"I can take myself home." I pinch my lips as soon as the words are out. Retorting something the second someone wants to help me is a reflex I can't help. But I want to go home with him; I just need to get used to being honest.

"It's hard, isn't it?" he asks, his hand already holding the door handle to the locker room. "To just let go."

He doesn't expect an answer, walking inside and leaving me alone with my racing heart. He ruined our friendship, and now he's set on ruining me. It's only now that I realize I'm enjoying every single second of it.

I take my time showering and gathering my stuff before I go wait in front of the men's locker room again. Wren isn't out, so I pull out my phone, sign up for a shift at the shelter and read an email from Professor Lopez asking for another meeting. Apparently, I missed a lot of points in my last edits of the article. From the corner of my eye, I can see players walking out in small groups or alone, but it's never Wren. I catch up on some reading until my neck hurts, and when I look up, he's still not out.

"What the fuck," I mumble to myself. Does he think he can just make me wait here forever for him?

I slap open the door, striding in.

"Wren Hunter," I snap.

"Whoa!" Miles snatches a towel from a nearby bench to cover himself. "Only men in here, Peach."

I cross my arms over my chest, tilting my head to the side as my gaze drops to his crotch.

"What are you doing with that towel? From what I just saw, there's not much to hide."

"What, because you think you're so hot?"

I cock an eyebrow at him. "First of all, yes. But also, aren't you the one who just asked me to be your rally girl rather than Wren's? Don't suddenly pretend you're not into me because I hurt your ego."

There's movement behind him, and my mouth drops open when Wren walks out of the showers with nothing but a towel around his waist.

I struggle to swallow, suddenly deciding to look anywhere but at the drops rolling down his perfect abs. The lockers are a deep burgundy, each with a number on top of them and the last name of the player. My eyes automatically go to number seven. Hunter.

I lick my lips as I wonder what Wren looks like when he's standing in front of it, getting ready for a game.

"She's right."

My heart sinks when I barely recognize Wren's voice. It's cold, turning every word into a lifeless expression.

"You wanted her as your rally girl." He keeps going, stopping right beside him.

Wren and I are only separated by a paling Miles now.

"Man, it was a joke." He chuckles. "I was riling her up. Don't take it so seriously."

Wren nods, pretending to agree. "Yeah." His face falls, and his glare could punch a hole through Miles's head. "But shouldn't you know better than to make jokes about my girlfriend?"

"Not your—" I cut myself off when his deadly stare flicks to me. Scratching my throat, I mumble, "Never mind. Old habit."

Miles takes a step back and grabs his clothes from his sport bag, his eyes staying on Wren as he seems to lose composure.

"It was a stupid joke," he admits. "Peach is yours. Everyone knows she's yours. You've spent the last four years drilling it into our brains. Don't worry. We know."

"Good. Penelope baby, come here." He points right in front of him, and I cock an eyebrow.

"Yeah, sure will," I say sarcastically as I take a step away from him, crossing my arms over my chest.

He doesn't move an inch, but his voice is lower when he talks again.

"Don't make me repeat myself." He snaps his fingers, pointing at the exact same point.

He snapped.

His.

Fingers.

Calling me over like some sort of...*pet*.

He said it before, didn't he? Called me his new pet. And I get it now. Whenever Wren feels control slipping, he'll double the stakes. He'll tighten the leash. Execute when he asks nicely, and it'll go well. Fight back, and he'll ask for more.

This situation is getting worse before I can even think of taking charge. Because there's no way Wren Hunter will ever relinquish any control. And especially not in front of someone else.

My gaze darts to Miles, and his wide eyes are on Wren's finger pointing at the floor.

I walk to him slowly, knowing any pushback will only make it worse. Even when I'm standing right in front of him, his finger stays pointing at the ground.

"On your knees, Trouble."

"Don't do this to me," I murmur, my body starting to tremble at the humiliation. I can feel Miles's gaze burning into the side of my face.

"Let go," he replies softly. He puts a strand of hair behind my ear to lessen the blow. "For me."

And that's one way to switch off my brain.

He snaps his fingers again, and it's the only reminder of my place in this new relationship we're trying to navigate.

I get down on my knees in front of him and look up into his eyes. A god seems like a weak being next to him. We grew up thinking there's no one above this man, and it's turning into a belief I can't control.

It doesn't matter how hard I fight back. Wren Hunter always gets what he wants. Even if it takes years. Even if it's me.

"Open your mouth and show me your tongue."

I lick my lips, unsure I can handle the surge of desire electrifying my body.

I slowly open my mouth, showing him my tongue.

"Atta girl. Put your hands behind your back."

I try to execute quicker this time, closing my eyes to avoid seeing Miles in my peripheral.

My eyes snap open when I hear the towel drop, and I feel them round. This is the first time in my life I get to see Wren's dick so close. I've felt it inside me and saw it through the mirror yesterday. I know it's not small. But there's a difference between it sliding inside me when I'm wet and desperate and...and having it in my mouth. This is going to destroy me.

The veins throb angrily when he grabs the hard length in a tight grip. His other hand adjusts my hair gently, gathering it in his grip, and then he does that thing where he wraps it twice around his fist. Exactly like he did in that restaurant bathroom, and before I know what's happening, the wave of feelings I had then comes back.

"Spread your legs a little wider. There you go."

It's just a grip on my hair. It barely even hurts. But the effect on me is undeniable. My breathing accelerates as he pulls my head back and taps my tongue with the tip of his dick.

"You stay still and pretty. Don't move, don't pull away, don't suck."

Don't suck? Then what the fuck does he expect from me?

I find out the answer too quickly.

He pushes his dick in my mouth, and I almost pull back, except I can't with his grip on my hair. His girth stretches my lips, and I gag the second he hits the back of my mouth.

"Don't move. Let me set the pace."

I try not to, but when he pushes farther in, my body recoils, and a whimper escapes me. He pulls out, slapping my mouth with his dick.

"Stay still, Penelope. Give our friend a show. I want him to understand this is the one and only dick that will be going down your throat for the rest of your life."

I barely have time to catch my breath before he pushes in again.

"Breathe through your nose. Good girl. There you go."

I'm scared I'll suffocate as he keeps pushing, but he adjusts my head, and my throat somehow opens for him with the new angle.

"Atta girl. Look at you dribbling everywhere. Does my dick taste good on your tongue, Trouble?"

He shifts, and I startle when I feel his ankle between my legs, pressing against the tights I'm wearing under my uniform skirt.

He chuckles. "Try not to rub yourself on me too much."

Behind my back, I grip my right wrist tightly in my left hand, forcing myself not to bring my fingers to my clit. My thoughts feel heavy again, my head floating somewhere in the clouds as he pulls back and pushes back in. The choking, wet sound is almost ridiculous, and I should be humiliated. But somehow, all I feel is a sense of peace, and before I know it, my hips thrust forward, and a zap of electricity travels from my clit and all the way to my nipples.

I moan around his dick, and he accelerates, encouraged by my sound.

"Fuck," he rasps. "Fuck, Peach, had I known your mouth

felt so good, I would have stopped giving you a choice years ago."

I can't hold still as he keeps fucking my mouth relentlessly. I'm shamelessly rubbing myself against him, the pressure surrounding me with that strangely peaceful feeling where I lose myself and any sense of reality.

There's no more right or wrong. No more fighting back and no more pride. All that matters is Wren, what he says, and the pleasure it brings me to let him have control over me.

The sudden taste of his cum on my tongue barely brings me back.

He says something, but I only hear the end of the sentence. The order.

"Don't swallow."

Something else. I think he's praising me. Again, my brain chooses to only catch whatever next words are about his control.

"Up. Good girl."

Wait, am I standing up already? Did I listen?

My lips are sealed, his cum on my tongue as he turns me around. I moan a complaint. Fuck. I need to come.

"Shh, stay with me."

He settles behind me, naked, his heat passing through my clothes. With a hand still in my hair, he makes me face Miles.

Miles.

I forgot he was here.

My eyelids feel weighted, and I can barely see straight anymore. I just want to lean back and relax into Wren. I want to hear another order.

I want to *please him*.

His thumb pulls at my lower lip.

"Open. Show him how beautiful you look with my cum spilling out of your mouth."

I part my lips and let him press his thumb against my tongue to the point that his cum dribbles onto my chin, drops falling onto my shirt.

"Beautiful, isn't she?" I hear Wren, but I can barely keep my eyes open. "Wouldn't you love to have her as your rally girl, Miles?"

I don't see him, but he must nod, because Wren keeps going.

"Hm. But who do you belong to, Peach?"

"You," I rasp.

"Yes, you fucking do. Swallow."

Without the shadow of a second thought, I swallow whatever is left of him on my tongue. He wipes my chin with his thumb, and I lick him over and over again until there's nothing left.

I hear him tell Miles to fuck off, then I hear the door click shut.

"You're very special to me, Trouble."

My eyes open, and Wren is in front of me, holding my head between his palms. Where do these pieces of time go? Everything feels like it's passing by without my knowledge.

"So special." He kisses my forehead, and I sigh as my shoulders relax some more.

I'm in heaven. And the worst thing is, I still haven't come. Since yesterday. In the bathroom.

I barely feel like my soul is back in my body by the time Wren opens the door to his bedroom. He helps me in, sitting me on the bed, and caresses my hair to keep my attention on him.

"I'm going to get you showered, and since I'm sure you want to do some work, you can work from here."

I blink up at him. "Where will you be?"

"I have to be at the temple tonight."

"I want to be with you." The words slip out so naturally, I wonder who of us is the most surprised.

He settles between my legs, kissing the top of my head, my cheek, and then softly caressing my lips with his.

"There's absolutely nowhere in the world I would rather be than by your side. I'd spend the entire night quietly watching you exist if I could. But I have no choice when it comes to the Circle. I have to be there tonight."

I lie down in bed, refusing to leave that perfect state I've reached. "Then you'll come back here."

"Of course. I'll always come back wherever you are."

I smile to myself. It's true. Wherever I am, Wren always finds his way there.

"Easier to have me here than break into my room at night, isn't it?"

He leans over me, wrapping his hand loosely around my throat, and my body melts from the touch.

"Did you ever see me?"

I take a trembling breath. "You're the one who told me."

He tightens his grip. "That wasn't the question." And he releases, letting a rush come over me.

My eyes flutter shut, and I nod. There's a need inside me that only Wren can satiate.

"Once. I thought it was a dream," I murmur. "At first."

Caressing my pulse with his thumb, he keeps me on the edge of sanity. "What happened when you realized it wasn't?"

He squeezes delicately again, and I gasp when he releases, my back curving as I try to lift off the bed. I want to be closer to him, but he keeps me trapped on the mattress. "Wren..."

"Tell me."

"Nothing," I rasp. "I...I liked it. I felt safe."

Our gazes connect when I open my eyes. The surprise and satisfaction on his face is a sight I wouldn't have wanted to miss. He's the most handsome man I've ever had the pleasure of looking at. I don't even remember why I refused to see it before. I don't know why I stopped myself from enjoying it when he's always been right here. Waiting for me.

"It's so precious to see you in subspace. All for me. Your body and mind become so malleable." He takes a deep breath and exhales. "You are entirely mine, Peach." He sounds like he can hardly believe it. "Forever."

I don't know what comes over me, but I nod. Pressing my hips forward, I release a sharp breath.

"Touch me," I say as I wrap my hand around his wrist. "Please, sir, touch me."

He smiles, and by the smugness in it, I know I lost the game. "Absolutely not. This isn't how it works between us anymore. You suffer, and I play."

I feel my blood coloring my cheeks, the heat making me dizzy.

"Oh, you mother—"

His grip tightens around my throat. "You were doing so good." He chuckles. "I'm not going to touch you now. But if you keep up the good behavior, and if you start begging with a little more enthusiasm, I might change my mind by the time I come back from the temple."

377

I pout and try a different technique. "But how am I meant to beg if you're not even here to hear it."

He licks his lips, his eyes roaming over my face like he can't get enough of me. "You've got a phone, don't you? Use it. Make up for all those times you ignored my texts."

When he lets me go, I throw a pillow in his face. "Fuck off."

All I achieve is tearing a laugh out of him. Then a weird noise resonates in the room.

"Is that your laugh?" I sit up, and it comes back.

Woof!

Definitely not his laugh.

"Oh. My. God," I coo. "Oh my god, look at you." The tiny, long-haired golden Dachshund yaps as it tries to jump on the bed. "Wren, where did you get him?"

"Found her," he mumbles, scratching the back of his neck.

I grab her, and she starts climbing me, attempting to lick my face.

"I love her," I say as I look at him. "Does she have a name yet? Are you keeping her?"

"Uh...her name is currently Little Sausage."

I look at him, deadpan. "Original."

"I'm not planning on keeping her," he adds, with no care for the pretty dog whatsoever.

She barks at him in return, and he rolls his eyes. "She's unbearable."

"Yes, so what?" I snap. "Where the hell is your heart? You're just going to abandon her? What the fuck is wrong with you?"

"I kill people on a regular basis, Peach. I don't know what made you think I have a heart."

I pause and narrow my gaze at him. "Killing people is

one thing, but abandoning a dog is seriously fucked up, Wren."

Tilting his head to the side, he observes me playing with her. "You know what. I already have one unbearable woman in my life. I'm not sure another one would be good for my sanity."

"No one cares about your sanity." I scratch Little Sausage's head, and when she licks my face, I laugh so hard, a squeal escapes me.

Wren freezes in front of me. "Did you just...squeal?"

"Oh, shut up, you know it happens sometimes."

Out of nowhere, his strange fascination with me returns. "Yes, I do. Except you haven't in years. The last time was freshman year."

It's my turn to pause, and Sausage jumps off my lap and onto the bed.

"Why do you know the last time I made this horrible noise?"

"Because it was when I gifted you that chocolate coin I had made into a Nobel Prize for Easter."

I can only blink at him until Sausage jumps back on me and nibbles on my arms.

"It could have happened again since."

"Except it hasn't," he retorts right away. "I would know. It's my favorite sound in the world."

I open my mouth to say something. Anything. Any insult, mockery, expression that could show in one way or another that this is weird, and he's too obsessed for our own good.

But I can't.

Because my heart is beating too hard for me to even hear my own thoughts. And suddenly, a cute dog doesn't feel like enough endorphins to match the way Wren makes me feel.

"You're sick," I say in the most loving way I ever have to him. "Your obsession with me. It's...it's sick," I repeat.

He nods, almost proud of himself. "I know. You're an illness inside me, and I never want to be cured."

I'm too speechless to answer. All I've ever wanted in my life was to be loved so strongly I'd finally feel whole. I'd finally stop wondering where I wasn't enough.

Wren doesn't make me feel like I'm enough.

Oh no. It would be too weak of a way to describe how he makes me feel.

A better way to put it would be that I'm so much more than enough, yet he'll never be sated. Like there's nothing I could do or say that would stop him from keeping on exploring every part of my being.

"We'll keep Little Sausage," he finally declares, his eyes going down to his phone. He's typing something.

And I'm still too shocked to talk, so I nod like an idiot and hug her close to my chest.

He leaves a couple of hours after my shower. He let me work at his desk, among the Scrabble pieces he uses to play against himself and shove down people's throats, and all the books he references for his own essays.

"Make sure you're here when I come back," he says as he drops a kiss at the top of my head.

When I don't look up and don't answer, he wraps a hand around my jaw, forcing me to face him, and presses his mouth to mine.

My body heat rises the second his tongue breaches my lips. I melt into his touch. This effect he has on me is becoming a serious problem.

"No touching yourself, but you can beg prettily. I'll

check my phone," he murmurs against my mouth. "And no leaving the house. Understood?"

"Understood," I breathe out.

He's barely gone when a notification pings on my phone. And my heart stops.

> Hermes: Did you miss me, little murderer?

My ears are ringing as I open the SFU app. At first, there was a part of me that believed Wren was Hermes, and that once he'd gotten me to the initiations, he would drop this. But then I learned the person who sent me the invite was Monty Hunter. That man certainly isn't running an SFU gossip account that blackmails students. So I'm back to square one, having no idea who's using Ania as leverage to get what they want out of me.

I don't know when it's going to stop.

And I don't know what their ultimate goal is.

I didn't mention anything to Wren, because why would I want to talk about his ex who was murdered? Especially when I'm being accused of it. *Especially* when I was with her that night, and that we argued over him. But it's different now. We're together, and I chose that. I agreed there would be no more lies.

Another message appears.

> Hermes: Congratulations on becoming a Hera. But you didn't think our little game was over, did you?

"Fuck," I panic, standing up and pacing. "Fuck. Fuck. Fuck."

I'm chewing on my hair before I can control it, and I

don't even care. This is bad. Instead of passively waiting for his next message, I send one.

> **Penelope S.M.:** What the hell do you want from me?

> **Hermes:** I want you to see something. Go to the temple tonight. There are rooms underground. Just have a little look for me.

> **Hermes:** And as always. This is our little secret.

Wren's warning comes back. To not leave his house. The one time I didn't plan on disobeying him, I'm not even left with a choice. I'm forced to lie to the man I love so I don't get sent to prison by the person blackmailing me. The situation is completely slipping from my already loose grasp.

> **Hermes:** Did I pique your interest? Or should we talk about those pictures of you and Ania again?

-metal IS NOT the same as punk.

-She's still allergic to shellfish and cat hair

-Always leave the green olives to her

-We don't like metal anymore.

~~-Tea tree and peppermint shampoo~~

~~-Don't forget the peri-peri powder on her fries~~

-Bake and shake every first Tuesday of the month.

-No more sugar in her coffee. It makes her feel sick

-DO NOT bother me during girls' night Wren

-Spiced honey on pepperoni pizza

-Check the triangle freckles on her right shoulder frequently. Dermatologist said to keep an eye.

-New vision results: Right eye -2.75. Left eye -3.25

-If she gets in next September's yearly release of the EEAJ, the announcement will be in August next year.

~~-Her brace needs to come off in a week~~

-New shampoo: coconut oil in it

-No more peri-peri on her fries

-Keep the stupid dog

Chapter Twenty-Eight

Wren

Trouble - Camylio

My gaze drops to my phone on my lap as I check for another message from Peach.

Nothing. The little Vixen.

The door to Duval's office opens, and he walks in, nodding at his security guard. I've been waiting for half an hour, but I say nothing, standing from my seat because that's just how it works within the Circle. If Zeus enters a room, everyone in it shows respect.

He waves at me to sit down, and he leans against his desk rather than sit behind it.

"Long day," he huffs, then shows me the book he's holding.

Great.

I smile, tilting my head to the side. "Aw, did someone bully you at work? Now his name is on the list?"

He chuckles to himself, certainly not hurt by my comment. If anything, I think he likes it.

"Actually, a Hera cheated on her Shadow. This is the man she cheated with."

I can't suppress my surprise. "She did?" I do try to hide my eagerness to know more, though. "So, I kill him. What about her?"

He shrugs. "That's up to her Shadow. But she's in the dungeons right now, hence nothing romantic, I assume. And she'll know she cost a man his life. That's not something everyone can live with."

His accusing stare doesn't leave me as I grab the book.

"What do you want me to say? I *can* live with it. That's why you forced me to join, isn't it?"

He snorts. "Forced you. You asked for a favor, Wren. We gave it to you. Then you paid back your debt. No one here was forced to do anything."

I keep my anger well hidden, but it still burns my lungs. "I was a teen."

He cocks an eyebrow in a silent, *so what?*

"A lucky teen who didn't go to prison for what he did, so know what's good for you."

I look away, attempting to contain the buzzing in my body. "You know..." I chuckle. "For someone who's perfectly aware of what I'm capable of, you think yourself very safe in a room alone with me."

He pales instantly. The difference in his behavior is stark when he straightens up and decides to round his desk to hide behind it. I smile at him, and I don't need to wonder if he understands it's not the charming smile most people think it is. Oh, he knows it's not.

"All I'm saying..." His voice is quieter, so he clears his throat and tries again. "All I'm saying is, your dad had connections, and I'm glad we were able to help you."

"Talking about my dad. What does he want with Penelope?"

"That I don't know."

"For god's sake, Duval. You're such a pathetic man. Look at you, barely able to hold it together. What are you thinking? How I'd do it?"

"I don't know what your dad wants with her, Wren."

I readjust myself in my seat, and he startles, tearing a low laugh out of me.

"I'll tell you what the other side of me has already noticed. The letter opener that I could push into your jugular. The corner of your desk, where I could hit your head so many times you'd be unrecognizable. And I quite like that little tie of yours. I'll just tighten it very slowly until your eyes bulge out of your head."

"Joe!" he shouts, and his guard is in the room a split second later.

Duval is sweating so much he has to dab his forehead with the handkerchief he keeps in the breast pocket of his suite.

"Yes, sir?"

"Escort Mr. Hunter out of the building, please. We're done for tonight."

I nod as I stand, waving the book at him. "I got what I needed."

"Wren," he calls out as I'm about to cross the door.

I stop, but I don't turn to him. Who knows if I'll be able to hold back from ending his life.

"Your dad is a titan. He doesn't have to get the board's approval to invite a woman to initiate, and he doesn't have to give a reason. I promise you, I don't know what he wants with Penelope."

"My fucking misery," I mumble. "That's what he's always wanted."

I leave before he can say anything else. I could already hear his response. *After what you did, surely you can understand him.*

I'm grinding my teeth to dust as I follow Joe down the stairs. Before we cross the hallway to the exit, we hear a commotion from our right. It's behind the door that leads to the Aphrodites' rooms. Technically, they're dungeons the Shadows can use whenever they want. Sometimes with the Aphrodites, sometimes with their Hera if they feel like it.

"Probably that cheating Hera being punished," Joe says, sounding disgusted.

"Keep your comments to yourself," I answer, voice low.

I have every intention to leave the temple, but something stops me. I can't explain what, exactly. An instinct that makes the hair at the back of my neck stand to attention.

I realize what it is when I turn toward the door, listening more closely. There was a scream. Barely audible, because the rooms are soundproof, but I heard the faint call for help.

And something deep inside me recognized that voice.

The second I hear it again, I'm ripping the door open and running down the stairs two at a time.

"Fuck you, *fuck you!*" I hear Peach shout.

I can't see her yet, only two men's backs as they try to push someone into a dungeon, but I have no doubt it's her small body holding them back.

I stop right behind them, seeing her red hair flash between them.

"I've seen you suck a cock, Peach. You love that shit so much, you'd die to have two in you at the same time."

That's Miles. My lacrosse teammate, who I already taught a lesson to when it comes to her.

"If you're going to disobey and come to the dungeons unsupervised, you should know there are consequences to pay, Hera."

And that's his dad, Paul, who somehow got his useless son into the Circle this year.

"Touch me with your pencil dicks, and I will bite them off," she hisses.

God, I love this woman. Her bravery is truly unmatchable.

"Did you know she once threw a chair at a coffee shop barista who told her to 'give him a smile'? He said it once, and she warned him not to say it again. And he did. Always listen to her warning," I say.

They both turn around at the same time, but my gaze is taken hostage by Peach. Her hands are holding the wooden door frame in a white-knuckled grip, and her hair is a mess, like someone dragged her by it.

"Oh, that's bad." The lack of any emotion in my voice keeps everyone's attention on me, and the world might as well have frozen from how still they all are.

I realize that having said that while staring at Peach makes it sound like she's in trouble, and I'm proven right when she takes a few steps back, taking herself into the room.

"Wren." Her voice has gone from the fiery woman she is to a low rasp. "They-they. The things they do to women down here..."

I cock my head, and she can see it—that I've already snapped. This woman is *part of me*. A subtle, practically invisible shift in my behavior is clear as day to her.

"She broke into the temple. She came to an area

forbidden to Heras," Paul says behind me. "Rules must be respected, Wren. Actions have consequences."

I ignore him, watching Peach's lower lip tremble as she keeps trapping herself farther into the room, trying to get away from my advancing body. Her back hits a dresser, which I know is full of all sorts of sex toys that would terrify her. I stop a hair's breadth away, and she tilts her head all the way back so she can see my eyes.

"I know," she whispers. Not because she doesn't want to be heard, but because I don't think she can breathe properly. "I know you said not to come. I-I—"

Her eyes are flicking between mine wildly, showing she's aware she crossed a line. That this is the kind of trouble she's not going to get away from unscathed.

"Finish your sentence," I say calmly, encouraging her to talk.

She inhales sharply, then breathes out, "I'm sorry."

She flinches when I reach my hand to her face to push wild strands of hair behind her ear.

I tut, shaking my head. "Why are you afraid of me?" I murmur.

"Because..." Her chest shakes as she tries to breathe. "You're different." Her last word is barely audible. She doesn't even want *me* to hear it, let alone the two clowns behind me.

"I am."

"You're scaring me."

I smile softly at her. "I think being a little scared of me can only do you good, Penelope baby. It might stop you from being so careless and putting yourself in more trouble than you can handle." I caress her cheek with my knuckles. "But I need you to remember that when I'm like this, when I'm *different,* you're the only one who's safe from me."

My hand drops to her neck, and then her collarbone. That's when I notice how scraped her shoulder is. It's fresh, the blood still forming little dots all over her skin. It's big too. Her whole shoulder and upper arm.

"Tsk, this is bad too."

"I know I—" She gasps, cut off by my hands now gripping her waist.

I lift her up and put her down on the dresser behind her.

"Don't move."

"I just want to say—"

"In a minute." I kiss her forehead and turn around.

"Mr. Ellson." I nod. "Miles."

Paul takes a step toward me. "This is completely unacceptable. And if you won't punish her, we will. Like we'd planned."

"I know, I know," I say lightly as I undo the cufflinks of my black shirt. My tone is a contrast to his tight and angry voice. "And believe me, she'll be punished accordingly."

I put the links in my pocket, roll up my sleeves, and look at both of them again. "Okay," I say on an exhale, then smile. "Who dragged her by her beautiful hair? And who hurt her shoulder?"

Miles opens his mouth, but he's cut off by Peach.

"Wren—"

I don't turn around, too busy observing the dead men walking in front of me. "I said *in a minute*, Trouble. Don't add to your own punishment."

"Listen," Miles sneers. "If you didn't want us touching your Hera, maybe you shouldn't have had her suck your cock in front of me, don't you think?"

"She's mine. I do whatever the fuck I want with her. I'm pretty sure that's the whole point. And no, it's not an invite for you to touch. I own her, Miles. You don't. I could put her on all fours in front of you and fuck her until her voice is raw from screaming my name and it *still* wouldn't be an invite to touch."

"Her breaking into the temple is," Paul intervenes.

"Spare me, will you? She's not allowed to enter because *I said so*, and I told the guards about it. Not because it's a punishable offense." I walk closer, my voice getting smoother and smoother.

God, this feels so pure, so perfect.

I cock an eyebrow at them. "Now, back to my initial question. I want to know who touched my Hera's hair, and who touched her shoulder. One each? One did it all? Both of you?"

When they stay completely silent, I know I've reached the end of my patience.

"Both of you, it is."

I throw a punch so hard into Paul's face, I feel his jawbone crack under my knuckles. That'll hurt tomorrow, mainly for him.

He drops on the floor, unconscious, and I turn to a screaming Miles.

"What the fuck? *What the fuck!*"

I grab him in a headlock and press my forearm and biceps together. He squeaks, tapping my arm and attempting to push me away, to no avail.

"Wren!"

"One minute, Penelope baby. I'm kind of busy right now," I answer cheerily.

I keep squeezing until Miles is weak enough that I can drag him to the doorway. Holding him by the back of his collar, I place his head by the frame, and I smash the door into it.

"Wren!"

Peach's scream is a fair indication I might be going a little too far. But the violence is the only thing that's going to calm me down. I slam again, but her little gasp of distress pierces through the fog, and suddenly, there's something more important than killing Miles. And that's giving Peach all my attention. So, like a cat not interested in playing with an unconscious mouse, I drop him, dust off my shirt, and turn back to her, facing away from the two men at my feet.

"Yes?"

She hasn't moved, still sitting on the dresser, her arms wrapped around her waist, hugging herself. Her eyes are wide with shock, and she can barely keep her gaze on me.

"I wanted to say...that the, uh, the scratches on my shoulders..." She gulps and starts playing with strands of hair. "They're from when I climbed the wall to get into the temple's gardens."

I blink at her.

Oh.

Now that's a rather unfortunate misunderstanding.

My silence has her word vomiting.

"You know, so I could sneak into the temple through the back doors? I slipped on my first try and just crashed back down. And I scratched my shoulder in the process. And it's fine, it's not even hurting that bad, and mainly, it wasn't... well, it wasn't them, you know?"

"Huh."

I look over at the two bodies on the floor and back at my beautiful yet absolutely insane girlfriend, who's now anxiously chewing on her hair.

"Well, did they touch you?"

I need *something* to justify this mess, and she sees it right away.

She nods eagerly. "Oh, yes. Yes. Miles pulled me by the hair. That hurt." She's exaggerating to defend my actions, and I think I love her even more for it. "And his dad pushed me, and I hit my elbow against the door frame."

She dramatically lifts her arm to try to look at her elbow, bending it this way and that. "Yeah, I think I have a bruise," she adds with a slight wince for show.

I smile at her, feeling myself coming back from my trip to the other side. When she shows me her index finger, I laugh. It has a micro cut on the side, probably a splinter from when she was holding the door frame so hard.

"Ow," she whispers. "That's them too."

I grab her hand, kiss her finger, and then her mouth. Deeply. I show her exactly how I feel about her little act.

"You, young lady, are a serious troublemaker who can't spend more than a few days without hurting herself some-how." I kiss her again, an unstoppable need coursing through me. "And you directly went against something I said." It gets worse when she wraps her arms around my neck, keeping me close.

The kiss gets more violent, more possessive. I bite her lower lip, and she whimpers as her legs spread open to let my body closer. I only pull back to open one of the drawers to the dresser as far as I can with her legs in the way, and I grab the first thing I find in there. Metal handcuffs. That'll do.

"Put your hands behind your back," I growl against her mouth.

She doesn't need to be told twice, her wrists disappearing behind her. As I slip on the cuffs, I love the way her eyes round at the clicking sound of them closing. I do the other wrist in a rush.

"Test them," I say, voice lowering. A smile spreads on my face when she pulls at them.

"These are real handcuffs," she mumbles, hardly believing it's not the breakable furry ones from online sex shops.

I pop open the button of the black jeans she put on to come here and slide them down, pulling harshly to get them over her beautiful ass and all the way below her knees.

"Well, I have to make this fun for me, don't I?"

I smile as I undo my pants, freeing my hard dick.

She's already panting by the time I'm rubbing the tip against her wetness. As I tap her clit, her head falls back.

"Wren," she moans. "I need you."

I fist her hair, making her look at me as I grab my cock and press myself against her entrance.

"To be clear," I say as her mouth falls open. "This is not your punishment. This is because you are irre-fucking-sistible, Trouble."

I thrust inside her violently, my stomach seizing as she whimpers, and I feel her stretching around me. She was wet, but I don't doubt my size is too much to take, and her beautiful struggling sounds are making it hard not to destroy her just to hear more of them.

I pull back and push back in, filling her entirely.

"Fuck," she chokes out. "D-deep. Too deep."

"Look at me," I order through clenched teeth. "Who's in control?"

"You."

"Who does your body belong to?"

"You," she moans.

"That's right. And I do what I want with it, don't I?"

"Y-yes," she groans as I move slowly and deeply inside her.

"So take my cock like a good little slut and scream my name when you come, baby."

After that, I don't bother holding back anymore. I thrust into her mercilessly, forcing her to look at me with her lush, long hair rolled twice around my fist. Without losing momentum, I bend my knees slightly and make sure I hit the perfect spot every time I push back in.

Her eyes start rolling to the back of her head, and the way she contracts around me is going to be the end of me.

"My. Fucking. Name," I growl as I press my forehead against hers.

"W-wren. Wren... *Fuck, Wren!*" she screams as she detonates around me, her entire body shuddering. And I last about one extra millisecond before I come inside her with a roar.

It takes us a few minutes to catch our breaths, and I don't pull out until she starts squirming.

"Can we take these off?" she asks as she tugs at the cuffs.

"Shit," I hiss, and I watch her face tense with worry.

"What?"

"The keys. I don't know where they are."

She twists out of my hold, and I zip up my pants as I look around. Oh, Paul and Miles are still there. That slipped my mind.

"Wren Hunter," she snaps. "Are you for real?"

I shake my head, smiling at her as I grab the keys from the drawer. "No." I laugh softly. "I just wanted to kiss the pretty angry vein on your forehead," I admit as I do exactly that.

I undo the cuffs, and she looks over my shoulder.

"Do I have to worry about those two showing up dead somewhere?" she asks.

I look at them, then back at her. "No. They got what they deserved already."

"Promise?"

"Yes." I nod. "Let's get you back where I had left you, huh?" I murmur against her lips. "In my bedroom, where you should have stayed."

"Yes, please. Get me out of this place. It's fucked up."

-metal IS NOT the same as punk.
-She's still allergic to shellfish and cat hair
-Always leave the green olives to her
-We don't like metal anymore.
~~-Tea tree and peppermint shampoo~~
~~-Don't forget the peri-peri powder on her fries~~
-Bake and shake every first Tuesday of the month.
-No more sugar in her coffee. It makes her feel sick
-DO NOT bother me during girls' night Wren
-Spiced honey on pepperoni pizza
-Check the triangle freckles on her right shoulder
frequently. Dermatologist said to keep an eye.
-New vision results: Right eye -2.75. Left eye -3.25
-If she gets in next September's yearly release of the
EEAJ, the announcement will be in August next year.
~~-Her brace needs to come off in a week~~
-New shampoo: coconut oil in it
-No more peri-peri on her fries
-Keep the stupid dog

Chapter Twenty-Nine

Wren

No Angels - Stellar

I startle awake, unsure of where I am for a few seconds. It's my room, my bed, but it smells like Peach. It's that very specific mix of flowery and fruity. Specifically, it's rose and lychee, but that knowledge is only because I looked up her perfume a long time ago. Before that, I just knew it as the smell I'm addicted to.

Speaking of something I'm addicted to, Peach isn't next to me. I brought her home yesterday, and we fell asleep together in my bed. I can hear the shower running, and I'm ready to join her, but the second I become fully aware of my body, I feel something in my hand.

A piece of paper.

My entire being freezes.

I know for a fact that I did not open the book Duval gave me. I have no idea who I'm meant to kill for the Circle, so how could I possibly have done it?

No, there's only one answer to who I could have killed,

and my heart races as I open my fist to look at the bloody paper in it.

"Fuck," I hiss as I read the names on it.

Paul Ellson

Miles Ellson

"Shit." I wipe a hand across my face.

I remember perfectly well leaving them unconscious on the dungeon floor. I remember taking Peach back to my place and falling asleep with her in my arms.

I don't remember going back for them.

This is bad. It's never been that bad before. The more of Peach I allow myself to have, the more she gives me, the worst I become.

Duval is going to lose it, and I have no excuse for what I did, apart from they touched her. That they tried to punish her. They didn't actually hurt her. It's not the first person I've killed for Peach who's part of the Circle. Bodies are piling up, and I don't think they're going to keep letting me get away with it. I could get into serious trouble with the Circle.

The shower stops, and my heart stops with it. I have to throw this away before Peach sees it. I promised her I wouldn't hurt the Ellsons any more than I had. If I think I'm in trouble with Duval, I don't even want to know what she'll put me through.

I'm too late to move. The door to the bathroom is opening, and I shove the paper in my mouth. Peach walks out with a towel around her and another she's using to dry her hair. She's bent forward, looking at the floor as she wraps it around her hair, and I use this occasion to chew like a maniac until it's a disgusting paste on my tongue.

She will fucking end me if she learns I killed them for what she'll consider nothing.

She straightens back up, her strong gaze on me, and I gulp, swallowing the paper.

"Wren." Her hard voice requires no further explanation. She knows.

I just swallowed a piece of paper for no reason.

Fuck my life.

"Yes?" I ask innocently.

"We need to talk." She advances, her spine straight and her eyebrows drawn together.

I clear my throat and stand. I need something on her. My height will help. "About?"

She stops in front of me, shaking her head. "About Miles and his dad."

My shoulders slump as she cocks an eyebrow at me. "I know. I'm sor—"

"I'm weirdly touched."

I pause, blinking at her as confusion takes over me. "Come again?"

"I know," she huffs. "I don't know what's happening to me. I feel like you've been eating at my brain with a little spoon and turning me even more twisted than you, but you beat up two guys because they hurt me, and I'm...touched."

"Beat up?"

"Yeah." She cocks her head to the side like a cute little puppy. "You were there, weren't you? Or do you forget what happens when you don't go all the way too? How does it work when you become Mr. Hyde?"

She doesn't know. Fuck. She doesn't know.

"I remember." I nod. "And I would do it all over again."

401

"Yeah, well, let's not make a habit out of it."

I smile softly, putting a hand on the back of her neck as I bring her closer and press my lips against hers. Kissing Peach is the kind of gesture that makes me feel *giddy*.

Every time, I become a teen again, unable to believe that the girl I have a crush on notices me. My head fills with dreams and hopes for our future.

It all comes from her, from her lips on mine and the way our tongues intertwine. It's her little sigh that escapes the second our mouths touch, and how I feel her turning compliant in my hold.

Peach and I have a lot in common. And one thing among many others is that we're scientists. We're not big into literature. We don't really get the way poets express themselves. We like facts. Data. Science-backed information. It's a passion of ours.

I always thought love doesn't happen in the heart. It's all in the brain. We have triggers, they're passed on to our brain, and it releases neurotransmitters like oxytocin, dopamine, and serotonin that make us feel all sorts of crazy things. Love is physiological. It's a reward system, and biological rewards motivate our actions.

I know that for a fact. A fucking scientifical fact.

But then why is it that when I kiss her, I suddenly believe I'm capable of understanding things further than science ever has. When I'm with Peach, I'm capable of quantifying and feeling infinity. It's the love I have for her. *Infinite*.

When her skin is against mine and her perfume wraps around me, I have the answers to questions that scientists can't comprehend about love. What was the initial trigger? Why that person? What caused the chemistry? Is there a pattern, a choice we actually make?

Yes. It's Peach.

Peach is the answer to all those questions.

I can explain obsession and murder when she's far from me, when she doesn't notice me, when she's hurt.

I'm knowledgeable about everything because Peach makes me feel it all.

She falls flat on her feet, forcing a separation, and my heart shrinks a little. It's almost painful.

"Wren." Biting her lower lip, her green eyes observe my face as her hands wrap around my biceps. "I want to talk about last night. About you not being you."

"I don't want to talk about me snapping."

I try to look away, at anything in the room apart from her, but she places a hand on my cheek, softly and silently compelling me to look into her eyes, and I melt into her touch.

"Let's start by not calling it *snapping*. This concerns both of us, as a team. I'm not here to accuse you of anything. I'm here to help, alright?"

I put my hand on hers, pulling it away from my cheek only so I can kiss her inner wrist.

"Alright," I whisper, my chest strangely light compared to the lump in my throat.

I feel understood when it comes to Peach, and that's what has always put her above everyone else. This woman creates a new feeling in me every single day, and even the worst ones feel like heaven.

I massage the back of my neck, desperate to ease some tension before I take it a step further.

"Are you scared of me?"

"No." Her answer is automatic. That's what she says to anyone. Even when she's terrified.

I roll my eyes, and she laughs a little.

"I promise you, Wren. I am not scared of you. And especially not after last night."

"I killed them."

I don't need to tell her who. I don't need to tell her why. She's not stupid.

There's a beat that lasts for an eternity. That, too, I can quantify when I'm around Peach. One second of her eyes off me is an eternity. One minute of attention she gives to someone else. One hour I have to watch her from afar in class. It's all the same.

Eternity.

And this, right now, her mouth slightly agape, her eyes fluttering shut, the barely noticeable shift in her position as I wait for reassurance. God, eternity is so long.

"Are you scared of me?" I ask again, my voice barely a rasp now.

And she takes her time to think before she answers. She lets me fear for my equilibrium.

"I'm not scared of you," she whispers.

I take her in my arms with a forcefulness that makes her gasp, but she still wraps hers around my neck.

"I love you," I breathe against her neck, burying my face against her skin.

I inhale her perfume like it's the oxygen keeping me alive.

Until now, I had her physically. She couldn't leave me. But Peach is falling for me the way I did with her. And I'm getting everything I've always wanted.

Her heart.

Her soul.

I am certain of that because they're both tightly woven with mine.

"If you do," she says confidently, even though I feel her

racing heartbeat against my torso. "You'll share every part of you with me. Even the one that scares *you.*"

I straighten up and push her hair over both her shoulders.

"I promise I will. But first, there's the matter of your punishment, Penelope baby."

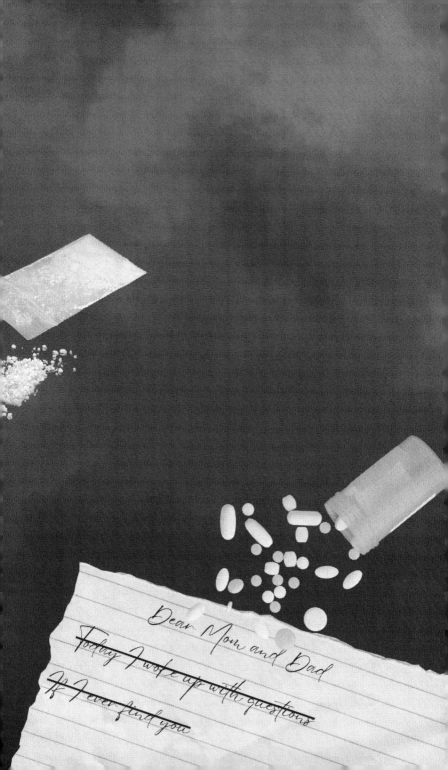

Chapter Thirty

Peach

Cravin' - Stiletto, Kendyle Paige

"I can't breathe," I rasp.

My knees hurt from kneeling on the wooden floor in his living room, and on top of feeling like it's been forever, I'm scared Achilles is going to walk in at any time.

Wren showered, fed me breakfast, and barely talked to me the whole time until he asked me to kneel in my underwear, keep my hands behind my back, and be quiet.

I'm struggling with the last part. Especially now that he's put a thin leather choker around me. He attached my Hera pendant to it, and the lotus flower now falls in the hollow of my throat.

No more hiding who you belong to, Trouble.

He circles me slowly, stopping behind me. I feel one of his fingers on the back of my neck, and he pulls until the choker becomes the rightful owner of its name.

"See, *now* you can't breathe."

Instinctively, I bring my hands to my throat, trying to pull it away from my trachea.

"Hands behind your back. Now."

I'm quick to put them back, hoping obeying will make him stop. And it does. I take a gulp of air as he steps back in front of me.

"Most of your fears are just your stubbornness fighting me. But you know deep down that you're safe with me, Penelope. All you need to do is let go. Can you do that for me?"

I eye the door, then him again. He reads my mind and answers so I don't have to break the rules again.

"Achilles is busy today." He squats in front of me, gripping my chin and forcing me to look into his eyes. "But even if he comes back early and walks in on you like this, you won't move. I'm the one in control. I own you, I own your body, and it's up to me whether anyone else sees it or not. Do you understand?"

I nod, and he kisses my lips before letting go. I don't know if it's his words, his power, or his deep voice that makes my insides shake, but I'm embarrassed by how wet I am already.

"Good."

His fingers delicately trace my collarbones, and he pushes my bra straps to the side. Slowly, he pulls the cups down to reveal my hardened nipples, and I tremble when he rubs them with both thumbs. Goosebumps break all over my skin, and my lungs wheeze as I exhale.

"I was thinking," he murmurs. "We could go on a walk in the forest today."

He talks like we're at the breakfast table planning our day, but his fingers are unrelenting, and I can't focus on anything as electricity keeps zapping to my core.

"We could take our new puppy with us."

He pinches one, then the other, and I gasp, squirming on the spot.

"And then maybe some lunch at the Acropolis, or we could go off campus."

"God, Wren," I whimper.

"Stay quiet." His strict voice is a stark contrast to the soft way he's talking about our day.

I bite my lower lip, throwing my head back, and his hands are on my waist. He pulls me up until I'm not resting on my upturned feet anymore.

I only understand why when his mouth unleashes on one of my nipples. He wanted to make me more accessible. He switches, and I'm moaning loudly, my hips shifting back and forth as I curve into him.

"I'm going to give you something to wear. It'll be difficult, but I want you to remember this is a punishment." He's talking against my skin, and the mix of his spit and his breath heightens the sensations. "Then we'll go on our walk, and until your punishment is over, you're only allowed to talk to beg me to fuck you. Clear?"

I nod, and that's enough for him. He stands and points a finger at me.

"Stay."

He leaves the room, and my knees are aching by the time he comes back. This isn't a comfortable position to stay in. Coming to a stop in front of me, he puts his foot between my knees, just past them.

"Sit."

I could kill him. I'm not his dog. But fuck, I'm so horny I might as well be, because I lower myself faster than I can think. My pussy lands right on his leather shoe, and I'm close to losing my mind.

"Atta girl, straighten your spine. Show me those beautiful tits, Trouble."

The second I do, he shows me what he's holding.

"Wren..."

"Shh. They're going on whether you want it or not. Stay still."

He lowers himself again, and this time, he's got two nipple clamps linked by a chain. My worried eyes are stuck on my nipples. He plays with them once more, making sure they're harder than before, and then he clamps them. One after the other.

Okay...I can survive that. It's not that bad—

"Fuck!" I scream as pain shoots through my right nipple. His fingers are on the little wheel, and he's slowly tightening the clamp. "Stop...stop...stop."

He does, but only to do the same with the other one. My eyes are scrunched tight by the time he's done, and I'm panting from the pain.

"You're taking your punishment really well, Penelope baby. Keep being a good girl for me."

The words somehow soothe the ache, and when his thumbs come to caress my clamped nipples, pleasure shoots all the way down past my stomach.

My mouth parts, and I look at him again.

"Beautiful," he rasps as he brings his thumb to my lips, pushing until he's resting it on my tongue. "Fucking gorgeous."

He's rock hard, I can see it through his jeans, and knowing that he finds me sexy like this doubles my need for him.

Pressing on my tongue, he switches his thumb for two fingers, pushing farther into my mouth this time, as if he's about to fuck my throat. They turn into three, and I'm drooling all over myself, wanting more of him, desperate for anything he has to give.

I move my head, sucking his fingers like it's his dick, and before I know it, I'm moving my hips and rubbing myself against his shoe.

"Fuck, Peach." I look up at him, his jaw slack from surprise or pleasure, I don't know. "Look at you. You're everything I've ever needed."

That spurs me on, and when he pulls his fingers out to press on the back of my head, I end up with my face against his jeans. I'm insatiable as he keeps me against him.

"I want you," I moan. "I want your cock in my mouth."

He tuts, pressing harder. "Good girls ask politely."

"Please," I whimper. "I want to taste you. I want to feel you."

He pulls away, staring down at me like I'm the most precious jewel in the world.

Smiling, he says, "Three weeks ago, you were in this exact position, telling me you didn't want me. Look at you now. Who would have thought I could make such a compliant little slut out of you in such a short time."

My world comes crashing down when he steps away, leaving me empty and needier than ever. His words don't mean a thing when I feel like I'm on the edge of losing myself from desire.

"Now go get dressed. We still have our walk. And don't you dare take those clamps off."

I'm in a pair of leggings and Wren's large lacrosse sweatshirt that falls mid-thigh. Should I be freezing? Absolutely. This isn't nearly enough layers for the fall season here. Am I freezing? No. I'm hot, waves of desires coursing through me as Wren holds my hand while he walks us through the forest. It's barely a hike, but we're deep in the middle of the woods, and the fact that I'm so turned on is making me feel like I ran a marathon. Little Sausage is running ahead, grabbing sticks that are three times her size.

"Wren," I groan for the tenth time. "Please... I can't do this anymore."

"Do they hurt?" he asks softly. "Are you desperate to take them off?"

I stop, forcing him to stop too, and when he turns back to me, I slam my lips against his. "I'm desperate for *you*," I pant. "I need you inside me. I need to feel you. I need to come. Please, I got the lesson. Stop torturing me."

One second, his hands are on my ass, and the next, he's lifting me, allowing me to wrap my legs around his waist.

"What lesson?" he growls against my mouth.

I'm pushed against a giant tree trunk, and I can hardly formulate a sentence when he starts kissing my neck, all the way down to my shoulder.

"That I'm not allowed to go to the temple. Th-that if you tell me to stay somewhere—*fuck*—I'll stay."

Lowering my leggings as far as they can go, he does the same to his jeans, and then his dick is against my entrance. He stays there, barely in, driving me completely insane with one hand holding me by my ass, and one pulling the sweat-shirt above my boobs.

"Why did you go there yesterday? Do you just love chal-lenging everything I say? A sucker for punishment, maybe?"

My brain can barely function anymore, but I know I can't say anything about Hermes. So, I nod.

"I don't like being told what to do, and I wanted to see why you didn't want me to go there." The lie is bitter, but it's impossible to admit the truth. Hermes would make me pay.

I whimper as he starts undoing the clamps, the pain unbearable as blood flows back to my nipples, but for every turn of each wheel, he sinks a little deeper, and I'm seeing stars by the time I'm full of him.

"Do you understand now what happens when you don't listen? I will always protect you, no matter what you do. You put yourself in trouble, I will *always* pick up the pieces. But *do not* disobey me."

He throws the clamps on the ground and rubs one nipple, then the other. They're throbbing, and I try to roll my hips to feel friction.

"You, my pretty girl," he rasps as he starts slowly moving deep inside me, "keep me on the edge of sanity. And I'm a sucker for it."

He doesn't thrust harshly. It's languid, deep, stealing my breath away every time he shifts in the slightest, and the range of emotions barreling through me is messing with my head.

"Shit," I say through the passion swelling in my throat. "I love you."

He hits a little harder. "Do you love me or the way I fuck you?"

"*You*, Wren. I love you and everything you make me feel inside."

He holds me closer to him.

"It's overwhelming," I gasp. "I'm bursting with it."

His hand leaves my boobs to press on my mound.

"Fuck, no, no, no..." I cry out as the world around us disappears.

He pulls out farther, rubbing against my G-spot every time he slides back in.

413

"Don't make me squirt," I squeak. "It's embarrassing."

"Oh, but you're going to do exactly that for me, Trouble. And it's not embarrassing. It's fucking beautiful."

I squeeze with everything I have, but all it does is make me feel more of him, more of the delicious torture.

"We're outside," I pant. "We...we..."

"I'll take you straight back home. I'll shower you. I'll fucking lick all of you the second we're done, if that's what you want. Now, *let go.*"

I come so hard, I feel like I'm blacking out. Being in his arms is so safe, I can't even feel anything else but his over-powering need for me as he makes me squirt all over him. He comes at the same time, his fevered body trembling from the pleasure.

I don't know where I am anymore. I'm blinking and he's out of me, still holding me close.

"I love you," he says. "I love you so much, I fear I might die if I ever lose you."

I smile against his neck as he pulls my leggings back up. They're damp, and my cheeks flush.

"Let's go home," I mumble. "*Together.* That way, you don't die."

We're on our way out of the forest when both our phones chime. Recognizing the Hermes sound, I look up in a panic toward Wren. I did everything I was told yesterday. Surely, they can't be exposing me. Right?

Wren's face falls as he opens the app, and my heart falls with it.

"Fuck," he murmurs.

"What? What is it?"

"Paul and Miles," he says as he runs a hand across his face. "It looks like I left the bodies on campus. *Again.*"

-metal IS NOT the same as punk.
-She's still allergic to shellfish and cat hair
-Always leave the green olives to her
-We don't like metal anymore.
-~~Tea tree and peppermint shampoo~~
-~~Don't forget the peri-peri powder on her fries~~
-Bake and shake every first Tuesday of the month.
-No more sugar in her coffee. It makes her feel sick
-DO NOT bother me during girls' night Wren
-Spiced honey on pepperoni pizza
-Check the triangle freckles on her right shoulder
frequently. Dermatologist said to keep an eye.
-New vision results: Right eye -2.75. Left eye -3.25
-If she gets in next September's yearly release of the
EEAJ, the announcement will be in August next year.
-~~Her brace needs to come off in a week~~
-New shampoo: coconut oil in it
-No more peri-peri on her fries
-Keep the stupid dog

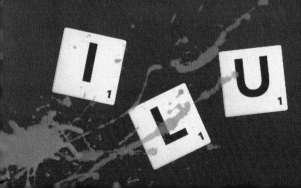

Chapter Thirty-One

Wren

Used to This - Camila Cabello

"Talk to me," Peach says as she sits up in bed and the covers slip down to her waist, exposing her naked chest.

We went home, showered, had food, but there's a hunger for each other we can't seem to satiate.

She pulls the sheet back up, tilting her head to the side and cocking an unimpressed eyebrow at me. I interlock my fingers together behind my head as I get more comfortable on my pillow.

"I was enjoying that view."

"Wren Hunter, focus. We said we'd talk. Except you've refused to utter a word that isn't filthy talk since we saw that Hermes post."

I look at the ceiling, not knowing what to say. She's right, I haven't talked about it because I don't even know where to start. An email from campus security followed the Hermes post. Some of the sentences are still bouncing in my head.

If you heard or saw anything, please contact the police.

Someone is targeting students and possibly their family members. Please, do not leave accommodations unless it's to go to classes.

We are working hard with the Silver Falls University Police Department to arrest the culprit.

They're still not revealing anything about the Scrabble tiles. Probably to avoid saying they're looking for a serial killer, and surely so they don't take the risk having any copycat going around.

I huff. Not so worried about the police, but rather anxious that the Circle hasn't said anything yet. I know they won't let me get away with it.

"I can't force you to talk about something," Peach says softly. She runs a hand through my hair, and a shiver travels down my entire body.

Penelope Sanderson-Menacci is naked in my bed, running her fingers through my hair. She's so close, I can feel the heat of her body under the covers. Lying back down, she faces me on her left side, and one of her legs comes to rest on mine.

God, this is heaven.

"I wrote my first letters to my biological parents in middle school," she whispers.

My head snaps to the side, eyes wide.

"Peach, I know you're not the kind of person to open up about these things. I would never force you to."

"I know." She smiles. "I want to. I feel safe with you. I've always felt safe with you."

She waits until I'm fully turned to face her, and in my bed, naked under the sheets, she makes herself vulnerable to me.

"I was thirteen, and Stoneview Middle School had organized that stupid event where parents were coming to spend the day with us. It was the weirdest shit. Neither of my dads could come. Sanderson was in D.C. for work, and Menacci had gone to Italy to visit his dying mom."

She looks up, and to anyone, it could look like she's searching through her memories, but I can tell she's taking a break from the vulnerability.

"Anyway, one of the kids—and I won't say who, because I don't want them in a body bag—said that no one came for me because I had no real parents. And then he made the joke that I'd been abandoned again." Her voice breaks, and she smiles at me as she swallows. "As you can imagine, I threw a few books at him and told him to shut the hell up. The thing is, so many parents weren't even there. It's Stoneview, so most of them were working somewhere around the world and leaving their kids to the house staff."

She bites her inner cheek, and under the sheets, I take her hand in mine.

"Well, I think that kid really got to me." She chuckles. "I went home that night, and I grabbed a notepad because I wanted to write something to my dads to tell them that they had ruined my day by not being here. But the second I put pen to paper, I subconsciously wrote *Dear Mom and Dad*."

She gulps again, and I can only imagine the way her throat tightens.

"It was a very short letter. Barely a few sentences. *Dear Mom and Dad, I never wrote to you, and you'll never read this because you put me in an orphanage. But what if you do read it one day? Then I don't want you to say sorry, and I don't want you to take me back. I just want you to answer one question. Why?*"

I blink a few times, feeling my eyes stinging.

That letter.

She knows it by heart.

My chest tightens, and so does my grip on her hand.

"God, Wren." She pretends to laugh, but I drown in the sadness that escapes her. "I went down one hell of a rabbit hole after that. I became obsessed. *Why, why, why?* Years went by, and every single insecurity that crossed my teenage mind was put on the list. Because I can't control my emotions? Because I talk too much? Because I'm too opinionated? It made no sense, because I knew, my *brain logically knew*, that they couldn't have known how I'd turn out. But your emotions? Your nervous system? Your body? It doesn't know. You can't regulate how you feel, no matter how many times you tell yourself something."

She takes a shaky breath, her lower lip trembling.

"After that, the letters would just write themselves. I look like neither of my dads, and it made me wonder who I look like. I wanted to know which of my parents was a redhead, which had the green eyes. I wanted to know who thought about it first, to leave me all alone. Him or her? Are they alive?"

A tear runs down her face, and she sniffles in the cutest way possible.

"Those questions, they go on repeat in my head like some stupid broken record. Some days, I add new ones, and some days, I forget the ones from the night before. Sometimes, I lay down in my bed, and I imagine the life we could have had. And I'm ashamed because my dads have given me everything. They're not perfect, but fuck, they love me. But I'm in bed, paralyzed and playing scenes about my biological parents, and I imagine them and me when I was three, and they're parking in front of the shelter where they'll leave me, the same shelter that will give me to an orphanage and...and..."

Her voice is so quiet from now on, I'm scared to breathe, or I'll miss a word. The tears are streaming down her face, and I don't dare wipe them away.

"They look at me and...and they change their mind. They can't go through with it because they love me too much."

A sob bursts from her throat, so profoundly painful that it rips through my heart, and I feel tears running down my own face.

"Except they didn't."

This hurts.

So.

Fucking.

Much.

"They didn't love me enough to change their minds," she whispers when she can talk again. "I don't remember that day. I don't remember anything from before the orphanage. I was too young. I don't even remember how I felt. But fuck do I play all sorts of scenarios in my head. And you know what helps? Keeping myself busy. Drugs. All the things about me that you hate, they would help me feel just a little less lonely."

She shakes her head. "Don't worry. I know they're bad for me. Sometimes, I just can't help it, because it's...easy." Trying to bring an ounce of humor into her voice, she adds, "Anyway, that's my story. So feel free to share yours whenever you're ready."

We hug for so long after that I lose sense of time.

But I don't say anything I usually do. I don't tell her that I will never abandon her, or that anyone else who did is insane. Because that's not what she needs. I understand that now.

I always categorized Peach's belief that she doesn't

deserve love as something that would fix itself if she one day accepted how much I love her. But the selfishness of my thoughts is stark tonight. Her being abandoned as a child is part of who she is. The consequences it had on her aren't something we can run away from or try to fix with a bandage. My love or her dads' cannot replace the love she should have been given by those strangers.

She will live with it for the rest of her life, and I will be there every time she feels vulnerable about it. Without judgement and without quick fixes.

For now, I just keep on holding her tight.

"That's amazing, Dad," Peach cheers as she chops carrots. Her phone is propped on the coffee machine, and she's nodding along as Sanderson smiles on the screen. "And of course, I'll be there. I wouldn't miss election night with you for the world. You're going to be mayor of Stoneview, I know it."

She pushes her chopped carrots into the pot full of water and potatoes. After our talk upstairs, she said she wanted soup and categorically refused to let me cook or order in. When I understood she wanted to keep her mind busy with something, I let her go down to the kitchen and worked in my room for a bit.

She sees me appear behind her through the video call and stiffens when I put an arm around her waist.

"Hello, Mr. Sanderson," I say politely. "How are you?"

He blinks at the image in front of him, his only child being held by her best friend in a way that shows they're clearly dating.

"Well, you know what they say..." He chuckles. "Better

late than never." Pausing, his eyes stay on Peach rather than me, because it's no secret that he loves her like the most precious thing in the world. "Your dad is going to be so happy."

She probably doesn't notice she's chewing on her hair, so I pull it out of her mouth. I can feel the guilt seeping out of her. She was sobbing in my bed, heartbroken about being abandoned by her biological parents, barely over an hour ago. Anyone would struggle to reconcile that with feeling the love from your adoptive parent.

"You'll be Penny's date to the release party at our home, Wren, won't you?" he adds.

"Of course, sir." I nod. "I'm looking forward to celebrating your win."

He laughs to himself, his eyes wrinkled with genuine amusement. "I always knew you were a good man. Alright, I'll leave you two to it now. I love you, Penny Pickle."

She pulls her hair out of her mouth, finally realizing what she was doing.

"I love you, Daddy," she says with a voice full of affection.

As she hangs up, I put my hands on her hips, turning her around until she's leaning against the counter. I press my lips against hers. And just like every time I think I'm going for a quick kiss, an overwhelming need takes hold of me. I kiss her once, twice, three times before I move to the corner of her mouth, her cheek, her temple. I leave a few on her forehead and finally separate when I've kissed the top of her head.

"Let's take Little Sausage for her evening walk," I murmur against her hair, breathing in her expensive perfume.

"I'm making food," she mumbles in the crook of my neck.

She always finds her way there somehow. "You go without me."

My heart sinks, and I step back with a forced smile on my face. "Alright." I leave another quick kiss on her forehead.

"Wait, wait, wait," she calls out as soon as I start walking away. She's pressing buttons on the cooker. "I'm coming with you."

"That was a quick change of heart." I chuckle just before whistling for the dog to come.

Her little paws click on the floorboard as she runs from the living room, and we meet her near the door.

"You do that thing when you're annoyed with me," she explains, a smile lifting the corner of her mouth as she puts her heavy wool coat on.

"What?" I scoff. "I don't have a thing when I'm annoyed." I squat to hook the leash to Sausage.

"Yes, you do." While I'm still on my haunches, she leans down and presses a kiss on my forehead. "This."

I have to press my lips together not to smile. She's right. I don't do it on purpose. I guess it's just a way to remind myself, even when I'm annoyed, that I'm still the luckiest guy on the planet to have her.

"Whatever," I say as I stand up, but I can feel my cheeks heating from the fact that I got caught.

Keeping the end of the leash in my hand, I snap my fingers, pointing at my foot. Sausage runs to me, standing there with her tail wagging. "Stay," I warn her as I open the door.

I look back at Peach. "Ready?"

Her eyes are wide, her mouth agape, and she doesn't move.

"What?" I look behind me, but no, she's clearly staring right at me. "What?" I insist.

"You talk to her...the same way you talk to me in the bedroom."

I wipe a hand across my mouth, trying to hide my smile as I see that little vein starting to pulse on her forehead.

"Baby, don't be jealous. If it's any consolation, you're my favorite." It's just too tempting to provoke her. So, I snap my fingers again and point toward my foot. "Come on, let's go."

"I will break your fucking hand, Wren Hunter," she hisses as she walks past me to go out.

I follow her, laughing so loudly it makes Little Sausage bark with excitement.

We're about five minutes into our walk, holding hands as we make our way through the streets of our campus and passing through Greek row, when I take a deep breath and look around.

It's a quiet night. People are probably at the Acropolis or having a night in. Following the email from campus to stay in as much as possible, there are no house parties going on, no one on the streets. Peach and I can have a conversation without being heard.

I huff, playing with the leash I'm holding to release some tension. Sausage is free of it, running ahead. Peach catches my sudden awkwardness.

"What's wrong?"

We keep walking, and everything else is suddenly catching my attention. As long as I don't have to look into her eyes.

Licking my lips, I swallow thickly and say, "The Silent Circle has a habit of collecting favors."

It's clear as day that she understands where I'm going. She stops, her eyes digging into mine.

"Don't force yourself."

"I'm not," I tell her. "I want to share this with you. The same way you did with me, but I'm not going to beat around the bush. I'm going to tell you what happened, and we're going to move on. Because you're stuck with me, Peach. So if this makes you hate me, there's nothing you can do about it."

The reminder seems to shock her. We've been acting like such a normal couple that she forgot she can't actually leave me. She finally nods, encouraging me to go ahead.

"Sometimes Shadows will offer help to people who aren't part of the Circle, but warn them that they'll owe a favor back, and it can be asked for at any time. I can't begin to express how dangerous it is to owe a debt to the Circle. They will *always* collect it."

I look away from her. "When they collected mine, they asked me to join. That's why I didn't have a choice. Because I owed them, and there was nothing else I could do but what they asked of me. They wanted a reaper, or *Thanatos* in their own term."

"Thanatos," she repeats. "The god of non-violent death."

"Yeah." I chuckle. "Well, don't expect the Circle to stick to the non-violent part. As long as I kill the targets, they don't ask how. They just make sure to get rid of the body." With a huff, I run a hand through my hair. "Since I was fifteen, I knew I was going to have to repay them at some point. I had just hoped it would be one favor and done. Except the favor was to join them, and now...well, now, here we are."

She wants the rest, I can tell. It's just a little harder to push out of me than I thought.

"What happened when you were fifteen that meant you needed a favor from the Circle?" she asks.

"Do you remember my dad's brother, Vincent?"

"Yes, of course, I remember him. He was a bit of a creep, wasn't he?"

My jaw clenches, ghosts from the past waging a war in my mind. I crack my neck, left then right. Fuck, this is harder than I thought.

"He was a creep, yes. To say the least." I massage my shoulder. My body feels like it isn't mine anymore. "Peach, there's something you need to know about my childhood. Something I hid from you as your best friend, and I didn't do it because I didn't trust you, but because I love you."

I lick my lips, trying to keep my focus. Her beautiful eyes open a little wider, eagerly awaiting the truth.

"I was a child with serious violent outbursts. It started small, but slowly, they would get worse and worse. I'd hit Elijah for the smallest reasons. I even hit my mom once. There was nothing to justify them and nobody understood. So, despite my dad believing that beating me up to keep me weak was the only solution, my mom took me to see a psychiatrist. It took months. They ruled out a lot of diagnoses first. They did tests, physical, mental—it was so fucking invasive—and they concluded I suffered from Intermittent Explosive Disorder."

She swallows thickly, her eyes observing my entire body. "What is that?"

"A label they stuck on me to give us some sort of explanation. Except it doesn't help, and it only got worse."

"You... You never had that around me. Or at school, sleepovers–"

"No." I chuckle bitterly, looking everywhere but at her. "Because there were no triggers there. No dad who beats you up and forces your body into constant survival mode." And then I look into her eyes. "But mainly, there was you.

And nothing puts me at peace the way you do by simply existing around me."

I lift a hand to her cheek, caressing her soft skin with my thumb. Her eyes flutter shut, and when she opens them, they're begging for more.

"Wren, tell me how this is linked to your uncle or the Circle."

"Okay," I rasp, having no choice but to get to it. "Uncle Vincent is the first time I dissociated. He and my dad came back from the Stoneview Country Club one day, and they were smoking cigars in my dad's office. I wanted to join because they had invited Elijah to. So, why not me?"

My heart starts racing, and my hand refuses to move from Peach's face. "They didn't invite me because they hated me. They've always hated me. So all I did was stand behind the door and listen to their conversation. Until that conversation turned to you."

"Me?"

"Yes, you. And how Vincent thought you were so beautiful for a fifteen-year-old. Your tits, and your ass, and that sassy mouth was so *hot*," I hiss disgustingly. "You were *fifteen*."

I throw my head back, desperate to remember what happened, exactly. Except I never will.

"All I know is that one second, I was opening the door, and the next, I was coming to my senses. Vincent was on the floor, his throat slashed, and I was the one holding the letter opener. My brother had a bloody nose, and my dad a ripped shirt."

I blink at the dark sky before looking back at her. Her chest rises up and down so quickly, I wonder if she's about to bolt.

"My dad told me he knew people who could get rid of

the body. No one would ask anything, and my aunt would never know the truth. It would all just disappear. I wouldn't get in trouble with the law, but that I would owe them a favor. Those people were the Silent Circle, and they saw an opportunity in a teen who was capable of murdering his own family."

My gaze drops, my shoulders deflating. "My family already didn't like me, but after that, they never looked at me the same. My dad... Fuck, I killed his brother, Peach. No wonder he *loathes me*."

My hand is still on her cheek, and she places hers on mine too, forcing me to look into her eyes. "I love you, Wren. No matter what, no matter in what form, friendship or more, I will always love every single part of you."

This is it. The kind of love I never felt from someone else before. *Unconditional.* And it's so intense I can hardly process it.

She huffs, shaking her head. "But I don't want to be the reason people die."

Her green eyes are only lit by the light of the moon, but they've never looked so demanding.

"What if you're the reason I'm alive? Because only you keep me sane, Trouble. That thing inside of me can only be tamed by you. And all the times I've wanted to give up and just let it take over, I thought of you. How I might lose you if I do. I live for one and only one reason, and that's you."

She wants to smile, I can tell. It's shining in her eyes.

"Why are you always sending so much love my way, Wren Hunter?"

"Because keeping all that love to myself would be inhuman."

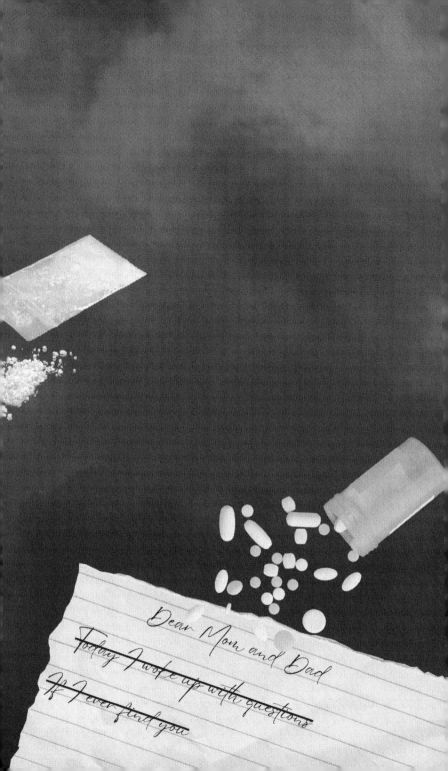

Dear Mom and Dad

Today I woke up with questions

If I ever find you

Chapter Thirty-Two

Peach

Sinner - Shaya Zamora

My heart thumps powerfully.

I hear every single beat in my ears, drumming against my brain and stopping me from thinking straight.

In the women's bathroom of the science building, I look at myself in the mirror. I'm so pale.

And I think I'm going to be sick again.

Penelope, what happened? You've made no real progress on this paper. This looks like self-sabotaging.

Professor Lopez pulled out today's Hermes post about me. A picture of me at a party, head down, straight up snorting cocaine.

It's a very old picture, Professor. I promise you. Look, my hair isn't even the same length!

The disappointed look on his face was enough to make me want to cry.

The picture exists. That's enough to give you a reputation.

Lopez's voice bouncing in my brain sends me straight back to the stall, and I throw up bile since I've got nothing left in my stomach.

The bathroom is the only updated room in the old, historical building, and I'm suddenly hating how bright it is in here compared to the creepy hallways.

Has anything happened since the last time we met?

Yes, actually. I was forced into a secret society, signed a deal with the devil so he could make me his. I lost my best friend to a murderer, but they're the same person. And I was promised life-changing information that would help me heal, yet I've seen barely anything. But the worst thing is? It's now been almost over a week since that man showed me his most vulnerable side, and I showed him mine, and I now deeply believe that he's my soulmate.

My sanity is hanging by a thread. I still don't know what Hermes wants from me. I saw what those sick men do to women at the temple. I witnessed a Hera being punished for cheating on someone she'd been forced to marry. Now what? Why did Hermes want me to see that after they blackmailed me into going to the initiations? So I could see how stuck I am? How I should behave if I don't want to end up like her?

I'm going to lose my chance at being something. Something real, outside of that vicious cycle Wren forced me into. Because I can't focus. Because all I think about is him, and his hands on my body. Him and the way he punishes, and loves me, and makes me experience every feeling possible under the sun. I want his mouth on mine, his hands on my hips, and *him* inside me.

I want his cruelty and his control.

And I want his love.

His. Fucking. Love.

I wipe tears from my eyes as I stand up and go back to the sink. Washing my hands, I clean my mouth and pull out the toothbrush I keep in my bag. I've done many library all-nighters before, and I always keep a little kit with me.

My eyes catch the pills I picked up earlier, and I shake my head, but then Professor Lopez's voice is back, telling me we won't be able to submit the paper if I don't get a grip. I reach for them, fisting the small packet tightly, and pull out one of my notebooks.

I set the book flat on the counter, and then two pills on it.

Placing another book on top of it, I put all my weight down until I hear the pills being crushed. I do it again a few times before pulling out my credit card.

I need to seriously work on this paper, to focus on my future and nothing else. My biggest dream is a Nobel Prize, and Wren has reduced me to a fucking sex toy...who enjoys being a sex toy.

My lines aren't perfect, but they'll do. I bend over, press a finger on one of my nostrils...and I pause.

I would prove Hermes right. I would betray Professor Lopez. Mainly, I promised Wren I wouldn't. I haven't done any drugs, haven't even drank anything since the last time we argued about it. And he keeps me busy, loved, occupies my mind so well that I haven't felt the need to do this. I can do some fucking work without Adderall. I'm stronger than that.

I blow on the powder and dust off my books. Putting all my stuff back in my bag, I make my way to the library.

I pick a quiet table rather than the usual one people know belongs to my friends and me. This time, I'm at the back, between two giant rows of books and surrounded by a few empty tables.

No one bothers me. I'm going to be in the Environmental Engineering American Journal.

I'm probably an hour in when I feel a presence by my table. Looking up from my laptop, ready to tell whoever to fuck off, I barely hold back my surprise when I see Elijah.

"Hey," I say softly.

I don't know how to act around him.

I feel guilty for not keeping in touch with him. All because of Wren. This is the one thing I won't let my Shadow take control of. I will not stop being friends with Elijah... Or I thought I wouldn't. Because the truth is, it's been two weeks and we haven't spoken, texted, or spent any time together.

He's got a sorry face on, and I don't know if it's because he's mad at me or is about to tell me something I don't want to know.

"Can I sit down?" he asks.

I look around, realizing that some people have taken the few tables around me. On one of them, Chris Murray, Ella's boyfriend, is studying with other people from law school.

"Uh," I hesitate. "Maybe we should go somewhere else."

His eyes follow my gaze, and he notices Chris too.

"Do you think he'll snitch to your Shadow that you're hanging out with me when you're not allowed to?"

I roll my eyes. "You're saying it like I actually care what Wren says I can or can't do."

"Don't you? You're the one who wants to move."

That pokes my pride, and I narrow my gaze at him. "I was more worried for you, but sure, sit down."

He sits, putting his backpack on his lap.

"Are you working on your paper?" he asks as he eyes the books around me.

I nod. "It's not going well. I just... I want this so bad, you know? And I worked so hard on it that now I don't even know how to push myself further. But I'm no quitter."

He looks around and murmurs, "The Circle could just get you in that journal, Peach. Has Wren not offered?"

My mouth drops open, and it's hard to keep my voice down. "No, of course not. It wouldn't even cross his mind." It's never been so obvious that Wren knows me much more than Elijah does.

"Elijah, I would never want my success to come that way. I want to earn my place. Wren knows that, and he'd never disrespect me by even suggesting using the Circle to get me in the E.E.A.J."

His eyebrows pull together, and he forces a smile, clearly disliking me defending Wren.

"Of course. I'm sorry." He scratches his throat and adds, "So, has he been able to come up with anything else regarding your parents?"

I open my mouth, but shut it right away. I was about to defend him yet again.

"No," I admit quietly.

"And do you know if he's still looking?"

Elijah feels different today, less like my sweet friend. Maybe it's because I'm not used to him talking with so much confidence. Or maybe it's because Wren opened up about his family hating him, and I have a problem with how Elijah sides with his parents in the way they treat Wren at home.

"He is," I say curtly. "He'll find something."

Nodding to himself, he pulls an envelope out of his bag.

My heartbeat picks up, noticing the string sealing it shut. It's the same kind of envelope Wren had brought back to my house. The one that had the certificate in it.

I can't breathe for a few seconds, trying to keep calm,

435

and I fail. My hand goes for the envelope, and he slaps his on top of it.

"Don't," I snarl.

"Before you open it, I just want you to know, this is going to be hard. But I'm here."

"Move. Your. Hand."

He lets go, and I snap the string rather than unroll it. Pulling out the single sheet, my heart sinks further than I thought possible.

"No," I whisper, my eyes moving faster on the page than my brain can catch up with. "No, no, no."

My throat seizes, the ball forming in there making it impossible to inhale a full breath.

Death certificate.

I look up, and Elijah's eyes are so full of sorrow it starts a storm in my head.

"My mom," I rasp. "She's...dead?" I read more, and my eyes widen, allowing tears to fall. "Oh my god," I gasp weakly.

Cause: Homicide. Bullet wounds.

"She was murdered," I choke out. "She was...she was shot."

He nods, lips pinched and unshed tears filling his eyes. "I'm so sorry, Peach."

"How did Wren not find this?" I rasp. "He's been looking."

He stays silent, his gaze dropping as his grip on his bag tightens. I need no other explanation.

"No." I shake my head. "Don't say it. Because it's not true. He didn't know."

"Peach—"

"What do you do for the Circle?" I insist. "You clearly

have more power than he does. You work with people who are more connected."

"I'm good with numbers," he explains calmly. "I'm nothing more than an accountant to help them with tax evasion."

"That's not true." But how much more can I lie to myself?

"Wren knows, Peach," he says with more strength. "The same person who gave this to me told me he gave it to him." And in case this doesn't hurt enough, he repeats, "He knows."

"But..." I croak. "Why wouldn't he say anything?"

Elijah doesn't get a chance to give me any sort of reassurance, because a shadow is right here, quick as lightning, and before I can blink, Wren is holding my friend by the collar of his uniform, slamming him against the shelves.

"Wren," I gasp, standing up so quickly my chair falls back.

"You know what, Brother?" he hisses. "You're the only person I've given multiple warnings to in my life. And yet, you never took the chances I've given you to *stay. Away. From her.*"

"Let him go," I hiss as I look around.

There's a crowd of hungry eyes surrounding us, all supporters of our college golden boy and looking forward to finally seeing him put his "loser" of a brother in his place. Standing closer to us, apart from the crowd, Chris Murray is watching, arms crossed, a vigilant look in his eyes.

Yet he doesn't intervene.

"You fucking snitch," I spit at him. Wren has classes in the science building until the end of the day. Chris is obviously the one who told him about this. "Can't you mind your own business for once?"

Turning back to the brothers, I freeze on the spot when I realize that Wren is done with the warnings. He's holding Elijah by the throat now, and he slams him against the shelves again, causing his brother to wince in pain.

"Look at her," he snarls in his face. *"Look at her."*

Elijah's wild eyes are on me, his face red from the lack of oxygen. It's terrifying. He looks like a twig in Wren's hold.

"You do not approach her. You do not talk to her. Fuck, Elijah, I don't even want her crossing your mind. Do you understand?"

He tries to nod, but his eyes roll to the back of his head instead.

"Wren, let him go," I panic, still unable to move my body from the fear keeping me locked in place.

He releases him for a split second, only to punch him so hard Elijah loses his balance. But as he starts to fall, Wren grabs him by the throat again.

"Oh, no, no. You're not fainting on me. You're going to learn your fucking lesson," he growls. "You're going to keep looking at her while she defends you and pisses me off even further. You love when she feels bad for you, don't you?"

I notice the blood spilling from Elijah's mouth, and that finally gets me going.

"Let him go, you fucking asshole," I hiss. "At least he doesn't lie to me."

I snatch the paper from the table as I stride to them, gripping it in my hand with the same tightness I feel in my chest.

"What the fuck is this, huh?" I say as I shove it in his face.

He doesn't let go of his brother, but his face falls, guilt so clear in his eyes that I want to rip my heart out and show him what he did to it.

"Peach—"

"Let him go. Right. Now."

My order doesn't have the effect I thought it would.

"You're dead, Brother." And I hear the shift in Wren's tone. He's gone. Past what he can control.

The other part has taken over, and Elijah knows it because his eyes are screaming, *He snapped!*

"Don't. Don't, don't, don't." I grab him by the shoulder, attempting to pull him away. "Chris," I call out.

Elijah is on the floor in the next second, Wren kicking him everywhere he can reach as his brother cries out and puts himself in a fetal position.

Wrapping my arms around Wren's waist, I pull as hard as I can. "Chris! He's going to kill him." My throat is so tight, I struggle to scream. I'm in a nightmare and nothing I do has any impact.

"Wren, enough." Chris's voice is calm, but there's a haste in it that shows he's aware he's running out of time.

He pushes me to the side but has to try three times before he finally manages to pull Wren away. Wren fights back for a few seconds, but there's a calmness to him as Chris holds him back from behind, hooking his arms around Wren's so he can't swing as Elijah rolls to his side and attempts to stand up.

I face my boyfriend, my heart breaking into the kind of tiny pieces I know I will never be able to put back together.

"You lied to me," I croak.

He's panting, clearly not back from his trip to the other side. His shirt is ripped open, buttons on the floor from when I tried to pull him back. And his abs are covered in red marks, some bleeding, because I clearly scratched him in the process.

"You lied to me," I repeat shakily. "About something you knew meant *everything* to me."

His eyes go to the paper in my hand.

"Peach, let me explain," he wheezes, attempting to catch his breath.

And that's when it really hits. Because I think a part of me was still hoping that this was all a huge misunderstanding. That Elijah was wrong. The part of me that has desperately fallen in love with Wren and would excuse him of anything just wants to believe that he would never do this to me. Not as my best friend, not as my boyfriend.

Not as the love of my life.

A fury like never before takes hold of me. Against him, against his lies, against everything he's put me through this year.

"You lied to me!" I yell as I push him.

Chris is still holding him, and he can't do anything. They don't move, and it angers me even more.

"How could you do this to me?" My scream resonates in the entire library, ripping from my throat like thunder from the clouds.

"I wanted to tell you. Please, please, listen to me. I was protecting you. *Let me go,*" he throws out at Chris before talking to me again. "I didn't want to hurt you further than you already were. This was too hard for you to take."

I slap him with the paper. "You don't get to make this decision for me!" His chest, his face, I keep hitting him with a single sheet of paper that rips to pieces.

"How...how...Wren, oh my god," I sob. "How could you do this to me? You made me love you, you *changed me.* You threw away our friendship for your *selfish, obsessive love.*"

I can't control my tears. The paper is crumbled, ripped, destroyed. Just like my trust. I drop the remaining piece to the floor, slapping his chest with my palms.

I lose strength quickly, and he's incapable of doing anything, still held back by Chris, who is smart enough to not get in the way.

Panting, I look up at his face. My heartbreak reflects in his eyes, his guilt seeping through me.

We are one. We are soulmates.

This was never meant to happen.

"I let down my walls for you because I trusted you to keep me safe."

Taking a step back, I shake my head.

"You ruined me."

And I turn around because I can't look at him anymore.

I hear the commotion of Wren trying to get out of Chris's hold, and then I hear the calm, "Leave her alone. Give her time," from him as I push through the crowd of shocked students.

He threw it all away.

The way I was with him...I'd never been like that with anyone else. I've always been the strong girl. Because that's who I grew up to be and what the people around me needed me to be. The problem once you show strength is that even if you ever allow yourself not to be strong, people won't let you. It doesn't fit their narrative, and they need someone invincible they can always turn to. If you show weakness, it scares them.

It didn't scare Wren Hunter.

He *pushed me* to show my weaker side.

He let it happen. He tore our friendship apart to build it into a loving relationship, broke me into pieces, and put me back together so I would be made for him only.

441

And then he lost me.

But mainly, after weeks of falling deeper and deeper in love with him...

I lost him.

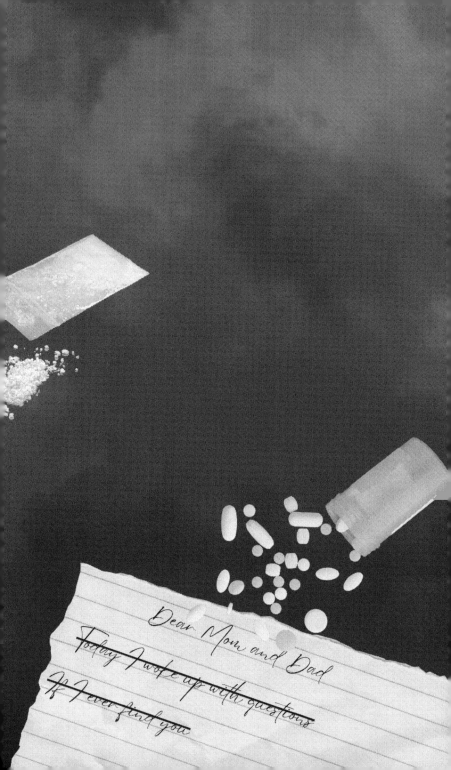

Dear Mom and Dad

Today I woke up with questions

If I ever find you

Chapter Thirty-Three

Peach

Reflections - The Neighbourhood

"Here you go, sweetie," Alex says as she passes me a steaming mug of tea.

I'm curled up on her sofa under three fluffy blankets, and I have one of her pet bunnies chewing some cilantro on my lap.

I look down at my phone that's lighting up for the hundredth time. It's late. He called me all day and all evening. He keeps alternating calls and messages. Every time there's a new text, I re-read all the other ones.

> Wren: Where are you?

> Wren: Peach. I'm so sorry. You have to let me explain.

> Wren: Where did you go? Are you on campus? Your house is empty.

> Wren: I'm sorry. Please pick up.

> Wren: Pick up, Penelope.

> Wren: Peach, baby, please. We need to talk. Where are you?

> Wren: Talk to me. I'm begging you.

> Wren: I'm worried. At least tell me you're safe.

> Wren: Penelope, pick up the fucking phone.

There are a few reasons I came to Alex and Xi's house on the North Shore of Silver Falls the second I left the library. The first one being I couldn't go to Ella's because Chris can't be trusted. He would have told Wren where I am right away. The second is that Wren has never been here. He knows Alex lives on the North Shore when she's not on campus, but he has no idea where exactly.

Alex sits next to me on the sofa and puts her hand on my lap.

"Hey." She smiles softly. "Did you change your mind about talking about it, or should we just binge watch something super violent?"

I chuckle softly, petting her bunny. His name is Jean-Paul Sartre. Yes, like the French philosopher. She's such a nerd.

Alex has the kindest heart, and no matter that I've been distant, she knows I'm hiding something, and she still welcomed me with open arms when I knocked on her door.

Xi walks into the living room, nodding a hello at me, but nothing more. He's not the friendliest, most talkative guy. He's clearly coming back from the painting studio he set up in his shed. He's got pink paint smudged on his shirt, fingers, and hair. It's Alex's favorite color, and Xi might be a big, bad ex-drug dealer from the North Shore, but it's clear when you look at their house who owns his ass.

The front door is painted fuchsia, and there are frames of the couple everywhere on pink shelves she probably made him put up. Some are of them and the bunnies. Some are only the bunnies. So when Xi walks in, wearing jeans and a white tank top, and I notice how big his arms are, how lethal his entire body is...when I think about the fact that he's probably killed people for the gang he used to be in, I want to burst out laughing. The man has pet bunnies.

"I think I'll choose the violent movie, if you don't mind," I tell my friend. "I'm not sure I feel like talking about anything."

She nods, completely unsurprised. I'm not one to talk about topics that feel a little too real. As she grabs the remote, she hesitates.

"Are you and Wren still together?" she whispers, barely able to look at me. She sounds like a kid whose parents are about to divorce.

Except it's a lot more complicated than that, isn't it? I'm furious with Wren. Betrayed. But he's my Shadow. There are forces more powerful than my will that get to decide if he and I are still together or not.

And there's also the issue that I'm in love with him, and that isn't a feeling I can simply shut down.

I've never felt so lonely while being linked so strongly to someone.

I take too long to answer, my thoughts swirling like smoke in my head. It's impossible to take hold of one to make sense of anything.

"Something violent," Alex says reassuringly, stopping the war in my head.

"Where the guy gets his dick chopped off will do," I say playfully.

"Intense," I hear Xi mumble behind the couch. He's now

447

throwing carrot peels into the fenced space the bunnies have in the living room. They have three of them. Why do they need so much space? This house is tiny, too.

"This is how girls cope," Alex throws back as we both look over our shoulders at him. "I don't tell you how to deal with heartbreak."

"Cupcake." He smiles, but there's nothing reassuring in it. "Break my heart, and you'll be the one having to deal with putting it back together. Spoiler alert: won't feel like a trip to Disneyland for you."

She giggles as I roll my eyes, and we're cut off by her phone ringing. Her wide gaze comes to me as she shows me the name on the screen.

Wren.

"Motherfucker," I groan, throwing my head back.

"I'm going to see what he wants. I won't tell him you're here," she assures me.

"No, no. Alex, you're a terrible liar—" I cut myself off as she picks up and puts him on speaker.

"Hey, Wren," she says in a fake cheer. "What's—"

"Is she with you? Because she's not at your campus house. She's not at her dads', and she's not with Ella."

Alex's eyes go from me and to Xi, who's now slowly walking to the sofa with a scowl on his face.

"Um, she's not here," she says meekly, making me slap a hand against my face.

"You're a terrible liar."

I mouth *I told you* to her, and she shakes her head, not knowing what to do.

"Please, please, tell her I'm sorry. Tell her to come home. I need her."

"What did you do?" my friend asks, her eyes on me and her face falling when she notices my eyes tearing up.

"I fucked up. But I never meant to hurt her. I would never hurt her. I was... I was trying to keep her happy. Please, give her the phone. I need to hear her voice."

Her eyebrows rise slightly, her puppy eyes begging me to say something. She's fucking falling for it. So, I shake my head vehemently.

"Give me your address, Alex. Let me bring her home, and you won't have to worry about anything else. Please, we're both your friends." He sounds so desperate, he's even pulling at my heartstrings. I can't imagine Alex, who wears her heart on her sleeve, resisting him much longer.

Hang up, I mouth. But she shakes her head.

"Wren." She hesitates. "Maybe you could give her the night? And try again tomorrow?"

"No." And the switch in his voice makes her blink a few times in confusion. She doesn't know that side of him. She still knows him as Wren, our best friend.

"N-no?" she stutters. I catch Xi's eyes narrowing at the phone as he crosses his arms.

"No. And actually, I'd like you to remind her of something for me. Can you do that?"

"Uh..." she hesitates, wide eyes now looking around the room.

My jaw tightens. He's scaring her.

"Tell her that she can hide all she wants, but there's no escaping me." His smooth, low voice is terrifying, sending goosebumps to my forearms. *"Remind her that her choice is an illusion I can take away at any time, and that the same system we both hate will support me in finding her. She can hate me, and she can be mad for the rest of her life, but she will be mad by my side."* My mouth drops open to help my struggling breath. I can't believe he's giving her hints of the Circle even existing.

"And you two stay at your house, Alex. I can find you, don't you worry."

She's frozen on the spot, but it doesn't matter, because Xi snatches her phone out of her hands.

"Do you know who the fuck you're talking to, Hunter?" he growls. "I've killed men for a lot less than being threatening to Alex. So watch your tone and stay away from our house. Because if I see you here, I'll show you how we deal with clingy exes on this side of the river."

Hanging up, he turns back to us, throwing the phone on the couch. He looks me up and down and says to Alex, "If she becomes a problem for your safety, she's out."

"What?" Alex gasps. "No, she's not. Take that back."

He shakes his head. "Her ex-boyfriend surrounds himself with seriously dangerous people, Cupcake. I'm not taking any risks."

"What?" The word slips out of my mouth with barely any emotion in it. The shock is too great. "What do you know?"

"Enough to know I don't want him and his little friends anywhere near my woman."

"What little friends?" Alex jumps back in. "What is it? What are we talking about?"

"How do you know anything?" I ask as I get to my feet, rounding the sofa to where he's standing.

"Those guys keep their power by owning everyone. They're intricately linked with mafia men. And I happen to know a few of those men. That's it," he explains in his unbothered tone.

"Wait, wait." Alex shakes her head as Jean-Paul Sartre jumps on her lap. She grabs him, petting him as she stands up. "Are we... Are we scared of Wren now or something?

Why is he dangerous so suddenly?" Her eyes grow wider than saucers. "Xi, are *you* scared of Wren?"

She looks like her world is about to fall apart, and mine too. To Alex, there's no one who can keep her safer than her ex-gang-member boyfriend who grew up in the roughest town in the tri-state area. She's looking so vulnerable like this, a little girl who's finding out for the first time that parents can be scared too.

"All I'm saying," Xi says calmly, "is that Wren Hunter is someone you don't necessarily want to mess with. So if your friend being here becomes a danger to you, she's out."

"But you just *threatened him*," she says weakly. "Why would you threaten someone you're scared of!" She walks around, petting her bunny until she freezes. "Wait, that makes no sense." She laughs to herself. "Wren is our best friend. Xi, you're being paranoid. Again."

He approaches her at the same time I do, and he puts a hand on her cheek.

"I'm not scared of *him*. My threat is very much valid. He shows up here, he's dead. Buried by tree thirteen and all. But then we might, you know, have to move across the world or something. Because the people he associates with are more powerful than I can handle on my own."

Alex rubs a hand down her now pinkened face. "You've lost your mind. Wren doesn't associate himself with anyone but *us*. Is that who you're scared of? Me and my friends? His lacrosse team? This is insane."

"What's tree thirteen?" I ask, heart racing. I feel this is useful information I should know.

They both turn to me. And Alex forgets all about Wren and the people she should fear. Good.

"Um," my friend hesitates.

Xi doesn't.

Lola King

"It's a place on the North Shore, where we bury all our bodies. There are so many, it would be impossible for the cops to trace them back to anyone."

I stay still for a while, my thoughts running a hundred miles an hour. Today is a heavy day. A lot on my mind. A lot that's going to stick with me and haunt me. And I'm struggling to put words to my emotions.

Xi observes me as Alex goes back to the couch, sitting down and sighing that "this is too much to process."

He crosses his arms over his chest, his eyes growing more intense on me. "Why are you interested in tree thirteen?"

"Because you just threatened to put my boyfriend six feet under by said tree," I snap back. "Can I have a minute to process it?"

"Still your boyfriend, then." He continues with his unbearably flat tone.

He doesn't move, observing me from head to toe, and back up... Then something flashes in his eyes. Recognition.

"Do you have a sister?"

"I'm an only child," I reply right away. "Adopted."

"Right. Of course. You just remind me of someone."

The entire conversation feels robotic until stupid hope flares up my chest.

"Who? Because I could have a mom." And I know I read she had been killed, but that's the thing about hope. It comes back, because it keeps you going. A survival mechanism that's kept humanity alive for hundreds of thousands of years.

Sweat coats my back when I take a step toward him.

"I could have a mom," I repeat, and the vigor in my words makes him take a step back.

"Xi," Alex insists. "Do you know a woman who looks like Peach and is of age to be her mom?"

He shakes his head. "No, sorry. She's young. Early thirties or something."

Alex looks at me with eyes full of apology and smiles to try to reassure me that everything is going to be okay.

"But how much does she look like me? It has to be a lot if you thought of her?"

His gaze darts to Alex, and I catch her shaking her head. I know she isn't holding something back from me. Alex is too bad at that. She probably doesn't even know the woman. What she's silently telling him, though, is to not give me false hope.

Xi runs a hand through his thick dark hair. "Maybe all redheads look a bit the same to me," he mumbles.

"Are you only realizing now that I look like her, Xi?" I ask, annoyed. "You've seen me how many hundreds of times since you've been with Alex? And you see it *now*?"

"I'll be honest with you. When Alex is in a room, I don't really look at anyone else."

Can't blame him for that, I guess.

I turn to Alex. "Do you know her?"

Negative.

I'm about to ask for her name when my phone beeps again, and I look down, expecting another message from Wren.

It's not him.

It's Hermes.

Hermes: Did you know there are secret rooms under the campus castle?

"No," I whisper to myself, despair clinging to me like a heavy blanket weighing me down.

This is the last thing I need right now.

> Hermes: Well, there are. There's a secret passageway to access them. In the middle of the quad, the statue of Athena stares at the entrance. The young men from the Circle like to use the place to play with their Heras without the older members keeping an eye on them.

"Peach, is everything okay?"

I startle, nodding at Alex, but I feel like my soul is leaving my body.

> Hermes: Go check it out, little murderer. Hurry up. Or you'll miss the best part.

It takes all of me to stay standing, my legs threatening to give up on me. I can't take any more of life today.

"All fine," I croak. "I...I have to go."

"Are you okay? Was it Wren? Was it...those people Xi is talking about?"

I shake my head. "No. No, but I have to run."

"Peach." Alex gets up, nervous energy wafting from her. "Who are those people?"

I glance at Xi. "I can't say anything, but you're not part of it. Whatever you know and share with her won't get anyone in trouble. I have to go."

Of course, I feel horrible lying to my friend after she let me stay all day and was going to let me hide the whole night at her house so Wren wouldn't find me.

But when Hermes calls...I have to act.

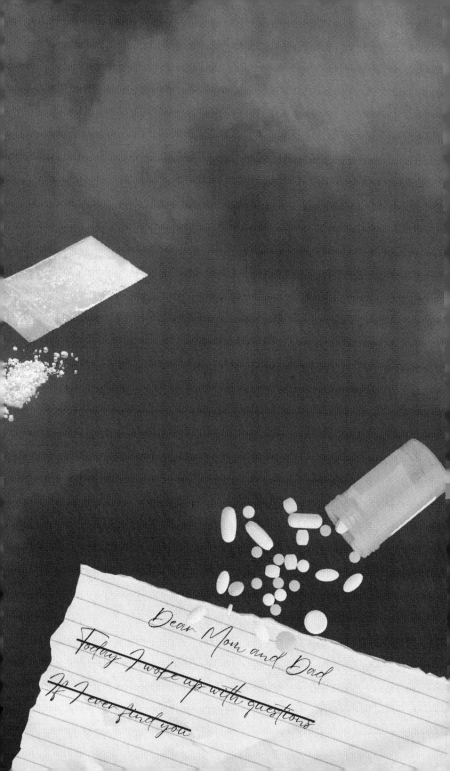

Chapter Thirty-Four

Peach

Carry You Home - Alex Warren

S tanding in the campus castle's west quad in the middle of the night, trying to see where the statue of Athena is staring, isn't exactly what I had planned to do to heal my heartbreak.

But here I fucking am.

She's looking across the square, but down, and I always assumed it was because she's a goddess, and that's what gods do. They look down on us as they play with our lives. At least that's what Wren Hunter, God of SFU, does.

I follow all the way to the edge of the building, staring at the red bricks. One of them is clearly more used than the other ones. It doesn't quite fit into the wall. I graze it with the tips of my fingers and try to pull it out. If I get caught, I don't know how I'm going to explain this.

I heard there are secret rooms under the castle, and I wanted to have a little look. How do I know, you ask? Well, because the campus gossip account has been blackmailing me and told me to have a look.

I huff, acknowledging I'm fucking losing it, when the brick finally pulls away and a small handle shows behind.

"Oh, how I wished this hadn't worked." I groan, turning the round handle. The hidden door pushes in, and I enter a hallway only lit up by burning torches against the wall.

The second I'm in, the door closes.

"Awesome," I whisper. "Not the creepiest thing ever."

Actually, maybe being chased through a maze was worse. God, that feels like a lifetime ago.

I rub my eyes and proceed forward. The quicker I get this over with, the quicker I can go back home. But then Wren will probably be waiting there for me, so maybe I should just die down here.

My thoughts keep battling against my inner peace as I advance toward a wooden door. I can already hear voices behind it, mainly whimpers and crying.

I'm careful opening the door. I have no idea what I'm about to walk into, but if someone is getting hurt, it'll be Heras. And I can't let that happen.

It's only when I'm inside that I'm able to realize there was no way to enter discreetly. The room is too small for that. The walls are old stones curving at the top, meaning everyone standing is practically touching the ceiling.

It's an old basement, maybe a cellar at some point. The floor is some sort of red clay that has slowly turned to dust over time. All heads turn to me as soon as I enter. Four topless men stare at me, and a fifth one is already walking out by another door.

Hermes.

I don't know how I know it, but it has to be them. Proba-bly...him?

Hermes is a man, and he's escaping the second I'm entering.

"Peach," someone calls out. "Fuck, did Wren finally accept our invite?"

"What?" I ask, completely lost as I recognize Simon Dresner. He goes to SFU, but I rarely see him or hear of him.

I can't linger on him too long, my gaze catching the four women on the floor. They're naked, playing some sort of sexual version of Twister. But what's catching my attention the most is that they're bleeding, cuts all over their bodies, looking like they're not really here.

"What... What the hell?" I try to push past the tightness in my chest. "What are you doing?"

"She wasn't invited," one of them says. I don't know him. "She found us."

Their behavior changes quicker than I can catch up, and I instinctively take a step back toward the door.

"Did you drug them?" I ask. My eyes don't go back to the women—I have to keep my focus on the danger—but they haven't moved one bit, and I hear their whimpers.

"We do what we want with our Heras, don't we?" Simon sneers.

"You're *torturing them*," I hiss.

"Where's your Shadow, Peach?"

I swallow thickly, and I decide survival is more important than pride. "On his way. He told me to meet him here. How else would I know about this place?"

As I take another step back, two strong arms wrap around me from behind in a bear hug and lift me up. One of them must have moved while I was focused on the others.

"Let go!" I shout, twisting in his hold as my nerves kick into high gear. "Wren is coming, and he's going to kill you!"

"Yes, see..." Simon snorts as he gets closer to me. His breath smells of alcohol, and I choke on it when his lips press against my ear. "That's kind of how I know Hunter isn't coming. He turned down our invitations to bring you here so many times. He threatened to kill us if we ever tried again. If we ever..."

It's only when I feel cold metal against my cheek that I understand he had a knife in his hand the whole time.

"...touch you."

With my heart beating in my ears, I press myself harder against the man holding me.

"We have to play here with our Heras," he explains, the blade caressing along my jaw, and then my throat. "Because the more established Shadows have a little bit too much respect for them. We just don't care. Heras, Aphrodites, you're all little toys to us."

"Simon," I rasp, too scared to even move. "Let me go."

He steps away, smiles at me, and shakes his head. "I think it's time for Wren to share his toy."

The guy holding me brings me to where the four women are all twisted together, panting from pain, blood running from their cuts.

"Stop, stop, stop," I shout as desperation thrums through my veins. "Move! Don't stay like this!" I scream at the girls. I twist harder, my heart bruising my ribcage.

But they all just slowly blink at me, pumped with whatever drugs they've given them. One isn't even looking at me, staring at her flat palms on the floor and the blood dripping down her trembling arms. They're a pyramid of broken dolls.

I'm sweating when the knife comes back.

"Fuck you!" I shriek, attempting to kick the man behind me. Another moves closer, leaving the shadows to play with me too.

"Oh my god, Dustin." He's good. He's part of the college

newspaper. He's just a nerdy guy who never causes any trouble.

"Do you know what I was thinking?" he says lowly, his eyes shining with anticipation.

Dustin isn't going to help me.

Dustin is going to make it worse; my instincts already told me everything.

"What's that?" Simon asks as he rips my uniform shirt, buttons flying everywhere.

Another blade shines, reflecting the low light from the torches. That one is being held by Dustin.

"I think," he purrs, "that Peach is a strong girl. Or so she always says. And strong girls don't need drugs to deal with the pain, do they?"

I shake my head madly, a sob getting stuck in my throat and turning the words I want to push out into a meaningless whimper.

"Stop... Wren... He'll kill you when he learns what you did."

I'm shaking as Dustin presses his blade to my sternum.

"Wren can't kill *everyone*." Simon smiles. "See, Peach. The problem is, we're privileged men. We've always gotten everything we wanted. More money than we can count, no consequences for our actions, and after a while...you get bored, you know? We keep having to up the stakes to feel something. We just want to have fun."

"Let us have fun, Peach," Dustin says, almost softly.

"No." My god, I can't breathe. "Please, don't."

Is that what Hermes wanted? For me to suffer? For what I did to Ania?

The blade presses against my skin, tearing a cry out of me. I fight for a while. Fuck, I fight with all I have, because

461

screaming and kicking and twisting in this man's arms is all I can do to survive.

But it does nothing.

Because at the end of the day, I'm just me against four men who think they have every right over the women of the Silent Circle. They think my body is theirs to play with.

And they do just that.

Pain. That's what they want. They make small cuts, agonizingly shallow, so they don't become lethal.

They don't have to keep holding me. Weakened, I give up quickly. Because I'm not strong. I'm tired. I'm tired of fighting against everything and everyone for basic decency. I'm tired of arguing with people who won't hear me.

And I'm exhausted from fighting men who will never see me as more than a body to use and a mind to break.

My tears burn my face when they lay me down next to the other women, and I realize it's because they cut my cheek.

Will it scar?

Will I forever look in the mirror and be reminded of the night Hermes trapped me in a room to be tortured?

"Please...stop." My voice is barely above a whisper when they all line up by us, observing, thinking what they could do next.

"Okay, I'll spin," Simon says as he takes the Twister spinner from the floor. "Peach, you have to put your"—he spins—"left hand on blue."

I shake my head, my eyes fluttering shut.

"Oh, come on, you're a cheerleader. Show us what you can do."

"Stop," I croak as another sob pushes painfully against my chest.

"She's so boring." Dustin huffs as he walks toward me. But he doesn't reach me.

The door slams open, and I don't understand what's happening until Wren is right in front of me.

Except Wren doesn't look like my best friend, or my boyfriend.

He looks like the God of Death. He looks like that man the Silent Circle calls the reaper.

If the reaper had a heart. And said heart had been torn into a million pieces from worry and anguish.

Relief consumes me, even if only for a moment.

"Wren," I rasp, my eyes so heavy.

"I'm here, baby, don't move." He leans down, picking me up in his arms. One under my knees, one at my back.

I settle my head in the crook of his neck, breathing him in. There's movement behind him, and I tense again.

"It's Achilles," he says. "He's checking on the Heras. Those guys aren't moving. Don't worry. They know what's good for them."

Everything happening is cut by moments of darkness. One second, he's picking me up, and the next, we're coming out of the tunnel that led me here.

I close my eyes again.

"You're going to kill them," I rasp against his neck. I thought we were in the quad, but we're already walking into his house. When did that happen?

"I'm going to take care of you. What comes after that doesn't concern you."

"You didn't snap."

He says nothing.

"You didn't snap because you can't kill all of them. They said you couldn't kill all of them."

"And they were right." That's not Wren. That's Achilles.

"You can't murder all of them, Wren. The Circle will have your head if you kill so many members."

I'm lying on a bed that smells like Wren.

"I'm still mad at you," I croak.

"Of course you are," he mumbles. "I don't expect being tortured would do anything to your stubbornness."

"You didn't snap," I repeat.

"Good. Because he can't lose control on this one." My other friend is by my side too, and I feel his hand in my hair. "Stay with us, Peach, will you? I'd be a bit annoyed if you died. Who will save the polar bears?"

I groan. "Achilles, shut up."

There's something raining on my forearm. It's a spray and it really fucking stings, tearing more cries out of me.

"How did you find me?" I ask.

"Simon stupidly thought I'd want to have fun with them," Achilles explains. "He sent me a text to tell me they were...*playing* with you."

"It's almost over," Wren says softly.

He dabs what feels like a cloth. He does it again, on my torso, on my thigh, and on my cheek.

"If I want to kill them, I'll kill them," he mumbles to himself.

"But you didn't," I say again, feeling like I'm in a fever dream. "You didn't snap."

"I didn't snap because I'm too worried about you right now," he finally says. "Don't you think I walked into that room thinking it was going to be a bloodbath? Of course, I thought I was going to kill them, but my priorities shifted when I saw you bleeding on the floor. Now please, just stop talking, and let me take care of you."

"I deserve this." My heart is beating really slowly. Not

because I'm dying, but because I feel safe again. Safe, and a little dizzy, but I know I'll be fine.

"You do not deserve this," Wren growls before turning to Achilles. "They're shallow. Just give me the Band-Aids. I need..." He hesitates, scratching his throat. And I understand it's because he's not feeling confident in what he's doing. I'd go as far as saying that he might be a little afraid. I didn't think Wren Hunter could get scared. Gods don't get scared. "...I need to put something on the cuts."

"Yes, I deserve it. Hermes forced me to go there to punish me."

The silence around me is loud. Loud enough that I open my eyes again.

"Hermes?" Wren inquires, his eyebrows scrunching together. "Hermes talks to you?"

"Yes." I close my eyes again, then whisper the rest of my sentence like the secret it is. "Hermes is punishing me because I killed Ania."

There's a snort from Achilles. "I told you she killed her."

I don't open my eyes after that. I'm just too exhausted. I just want to forget and not be here.

-metal IS NOT the same as punk.
-She's still allergic to shellfish and cat hair
-Always leave the green olives to her
-We don't like metal anymore.
~~-Tea tree and peppermint shampoo~~
~~-Don't forget the peri-peri powder on her fries~~
-Bake and shake every first Tuesday of the month.
-No more sugar in her coffee. It makes her feel sick
-DO NOT bother me during girls' night Wren
-Spiced honey on pepperoni pizza
-Check the triangle freckles on her right shoulder
frequently. Dermatologist said to keep an eye.
-New vision results: Right eye -2.75. Left eye -3.25
-If she gets in next September's yearly release of the
EEAJ, the announcement will be in August next year.
~~-Her brace needs to come off in a week~~
-New shampoo: coconut oil in it
-No more peri-peri on her fries
-Keep the stupid dog
-The letters started at 13

Chapter Thirty-Five

Wren

Hayloft II - Mother Mother

I'm woken up by the sound of Little Sausage yapping next to me. My heart sinks the second I become aware of my own body. Peach isn't next to me. I know that because I fell asleep holding her so tightly, I was worried she wouldn't be able to breathe. But at least no one could take her from me. I wasn't going to not keep her close after I found her in that secret room.

Something is off.

It's more than the fact that I can't feel her soft skin or smell her perfume. I feel strange. And I can smell blood on me. Did Peach bleed some more during the night?

My body cracks in all the wrong places as I move, lethargy dissipating until I can feel my whole self.

My hand is in a fist.

Wait.

My hand is in a fist.

Fuck. Fuck. Fuck. Fuck.

I sit up quickly enough to make myself dizzy. And I

notice Peach standing in front of my bed, showered, a towel around her body and one twisted in her hair. She's facing away from me, looking at my laptop open on the desk. A local news anchor is talking on the screen. She's holding a mic, standing in a familiar place. Squinting my eyes, I recognize the castle's west quad. This is our campus. This is where there's a tunnel that leads to the room where I found Peach yesterday.

"The three bodies were found in the early hours on the Silver Falls University campus, which had already seen four murders since last summer. The number has now risen to seven, along with a student in the hospital who's yet to wake up from his life-threatening injuries."

The journalist pauses as a group of students walk behind her, throwing dark looks at the camera, and she attempts to smile politely. If there's one thing the one percent hates, it's attention from the outside world. We prefer to stay in our bubble where everything is possible, and we don't want cameras here.

"Each of the men was found in their respective bedrooms. The police aren't revealing everything, but they agreed to share information with us that they hadn't before. According to the SFPD, it looks like we're looking at a serial killer with a ritual. Not in the way they kill their victims, but with what they leave in their mouths and throats. The letters I, L, and U, from a Scrabble game. Could they be crimes of passion? We'll keep you in touch with any new information we get. In the meantime, the police are calling out to any witnesses who could help with the investigation. Our condolences and prayers go to the families of Simon Dresner, Matt Robinson, and Byron Wallace."

Peach turns to me so slowly, I wonder if she'll ever look at me. Her face is pale, and she replaced the bandage I'd put on her cheek yesterday with a new one. The other wounds seem to have stopped bleeding, so she didn't cover them again. She's holding her towel tightly around her as her eyes drop to my fist.

"Open your hand, Wren," she says with a softness I've never heard from her.

I shake my head as anguish takes hold of me. I'm out of control. I remember nothing. Not even leaving this room. But there are dozens of Scrabble tiles scattered on my floor, because I was clearly searching for four I's, four L's, and four U's.

Slowly, I relax my fingers. They hurt from being held so tightly, for God knows how long. The piece of paper is bloody and, unsurprisingly, there are four names on it.

Dustin McCarthy
Simon Dresner
Matt Robinson
Byron Wallace

"Dustin isn't dead," Peach says, the blood draining from her face. "He isn't dead."

"Fuck," I rage as I throw the paper on the bed and run a hand across my face. "I'm losing it," I pant. "It's getting worse." My voice is barely above a rasp. "And now that fucker could wake up and ruin my fucking life."

Peach stays far from me by the end of the bed.

"Please," I say, distress dripping from the vowel. "Don't be scared of me."

"I'm not scared of you," she admits. "I needed protection from those men. Their Heras needed protection from them." Yet her voice is cold, the tone telling me to not try to approach.

"Trouble," I sigh. "I was so worried about you. Fuck, worry is an understatement. The fear I felt when I saw you...that's why it happened. I didn't want to. It's... It's that *thing* inside me."

"They got what they deserved. But you are getting what you deserve too, Wren. You lied to me, and you saving me doesn't make up for what you hid from me."

I take a deep breath, keeping my calm.

"I promise you, I was going to tell you. I just... Your heart broke the first time you got bad news regarding your biological parents. I didn't have the strength to hurt you again. You don't understand what seeing you in pain does to me."

"Then you're selfish. What you didn't want was to hurt yourself. Because keeping that from me broke my heart more than if you'd shared it and offered me comfort."

"I know," I rasp. "I'm sorry, and you need to let me make it up to you. Please."

"You can't always just *make up* for things!"

That's when despair hits me. And when I'm desperate, scared of losing her, scared of her *not loving me*...that's when I do bad things. That's when I tighten her leash.

So, instead of apologizing again, I ask, "How will you make up for killing the girl I was dating, Penelope?"

Her mouth drops, and she stumbles back from the shock.

"You want to talk about hiding things from each other? How will you make up for hiding from me that Hermes has been blackmailing you with a murder you never mentioned."

She shakes her head. The panic taking hold of her is

making her stutter, and she's looking around the room, as if checking to make sure no one can hear us.

"H-how do you know?"

"You talk when you feel safe, baby," I say as I stand up. "And you were deeply vulnerable yesterday. Don't you remember? When I was taking care of you?"

God, I'm an asshole. I should be on my knees, begging her to forgive me for hiding the truth from her. Instead, I'm pulling out things I can use against her. Because apologies... she could refuse that. She could turn me down. But black-mail? That works every fucking time. And that's the only chance I have at keeping control.

Her chest trembles as she tries to breathe.

"Those men deserved to die," I say, pointing at the laptop screen. "Ania? What did she do except take my attention away from you?"

"I don't remember what happened," she defends. "We had an argument, but I don't know what happened after that. We argued at the house because I was being jealous. I was very drunk. She texted to apologize and then... Fuck, I was on drugs. I don't remember following her to the river..."

I laugh, but the sarcasm in it sounds more like despair. "Take it from me, Trouble. Not remembering doesn't mean you didn't do it."

She brings her fingers to her mouth. "But she—" Gulp-ing, her gaze drops. "She was so sweet."

I'm close to her now, and I bring a hand to her cheek. "Now we've both got blood on our hands."

Her eyes are full of tears as she looks up. "She didn't deserve it. Those men, they deserved it. *They fucking deserved it, Wren.*" The way she hisses her sentence stirs confusion in my gut. An instinctive feeling that comes with her hatred for them. "But Ania..." She shakes her head. "All she did was love you before I realized how much I loved you. I will regret killing *her* for the rest of my life."

I open my mouth.

Stop.

Think.

Freeze.

"Oh." That's the only word that passes my lips, but she can read the understanding on my face.

On the outside, I'm blinking at her, steady and unmoving. On the inside, my thoughts are bouncing, adding up, problem solving. No wonder she's so scared of Dustin waking up.

"You're the kind of trouble I should have warned my heart and sanity about, Peach."

"And you're the kind of trouble who will never control all of me."

I nod. Yes, don't I fucking know it now. Still, a pride I've never felt for her before rises in my chest. It's better than how I usually feel when she achieves something. It burns hotter, makes me giddy, could drive me to do *anything* for her. The way I feel right now, it's an attraction to danger, to the risk, the adrenaline. To my entire life hanging on by a thread and wanting to be the one to break it with a snap of my teeth. Just so I can fall deeper and deeper under Peach's manipulation. I'm not the one in control. I never was.

"Penelope," I purr, giddy from her genius. "When did you start killing people and pinning their murders on me?"

A slow smirk spreads on her face. It's the sexiest, most terrifying thing I've ever seen in my life.

"When you made me join a secret society that disrespects women. When I realized you could kill for me."

She takes a step closer. "When I understood that you don't remember when you do."

As she presses a hand to my chest, my heart forces itself against my ribcage. It recognizes its owner. It wants her to dig in and wrap her delicate murderer's hand around it.

"I learned your M.O.," she whispers. "The letters. The paper in your hand. You have no idea how scared I was when I killed the first one. I thought...what if Wren *does* remember? What if he *knows* he didn't do it? But then you ran after me when I left the library, and I asked you if you'd killed Josh. You really thought you had." She laughs to herself, almost like this whole thing was too easy for her.

"Josh? That was you?"

"Well, it wasn't you, baby." She chuckles. "You were your own judge and jury that day, accusing yourself like there was no other option. But who's the reaper now?"

Her tongue darts to her lower lip. The purr in her voice lowering her tone is the most captivating sound I've ever heard.

"I think between making our deal and having me beg for orgasms, you forgot who I was, Wren. You lost yourself along the way. Take this as a lesson to know your place when it comes to me."

I swallow thickly, my body buzzing with a need for her that makes it hard to stay in place.

"Miles and his dad?"

She bites her lower lip and looks at me with beautiful innocent eyes under thick light-brown eyelashes.

I'm getting hard. I'm getting hard from my girlfriend manipulating me into thinking I killed people I hadn't. From her driving me completely crazy. I now understand all those women who fall in love with serial killers. If Peach was arrested, I, too, would send her letters telling her how much I love her.

473

"Simon, Matt, Byron..." I can barely articulate their names.

She rolls her eyes, annoyed that I can hardly believe this tiny fucking thing of a woman in front of me killed six full-grown men. When she realizes that, she huffs.

"Josh assaulted me in the maze. So, I took him by surprise like he did. Late at night when he was going home drunk. He walked past the library, and I was there, waiting, lurking. He couldn't defend himself. I strangled him, and I put the letters down his throat. And then I wrote his name on a piece of paper and put it in your hand while you were sleeping."

My hand reaches up, caressing her arm, her shoulder, clamping the back of her neck. I can hardly breathe from how aroused I am.

"I watched Miles and Paul Ellson rape that Hera, telling her that it was because she cheated on her Shadow. And when I tried to stop them, they attempted to push me into that room to do the same to me." She continues, her gaze strong and vengeful. "You had already weakened them, so all I had to do was wait for Paul to drive his son back to campus. Got them in the parking lot. I even used your knife."

My other hand comes to her cheek with an increasingly violent need, and I bring her even closer to me.

"Keep going," I growl and press my hips against her.

"Those four who tortured me were the best." She smirks. "Because I was feeling weak, and I was hurting. And it was so hard to get out of the safe space you created for me in your arms. You'd just saved me, and I was going to put four more murders on you. But at a point when I thought I wasn't capable of doing it, I got a message from one of the Heras who was with me in that room. I know her from cheer. She apologized for not doing anything to help me."

Her voice becomes quiet, but her smile is peaceful.

"Yesterday was the best, because I was helped by other women who were pushed so far, they were ready to kill. I told her to contact the others, and all they had to do was give me their addresses, and when they went to bed with their Shadows, leave the front door or their bedroom unlocked. They were hurting. I didn't want to ask anything of them but the minimum. *Just leave it unlocked.*"

Her nostrils flare as her eyes shine with tears. Jaw tightening, she pushes the rest of her sentence past her gritted teeth. "And all of them did."

I wipe the tear that falls with my entire palm, keeping her tightly in my hold.

"Men should be more careful of the women who take their shit silently. They suffer and smile through injustice. They suffer and watch men enjoy their tears. They suffer and suffer and *suffer.* And one day...*boom.*"

She looks like the devil. She's beautiful.

"You took on a fight not only to protect yourself," I say, in awe, "but the other Heras too."

"Never forget that women who fight back get nothing out of it. They stand their ground against fear, threats, manipulation, not for themselves, but for all the other women around them. No woman has ever shouted that they're fighting back because it'll fix whatever they've endured. No. It's always 'for other women out there.' And none of you men will ever know what that's like. You don't protect us. We protect ourselves."

"I hurt you," I rasp. "I made you submit, and you let me live." There's an excitement in my tone I can't control. She's a serial killer...and she chose to let me keep my life.

"There's only one difference between you and those men, Wren," she explains, softening. "At the end of the day, with you, I know I always have a choice. Because no matter what, you will never hurt me. You said it yourself. And that doesn't only apply to you being a murderer. It's in the safe space you created for me, for both of us. I will never forget that you're not the one who invited me to the initiations. You asked me, I said no, and you left it, no matter how much it hurt you. You're not the one who dragged me into this. *Choice*. That's what you've given me. That's the difference between you and them. I never did anything I didn't want to do deep down when it comes to you."

"I love you," I whisper. "You used me. I thought I was losing my mind, Trouble. But *fuck*, I'm in love with you."

"You still love me?" She smiles as she grabs hold of my wrist and forces me to let go of her.

My arms fall by my sides as she steps back.

"You're in love with the woman who drove you mad?"

She presses her back against the desk behind her and slightly opens the towel by her side, showing me a glimpse of her perfect pussy.

"Prove it," she sneers. "Crawl to the woman who owns you, Wren."

My heart can barely beat anymore. My jaw drops open, and I lick my lips. She thinks this is going to deter me? I would crawl all the way to hell to save her, only to realize she's the one ruling the darkest depths of it.

I would kiss the ground of the kingdom she rules.

I would kneel beside her throne for the rest of my life if it meant she allowed me to be hers.

I drop to the floor, putting my palms flat in front of me, and as I crawl to the woman I've loved my entire life, I realize that my dick has never been harder.

Kneeling in front of her, I let her grip my hair with one hand as she spreads her legs.

"Do you know why I never doubted it was me killing those people?" I murmur, looking up at her.

She shakes her head silently as her eyes shine with lust.

"Because you're the love of my life, Trouble," I growl against her mound. "I would kill them all over again for you. And a hundred more. If you want to do it yourself, I'll hide every single body you leave behind. And if you get caught, I'll take the blame. If your wish is to kill, I'll hand you the knife. If you need to hide from the law, I'll hide you. And if what you desire is to have me at your feet, I'll kneel."

I inhale her and hear her little gasp, but she stays standing, strong. She still smells of the shower gel she just used, but it mixes with the faint scent of her desire.

On my knees, I use my hands to spread her lips apart, and I bring my tongue to her heat. She's soaking wet, and she tastes like nothing else in the world. She tastes of euphoric pleasure, undying love, lethal lust.

Her hand tightens in my hair when I trace lazy circles around her gorgeous clit. It's swollen, so needy and ready to be devoured. But before I put all my focus there, I run my tongue flatly from her entrance, through her lips, all the way to her clit. I repeat the gesture religiously, barely holding myself back from burying my face into her, because I want her to feel every second of my devotion. I kiss her, my lips coated in her wetness, and her hand in my hair becomes two.

"Fuck," I hear her gasp above me.

Needing more access, I take one of her legs and put it over my shoulder. She's less balanced, but I've got her. Always.

"Wren," she moans when I harden my tongue and

repeatedly go over her clit. I press hard because that's how she likes it.

I know Peach by heart because she imprinted herself on my soul a long time ago. But discovering her body, learning every detail that makes her tic, has been a new passion in the last few weeks. She gave me access to her, and I had to prove I would never disappoint.

So I learned it all.

And not just the easy things, like the fact that she likes hard pressure on her clit while I'm licking her. There's so much more. There's how she moans if I play with her right nipple, but she can't breathe from pleasure if I pinch it harshly. Which drives me to pull at the towel with one hand and graze her taut stomach with my fingers until I find her nipple already hardened.

When I pinch, she freezes for a second, whimpering, before relaxing in my hold as her breathing stops and her wetness doubles.

That's my girl.

She pushes her hips against me, and I decide to pull out another weapon I put in my arsenal while I was discovering her body. Leaving her breast, I bring my hand between her legs from behind and my thumb to her entrance, pushing inside her. I soak my finger with her pleasure and drag it backward until I find her tight hole. When I rub it carefully, barely pushing in, her desperate moan encourages me as I keep licking her clit with careful slowness. I don't want her to fall over the edge just yet.

I bring my other hand to her slippery entrance, pressing two fingers inside her and languidly rub against her G-spot as my tongue accelerates in opposition.

"You're the most dangerous kind of murderer," I growl against her heat.

She tenses, trembling around me, and feeling her orgasm coming as her moans get shorter and sharper, I add, "You are a queen."

I pull away in the slightest.

Her hands tighten on my hair, gripping to the point of pain.

"Penelope baby?" I ask, making sure she feels my breath on her sensitive skin. "I do have a question."

"What?" she snaps above me, but when I move my fingers inside her, she melts under my touch, dripping onto my palm.

"What?" she repeats softly, like the good girl I know she can be.

It makes one feel incredibly powerful to tame a lioness. That's just the law of nature.

"Tell me, if I can make a queen beg...does that make me a god?"

The smugness in my voice would make her furious if I wasn't holding her one small movement away from an orgasm.

"Don't..." she pants. "Wren..."

"Answer."

I slowly push my thumb into her ass, making her knee buckle.

"*Yes!*" she whimpers. "Fuck, yes. It does."

I lick her slowly once more as a reward, but it's not enough.

"Then beg, baby. And scream at my altar when you come."

"Please," she moans as both my hands start moving again. All she's missing is my tongue one last time. "Please, *please, God, please.*"

479

I bury my face in her pussy, unable to hold back any longer.

It barely takes her a few seconds to scream out my name, becoming a trembling mess in my hold.

"Good little slut," I finally say against her skin.

And as much power as I have over her body right now, she's close to turning me into a teenager exploding in his pants.

I'm careful when I pull away, putting my hands on her hips and making sure she's stable before I stand up. The towel that was in her hair fell on my desk, and the other one is on the floor, so I pick it up as she catches her breath.

I kiss her as she tries to grab it, forcing my tongue inside her mouth as she gasps. She hums against me, wrapping her arms around my neck.

"That wasn't fair," she murmurs into the kiss.

"I'll teach you to top from the bottom one day if you're good."

She bursts into a laugh, throwing her head back as she pushes me away from her. "I love you, asshole."

"I love you too. And I thought... I thought I was cursed, Peach. That I would never change. But it turns out that after getting rid of those initiations' goons...I didn't kill anyone. And do you know what that means?"

She shakes her head.

"That I'm no monster when I'm with you."

Biting my lower lip, I smile, observing her so closely my eyes could burn. Like an idiot who thinks he can somewhat look at the sun.

There's a knock on the front door that's too violent for me to ignore. Every single ounce of happiness in me disappears in a blink, and Peach catches it right away.

"What?" she murmurs.

"That's the Circle."

I take a step back.

"You're not getting out of this room," I say. "I have to go."

The clock is ticking. Dustin could wake up at any time, tell the police who attempted to murder him. Worse. He could talk to the Circle. Not only will they not save a member if things go public, but they'll also kill Peach.

Her brow pinches, eyes narrowing on me. "What do you mean, I'm not getting out of this room? Why?"

"You know why," I say calmly as I grab the key in the keyhole. "Dustin is alive. I need to protect you."

"Did you just learn nothing? I can protect myself."

She takes a step, then realizes she's still in nothing but a towel, but after a pause, she seems to decide it doesn't matter as long as she can get out.

I slam the door before she can leave, locking it just as she tries to open it.

"Open!" I hear the sound of her palm slapping against the door. "Wren, open this fucking door!" She sounds like she's body slamming into it now. "I'll fucking kill you!"

Yeah, I have no doubt about that.

"I'll be back. Do not go anywhere," I call back, as if she could go anywhere.

-metal IS NOT the same as punk.
-She's still allergic to shellfish and cat hair
-Always leave the green olives to her
-We don't like metal anymore.
-Tea tree and peppermint shampoo
-Don't forget the peri-peri powder on her fries
-Bake and shake every first Tuesday of the month.
-No more sugar in her coffee. It makes her feel sick
-DO NOT bother me during girls' night Wren
-Spiced honey on pepperoni pizza
-Check the triangle freckles on her right shoulder
frequently. Dermatologist said to keep an eye.
-New vision results: Right eye -2.75. Left eye -3.25
-If she gets in next September's yearly release of the
EEAJ, the announcement will be in August next year.
-Her brace needs to come off in a week
-New shampoo: coconut oil in it
-No more peri-peri on her fries
-Keep the stupid dog
-The letters started at 13
-The love of my life is a serial killer

Chapter Thirty-Six

Wren

Bonnie and Clyde - Dutch Melrose, HARRY WAS HERE

I'm rushing down the stairs two at a time because I have no time to lose. None. Not a second.

"Hunter, for fuck's sake," Achilles hisses as soon as I show up in the living room. "For someone so obsessed with control, you seem to have lost all of it. Or is it your rationality you left somewhere behind?"

"I can't explain. I can never explain. Let's not." I'm already by the door, putting my shoes on. I still have blood on my hands. I'm not showered. I'm wearing yesterday's clothes.

"What are you going to do now that the Circle is showing up at our door?" he asks, tone low, making sure they don't hear us. "They're running out of members because of you, Wren. I *told you* not to kill them all."

"Yes. Yes. I heard you. Listen, while they talk to me, I need you to call Xi. I need someone outside of the Circle to help me get rid of Dustin. The Circle is just going to give me a big slap on the wrist, but after that, I need to clean up my mess."

Because that's what it is. Peach's mess is my mess. Through thick and thin, I'll be there for her.

"A slap on the wrist? You think?" he snaps sarcastically. "I'd go with killing you, maybe."

I shake my head. "They need me. They won't kill me. At least not this time. But if bodies keep piling up, they might."

"So *stop. Killing. People.*"

"Here's the thing I understood today. As long as we're part of the Circle and Peach is at the mercy of those men, the bodies will keep piling up."

Because my girlfriend is a serial killer, which I'll keep to myself for now.

His jaw tightens. "Wren, I need you to see the way you don't make any sense. Please."

"I am making sense. No body, no crime. Ever heard of that? I need someone who will make Dustin disappear. I don't care how, as long as it's not linked to me. That's something Xi could help with."

"Yes, I'm sure he can't wait to help you after you threatened his girlfriend yesterday."

I stop, turning to him and taking a deep breath. "I did *not* threaten Alex. She's my friend. I said I'd find out where she lives." I shake my head. "Xi's just too sensitive," I mumble.

He looks at me, deadpan. Lost for words.

"I'll call Xi. You need all the help you can get, you fucking maniac."

He disappears upstairs, and I open the door to Eugene Duval, my dad, and two bodyguards.

"Zeus," I say politely. "Dad." I eye the two guards who could crush my skull with their bare hands. "Gentlemen."

"We need to talk," Duval says as he walks in without waiting for an invitation.

My dad doesn't bother with any acknowledgement.

I close the door behind them, then follow them to the living room as the bodyguards stand behind the couch while the two men sit down.

"You're killing our own, Wren," Duval says slowly, as if I was too stupid to understand until now.

I refuse to sit, preferring to look down on them. So I cross my arms and stay a safe distance away.

"You wanted a reaper, you got one."

"You cannot kill within the Circle without consequences. We have laws in place. It's important to respect them, or it would be anarchy in our society."

I smile softly at them.

"You've always known what happens when I snap. I warned you when you came to collect your favor that if I joined the Circle, it wouldn't change who I am. You made me join anyway, labeled me as Thanatos. Now I snapped, and people died. *That's* consequences."

My eyes dart to my dad. His constant disgust when he looks at me has stopped having an effect a long time ago. Next to him, Duval purses his lips.

"Listen," he says, keeping his calm. "Nothing bad is going to happen to you as of now. You're right; we wanted you for the things you can do, risk included. That's why we didn't say anything until now."

My father doesn't look like he agrees with this, but no matter how powerful he is, he's not the president of the Silent Circle.

"But this can't continue, and we must get to the bottom of why you're killing members who have done nothing wrong. Unless you'd like to tell us why?"

"I don't know. I don't remember. Never do."

My dad narrows his eyes at me, as if he can read me clearer like this. After all, he made me the monster that I am, didn't he?

"It wouldn't have anything to do with Penelope, would it?"

I shrug. "I *don't* remember, Dad."

"Monty, it's okay." Duval puts a placating hand on his friend's shoulder. "When Dustin McCarthy wakes up, we'll talk to him and clear things up. Until then, Wren, you are forbidden to enter the temple, participate in any event with the Circle, and cannot ask for favors from other members."

"Oh no," I deadpan. "What will I do? Enjoy a normal college experience? How boring."

Duval stands, arranging the jacket of his suit, and my father follows.

"For now, this is a warning, Wren," Zeus says. "But if Dustin shares information you withheld from us, or if you do anything to him before he can talk, you'll be treated like any other man who betrayed the Circle. Traitors do not live."

"Sounds about right. Good thing I'm no traitor."

Ignoring my sarcastic answer, Duval walks past, but my dad stops right in front of me, his piercing eyes seeing through any mask I'm capable of putting up.

"Where's Penelope?"

"Getting ready. It's election day. She has to go to Stoneview to be with her dad."

He lets out an unconvinced *humph* and takes a step back, but this time, I'm the one who stops him with a hand on his shoulder.

"I know you're the one who invited her to the initiations. I know you said you had plans for her." I force a bright smile, which I have no doubt he knows is the most threatening thing you can see on my face.

"You want to hate me? Hate me all you want. Have Peach in the Circle to keep me in check? Go for it. Hurt me, too. Because you've done that my entire life. But hurt *her*? Oh, Dad..." I laugh softly. "There is only one thing that matters to me, and it's keeping a smile on Penelope's face. If that smile even falters because of you...there will be nowhere for any of you to hide."

He's getting red from the anger rising in his body, and I wonder if he's going to hit me. Because it's instinctive for him. So I step closer, so close to him, I can almost hear his heartbeat.

"If anything happens to her, I won't care about any of your threats. Because I promise you, the entire world will go down in flames, and you with it."

I let them leave after that. There's nothing else to say; the message is clear. And even though my dad hates being threatened, I'm safe. At least until they talk to Dustin McCarthy. I need to get this sorted.

Achilles walks back into the living room, phone in hand. "Xi is on his way. He's taking you to see someone who can help."

"You convinced him?" I ask, surprised he was able to take something seriously for more than two seconds.

"Wren, please. Have more faith in me. I'm a sweet talker. It doesn't only work on women."

I cock an eyebrow. "Alex convinced him, didn't she?"

"Yep. Let's go." He gives me my coat and grabs his.

That woman truly is an amazing friend.

Xi parks his truck in front of a Stoneview mansion. I drove past here a few times, but never really took notice of it.

Before leaving, all I told Peach was to get ready and go to her dads'. She'll be safe in a place where they probably have at least five journalists that will be roaming around all day for the elections. The most important thing is her safety, and I'm ready to deal with all kinds of wrong people to make sure she's unharmed.

"So, this guy," I say. "He lives in Stoneview. And you are *sure* he's not linked to the Circle?"

"Positive," Xi responds, observing at the main gate. He opens his window and presses the intercom. "He knows of them. But he would never work with them."

"And he can make people disappear?"

"That's his favorite pastime."

"This is a private residence," a man says through the interphone. He sounds more like a bodyguard than a butler.

"Tell your boss Xi is here," my friend throws back.

"Hold on."

Xi closes his window and turns to me. "Listen. This guy is no joke. He owns the North Shore and married Kayla King, the girl who used to be the head of the Kings Crew."

"Was that your gang or the gang that kicked your ass, I can never remember," Achilles asks from the back seat.

Xi looks at him through the mirror. "I was part of NSC." That's all we'll get as far as who kicked whose ass.

"Initially, Nate comes from the Cosa Nostra. He was meant to become the head of one of the families, the Biancos. Except he went rogue instead, got rid of his boss, and did his own thing. He united the North Shore when we were at war. He built his own army. And now every-fuck-ing-one eats from the palm of his hand. The Italians, the Irish, the fucking Russians."

I smile to myself. "Perfect. This is exactly what I need."

"Yeah, okay. Before you scream victory. My help stops here, got it? As much as she wanted me to help because it's for you, Alex doesn't like me involved in this kind of shit. I promised her I would bring you here, and that's it. I don't break her trust. Ever. The man is a complete psychopath, and whether he ends up helping you or not is not my problem."

"How do you even know the guy if he's married to the head of the opposite gang?" Achilles asks as the gate finally opens. That's a good sign.

"First of all, no more opposite gangs. Secondly, his wife's brother is engaged to my stepsister."

There's a long silence, Achilles and I eyeing each other, my friend mouthing *the fuck?*

We don't get to ask what he means, exactly, because Xi is already driving forward and up a driveway that snakes through the woods. We're in the hills, the part of Stoneview that has the best views. My family house is around here. So is Achilles's, Alex's and Chris Murray's. Most of the other houses are in the main town.

Xi parks by the front door, and I'm not even surprised to find two armed men on either side of it. Looks about right. The door opens before we reach it, and a man I'm assuming is Nathan White is standing in the doorway.

At first glance, there's nothing threatening about him. He's tall but not that big, more on the lean side. He's handsome, a small blond bun tied at the back of his head, with unthreatening features. He's not really the kind of guy I would think is dangerous.

Standing there in a dark blue suit, his hands rest casually in the pockets of his pants. He's not scowling at us, not broody. He actually looks welcoming enough that I wonder if he's a right hand rather than Nate.

But it's when I notice that his suit matches his eyes behind the black-rimmed glasses that everything falls into place. Those eyes are empty. Xi said he was a psychopath, but I imagined it as more of an expression. This... This is death in one look. In fact, I'd go as far as saying that it makes the man terrifying.

He observes us as we approach, Xi at the front and Achilles and I behind him.

"Dean told me Xi is here," Nate says as we approach. He cocks his head to the side. "But funnily enough, he didn't mention you had two friends with you. And Dean isn't known to be a liar, so I'm going to guess you kept this little secret from him."

Xi shrugs. "You weren't going to let me in if I said I was with two people."

"Well, my family lives here. Put two and two together." His tone makes the simple words feel like a death sentence.

"They're harmless. But they need help."

"Harmless?" Nate observes Achilles and me, so unimpressed, a lesser man would melt into a puddle of tears on the spot.

"This one looks like he enjoys mind-fucking people." He nudges his chin toward Achilles, then adds, "I've seen you somewhere."

"Dance class," Achilles replies casually. And I can't control the surprise on my face as I look at my friend. "Long story," he tells me.

"Right," Nate confirms. "And this one is obviously a murderer. It's written on his face."

Fucking hell, he's weirdly accurate.

"You a mind reader now, are you?" Xi grumbles. "Can we come in or not?"

Nate looks at the three of us one by one.

"You can come in." He steps to the side, and we're all about to walk in when he raises a finger. It's enough to stop all of us. "I was having a celebratory lunch with my family, Xi." He says his name, but his eyes are on me, the *murderer*. "Having strangers near me when they're here puts me on edge." When he smiles at me, I know that kind of smile. "No funny moves."

By the time we're in his office, the others have relaxed, but the clock is still ticking, and I need Dustin gone.

"How can I help?" Nate asks as he sits down at his desk. "And before you answer, think of what you can offer me in exchange."

I stay standing, Achilles already sitting down on a couch on the opposite side of the room, and Xi near the door.

"Then before I answer your question, tell me what you want," I say. "Because I'll give you anything."

Licking his lips with excitement, he smiles widely. "Is this for a woman? It sounds like it's for a woman."

I nod, not wanting to look too desperate and become entertainment for him, but at the same time...I *am* fucking desperate.

"Listen, time is running out. Said woman killed members of the Silent Circle, and one of them is not so dead. We're currently waiting to see if he'll wake up at Silver Falls Hospital. If he does and tells anyone she's the one who did it, I'll lose her."

I can hear Achilles shifting in his seat, understanding Peach is the real reaper. Not me.

"Then kill him," Nate answers with the voice of someone helping me choose a flavor of ice cream.

"I can't." I'm getting impatient and trying my best not to sound forceful. "If his death is linked back to me, they'll kill me. See, if I save my girlfriend from the Circle, I'd like to be alive to enjoy her company. Not six feet under."

He cocks his head to the side as he observes me. "Makes sense. Alright, you want me to make sure he doesn't talk. Do we just want to scare him? Do we want him far away? Another state? Another country? Dead?"

"I don't care. As long as he can't talk."

"Sounds like he should die. Where will you be? You want somewhere public, have an alibi."

"I'll be here, in Stoneview, at the mayoral election party."

"Good," he answers, and I'm sure if he could portray emotions, he'd sound impressed. "Make sure they take plenty of pictures of you. The whole night. But especially between seven and eight p.m. when I send someone to get rid of...?"

"Dustin McCarthy." I can almost taste the relief on my tongue, but I have to confirm. "So, you'll do it?"

"I can do it."

"But will you?" I insist.

"We haven't concluded what you'll be offering in return."

My jaw tightens. I crack my neck, left, right. In the next heartbeat, a calm spreads throughout my body. This isn't good.

I hear Achilles standing up behind me, catching on to what's happening. "Don't make him snap. For the love of God, no more deaths, *please*."

I agree with him. I don't want to snap. I don't want to put everyone at risk, but I need to hear someone is going to help me protect the woman I love.

"I told you, Nathan. You can have anything. I'm a Shadow," I finally say. "You can have *one* favor from me. For free. Anytime."

He leans back, his index finger pushing his black, square glasses up his nose. "See, now you got yourself a deal."

The office door opens, and a woman walks in, brow furrowed and green eyes glaring daggers at Nate.

"Little sunflower," he says with what I'm sure could be fondness. "Start thinking of your biggest dream, a Shadow from the Silent Circle owes us."

She crosses her arms over her chest, her gaze narrowing. "My biggest dream is for my husband to stay at the table while we celebrate someone I consider a sister getting into her dream college."

Nate shakes his head. "No, I'm afraid even a Shadow can't make that happen. Nyx talks too much, I'm sorry. The girl is already bleeding us dry because she pulls at your heartstrings. And you want me to sit through an entire lunch with her. That's torture."

"Nathan White, you rich, stingy asshole, get your ass back to that table. Now."

He huffs as he gets up. "Gentlemen. The boss has spoken. It's time for you to go."

I nod, following everyone out of the office. We walk through a hallway, and a woman comes out of the kitchen, holding a cake, two little girls trotting after her. One is holding a cake server, and the other one a bowl of strawberries. Those kids aren't only identical, but also a perfect mix of Nate and his wife.

The woman stops as she sees us, her mouth dropping open, her eyes stuck on Achilles. Her half-blonde, half-black hair is in a messy bun, bi-color fringe falling into her eyes and making her blink.

"You're Achilles Duval," she gasps. "Oh my god." Balancing the cake platter on one hand, she undoes her bun, arranging her hair this way and that.

"Fuck, Nyx, *that's* the boy you can't shut up ab—"

"Kay," she hisses under her breath. "Shutupohmygod-shutup," she mumbles, turning beet red.

I huff, throwing my head back. As if I don't have better things to do than this. "Achilles," I groan. "How...even? You make them fall in love from a distance now?"

I've never seen this woman in my life, and I can tell she doesn't go to SFU. It's unfortunate to say, but *no one* looks like her in our little bubble. None of us are original, just carbon copies of the same styles.

The pause is awkward for them, but unbearable for me. I have life-or-death things happening, and I'm stuck in this limbo of a moment because Achilles has fangirls all over the tri-state area.

"I'm Nyx," she attempts to tell him. She clearly has no idea what she's getting herself into. "I...I love you—I mean, not *you*." She chuckles awkwardly. "Violin. You play the violin. *I* play the violin. You're so good."

This is painful to watch.

"And, uh, we met once. That dance class?"

What fucking dance class?

I pinch the bridge of my nose, unable to go through this any longer.

"Okay?" Achilles says casually, being his absolute asshole self and not giving a shit.

"Not helping, Achilles," I groan.

This isn't the first time it's happened. My friend might be studying medicine, but he's known for playing the violin in famous concerts all over Maryland and its neighboring states. And in case his face and body weren't enough to have everyone falling for him, they also all think that him being a musical genius means he has a lot of cute feelings inside him. What feelings? The man doesn't even own a heart.

The moment is finally cut short by one of the little girls running to me, hugging my leg so hard the cake server digs into me.

"Daddy, that's my husband! My husband, like you and Mommy."

What. Is. Happening.

"What's your name?" she asks in her little voice, giant midnight blue eyes looking up at me. "Your name. Your name, what is it?" My God, is she on coke?

"Uh..." I look at her mom. "Wren."

"Wren and Lia sitting in a tree..." she starts singing. The second she does, the other girl drops her strawberries, running to me and hugging my other leg.

Kayla bursts out laughing. "They have this weird thing at the moment, wanting to imitate us, and I made the mistake of explaining that their daddy is my husband. Now they're looking for a husband."

"*Livie, no!*" Lia shrieks. She starts hitting her sister on the shoulder. "I found him first! Mommy!"

I feel Nate near me before I can even try to get them off me. He squats next to his girls, smiling at them.

"Girls, why don't you step away from the man before Daddy puts him six feet under."

"What's sick fix under?" Lia asks.

"That's what will happen to anyone who touches my daughters. Now step back," he carries on in a fake light voice.

"Nate," Kayla snaps at him. "Stop this right now."

They detach from him, the quiet one going in his arms as Lia goes to her mom.

"Livie dropped the stow...staw...straws-berries," Lia explains to Kayla.

"You're going to pick up the strawberries," Nate says to the one in his arms. She smiles, shakes her head, and buries herself in the crook of his neck. That's enough to make him change his mind.

"Nyx, pick up the strawberries."

"Got it." She seems happy to have something to busy herself with.

"Right, so, now I have to kill you," Nate tells me calmly.

"Nate. Enough," Kayla jumps back in.

From the corner of my eye, I can see the whole situation is very amusing to Xi and Achilles.

"Daddy, I love him!" Lia screams.

"No, you don't," he tells her. "Little sunflower," he says to Kay. "He touched them." He's talking like he's waiting for authorization to kill me, and I'm not exactly loving this conversation.

"*They* touched *him*," she explains slowly.

"What is your point here?" he deadpans.

She huffs. "Nyx, can you take the girls back to the dining room, please? So our guests can leave."

"Yes, please," I mutter. "I'm on a deadline here."

Nyx does as she's told, and a minute later, we're crossing the marble entrance hall, Xi and Achilles at the front, me in the middle, and Nate and his wife right behind me. I can *feel* his eyes burning a hole into the back of my head. I didn't check if he had a gun. Should I be worried?

I look down at my phone. I've got a message from Peach, telling me she made it to her dads' safely. At least one of us is making progress. I can't believe I'm still in this house. I swipe the message away, leaving nothing but my phone background, which is a picture of her.

"Holy shit," Kayla says, and I feel her much closer than I thought she was. She points at my phone. "For a second, I thought that was Lucky."

"Who's Lucky?" I ask.

"Nate, look," she says lightly. "Doesn't that girl look exactly like Lucky?"

Nate leans over my phone, his eyebrows raising in surprise. "Exactly like her. Is that your girl? The one you said killed members of the Circle? Because if she's related to Lucky, it would explain where her insanity comes from."

He says it like it doesn't matter. Because it doesn't matter to him, but I stop walking, my hand falling to my side and my heart racing.

"Who's Lucky?" I ask again.

Nate waves a hand. "No one for you to worry about."

"How old is she?" I insist. "Is she old enough to be a mom? A mom to this woman?" I ask as I point at my phone.

Of course, I read the death certificate for Peach's mom. But it's clear her parents were trying not to be found. What if they're playing dead? Changed their names. What if... shit. What if her mom is alive? I could make it up to her, finally bring her some good news.

I keep pointing at my phone as Kayla and Nate exchange a look like I'm fucking insane. I am. I'm insane enough to try to bring a dead woman back to life to make my girlfriend happy.

"Peach is twenty-two," I finally say, already losing hope.

"You're weird," Nate says in a flat tone. "I like it."

Kayla rolls her eyes, taking my phone from my hand and observing the picture again.

"I mean, yeah, they look exactly the same. But Lucky

doesn't have any kids. And if she did before we knew her, she's what, thirty-one, thirty-two? She couldn't have a twenty-two-year-old daughter."

I nod. Of course, it would have been insane. Her mom is dead. I read it myself.

"Lucky's a weird name," Achilles comments to himself as I take my phone back. "Who names their kid *Lucky?*"

"Says the guy named Achilles," Xi mumbles as we start walking to the door again.

"Her real name is Lana Anderson," Kayla explains. "She's an enforcer in the Cosa Nostra. For the Luciano family. And they call her Lucky Strike. Lucky for short. It fits her, too, because she was born in the Irish Mafia. Her dad is their leader, Keith Anderson. Then the mom got shot, died, and he lost the fucking will to live. Lucky got put with nuns, and by the time she got out, her dad had focused his entire business on sex trafficking. She didn't want to go back to that, and the Lucianos welcomed her. That woman's had it rough; no wonder she's a psychopath."

I can't breathe.

I can't even react.

Anderson. That's Peach's biological name. *Keith Anderson* is her dad, according to her birth certificate.

Kayla keeps walking and talking, but I'm frozen on the spot.

"Oh my god," I murmur. "She's not Peach's mom. She's her sister."

"Lucky has a sister?" Kayla gasps.

"She does... I-I think so. Fuck. This is crazy." I run a hand through my hair, unable to believe what I'm hearing. "This... She probably doesn't even know about Peach. Where can I find her? Lucky?"

"Okay, time-out," Nate jumps back in. "If you know

what's good for you, *nowhere*. Lucky, whether she's aware of a secret sister or not, is not someone who's going to care about it. She won't. She's ill. Insane. Truly incapable of feeling anything. Trust me."

But I can't stop my brain from overworking. "The dad," I blurt out. "Keith. Is he still alive?"

"Did you miss the part where Kay mentioned sex trafficking? Is that who you want to lead your girlfriend to? Because that's what he does, and a lot of his good friends are in the Silent Circle. So I wouldn't get too close to him if I were you."

My heart sinks so low I feel sick. Because I know exactly who in the Circle is involved in sex trafficking.

"Fuck," I finally say.

"Uh, Wren," Achilles calls out. "We have a problem."

A problem? We have a million fucking problems, and I feel my sanity slipping from my grasp. The monster is knocking on the bars of his cage, growling and wanting blood, and I'm here, trying to keep it together when the world around me is falling apart.

"What is it?" I ask with a calm absolutely no one should believe in.

"Chris just messaged. Dustin is awake."

My head snaps to Nate again. "We're out of time."

Thinking for a second, he runs his tongue across his teeth. I can see he's weighing the pros and the cons. Should he make an effort? Am I worth it? But mainly, am I someone you want in your corner or that you don't feel would be a threat as an enemy?

He comes to his own conclusions, whatever they are, and says, "Go to the election party. That kind of thing starts early. Show yourself there. I'll send someone to the hospital now. Hopefully, they'll make it before he talks."

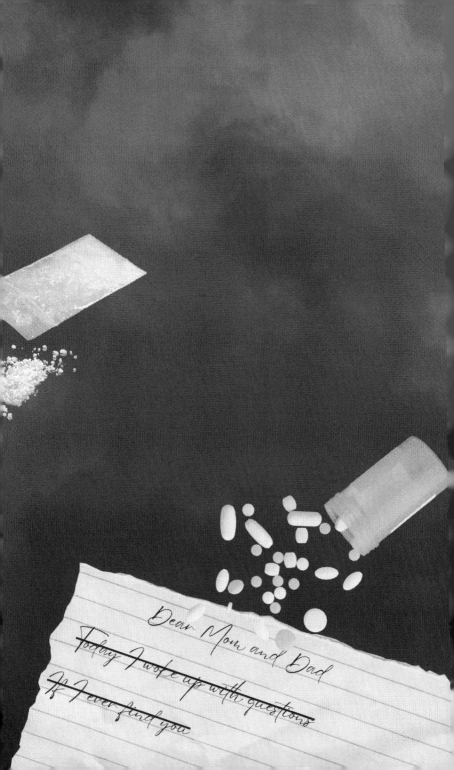

Chapter Thirty-Seven

Peach

Burning Down - Alex Warren

"Penny, *principessa*, what's wrong?" Dad Menacci asks as he watches the hired hairdresser and make-up artist work on me.

One is finishing straightening my hair to perfection while the other dabs the perfect amount of blush on my pale skin. I can't look like I put on too much make-up, but I have to look effortlessly perfect. In a few hours, we might be the family of the new Stoneview mayor.

"Nothin'," I mumble, but just as he can, I see the lines of worry on my face. The little vein on my forehead that isn't just for when I'm angry, but also when I'm desperately anxious.

It was hard to explain the cut on my cheek. Cheer accident, as if that makes any sense. They won't look too much into it, I'm sure of that, but Dad Sanderson was furious. It doesn't look good for the cameras.

"Is it because Dad took your phone?"

"I'm a twenty-two-year-old, and he's treating me like a

teenager," I throw back, even though that's not the only reason I'm stressed.

Dustin could wake up at any moment. The Circle is angry at Wren. I'm waiting for news that I can't see because my father decided to act insane. No one in the house should have access to their phone and what is said about us online until after the result. He thinks our reactions could get caught by the journalists and we don't want that.

"Is this going to be our lives if we win?" I insist. "Because I won't be visiting so often if that's the case."

Menacci shakes his head. "It's an important day for him. Let him have this."

I lower my gaze, observing my twisted hands on my lap. I hate feeling this way. Every movement makes me a little sick. And I don't want to look unwell to others.

"You're beautiful," my dad says, putting his hands on my shoulders the second the women step away. "And that dress is going to look perfect on you."

Through the mirror, I eye the dress hanging not far from us. Dad isn't wrong; I'll look beautiful in it, but God, it's the most boring dress I've ever seen in my life. It's an ankle-length beige dress with a fitted bodice, and a modest round neckline to make sure no one around can accuse me of showing too much cleavage. The A-line skirt is slightly flared, and in case someone could accidentally see my shoulders, there's a cropped smart jacket to wear with it, the same color of the dress and with gold buttons.

"It looks like we're having dinner with the queen," I mutter.

"We're not. But we might be having dinner with the mayor."

He tickles my ribs, and I can't help but laugh.

I giggle. "You're such an idiot."

My smile relaxes him, and his eyes light up. My dads are always happy when I'm happy, and another layer of emotion is coated on top of the current ones. Guilt.

"Dad," I whisper, looking down again. "I'm sorry."

My pulse pounds in my ears when his face falls.

"What? Why? Penny, are you alright? Do you need help with anything? You know you can always talk to me."

For a moment, I can't breathe as my throat tightens. My parents and I might not share the same DNA, but we share something more important. Our hearts. Because all it takes is a tone in my voice for my father to understand I've been going through something. It doesn't matter how many times I'm the one who parents them, and it doesn't matter that they drive me insane. Truly...it doesn't even matter that they didn't birth me. Because they raised me. Full of love and craziness. I might be the most stubborn child ever raised, but I am loved.

"I love you," I finally say, my mouth bursting with all the love I have for him. "I love you, and I love Dad, and I'm sorry if I ever make you feel like you didn't love me enough. Or that I wanted other parents. I'm sorry for all the questions about my biological parents when I was growing up. Because the truth is, they might have hurt me deeper than anyone else, but you and Dad spent your life putting me back together. And I love you for it."

There's a proud half-smile on his face despite his eyes being sad.

"Oh, Penny," he murmurs, giving me a hug from behind. He presses a kiss to my cheek. "*Principessa,* your dad and I love you so much. You're the proof of our love. Of everything we can accomplish as a family. And now is a good time to tell you that we're seeing that therapist again. We're going to make it through because we want to be a family for you. We're so proud of you, but I'm even prouder tonight that you opened up to me. Where is all this vulnerability coming from?" He chuckles. "I'm not complaining, but it's unlike you."

"Ugh." I roll my eyes and dab the tips of my fingers under my eyes to make sure the tears don't go any further. "Stupid Wren Hunter."

He smiles brightly at me through the mirror. "Always liked that boy."

My cheeks hurt from the strength I'm putting into not smiling back like an idiot. "Me too," I whisper. "I like him a lot."

"Can I borrow your phone? My dad thinks I'm a child." I ask Ella the second she crosses the entrance to the living room.

We both smile at a journalist walking past us. She nods at us, saying, "only one hour left" excitedly.

The second she's gone, Ella's face falls, and angry eyes come to me. "If it's to contact Chris, or Wren, or Achilles... you know the kind of man I mean, then forget about it. They're all not answering, and I have no idea where they are."

"You tried all of them?" There's a black snake of anxiety slithering its way from my stomach and to my chest, making me feel sicker.

"Yes," she huffs. "Chris hasn't been answering his phone, so I tried all of them, because something is wrong."

She has no idea how badly that's true.

I fake a reassuring smile, knowing there's no point in adding to her anxiety. There's nothing she can do right now.

"I'm sure they're just late. It's fine. Will you give me a minute? Alex is over there if you want."

I throw fake smiles and happy faces at whoever wants them as I walk through the crowd of my father's supporters, waiting eagerly to see if he'll be the next mayor. The second I find Elijah, I tap his shoulder and bring my lips to his ear.

"Meet me in front of the neighbor's house in five minutes. It's urgent."

I disappear discreetly, my small heels clicking on the stone outside our house as I jog down the long driveway. Exiting our residence through a side gate barely anyone ever uses, I make my way to the next house, standing on the street in front of their gates for long enough to go crazy.

I'm pacing when Elijah finally appears. He's still sporting bruises from Wren beating him up, and it's hard to look at him without feeling guilty for this whole mess.

"Oh my god," I sigh. "You took forever."

"I got us drinks," he says. "You looked like you needed one. Are you okay? Are your dads putting too much pressure on you?"

I snatch the flute of champagne from him and down it, not caring one bit that it's been a week since I've touched a drink.

"We have a problem. Wren...I...I think he's in trouble with the Circle."

His face freezes just as he opens his mouth, stuck in his thoughts.

"Okay, well, that's between him and the Circle."

"Elijah, please. I know you guys don't get along. He told me what he did to your uncle. You can fault him all you want, but he loves me, and he keeps me safe...and I love him. If we're friends, if you care about me, help me."

Something flashes in his eyes, and for the first time in my life, I see that Elijah has a side he struggles to control too. It's not necessarily violent, but it's not exactly friendly.

"How can you ask this of me?" he snaps. "He's bullied me my entire life. Do you have any idea what it's like to live in Wren Hunter's shadow? No, you don't. Because you and your friends are popular. Because you've always had Wren on your side. I never had that. He made me his enemy, hurt me, and now I'm supposed to, what? Go to the temple and save him? What did he even do?"

"He put his life before mine," I answer simply.

Nostrils flaring, he looks away. "Is he there, then?"

"I don't know," I say with a softness I hope he can reciprocate. "All I know is that he was supposed to be here, and he's not. He's not answering his phone, and the last time I saw him, Duval and your dad were threatening him."

"Ugh, Peach. Fuck. Fine. Let's get in my car."

"Thank you," I sigh with relief. "Thank you, thank you."

A minute later, we're driving down the Stoneview roads, on our way to the temple.

"All I can do is take you there, and we can ask about him, but we can't force any board member to release Wren if they're questioning him."

"I know," I answer, my tongue feeling a bit numb. "Ugh," I groan, suddenly lightheaded. "I forgot what alcohol feels like. It's not that nice."

"Yeah, well, stay awake, because I'm not sure I'll feel so nice facing this alone."

"Thank you," I say again. "I know you guys don't get along, but you're being the bigger person, and I love you for it."

The road ahead blurs, lines double. I close my eyes tightly.

"Fuck, I feel drunk. I..." God, my mouth can barely move anymore. "Is it because I haven't partied lately or something?"

"Oh no," Elijah says lightly. "That must be the sedative I put in your glass."

The sentence resonates in my mind just as my head falls forward. I force it back up, but it's my eyelids that struggle now.

"Wh-what?"

"You're losing consciousness because of the sedative I put in your glass," he repeats, as if it isn't outrageous.

The moment I try to stop my head from falling forward again, it flops back against the seat, and I can barely turn it to the side to look at him.

"I'm not feeling well," I mumble without any strength.

"It's normal, don't worry. We've played this game before, so I have no doubt you're going to be fine."

All I can hear clearly are my panicked breaths coming in and out of my mouth.

"Elijah..."

"I'm sorry, Peach. I like you, but I hate Wren more, and I think it's time he suffers. A lot."

He slows down as he enters a parking lot, and I recognize the back of Stoneview Country Club. We're at the temple. Already.

Wrapping a hand around my jaw, he holds my head up as the last grasp I have on my consciousness starts to slip away.

"If it can put your mind at ease, I know where Wren is. Here, in the dungeons. But I have some bad news for you, my darling." He smiles at me, and it's like nothing I've ever seen before from him. It's devilish, manipulative. *Sick.* "Dustin woke up, and he had a lot of things to say."

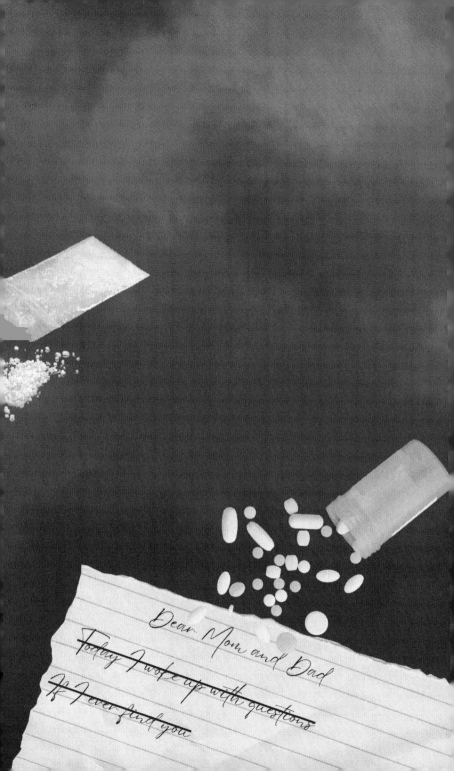

Dear Mom and Dad

Today I woke up with questions

If I ever find you

Chapter Thirty-Eight

Peach

Breathe In, Breathe Out - David Kushner

The first thing I notice is that my wrists are tied behind my back and attached to something. My eyes open slowly, a headache pounding on the side of my head.

Blackout.

It feels exactly like my blackouts, except I remember what happened before I slipped into the darkness. I remember everything. Wren and the guys were missing. Elijah, he betrayed me. Dustin... Dustin talked.

The kick of adrenaline jolts me awake, the lethargy replaced by fear and the need to survive. I'm sitting on an old stone floor, and I recognize the room. It's an Aphrodite's room in the dungeons. My wrists are in leather binds, and they're attached to what feels like a pole behind me. I press my back against it and use that balance to stand up. It takes me a minute, the muscles in my legs still asleep.

The door opening startles me, but I school my features, ready for whoever it is.

"Hey, Peach."

Elijah. He sounds so at ease, like we're meeting for one of our coffee dates. But the look on his face, the way he carries himself, it's nothing like the man I know. He's assured, his shoulders square. He's not big, never was, but he looks dangerous.

"Elijah, untie me." It's not a plea. It's not a strict order either. I'm putting myself on equal footing, because he needs to remember that's what we've always been. Equals.

"I'm afraid I can't do that." He stops in front of a dresser on his way to me, opens a drawer, and pulls out what looks like a riding crop. "Unlike Wren, I don't really care when a pretty girl gives me attention. I've got plenty of that already."

I pull my eyes away from the crop, only to blink up at him. Pretty girls giving Elijah attention? That's a first. I don't say it, though. I'm not exactly in a position to trigger his pride.

"We should talk," he says. "Get back down. On your knees. When I'm in the room, you always get on your knees."

My mouth drops open, and I force myself to shake my head to come back to reality. "What are you talking ab—"

The crop moves like lightning, and I cry out when it slaps violently against my cheek. My face. He went for my fucking face. The cut I had from yesterday opens, and I feel a dribble of blood coming down my cheek.

"I don't repeat myself."

My heart races, body shaking from the inside out as my legs slowly lower me to the floor. He didn't hesitate one second before hitting me. I have no doubt he'll do it again. Just like I have no doubt this isn't the first time he's done this.

"There you go. You'll learn quickly with me. I have a talent for it."

"What are you talking about?" I croak, looking up at him. My wrists are already hurting, and I'm wondering how long I was unconscious down here.

"You'll find out soon enough."

Not wanting to play his game, I look him up and down before saying. "You drugged me. You... The blackouts. How many times have you drugged me?"

"Well"—he turns around, pacing as he taps his palm with the length of the crop—"the first time was when I killed Ania. So I could pin it on you."

I feel dizzy as my heart stutters. My ears ring, nothing making sense anymore.

"What... *What?*"

"I drugged you. I chased her through the woods, I brought you to the river where she was, and when she looked at you, I pushed her in. I thought if you have flashbacks, you'll really think you did it."

"Oh my god," I squeak. "Oh my god, you killed her. Why?"

"Because my dad and I needed Wren to initiate with *you*. Not that useless girl he used to try to forget about you."

Something else pierces through my mind. "You're Hermes. You blackmailed me."

He pauses in front of me. "I'm not Hermes. I don't know who they are."

"I saw that he's a man. Yesterday, when I went into the room under the castle..."

"That was me. That wasn't Hermes. The second I saw you come in, I ran out with my Hera. Couldn't have you knowing the kind of games I play. I needed to keep your trust a little while longer."

"Elijah, please. I don't understand. Why are you doing this?"

When he sees the confusion still on my face, he carries on. "Well, two reasons. The first is that it's very hard to control my brother. He doesn't have many weaknesses. In fact, I would say he only has one."

He taps my cheek with the crop again, making me wince, despite the lightness in his action. "This pretty girl right here. And if you're going to have a reaper who can't control his urges to kill, you want the thing that controls him too. We needed you as his Hera."

My nostrils flare when he squats in front of me, coming face to face with me. "The second reason is your dad."

"My dad?" I repeat numbly. "Which one?"

"Not your adoptive dads." He waves a hand next to his head. "Your real dad. Him, Monty, and I work closely together. And he's been trying to fuck us over. You're going to be how we teach him a lesson. And I worked really hard on it, so don't fuck this up for me. I'm finally going to prove to everyone that Wren is a useless little shit, and I'm the son everyone should be talking about."

"My dad," I say again. "I don't..." God, my head is throbbing from the drugs, and this is too much to process. "You know my real dad. That's not...possible. I've been looking for him. You know I've been looking for him."

"Yes, Keith Anderson," he explains. "Peach, I have to apologize to you. I've been dishonest."

No. Shit.

My deadly stare must translate my thoughts because he laughs to himself.

"I lied when I said I was an accountant for the Circle. I'm not. See, what my dad and I do is find women to trade. Not often. Only the ones who will be the most expensive.

And your dad, well, I'm sorry you have to find out this way, but your dad participates in that trade. Monty and I find them, train them, sell them. Keith, he mainly sells what we provide him with. Often, we take them from our pool of Aphrodites. But for the first time"—he puts strands of my hair behind my ear—"I think we're going to take a Hera."

Stomach lurching, I press myself against the pole as his hand caresses my cheek. He smiles at me, pulls away, and stands up again.

"Keith Anderson has been playing dangerous games with us. It's about time he learns his lesson. He's going to watch his daughter get sold at an auction he organized. Dad and I just need to convince the rest of the board members. Thankfully, you going on a little killing spree has truly helped. And Wren protecting you? Chef's kiss. You two are going to be beautiful, tragic lovers. Thank you for your help."

The fear only truly kicks in when he mentions Wren. Is he going to hurt him? The man is talking about trafficking me, but the idea of Wren hurting, maybe dying? I can't process that. He's my soulmate. He's my protector. He's my everything. He waited his whole life for me. I'm not going to let anything happen to him.

"Elijah," I say, trying to keep a calm voice, but the tremor in it can't be ignored. "You're my friend. You've always been my friend. For as long as Wren has. Please, don't hurt him."

He cocks an eyebrow at me. "Don't worry, Peach. I'm only going to hurt you." Then he smiles, so proud of himself. "Oh, wait. I think *that* might hurt him a little bit."

As if on cue, the door to the dungeon opens, and Shadows dressed in black suits walk in. Eugene Duval and Monty Hunter are here. They come to stand near Elijah, right next to me. Three other older members are here too. I imagine they're the rest of the board, and my nerves rachet a little higher.

A crowd of Shadows follows, and once they're all in the room, two gigantic bodyguards walk in.

They're holding a hooded man by the arms. Topless, nothing but jeans hanging low on his hips. He doesn't walk rather than being carried by the guards, his feet dragging behind him.

I would recognize Wren among a crowd of men with black hoods covering their heads, and my heart stops beating when I see the blood on his chest. It's clearly dripped from his face. They tied his hands behind his back with zip ties, making him unable to defend himself.

"Wren," I whimper as they pull him farther inside. They bring him to his knees right next to me, and the grunt I hear from underneath the hood tells me he's at least awake.

"I'm here," I whisper, leaning as close to him as I can.

I feel him calm slightly, the energy within him shifting, and out of nowhere, something touches my hand at my back. I don't need to look over my shoulder. It's him. He's trying to hold me as much as he can with his hands tied.

His hand doesn't tremble like mine. I can feel his heartbeat at the tips of his fingers. It's fast. Not *scared* fast.

Fuming kind of fast.

I can tell the difference when it comes to him. I know the difference in his heartbeat when he's tired or annoyed with me. When his lust takes over. When his eyes cross mine.

And when he snaps.

Wren is far, *far* past snapping. He's been pushed too far; I can already tell.

"I'm okay," I murmur, hoping it will calm the beast a little more. "I'm not hurt."

His thumb caresses my wrist, and I want to cry. I love him. I don't want this to be the end. It's only now that our years of complicity come to the forefront of my mind. This man has always been there for me. He picked me up on my down days, and he celebrated all my wins. When I was scared, he held me, and when I wanted to push myself further, he was right behind me. Wren *always* puts me first.

"Gentlemen, you have been called to this emergency meeting to witness the board of the Silent Circle punishing two traitors," Duval says.

"This Hera." He points at me, and that triggers Elijah to grab me by the hair, showing my face to all of them.

I cry out when he twists his grip, and even though he can't see me, Wren grunts at my side. It's animalistic. His hand tightens around mine, and it brings me a peace even Elijah can't sever.

"This Hera," Duval repeats, "has killed our own. And her Shadow..."

Monty Hunter pulls the hood off Wren's head, and a desperate gasp tears from my chest.

"Wren," I whimper. "Oh my god..."

They've beaten him up so badly, both of his eyes are swollen. His nose is clearly broken, and there are constant strings of blood dripping from his nose and mouth. At this point, I don't even know which is feeding the thick liquid running down his chin, his neck, and to his chest.

"Elijah," I say through the sob constricting my throat. "Please...please, do something."

I don't know why I call out to him. Years of friendship have wired my brain into thinking he's got my back. Of course he doesn't. He just told me exactly why. His hatred for his brother, his vengeance on a father I never met. Nothing that makes sense to me. Nothing I can process in a way that would tell my nervous system Elijah is not an ally anymore.

The crop striking my face again would have sent me crashing to the floor if he wasn't holding me.

"Quiet."

"Let him go," I hiss through the pain.

The second strike turns Wren uncontrollable.

"Elijah, I swear to God, you're a dead man." Those are the words I catch through the garble of insults and blood pouring out of his mouth. Despite being beaten, he pulls at the zip ties, and for a split second, it looks like he's going to break through them. I take great pleasure in seeing every single member in this room step away from him.

But ultimately, there's nothing he or I can do, and Duval continues his trial.

"We're gathered here to decide on their fate and punishment for betraying the Silent Circle, a family who welcomed them and nursed them like their own children."

I would laugh through the irony if this wasn't so fucking tragic.

"Kill them!" some man throws out from the crowd. "That's the punishment for traitors. Kill them and kill them now."

This is more savage than a Vikings trial. No sense, no reason, just the need for blood.

Monty takes a step forward, putting a hand in front of him to quiet everyone.

"Death is the usual punishment, but we don't think they deserve such an easy way out. I know Wren. He's my son. Dying with his loved one would be a gift for him." He pauses, looks at us, and smiles brightly.

Monty Hunter said he had plans for me in the maze. He surely delivered on his promise.

"Keeping him alive while knowing she's out there somewhere suffering, that would be a real punishment. As for her, she deserves nothing more than to be sold as a whore to the highest bidder."

There's a round of approving sounds in the room.

"My son, Elijah, and I will take care of this."

Elijah releases me, distributing what looks like pictures to the Shadows. They pass them around, sneering and looking at me.

"I've got everything I need. She's been on the market for a while."

On the...market?

"And remember, she's drugged in those. We used them to attract attention. But she'll look a lot more alive during the auction."

Those are pictures of me.

A flash. I'm feeling cold.

Those are pictures he took when he drugged me. I thought I was blacking out from drugs or alcohol, but it was Elijah. That's why I always woke up feeling like something *bad* had happened. And that's the flash I remembered from time to time.

Wren's grip on my hand tightens, but I break anyway.

These men looking at what I'm assuming are naked pictures of a drugged me. Something Elijah has been using for months to attract attention to me on the black market.

"Don't worry, baby," Wren murmurs next to me, his words barely audible. "I'm going to kill him. I'm going to kill every single man in this room."

"No," I sob. "Enough. You won't do anything for me

517

anymore. I forbid you. You're going to let them send me away, and you're going to save yourself. That's it."

He doesn't listen. He doesn't agree. Of course not, because he lost his mind a long time ago when it comes to me. But I don't care. I don't care what Wren chooses. I've decided that I will take their punishment if it saves *him*.

After that, the trial is chopped into lapses of time I disconnect from. The board agrees on Monty and Elijah's proposal. The Shadows applaud their decision.

He'll keep working for the Circle, knowing I've been sent to be sold.

Wren is kept kneeling on the floor, but Elijah detaches me from the pole and brings me to standing.

I don't know what happens around me, exactly. All I know is that my eyes don't leave Wren's, and his don't leave mine.

"Don't be scared," he says. "This is going to be over soon."

I'm not too sure how he can believe that, but I nod to make him feel good. If this is our last moment together, I want to leave him thinking that everything is going to be okay.

"I love you."

"I will come get you, Trouble," he insists, clearly seeing I don't believe him. "I don't care how long it takes. You're going to hold on for me, do you understand?"

Those words pierce through my heart. I want to answer something, anything, but only a sob bursts from my lips.

"I promise you. *Write-it-on-my-arm-in-a-marker* promise you. You survive. You hold on, and I will bring you home. Say yes."

I open my mouth as Elijah drags me by the hair, but I can't breathe.

"Say yes!" Wren screams. "Say you'll hold on. Say *yes!*"

"Yes," I weep.

"Good girl. I love you. I love you..." he repeats. "I love you." Until I'm not in the room anymore.

And I still hear it. It resonates in my head until I realize I'm long gone. And we're far, far away from each other.

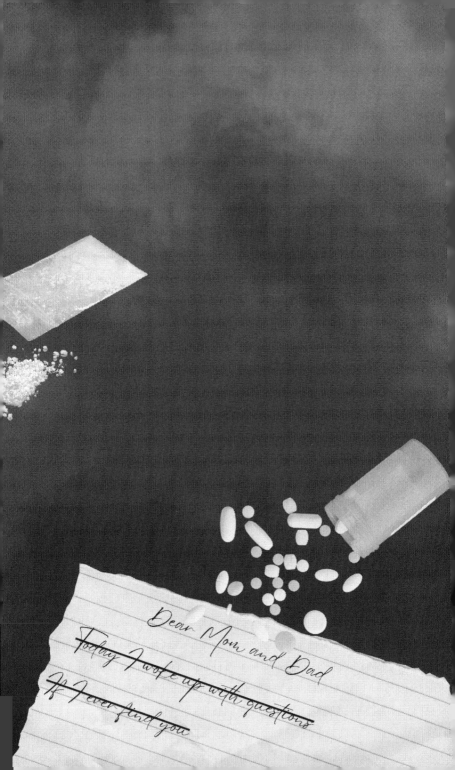

Chapter Thirty-Nine

Peach

LABOUR - the cacophony - Paris Paloma

I don't think we're in Stoneview anymore. I'm in some limousine, my hands finally free, my gaze straight ahead, eyes blinking slowly.

I'm still crying.

Not because of my situation, but because I want to know if Wren is okay.

"It's a long drive." That's Elijah on my right. "We'll stop twice. Sleep in a hotel both times. You don't ask for help, you don't try to run away. I don't even want to see you blink at a receptionist. Clear?"

I'm in a middle seat, but there's no one on my left. Opposite me is Monty Hunter, staring at me, waiting for my answer to the question his son asked.

"Is he going to live?" I croak, running my arm under my nose. "Wren."

Monty's upper lip curls with disgust. But no one answers me.

Elijah continues. "When we arrive at base, you'll get a

room, clean clothes. Bathroom is communal. You'll eat and share the common area with the other girls. I'll be training you. We have six months, so I need you to behave, Peach."

"You're not going to kill him, are you? He's safe now... now that I'm with you?"

Elijah's hand is quicker than I can even process. He backhands me hard enough to throw me against the window.

"You're going to be sold to someone who will do whatever he wants with you, and all you want to know about is *Wren?*"

Cheek throbbing, I drag myself back to a sitting position, look Elijah in the eye, and nod. "You can try all you want. You will never be half the man he is."

Elijah snorts, but I catch the flash of vulnerability in his eyes before he looks away.

"Don't worry, Son. She'll soon feel the consequences of her actions." Monty keeps his eyes on me as he says that, but I don't think he expected me to stare right back.

"The consequences of killing all your little friends, Mr. Hunter?" I smile at him. "Who says I won't do the same where you're taking me?"

"Shut up, Penelope," Elijah barks.

I don't. I keep staring at the man who had plans for me, but never realized I was more than someone who would take it without fighting back.

"You're dying to know, aren't you?" I say to Monty. "Why I killed them? Why I couldn't behave like the other Heras?"

He narrows his eyes. Pitiful man that he is. He has everything, but he wants more. Answers. So I give them to him.

"Do you know who controls the world, Mr. Hunter?"

"The Silent Circle, and it'd do you good to remember that."

"Yes, all of you," I agree. "From your grandfathers, your fathers, to you, and soon, it'll be the sons you raised to make the same selfish, dangerous, destroying decisions you did. And do you know who suffers?"

His gaze points at me, but I don't think he understands what that means.

"Your mothers. Your sisters. Your daughters. *Women*," I confirm. "Since the dawn of time, all you've allowed us to do is *suffer*. Every day, we're forced to live with the consequences of your actions. Hide your bodies, show yourself. Be quiet, smile more. Give us children. Raise our daughters to fear our sons and raise our sons to abuse our daughters."

"Are you talking about the Circle now, or the world." He chuckles mockingly.

"Being a woman in this world is the exact equivalent to being a Hera to a Shadow. It's just a different level. Become a Hera, you will get success and power, as long as you *submit* to the male ego. Stroke it, nurse it, and turn yourself meek when it hurts. Do you know what you've all done? Forced us to survive by hanging on to men's fake promises of protection."

I snort, and it turns into a loud, desperate cackle.

"*Protection.* What fucking protection? Every day in this world, you men start wars, celebrate your wins, mourn your fallen soldiers. But do you know what you forget? The women you raped. You crush laws under the heels of your shiny shoes, revert us to old times because you're scared. But do you know what you rejoice in? The women who bleed to death. You celebrate us if we stay in our place. If we don't become threatening. If the minorities who are smarter and more qualified than you don't get too close to power. If the privileged women stick to their internalized misogyny. If the people who are different from you keep fearing you."

I look him up and down with all the disgust I can muster.

"You are so fragile and weak that you would rather see us die than make space for us. I watch you murmur to a god who has died for men's sins. But watch my lips, we, women, *die* from *your* sins. Every day."

I take a deep, relaxing breath that seems to make him uneasy.

"So I killed you. One. By. One."

I smirk at him. Everything is going to be fine, just because I got to watch Monty Hunter lose his composure.

"It's your bodies," I say softly. "But it was my choice to bury them. And it was a pleasure to watch every single one of you die painfully. So..." I shrug. "Burn me at the stake, Shadows. Because this is what happens when you don't let us be part of the system. When you don't let us change things from the inside. A revolution. And if you think you're safe now that you're putting me away? Think again." I lean forward, lowering my voice to a whisper. "Who says I acted alone? And who says any of you are safe with your Hera?"

Monty shifts in his seat, taking my threat seriously. I enjoy my little win until Elijah pulls out a gun and points it at my temple.

"Did anyone help you?" he hisses.

I shake my head as my heart pumps a new wave of adrenaline through my veins. "No."

He presses the gun against my skin, and I can't stop the whimper pushing up my throat.

"Names."

"No one helped me. I promise you. No one helped me."

My fear makes Monty smile. "Not so strong now, are we?" He laughs.

That's until his phone rings, with *Duval* written on the screen. He picks up, putting it on speaker for Elijah to hear.

"*He burned it to the ground!*" Eugene screams on the other side. There're a million sounds around him, and he's panting, clearly running.

"Calm down," Monty replies, brow creased. "What are you talking about?"

"*The temple. He set the temple on fire.*"

I lean back in my seat, close my eyes, and smile to myself.

"Who?" Monty asks, in complete denial.

"*Who do you think? Your fucking son!*"

"Wren is tied up in a dungeon," he hisses.

"*He broke free. He killed them. Oh my god, he killed so many of them. It was a bloodbath.*" Duval pants, catching his breath. "*And now he's coming for you.*"

I look at them again, just to see Duval's call cut off by a call from Wren.

Monty's wild eyes go to Elijah as he answers.

"*I told you, didn't I?*" Wren's savage voice resonates in the car, and my nerves fade into butterflies at the sound. "*That if anything happened to her, there would be nowhere for you to hide.*"

He hangs up right away.

I lick my lips, look at both of them, and whisper, "I think you made him *snap*."

A second later, something crashes into our car.

-metal IS NOT the same as punk.
-She's still allergic to shellfish and cat hair
-Always leave the green olives to her
-We don't like metal anymore.
-~~Tea tree and peppermint shampoo~~
-~~Don't forget the peri-peri powder on her fries~~
-Bake and shake every first Tuesday of the month.
-No more sugar in her coffee. It makes her feel sick
-DO NOT bother me during girls' night Wren
-Spiced honey on pepperoni pizza
-Check the triangle freckles on her right shoulder
frequently. Dermatologist said to keep an eye.
-New vision results: Right eye -2.75. Left eye -3.25
-If she gets in next September's yearly release of the
EEAJ, the announcement will be in August next year.
-~~Her brace needs to come off in a week~~
-New shampoo: coconut oil in it
-No more peri-peri on her fries
-Keep the stupid dog
-The letters started at 13
-The love of my life is a serial killer

Chapter Forty

Wren

littlest things - Camylio

The first thing I do is pull her out of the limousine. I carry her across the road and lay her down carefully in the grass. She's bleeding from her hairline, but she's conscious.

"I'm sorry," I murmur, wiping the blood away. "I had to stop that car somehow. I couldn't let them take you to a second location."

"I'm okay," she croaks. "I feel fine."

"You stay here. Don't move. I'm going to finish this."

"No, Wren..." Her hand wraps around my forearm. "Elijah...he's got a gun. It's too dangerous. Please, I want to go home. Let's go home."

I shake my head, pressing a kiss on her forehead. "I warned them not to hurt you."

Standing again, I force her to let go of me. "Don't move," I repeat.

Elijah has pulled my dad's barely conscious body out of

their wrecked car in the ditch. He's stumbling as he walks toward me, thinking he can take me after what he did.

"You'll be last," I hiss as I stride toward him. He's not holding the gun, probably lost it as their car was tumbling, but even that wouldn't stop me.

I don't stop, throwing a punch and aiming for his cheek-bone. I want him in pain, but conscious. If I knock him out, he won't feel the way he dies. He falls to the ground, crying out like the little bitch he's always been.

But instead of taking care of him, I go to my father.

"Wren," he coughs, attempting to roll onto his side so he can get up. I kick him in the ribs and throw him onto his back again.

As I look down at him, my entire body buzzes with the need to kill.

"I let a lot of things go when it comes to this family," I say, rage rumbling from my throat. "You beat me up, and I did nothing." I kick him again. "You scared me, made me ashamed of myself, and I did nothing." I lift my left foot, crushing it down on his stomach. "You chose Elijah over me, as if a father *has* to choose a favorite son and let the other one suffer. You created something in me and never healed me from it. You roped me in the Circle, used me, tried to kill me slowly. And yet..." I laugh to myself, shaking my head like a maniac. "Yet it never crossed my mind to kill you."

He cries out when I put my foot on his chest. "You did all this to *me*, but your biggest mistake was not heeding my warning when it comes to *her*."

I kick him in the head, forcing him to look at Peach. She didn't stay where I put her.

"Trouble..." I laugh softly. "After all this, you still can't do what you're told, huh?"

She shakes her head as her eyes shine with vengeance. So I give her what she needs, looking down at my dad again.

"I *told you* if her smile faltered, it would be the end of you. Is she smiling right now, Dad?" When all he does is cry out, I lower myself to purr in his face. "Is she?"

"No." He bursts into tears. "Please, don't kill me. Please, please, please..."

"Did you really think you could take the love of my life away from me, and that *zip ties* would hold me back?" I snarl. "I killed your brother. Now I'm going to kill you. And I want you to die knowing I will kill your son, too."

"I'm sorry!" he yells with all the hope he has of staying alive.

"I don't care. See, the good thing is, I probably won't even remember doing this."

I kick him in the face. Once, twice. He grunts at the beginning, cries, but kicks after kicks turn him silent. His head is just a lifeless ball loosely attached to his body by the time I'm done.

I turn around to finish Elijah off, but everything happens in a flash.

He's got a gun pointed at me. And Peach is screaming.

I blink, and I'm weirdly losing my footing. Wait, I got pushed. She pushed me. And now I'm stumbling to the side as a shot booms around us.

I don't think twice, not even feeling the pain as I tackle Elijah to the ground. I punch him until I can't feel my hands anymore, and I take the gun from his grasp.

"You're shooting me, yet you're the one dying," I snarl, standing up as he tries to catch his breath. "Turns out, you do know your place." Not hesitating for even a split second, I shoot him in the head.

I tap my chest, my stomach, realizing I can't feel any pain. But he did shoot.

I run a hand across my bloody face. My ears are ringing as I look around.

And all I see is her. Her hands pressing against her stomach. And blood. A lot of blood.

Too much blood.

My eyes widen as a coldness wraps around my body.

She takes two steps back, blinking up at me, confused.

"Wren," she croaks, her voice barely audible.

She stumbles back again, her knees buckling, and I'm on her, catching her as she falls. Adrenaline shoots through me, and I go down with her, on my knees with her head on my lap.

"Peach." My eyes roam over her body. Her hands are bloody. "What did you do?" I say, my throat tightening. "What did you do? I told you to stay over there...I... Baby, what did you do?"

Her mouth opens, but no sound comes out as she takes a trembling breath. The world around me is swimming, falling apart. I place my shaking hand on top of hers and press with all my strength on her stomach.

"Breathe," I tell her with the little composure I have. "It's going to be okay. You're going to be okay."

Hand shaking, I reach for my father, right behind us, and pull his phone out of his pocket.

"I'm calling 911. Just breathe. Keep breathing and stay awake." Fuck, I'm the one who can't breathe, my lungs wheezing. "Can you stay awake for me?"

She tries to nod, but her eyes close instead.

"Penelope," I hiss. "I said *stay awake*."

This time, she manages to shake her head.

"Don't you play stubborn with me right now."

She smiles, but it's so weak I feel my heart shattering. "Trouble, please. Please, don't go to sleep. I need you. I can't live without y—" I gasp, unable to formulate the end of that sentence. There isn't a world I live in that Peach isn't in. "Why did you do this?"

"Because I'm in love with you." Her voice...it's got nothing left in it. No light, no sass. It has no strength. This isn't her.

"Trouble." My lower lip trembles, eyes blurring. "Hold on for me. I've got you."

"*9 1 1, what's your emergency?*"

"My girlfriend's been shot. We're right by the creek on Route 494. Right...right after Stoneview. She's bleeding. Fuck...she's bleeding a lot. Please."

"Wren..."

The phone clatters to the ground as she tries to grab my arm.

"Yes, baby, I'm here. I'm here. They're coming. Open— Show me your pretty eyes."

She slowly blinks them open, but they're dull. There's so little life in them, and a sob bursts from my mouth.

"Trouble, please don't leave me. I'm begging you. I can't... Without you, there's nothing. Please."

"I love you, Wren. I love you...so much."

I kiss her mouth, her bloody cheek. "I love you. That's why you're going to stay with me until they arrive. You're going to live. And... I'll make your life worth living, I promise."

I slap her lightly when her eyes close again, and I can see she's trying with all she has to keep them open.

"I'm sorry," she whispers so quietly I have to get closer to her face again. "That it took me so long to see how pure your love for me is."

"It's okay," I say in a rush. "It's okay, because you're going to live. And we're going to get your paper published, yeah? And... And I will make you coffee to stay up at night while you work. I will brush your hair in the morning when you're running late because you spent the night at the library."

My throat squeezes, and I hurt myself from forcing the words. But I keep going.

"We'll take Sausage on walks together. And I will bring you to that tapas place you love. I'll buy you ice cream and fries so you can dip them in it. No more peri-peri powder. I know you don't like that anymore."

She smiles, her eyes closing, and I know she sees it.

"Keep going," she breathes.

She sees it like I do, but her body isn't holding on. She's cold. And she's gray.

"I'm going to take you to the Philippines. Because... remember when we saw that documentary when we were teenagers? About that Island, Siargao. *Best place to surf.* And you said we should go learn how to surf over there. I'm going to take you."

She nods weakly, and all it does is tell me that she'll never learn how to surf.

"You're going to get a Nobel Prize. And I'll be there in the crowd, clapping so hard. Maybe that day, I'll ask you to marry me. Because you and I are going to get married, and we're going to have three children. They'll all have your hair because we both know you've got the stronger genes out of both of us– Oh God." She's not... I don't think she's...

"Trouble," I squeak. "Please. This life... This life isn't worth living without you." My tears drip onto her face, but it doesn't make her open her eyes again. "Please, live it all with me."

My hand leaves her bloody stomach to press against her cheek, smearing it with red. Still, she's beautiful.

"Live with me," I push out one last time.

Her mouth is slightly agape, her head heavy on my legs.

She deserves the world, the universe. Happiness, all the love there is. She deserves it all.

Instead, she took a bullet for me.

I can hear sirens in the distance.

But I know that they're too late. I know it within my heart, because it's so heavy, as if beating for two now.

-metal IS NOT the same as punk.
-She's still allergic to shellfish and cat hair
-Always leave the green olives to her
-We don't like metal anymore.
-~~Tea tree and peppermint shampoo~~
-~~Don't forget the peri-peri powder on her fries~~
-Bake and shake every first Tuesday of the month.
-No more sugar in her coffee. It makes her feel sick
-DO NOT bother me during girls' night Wren
-Spiced honey on pepperoni pizza
-Check the triangle freckles on her right shoulder
frequently. Dermatologist said to keep an eye.
-New vision results: Right eye -2.75. Left eye -3.25
-If she gets in next September's yearly release of the
EEAJ, the announcement will be in August next year.
-~~Her brace needs to come off in a week~~
-New shampoo: coconut oil in it
-No more peri-peri on her fries
-Keep the stupid dog
-The letters started at 13
-The love of my life is ~~a serial killer~~ my reason to
breathe
-Please...let it not be the last time I write something
on this list

Chapter Forty-One

Wren

My Home - Myles smith

The marker presses on the inner skin of my forearm. I write over the dozen other layers I've already inked on my skin.

I promise.

I promise if you wake up, I'll never leave your side again.

I promise if you wake up, you will never suffer again.

I promise if you wake up, you will never feel unloved.

I promise if you wake up, that I will spend every single waking hour making sure you're happy.

I promise.

I promise.

I promise.

But please...promise me you'll wake up.

There's a knock on the door, bringing me back to reality. Suddenly, everything is back. The beeping of the heart monitor, the smell of the hospital room. And Peach, in the bed, eyes closed.

What I would give to see the fire in her beautiful green eyes again.

The door opens, Chris and Achilles walking in. It's been three days since I burned the temple to the ground for trying to take Peach away from me, and those two are still sporting bruises from the whole ordeal.

They took Chris when he was walking back from the hospital, where he was keeping an eye on Dustin. They got Achilles and I the second Xi dropped us at our campus house. Beaten up, locked in different rooms. Dustin had already talked, and there was nothing we could do to defend ourselves. I went down and took my only two allies in the Circle down with me. Of course, I freed them before setting the building on fire.

I spared Duval. Not only because he's Achilles's father, but because he's a president I can handle. He's seen what I'm capable of now. It's impossible to kill everyone in the Circle; the organization will always keep on living. I'm better with Duval as the president. Protected by his fear of me.

He's already cleared things up with the police for the car "accident" and the bodies. Elijah Hunter lost his mind. Monty Hunter died in the accident after his son attacked the driver and they ended up in a ditch. Peach and I were behind them, crashed with them in the accident. Elijah, in his manic episode, shot Peach, and I shot him in self defense. Duval made sure that's the story, and it just so happens, the limo driver, acting as a second witness, approved all of it since he'll do whatever Duval tells him to.

And while he was at it, Zeus pinned the campus murders on Elijah too.

Antisocial, unstable student kills his peers.

The craziest part of this fake story is that for the first

time, I remember everything. The whole truth. Peach being shot was like a shock to the system, bringing me back to reality so fast I didn't get a chance to let my mind protect me from the horrors I'd committed.

Now I'm waiting to hear from Duval. We're only communicating through Chris and Achilles. He's too scared to see me.

"Wren, the nurse told you not to write on her anymore," Chris says calmly.

I look at Peach's arm next to mine. I keep writing on hers too, keep hearing her voice promising me she's going to wake up. Except she's not waking up.

I wipe a hand across my face. "I know," I say in a raspy voice. "I tried to stop."

It's weird. I can't find my normal voice without her. Nothing about me is the same. I feel empty. I have nothing to give to people.

They eye each other, but don't say anything more regarding my odd behavior.

"My dad agreed to your demands," Achilles says, approaching me. "You can't technically leave the Circle, but you will be a passive member. You have no official role anymore, and you can't ask members for favors. There will be no repercussions, but you can't access the temple...or wherever the new temple will be, I guess."

I nod. This is what I wanted, and Duval is scared enough to grant it to me. I don't care that I won't have the privileges the Circle brings. In fact, I couldn't care less.

"That applies for you and..." His eyes dart to Peach as his voice dies from emotion. "And Peach," he concludes.

She's his friend too. We all grew up together. And I might be the one who fell so deep for her there's no way out, but it doesn't mean he doesn't love her too.

"Alex and Ella are outside," Chris says. "They want to check on her."

I nod, taking Peach's hand in mine. "Of course. Can I just have another minute with her?" As if I haven't spent every second of the last three days in her presence.

The only time I left was because I was forced. They had to stitch me back together after the beating. She was in surgery, and I couldn't follow. That's the only reason I let them take care of me. I took a shower and was right there when she got out of surgery.

The guys leave, and I turn to her again.

"Everyone wants to see you. Everyone misses you," I say. "You have to come back to us, Trouble."

She bled so much, there wasn't enough oxygen going to her brain for her to stay conscious. She lost a kidney. They're still transfusing blood because of some internal bleeding. And she's not awake. Still. Not. Awake. Yesterday morning, the doctor came in, telling us her blood pressure was too low, and we don't know the brain damage that's been caused.

And he stomped on my heart with a sorry face when he said to her dads and me...

The next forty-eight hours are crucial.

Since then, I've been counting the minutes. Her dads don't leave her side either. They've just gone to get some food.

I open the marker again, writing on my arm. "I promise that you can be as strong headed as you want, whenever you want."

I take her arm. "If you just...promise to wake up," I say, my throat tightening again as I write on her again.

A tear drops on the ink, mixing with it.

"What the fuck are you doing, Hunter?"

Her voice is a rasped whisper, weak, barely audible. But it startles me, my eyes snapping to her face.

God, she looks so tired. Gray skin, matted hair, sunken eyes looking up at me.

But she's awake.

I open my mouth, no sound coming out. This can't be real.

She smiles smugly. "Don't look so shocked. I'm too stubborn to die."

My heart jumps in my chest, and I jump off the bed. "Oh my god," I cry out. "Peach! Don't move... D-don't move, baby. Don't hurt yourself."

She rolls her eyes, and I hear her mutter, "Where the hell am I going to go?" as I run out of the room.

"Doctor!" I yell. "She's awake... She's..." There are four people on me, none of them a doctor.

Alex, Ella, Chris, and Achilles surround me.

"Wait," I pant. I'm scared. So scared that this won't last. "We need a doctor. We need to make sure she's okay."

Nurses rush in, the doctor not far behind.

"Call her dads," I tell Ella as I follow the staff into the room.

They do all sorts of tests on her, getting her grumpy and sarcastic, and making me smile because grumpy Peach means she's alive. It lasts forever, and her dads are here by the time the staff leave, telling us she needs to rest, but that there's no brain damage, and her life is no longer in danger.

Her dads are surrounding her, holding her hands, kissing her forehead. Slowly, the brightness in her eyes comes back. She's shining, so her...so *alive*.

I wait hours for her dads to get their fill. They leave the room when she asks them to give her some space, and I finally step up to her bed, feeling like I'm walking on a cloud as I approach.

"Wren." Her smile spreads everywhere. To her cheeks, her eyes. It reaches my heart, seizing it harshly. "What is this?"

She points at the writing on her arm.

"That's you promising me that you'll wake up," I say, a rush of relief leaving my lungs as I sit next to her and drop a kiss on her forehead. "Thank you for keeping your promise."

"You're welcome." She giggles, and my stomach swoops. "And this?" She points at my arm this time. "What's this?"

"Those are all my promises *if* you woke up."

"Fun," she says as she looks up at me. "Which one do we start with?"

I rub a hand over my face, not believing that this is real. She's here. She's back. With me, in my arms.

"Whichever you want, Trouble."

"I did hear something along the lines of *I can be as strong headed as I want*?"

I laugh, the fear and anxiety of the last few days finally falling off my shoulders.

"I think you heard that wrong."

She takes my hand in hers, nestling against the crook of my chest. Where she belongs.

"Oh, no, Wren Hunter. I heard it loud and clear. Now I get to make your life a living hell because you wanted me back."

"Please do," I whisper, emotions still tight in my chest. "As long as I get to live this life with you."

She laughs, but the words are strong, and the affection intense when she says, "I love you."

"I love you too, Trouble."

This woman is incredible, and I've always known it. Deep in my bones, I knew she was made for me.

This woman is a miracle, and she's all mine.

This woman... I waited forever for her to love me, and I would have waited another lifetime for her to wake up.

Penelope Sanderson-Menacci. Who knew you could make me fall even deeper in love with you...by simply loving me back.

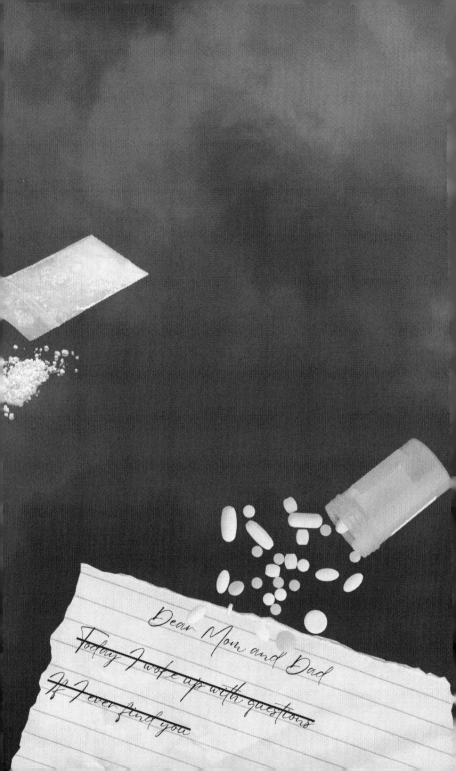

Epilogue

Peach

Ordinary - Alex Warren

T *en months later...*

Breathe. Breathe, Peach. It's going to be okay. Only a few minutes left. In for four seconds. Out for four seconds... Wait, was it eight seconds out?

My thumbs and forefingers are hurting from how harshly I'm pressing them together...the *Zen* way. Kind of. I'm cross-legged on the floor of the office that Professor Lopez offered me as his assistant, my eyes closed.

Peace. Breathe. Peace.

I open one eye, checking the clock. Still ten minutes.

Fuck. Ten minutes?

"She's in here." I hear Ella's voice as the door opens.

Oh, that traitor. I told her not to tell anyone.

I snap both eyes open, ready to annihilate whoever dares to bother my peaceful time.

Wren walks in, wearing light denim jeans that hug him perfectly, and a gray t-shirt I want to rip off his beautiful muscles.

Ella leaves and closes the door behind her. Yes, she knows what's good for her.

"Trouble," he says carefully, looking around the room I destroyed a minute ago.

I'm not exactly known for being the most patient person. And the stress got to me. I might or might not have thrown my books everywhere, swiped off everything that was on my desk. Maybe broke a chair. I don't know. Maybe.

"What are you doing?" Wren asks, approaching calmly.

"Meditating," I answer innocently as I close my eyes again. "You're impeding on my peaceful meditation."

I feel him squat in front of me, and his hand is on my cheek next, so I open my eyes. "Peaceful?" He chuckles.

"Oh, shut up." I huff as I uncross my legs. He helps me stand up, grabs me by my hips, and sits me on my desk.

"Anxiety getting a bit much?"

"Why is there an exact time to hear back from them?" I snap. "Can't Lopez just...I don't know...ask earlier?"

"Trouble, you survived a bullet to the stomach, three weeks in the hospital, four months of recovery, and you can't survive a few more minutes of waiting to know if your article will be published in the Environmental Engineering American Journal?"

I nod sternly. "Exactly."

He shakes his head, laughing softly. His hand caresses my hip, and slowly he drags it down between my legs. "Can I help in any way?"

Pushing my hips forward, I relish the pressure on my

clit. "I guess you can..." My eyes snap to the clock. "No more than six minutes, though."

He chuckles condescendingly against my cheek. "I can make you come in less than three, baby."

And then his hand slides under my summer dress, pushing my panties to the side.

"Especially when you're already wet," he adds. "Spread."

My legs automatically open, giving him better access. "Atta girl."

He pushes a finger inside me slowly. "Wren..." I pant, feeling my wetness double. "You're a fucking tease— Ah." I gasp when he pushes two fingers deep inside me, pulls away, then thrusts back in.

"What was that?"

"More," I moan, pushing my hips back and forth.

He wraps my long hair twice around his fist, thrusting until I can't breathe properly, and pulls my head back. "Look at me, hmm, so gorgeous. Do you want to come, Penelope baby?"

"Yes," I pant. "Y-yes..."

"Ask nicely." My heart kicks harder.

"Please, sir." I lick my lips, and his eyes catch it, making him smirk. "Please, sir, can I come?"

"Yes," he says tensely, just as he crashes his lips against mine. I whimper as my body shudders, pulsing around his fingers as he caresses my tongue with his.

I'm still catching my breath when my phone rings.

My eyes widen, going to Wren. "It's Lopez. Fuck, fuck!"

He takes my phone, answers, puts it on speaker, and gives it back to me.

"H-hi," I squeak.

"Hi, Penelope, how are you?"

I pause, breathe, and exhale. "Skip the small talk. I'm begging you."

He laughs softly, in that wise professor way. "Your article will be published in the next release. Next trimester."

Unable to process anything, I blink at the phone screen. "What?"

"You did it, baby," Wren says, making me look up at him. "On your way to that Nobel Prize."

I scream, a squeal that I know is Wren's favorite sound. Throwing my phone, I jump in my boyfriend's arms. He hugs me so tightly, I can't breathe, but I wrap my legs around his hips, my arms around his neck, and let him choke me from happiness.

By the time I'm looking at my phone again, Lopez has hung up, and I send him a text, thanking him for everything he helped me with.

"Pack your stuff," Wren says. "I'll bring the car around. People are waiting to celebrate."

"You...planned a party? What if I hadn't gotten published?"

"Please." He snorts. "I knew you would. I always believed in you." Kissing my lips briefly, he puts me down. "Even when you didn't believe in yourself."

"You don't need to bring the car. I can walk."

He shakes his head. "I'd rather you don't push yourself too much."

"Wren...it's been almost a year."

He smiles, petting my head. "I don't care. You wanted to be all brave and take a bullet for me? Now you put up with the consequences."

As he leaves the office, I turn around to pick up everything I threw on the floor earlier. My desk is almost as new when I hear the door open behind me.

"I'm ready—" I cut myself off when my mouth drops open.

In front of me stands a tall woman looking so much like me, I wonder if she's real for a few seconds. Her red hair is to her waist, like mine. She's taller, but we have the same body shape, on the skinnier side, rather straight than curvy. And our eyes...they're the exact same green. Except, like in the pictures I found of her, hers are empty of any life. It makes me shiver.

"Lana," I exhale, not believing my own eyes.

Wren told me about her. He told me everything he had learned. And while I have no desire to meet my biological dad, I've been looking for Lana Anderson...my older sister.

She approaches me slowly, like a hunter on prey rather than someone finally meeting her long-lost sister. Her dangerous aura makes me press myself against the desk.

She's the definition of power. Wearing a black suit perfectly tailored, her eyes narrowed on me, her posture high and mighty.

"I heard you were looking for me."

I nod dumbly, incapable of uttering a single word.

"That stops now."

I gulp. "Wh-what? No. No. I... My name is Penelope. I'm Keith Anderson's second daughter. We're sisters." The word feels foreign on my tongue.

She cocks an eyebrow at me. "Oh, no," she says, voice low. She points at me. "You're Penelope Sanderson-Menacci, the little girl who was adopted by a loving couple. Who was given a chance at a normal life." She points to herself. "I'm Lucky, the one who was sent to a place traumatizing enough, I now kill people without a second thought."

Tilting her head to the side, she observes me. "So you're going to stop asking around for me. Stop looking for me."

The death in her tone makes my chest tighten with dread.

"See, Penelope, most people who look for me too closely, *find me*. And they don't live to tell the tale."

I flinch when she brings her hand to my face, my heart palpitating, and my blood freezing. All she does is pull strands of hair out of my mouth. I was chewing on it.

"Nasty habit," she says.

I swallow thickly, nodding because it feels like I should agree.

"You saw me now. Stop looking for me," she repeats. "You're an only child who has two amazing, loving fathers." She looked into me. She knows me, my life. That sends a wave of relief through my veins. "You don't have to remember your mother being shot by the mafia. You don't have to remember your father abandoning your little sister."

"Oh my god," I whisper. "Do you remember the day I was abandoned?"

She nods. "Of course. I was thirteen. Keith couldn't live without his wife. Mainly, he was scared the same people who killed her would kill us. So he left you at the shelter, and he left me with the nuns. You got a good deal, Penelope. Believe me. Just enjoy the cards you've been dealt."

She turns her back to me, showing I'm no threat to her whatsoever, and walks slowly to the door.

Looking over her shoulder one last time, she says without an ounce of emotion, "Congratulations on your article."

And she's gone.

I stare at the door for another five minutes before Wren opens it. He knows something happened right away because there's no hiding anything from him.

"What's wrong? What is it?" he asks as he rushes to me.

"I just met my sister," I say, voice flat, still unable to believe it.

His hands come to my cheeks, forcing me to look up at him. "Lucky? Are you okay? Did she hurt you? Trouble, she's dangerous."

Smiling at him, I shake my head. "She's amazing."

His face falls. "Are you sure you're okay?"

"I'm sure," I repeat. "And now I know where I get my badassery from."

He throws his head back, laughing at my craziness. "I love you."

We celebrate my success at Wren's campus house for hours. My dads are here, and some journalists took a few pictures for the Stoneview press. *Mayor's daughter published in prestigious science journal.*

Our friends are here, too. Alex and Xi, Ella and Chris. Achilles is on his own, because God only knows when he'll settle down. Some of the cheer girls, three Heras I'm still close with. A few of Wren's lacrosse friends. It's magical. I don't drink anything, sticking to soda with Wren.

I'm walking out of the bathroom on the second floor when my boyfriend finds me.

"Come to my room. I have something for you." His beautiful blue eyes are shining with excitement. They're as indescribable as they've always been. Too dark for sky blue, too light for midnight blue. *Perfect blue.*

Once in his room, he points at one of the drawers at his desk. There are scrabble tiles on there, but he hasn't snapped in months, and I haven't had to teach anyone a lesson either. I think that's what happens when you're happy, in love. The rest disappears. The demons fade into darkness. You just...live.

I open the drawer, and there's a lot of clutter in there, but my eyes catch the small ring box.

"Wren," I gasp, bringing the box out. I don't open it, my stomach tensing with anxiety.

I turn to him, and his eyes go wild.

"Oh—"

But I cut him off.

"This is a lot," I say. "I know we went through things people will never go through, but...we're just about to start grad school. There are so many things we need to do before. I mean, I don't know... I don't have an answer for you. And... can you live on a maybe? Please, I don't want this to ruin us."

He approaches me slowly, taking the box from my grip and putting a calming hand on my cheek.

"Breathe, baby." Reaching behind me, he pulls something else from the drawer. "This"—he puts two plane tickets in front of my face—"is your gift."

My eyes round as I read the destination. Manila.

"The Philippines!" I gasp.

He nods, smiling. "I think it's time we live that life I promised you. We'll go island hopping and learn to surf in Siargao."

"God, I'll be such a better surfer than you."

He rolls his eyes "Sure. You lie to yourself."

I love the present. The destination is perfect. And he got us on a commercial flight. Because despite the fact that he owns a jet, he knows I hate the principle of it. No one needs a fucking jet.

My eyes fall to the box again. "So...this isn't for me?"

Why is there so much disappointment in my voice? I

was offering him a *maybe* a second ago. But just like always with Wren...I'm late. Late in realizing how I feel, late in understanding how committed I am.

He laughs softly. "I've had this since senior year of high school." He opens it, a beautiful golden ring with a deep emerald intricately attached to it that has my breath catching. "Of course it's for you. But I've had it for so long, I think I can wait a little more before putting it around your finger."

I swallow thickly. "You bought me an engagement ring senior year? We... We'd never even kissed."

"Oh, I know," he says, seemingly still a bit hurt by that fact. "But I knew, Trouble, that I could get through to the most stubborn girl around."

I lick my lips as tears well in my eyes. "Stupid boy, making me feel everything."

He kisses me softly. "I can wait. I can have a *maybe*. I waited my entire life for you to become my girlfriend. You'll become my fiancée whenever you're ready."

My eyes drop to the ring again. Heart hammering, body buzzing. In a sense, all those new feelings only came around for Wren. He taught me how to love because he needed something as strong as how he felt. And now...I feel it all. So vividly, so intentionally. I don't even remember how it was before.

All I want to know is how it'll keep on feeling.

"Now," I breathe out. "I want it now."

His eyebrows raise so high they practically disappear below his hairline. "Now?"

"Now," I repeat. "I'm done making you wait. I'm done making myself miss out on the most beautiful things in life. You, Wren Hunter, *your love*, is the best thing that's ever happened to me. Now put the pretty ring around my finger."

"This—" He chuckles awkwardly, looking around the room. "This isn't exactly how I imagined it would happen." But his voice is thick with love.

"I ruined a romantic moment. Are we surprised?"

He drops the plane tickets to the floor, takes the ring out of the box and throws that too.

"No," he says with a light laugh. "We're not, and that's why I love you."

He slides the ring around my finger, and my heart skips a beat. Just like the first time we talked, the first time he caught me when I fell, the first time he kissed me.

I go to kiss him, but he's pulling his phone out and starts typing.

"Oh my god, Wren," I snap. "Is it really the moment to send a text?" I snatch his phone from his hands.

"No, don't!"

Looking down, my eyes go round when I see a list in his Notes app. It's titled *College Peach*.

My eyes gaze over the list, murmuring random words.

"Green olives, shampoo, sugar makes me feel sick... spiced honey, freckles, new vision... Wren, what is this?" I ask, but I keep reading. "EEAJ, *new* shampoo, keep the dog...and the last one makes my heart stop."

Mrs. Penelope Hunter. Yes. Looks good on the list.

His cheeks are bright red when I look up at him.

"Do you keep a list of things I like or dislike?"

He snatches the phone back. "Stop looking. I just... It's to make sure I never forget anything."

"Why is this one titled *college*? Are there others?"

He nods, rolling his lips inwardly.

"High school?" I ask. "Middle school?"

He nods again. "Since I met you. I used to write them on

552

paper, but now I just write it on my phone and transfer them when I get a new one."

"You're insane," I say seriously, but I'm not mad. If anything...it's the most loving thing anyone has ever done, yet it's so simple.

"And you're my fiancée," he replies brightly.

His lips on mine are a new promise. That this moment of happiness will never end.

It's already been forever for us. And I'm ready to spend another eternity with him.

"I want to see it again," Alex says, grabbing my hand.

"I can't believe you're the first one of us to get engaged!" Ella shrieks for the tenth time tonight, looking at Wren and me. "I thought it would be Alex."

"Me too," Xi approves.

"*After* college," she says, like it's a daily conversation between them.

"Do you want to be the second one?" Chris asks his girl-friend. "Now?"

"Shut up." Ella rolls her eyes, but we all know the answer is yes.

We told my dads right away, then we told everyone downstairs, but it's just us now. Alex, Xi, Ella, Chris, Achilles, Wren, and I. Our chosen family.

"I would say it's a surprise if she was engaged to anyone other than Wren," Achilles says. "But who's really surprised here? The man had the plan in place since he was six."

We all laugh, and I eye my fiancé. He's not denying it, and his self-satisfied smile triggers questions inside me. It *is* weirdly convenient that the box was in the drawer. He's the one who hid the tickets in there. He knew I would open it.

"Did you put it there on purpose?" I ask him. "Was your plan for me to see the box and say we'd do it when I'm ready...just for me to realize I was ready?"

He winks at me, taking a sip of his beer. "I guess we'll never know."

A phone beeps in the room, and it's followed by many others, all in their own time.

It's a post from Hermes. A picture of a girl with half-bleached and half-black hair walking out of the admission office on campus.

Rags to riches! Our new favorite.

SFU has changed... I think they're giving bursaries now or something, because a little rat from the North Shore of Silver Falls got lost on our campus today.

Someone, please, for the love of God, get her to a hair-dresser.

Let her know in the comments how...welcome she is here.

#SFUcharity #don'ttouchmyHermesbag #pleaseleavealready

The comments, of course, are anything but welcoming.

"I know this girl," I say. "She's been at the women's shelter multiple times, temporarily homeless every time. Her dad is a gambler or something."

"Her name is Nyx," Wren says. "I met her once." He looks at Achilles, but our friend has put his phone away already. "You know her too."

"Or so she keeps saying," he answers blankly.

"We can't let Hermes get to her," I snap. "They'll destroy her."

They all know now that Hermes blackmailed me, that I almost lost my mind. We still don't know how they got the picture of me and Ania that night, or why they were after me, specifically. We don't know what they wanted out of me initiating and being part of the Circle, having me witness the things I did, but once it was announced that Elijah had murdered Ania–truthfully–and all the other people on campus–to cover for me–Hermes stopped messaging.

"We won't," Ella says. "We'll take care of her."

Achilles stands up, downing what's left of his beer, clearly ready to go to bed. He looks at all of us, a scowl on his face before he says, "What we really need to do is find out who that fucker is."

THE END

Want to know who Hermes is? Find out in the last book of
Silver Falls University: Loving The Tormentor

-metal IS NOT the same as punk.
-She's still allergic to shellfish and cat hair
-Always leave the green olives to her
-We don't like metal anymore.
-Tea tree and peppermint shampoo
-Don't forget the peri-peri powder on her fries
-Bake and shake every first Tuesday of the month.
-No more sugar in her coffee. It makes her feel sick
-DO NOT bother me during girls' night Wren
-Spiced honey on pepperoni pizza
-Check the triangle freckles on her right shoulder
frequently. Dermatologist said to keep an eye.
-New vision results: Right eye -2.75. Left eye -3.25
-If she gets in next September's yearly release of the
EEAJ, the announcement will be in August next year.
-Her brace needs to come off in a week
-New shampoo: coconut oil in it
-No more peri-peri on her fries
-Keep the stupid dog
-The letters started at 13
-The love of my life is a serial killer my reason to
breathe
-Please...let it not be the last time I write something
on this list
-Mrs. Penelope Hunter. Yes. Looks good on the list.

Also by Lola King

All books happen in the same world at different times

STONEVIEW STORIES

(*MF Bully*):

Giving In

Giving Away

Giving Up

One Last Kiss (Novella - includes spoilers from Rose's Duet)

ROSE'S DUET

(*FFMM why-choose*):

Queen Of Broken Hearts (Prequel novella)

King of My Heart

Ace of All Hearts

NORTH SHORE STORIES

(interconnected standalones):

Beautiful Fiend (MF, enemies to lovers)

Heartless Beloved - (MF, good girl/bad boy)

Delightful Sins - (MFM enemies-to-lovers)

Lawless God - (MF enemies-to-lovers)

HOLIDAY NOVELLA

Merry Christmas From Daddy to Little One (Prequel to Loving The Liar)

SILVER FALLS UNIVERSITY

(MF, elite college, secret society)

Loving The Liar (dark, second chance)

Loving The Reaper: (dark, best friends to lovers)

Loving The Tormentor: Coming soon!

Acknowledgments

I would like to thank my readers for their support and patience. Thank you for sticking with me through thick and thin.

A huge thank you to my editor, Mackenzie for working so hard with me on this book and always being available for me.

Thank you to Lauren for always being the first pair of eyes on my messy first drafts.

Thank you to my cover designer, Sherri, for bringing my imagination to life. I write stories for a living but everyone would be surprised at how badly I am at describing what I want on a cover. Sherri is a master at making sense of my nonsense.

Thank you to Valentine and all the girls at VPR for bringing my stories to readers and being an amazing team.

Thank you to Jay for once again holding my hand through the impostor syndrome that always creeps back in. You believe in me like no one else, even as a friend.

Thank you to my family. Your patience, support, and encouragement help me through my darkest hours. You're all insane, but I love you.